DEAR MR. BLACK

SHANORA WILLIAMS

DEAR
Mr. Black

Published September 2014
Editing by Yours Truly, The Editor
Cover Art and Design by Jersey Girl Designs

NOTE FROM THE AUTHOR

I WOULD LIKE to personally take the time out to enlighten every reader about a few details in *Dear Mr Black*. Since this story happens to have quite a unique premise, I'd just like to inform all of you that, though it may seem odd and wrong, it is purely **fiction**.

The cities/towns in which this novel is set are completely fictional and withhold no resemblances to an actual city/town, the people, cultures, or laws.

No, these are not events that have happened in my life or to anyone that I know. This just so happens to be a storyline that has been running wild in my mind ever since 2013, and I'm just *now* putting it out there.

I have worked on it, and then stopped. I have spent endless hours making it the best it can be, but wondering whether people would get it. I have wanted to give up on this novel and the characters because I feared many would truly misunderstand Chloe and Theo's struggle. In our society, most would consider it distasteful and ignorant.

I don't. This story is from my heart, I can guarantee it. This story is full of love, angst, and even some heartbreak. This story shows growth and maturity. This story, as one reader put it, is about life vs. love.

I hope people realize a certain pattern when it comes to my writing style. I write very realistically considering I've had a very realistic childhood and life. I don't see everything through color. Most of my life was spent looking through black and white binoculars.

Trust me when I say that I am a *firm* believer in HEA's, but please realize that not all stories will have that *rainbows and unicorn* mirage. Every single one of *my* stories has an HEA in itself. It all just depends on your personality, how you grew up, or how you accept it.

If you can grasp these detailed facts, then I encourage you to read *Dear Mr Black*, and I really hope you enjoy it! But if you cannot get with the age gap/differences, the lust, or if you are expecting a fairytale type of romance, then realize this may not be the story for you. I completely respect your decision if you are no longer interested in reading it.

Much love and BIG hugs,

Shanora
  xoxo

SWEET NOTIFICATIONS

To get notified about new release alerts, free books, and exclusive updates, visit www.shanorawilliams.com/mailing-list.

CONTACT SHANORA

Feel free to follow me on Instagram! I am always active and always eager to speak with my readers there.

Instagram @reallyshanora

Other Ways to Follow Me:
Twitter @shanorawilliams
Facebook @ShanoraWilliamsAuthor

ALSO BY SHANORA WILLIAMS

NORA HEAT COLLECTION
CRAVE

CARESS

DIRTY LITTLE SECRET

STANDALONES
TEMPORARY BOYFRIEND

100 PROOF

DOOMSDAY LOVE

TAINTED BLACK

UNTAINTED

INFINITY

SERIES
FIRENINE SERIES

THE BEWARE DUET

VENOM TRILOGY

Please visit www.shanorawilliams.com to check out my titles.

DEDICATION

Dedicated to the people who will sacrifice pretty much *anything* for the ones they love. You may feel like you aren't recognized, but you are special. You are loved, and you are appreciated. Your soul is precious and generous, and this world could always use more people like you.

ONE

CHLOE

I was twelve years old when I met the Blacks.

I'd just moved to Primrose Way, a suburban neighborhood in Bristle Wave County, California. Bristle Wave was right off the coast, a small, comforting area that travelers ventured to whenever they wanted to hit the pier, walk the beach, or even rent a boat to take out to sea.

My dad had gone into early retirement, so money was far from an issue when it came to staying in our new, high-dollar neighborhood. I'd heard plenty of horror stories about Primrose. Kids from school said people like me, girls with any trace of color, didn't fit in well. I considered it bullshit gossip. I mean, how would they know if they had never lived in Primrose? And how would they know if they had no pigment in their skin? My father, the man of *color*, was the one that chose the neighborhood. He didn't care for the snobby looks or turned up noses.

"As long as you're in a neighborhood like Primrose, you'll be fine." He said this when I complained about moving for the third time that year. Truthfully, all of the moving around was most likely the reason I had no one to personally call *my* friend. I was a loner, stuck in my house

wondering how to go up to the other kids on the block and ask them if they'd like to jump rope with me.

Let's just say my father was wrong. The girls in Primrose didn't like me. They were afraid to play with me, and none of them believed I was actually twelve years old because I was one bra size away from being a B-cup.

My mother tried arranging sleepovers, but no one would show up, which left me alone, drowning in a puddle of tears with my face down on a pillow as my mother rubbed my back. Dad didn't really know how to comfort me, so whenever I cried, he kept his distance.

He'd worked most of my childhood, but now that he was retired, he had no clue how to handle me—not that he didn't try or anything. He just knew how to make things really, really awkward. Mom worked endless hours as well but, unlike Dad, she hardly managed to spend two hours a day with me. Maybe an hour or so if I was lucky or if I decided to shop with her. I suppose I could have considered myself lucky because some of my friends at Bradshaw Heights Academy only saw their parents once a month. Having busy parents sucked.

Bristle Wave was boring for the most part. My daily routine was to ride my bike through the neighborhood park, come back home and read a book, and then wake up for school. During summer, it was worse.

My parents were hardly ever home—Dad most likely working or playing golf and Mom running her new art studio—so I stayed in the house reading young adult novels by Judy Blume and J.K. Rowling. I thought surely I'd be trapped in Primrose with no friends, no life, and no entertainment until I was off to college—that is, until the day the Blacks moved in.

They happened to move right into the home across the street from me. Mr. Clark lived there only months ago but was sent to a retirement home after falling down the stairs and breaking his hip.

The rumble of a motorcycle caught my ear, and I climbed off my bed, forgetting about the needless algebra homework as I stole a peek out the window. A moving truck parked along the curb, and a black Tahoe pulled into the driveway, parking in front of the garage door.

A woman and a girl climbed out of the Tahoe, the woman fanning the humidity away. The girl looked to be around my age, her nose stuck in a book, hooked on whatever story she was devouring. *Ahh*, I thought. *She likes to read, just like me. Check one.*

They entered the house, and a few moments later, the woman came back out, telling the movers where to carry the items as she pointed towards the ash-brick house, shading her eyes with the other hand above her brow.

The men carried a large, brown sofa across the lawn. Others carried small things like dining and patio chairs, but a small, red recliner caught my eye. The woman made sure it was handled properly.

Everyone seemed to be busy—everyone except the man sitting on the loud motorcycle he rode in on. It was rare hearing the growl of a motorcycle in Primrose. Everyone in the neighborhood drove classy cars—Mercedes, BMWs, and fancy Infiniti or Cadillac SUVs. I knew Mrs. Rhodes, their next-door neighbor, wouldn't be too pleased about that. She hated loud noises, yet she had a small Yorkie that yapped all day long until she came home.

The man sat on his motorcycle, wiping off his helmet with a brown cloth. He wore a fitted black T-shirt and dark wash jeans. His hair was a dark, beautiful, chaotic mess, a few tendrils hanging on his forehead, most likely from taking off his helmet. The haircut suited him—long in the front, short on the sides, and in the back, it parted on one side to uphold a classic yet modern appeal.

It was never like me to take full notice of anyone, but there was just something about this man that had me curious. He didn't seem to match the woman I assumed was his wife. She ran around like a chicken with her head cut off, telling the movers right from wrong. He seemed too laid back for her, but by the way he looked at her— watched as she swished her hips to get to the door in her snazzy high heels—I could tell he loved her.

Completely.

Utterly.

From this angle, he looked tall with a chiseled face, high cheek-bones, and a bone-straight smile that he revealed when his wife walked out the door. She sighed as she walked towards him and stepped between his legs, wrapping her arms around his neck. She held him close, sighed some more as she gazed into his eyes, and I could understand why. That man was absolutely breathtaking. From head to toe, he was perfection.

Curious as to where the girl went, I continued watching the little family. I assumed she was in her unfurnished bedroom, nose still buried deep in her novel. I instantly wanted to meet her. I wanted to know what she was reading. I hoped it was Judy Blume.

Collecting my house key and sliding into my favorite pair of *Sperry's*, I hurried down the stairs where my mother stood in the foyer, chatting on her cellphone while she peered out of the window. I wasn't the only one being nosey.

When she heard me coming down, she turned and asked, "Where are you going, sweetie?"

"I'm going to meet the new neighbors."

"Oh. Tell me how they are," she whisper-hissed as I swung the door open. I nodded and shut it behind me, standing on the porch. The family was no longer in sight. The movers were bringing in some more of their larger belongings.

I was being impatient. I wanted to meet the girl across the street first before any of the other prissy girls in Primrose got to her. Not that I needed a friend, but I *wanted* one. I wanted someone that had similar interests, and reading was a *huge* one for me. So, I walked across the street, up their driveway, and courageously knocked on the front door.

It opened right away, and to my surprise, it was the man from the motorcycle and the girl's father, I presumed. "Well," he said, slowly revealing a full smile. "Who do we have here?"

"Uh... hey." My cheeks turned rosy red, my chest going hot. I wasn't expecting him to answer the door. "I—I wanted to introduce myself. I'm Chloe Knight. I live right across the street"—I looked back and pointed to my house—"and I was wondering if I could meet the girl that went inside?"

The man raised a brow. "The girl? You mean my little Isabelle?"

"That's her name?"

"Mmm-hmm." One of the movers walked past him and me. The man looked down, gesturing back. "Come inside. I'll go get her."

My throat became thick, so I didn't say anything. I just bobbed my head and followed the man inside. The house felt full, and they hadn't even set up yet. Boxes were stacked in every corner, furniture piled high in the den and living room.

"Sorry about the mess," he teased, raising his brows. "Just moved in and all." He held his hands out, giving me a *shit happens* kind of shrug. I forced a smile, unsure of how to respond, and he noticed, stopping in his tracks before walking up the stairs. "I guess I should have told you who we are, huh?" He scratched the top of his head. "I'm Theo Black. My wife's name is Janet, and I've already told you my daughter's."

"Cool."

He pressed his lips to smile, and after informing me that he'd tell Isabelle I was downstairs, he was taking the steps by twos, calling for his daughter. I took the time to look around the home. A few tables were in place, and next to one of them was an open box of photo albums.

Glancing back briefly before focusing on it again, I reached forward and opened the album. The first few photos were of Mr. and Mrs. Black, but as I flipped through some more, there were baby photos of the girl. She wore a lot of pink and yellow. She had rosy, chubby cheeks, and she looked like a happy baby.

I noticed, then, that Mr. and Mrs. Black were very young when they had Isabelle. They looked to be in their late teens, early twenties. It was strange because they seemed so happy and content. While her parents seemed hip, cool, and lively, mine were nearing fifty, bitter towards each other, and mostly miserable. Hell, they hardly spoke to one another. And don't get me started on our awkward, scheduled dinners.

My parents decided to have a child once they'd established careers and traveled the world. By the time they were ready to settle, they were thirty-six. It was a decent age, but unfortunately, Mom was considered high-risk when she carried me. I figured it was the reason she never had more children.

For a while, I thought that was the key to happiness—living your life first with the one you love and then creating a tiny being that you will love unconditionally for the rest of your life. Apparently, I had the wrong mindset because as I studied the Black's pictures, I realized I didn't even have any of my own to compare them to. If I did, I had no clue where they were other than the few small frames on top of the fireplace and beside the sofa. All for show, of course. But through all their photos, they seemed genuinely happy.

"She'll be down in a minute." Mr. Black's deep voice startled me, and I snatched my hands away from the photo album, cheeks tinged red. "Sorry," I whispered quickly.

"Don't be." He walked around me, picking up the photo album I'd violated. Flipping past a few pages, he finally came across one and laughed. "This is Izzy when she was two. Completely naked, playing with her toes." He showed me the picture, leaning towards me. His arms brushed mine. I don't think he noticed or cared, but I did. How couldn't I? It was almost like I'd been shocked—it was electrifying.

I stepped aside, smiling with him. "She was adorable."

"Still is," he sighed.

Footsteps sounded seconds later, and the girl came rushing down. When she reached us, she put on a large grin, flashing pink braces. "You wanted to meet me!?" she practically shrieked.

"I—uh, yeah! I wanted to say hi and introduce myself to the new neighbors."

"That's so cool." She extended her arm, holding her hand out. I did the same. "Isabelle Black, but you can call me Izzy."

"Chloe Knight." I beamed.

"So nice to meet you."

"You too." We shook hands, and instantly, I freaking loved Isabelle. "Hey, were you reading a Judy Blume book earlier?"

She let out a girly gasp. "Oh my gosh! Yes! I love her!"

"I do too!" I squealed. "I can spot that blue cover from anywhere!"

"No *freakin'* way!"

"Your mom is gonna flip shit if she hears you talking like that," Mr. Black said, putting the album on the table.

Isabelle put her hand on her hip. "I wonder where I get it from."

He chuckled, and I laughed because he used a bad word right in front of us.

"Hey, how about I show you the rest of my books. I have almost all of Judy Blume!"

"Okay!" Isabelle grabbed my hand and led the way up the stairs, passing by her mother who was telling two of the movers how to set up the bed in the master bedroom.

"Oh!" Mrs. Black's eyes expanded when she realized there were two girls instead of one. "Who's this?" she asked, green eyes bright.

"Mom, this is Chloe. She lives across the street. I'm showing her my Judy Blume collection."

"Oh really? A new friend already! See, I told you this neighborhood wouldn't be so bad." Mrs. Black smiled, revealing dimples. She was a really pretty woman. Strawberry blonde hair, full pink lips, and a body I hoped I would get once I finally blossomed. She didn't even look like she'd had a child. It seemed she was still considering having babies.

"Hi," I said, waving.

"Hello gorgeous girl." She reached for one of my curls. "Your hair is beautiful. Did you do it?"

"I did!"

"You did a great job, sweetie. Maybe you can teach Izzy how to style her hair, huh?"

I shrugged, looking at Isabelle's frizzy, black mane. "Hmm, maybe."

Isabelle rolled her eyes. "Can we go now, Mom?"

"Go on. But please be careful, Izzy. You have a lot of fragile stuff in your boxes."

"I know, I know." She reached for my hand again. "Come on!" We ran down the hallway, stepping into a room with a bunk bed. The walls were already painted a light shade of pink, the fuzzy white rug on the ground making the color pop.

Isabelle showed me her collection of books. A large box was filled to the brim, piled high with novels, and not just Judy Blume. That day, Isabelle became my best friend, and I didn't even realize it. We connected and bonded, laughed and talked about books and Disney movies until the sun sank.

It was the most fun I'd had with anyone in a long time. I no longer felt lonely with Isabelle right across the street from me. Her room was the room on the second floor, only a few inches to the left of where my bay window was.

At night, if we couldn't sleep, one of us would blink a flashlight to see if the other was awake, and if we both were, we'd turn on our night-lights, talk through the walkie-talkies we went half on, and giggle about silly things. Most times, it was books, but sometimes it was boys.

We grew up with each other. We were closer than I ever thought possible. She'd become a sister to me. We gossiped. We watched girly movies and listened to the Backstreet Boys, Britney Spears, and TLC. We'd sing our hearts out, dancing in my bedroom or hers until we were exhausted.

We hardly ever fought, and if we did, it was about stupid things like what boy was hotter at school or which friendship bracelet we would buy from *Claire's*. Izzy and I were inseparable. And somehow, Mr. Black became closer to me to, but not in an unconstructive way.

Mr. Black helped Izzy and me with our homework and even took us to softball practice whenever my mother couldn't. Mrs. Black worked a lot at her bakery in Los Angeles, which left Mr. Black at home, caring for his daughter.

Not that Mrs. Black was a bad mother or wife, she just *needed* to be busy now. I'd heard from Izzy that her parents had struggled at one point in their lives, when she was seven and Mr. Black was in between jobs, trying to become a car technician, running his own business. They lived with Mrs. Black's mom in Los Angeles for almost three years.

Mr. Black was a good man—better yet, a *great* man. He'd take us to the park and to the movies, buying us all the candy and buttery popcorn we wanted, but when Izzy and I felt we were too old to hang out with him at the park (because let's face it, teenagers didn't like to be seen with their parents), he'd have no problem dropping us off at the mall and even giving us money to spend.

Things were great. My life was great. I had someone I could call a friend, someone I could consider a sister, maybe not by blood but by spirit and character.

From how I described the Blacks, you probably wonder just how I fell for Izzy's Dad. Let's just say it was very... unpredictable. It was something that just... happened—perhaps a simple crush that soon blossomed into something full and real and unique. I had always tried denying my feelings for him. I never wanted anyone to see, but there were certain things he said and did. Things that drove my young mind and body crazy.

Like the night when Mrs. Black wasn't home and he was drinking in his garage, listening to some R&B music. He moved his hips, dancing and twirling Izzy around playfully. She giggled, and I sat on top of a cooler in the corner, watching them bond. But then the song changed, and he flicked his fingers for me to join him.

I shook my head and waved my hands in a *no way* kind of gesture, but he insisted, marching forward and grabbing my hand. He tugged up, and I landed against his chest. He twirled me with a swift, charming effect, laughing as he held me close. I tried so hard not to fall victim to his touch. I tried hard to fight the chills he gave me, ignore the galloping of my heartbeat.

But his smile was too perfect.

And his natural scent was so comforting.

His lips were only a few inches away, and I'm not sure if he noticed, but my stomach was rubbing against his crotch. It was harmless. I was sure because he held Izzy the exact same way, but to me, it meant the fucking world to be so close... so intimate.

His laugh was hearty when he caught my embarrassed gaze, and I giggled when he finally released me and teased me about having two left feet. Izzy joined in on the laughter, telling Mr. Black that I'd always been a horrible dancer.

It was true.

I was glad they caused a distraction. I didn't mind being teased as long as neither of them took notice of my true feelings. God, I could remember that day so clearly.

I can also recall the time when I was sixteen and had just gotten my car and license. Just like any other teen, it was one of the most exciting times of my life—that is until I blew my tire going into the second week of driving.

I was stranded on the freeway, and it was freezing that day. As I shivered inside my coupe with my cellphone glued to my ear, I wanted to cry. I wanted to cry because my dad wasn't home and Mom wasn't answering her phone. Neither were there to help me, so with heavy tears, I called the one person I knew was always around and also happened to specialize in cars.—Mr. Black.

He answered, and after I sobbed into the phone, he told me to calm down. I mean, maybe I was being a bit dramatic, but only because it'd never happened to me and I hated the feeling of being stranded. Between sniffles and tears, a small glimmer of relief ignited as he told me he was on the way.

When he pulled up in the Tahoe, I felt my heart swell in my chest. He parked the truck and walked to my car. I sat in the driver's seat, and he tapped my window with his gloved knuckles, a faint smile playing on his lips as his head moved sideways.

His smile was comforting and silently whispered so many things, the main one being that everything was going to be okay and blowing a tire happened to people all the time. His smile gave me the reassurance I needed and the safety I longed for. He never failed to let me know that if I ever needed anything, he was only a phone call away.

Unlike my parents, Mr. Black made sure I was taken care of for the most part. However, I never considered him a parent. To me, he was a really, really great friend.

He opened my door as cars sped by, reaching beside my leg to pop my trunk. "Come on," he said, pulling away and going for the back.

Confused, I climbed out of the car and followed him, watching as he pulled out my spare tire. Propping it on the side of my car, he jogged to his truck and took out a wrench and a case of something, and then he came back in a quick pace, bending down to check out my tire.

"Can't blame yourself for this, Little Knight. Looks like this thing was about to give out way before you ever got the chance to drive it."

"Really?" I asked.

He gestured for me to bend down with him, and I did. "Yep. See that?" He pointed at a jagged piece on the tire. "The tear started right there. Something most likely stressed the rubber. Alright, come on," he grunted as he pushed the tire aside and picked up the wrench. "I'm gonna show you how to change a tire so we can make sure you're never left stranded again."

I nodded, but tears still hung at the edges of my eyes. Mr. Black took notice and sighed, reaching forward to cap my shoulders. Laughing, most likely at my overreaction, he said, "It's alright, Chloe. I'm here. Your car will be fine." Then he flashed me a crooked smile, one that made my heartbeat quicken.

"I feel stupid," I muttered as he used the wrench to unscrew the bolts.

"Don't worry. You'll live. Besides," he shrugged one shoulder, glancing my way, "I've been wanting an excuse to check out your car. A BMW? It's nice as hell, but what were your parents thinking giving you something this fancy for your first car?"

That made me laugh. I swiped my eyes. "I've always wanted one."

"Good taste, but I'd be damned if I ever gave Izzy something nicer than what I was driving."

I giggled at his remark and felt truly at ease as he laughed too.

Mr. Black did most of the work for me but told me to twist the wrench on the last bolt. Apparently, I was doing it wrong, not screwing it in enough, so without much thought, he reached over to help me. His hands wrapped around mine, and he held me in a sideways position, mixing in his strength to twist it. He made sure it was good and tight.

That day, I felt *everything*. I purposely smelled him, his scent making me want to curl into his chest on that lonely winter day and never move. And his arms, God, so large and welcoming. They were tight around me, tensing as he did one final spin around. The scruff along his jaw grazed my cheek, and my belly rolled, a fire replacing the chill I once endured. I could feel his body heat radiating, blending with mine, and for a split second, I considered us one.

I know he thought nothing of it because he was simply helping me, but I thought everything of the gesture. My heart danced in my chest, my mouth going dry, lacking full sentences as he told me how replacing a tire was supposed to be done.

That was the day I truly, honestly, fell hard for Mr. Black. That was the day he made me feel something I'd never felt before—a rush that was hard to describe. It was quick and sweet and whole. That rush made me lose all self-control, causing an ache within me when I realized he could never be mine and I shouldn't have wanted him to be anyway.

He was only helping, but I took his kindness as something more, falling and crushing hard on a married man. And he wasn't just *any* married man, he was a happily married man and the father to a girl I considered a sister to me.

So, I made sure my feelings for Mr. Black never showed and were never put on display. I slept on my love for him, burying it in a deep, safe place in my heart. I knew it would always linger and I would always feel my pulse go double speed when he was nearby, but my friendship was important, not only with Izzy, but with Mr. Black too.

In my mind, Mr. Black was a no-no. He was off limits. He wasn't mine. I could never have him. I wasn't even supposed to love him the way I did.

For the most part, I kept my feelings at bay, ignoring the racing of my heart, the fire, and the ache only his presence could conjure. It became manageable. I laid out restrictions for myself. I did it for his family. I did it for him. But most of all, I did it for Izzy.

Through the years, my set boundaries worked. I thought things between Izzy, Mr. Black, and me would remain perfect forever...

But then senior year happened.

Reality happened.

And it was far from gentle.

It hit the Blacks like a speeding monster-truck. It blind-sided them and even myself, ruining all happiness and blurring some of the bond I'd created with their family.

TWO

CHLOE

EVERY STUDENT KNEW that when the final bell rang on the last day of school, it was the official start of summer break. My fellow peers hollered, boasted, and laughed, tunneling through the exits of Bradshaw Academy and racing for their cars like wild bulls. Even the teachers smiled, their shoulders unstiffening and being replaced by a momentary touch of relief.

Izzy was eighteen, and due to starting school a year late, I was nineteen. We were excited to finally be done with high school, ready to tackle college. Sadly, we were going to different universities, but they were only two hours apart, so we planned on seeing each other often.

I drove home from school that day.

Before I could back out of my parking spot, Riley, my ex-boyfriend, banged his hands on the hood of my car with an annoying grin on his face. We gasped, our attention averting from each other to him, and I slammed on the brakes.

"What the fuck are you doing, dipshit!?" Izzy shouted, her upper half now through the sunroof.

Riley busted out in a laugh. I rolled my eyes, lowering my window. "Get out of the way!"

"Not until you answer my question from earlier!" Riley walked around the car and to my window. He bent down, placing his elbows on the top of the door.

"I already told you I would think about it." I looked back at Izzy as she sat down and folded her arms. "We have plans. Your little pool party doesn't seem like much fun."

"Oh yeah?" He flashed a crooked smile. It used to make me drool. I quickly got over it when I realized how much of a cocky jock he was. "And just what in the hell will you two be doing?"

"We'll be celebrating the start of summer elsewhere."

"Oh fuck. Don't tell me you're going to Joseph's party instead of mine."

"Well, his party doesn't involve a ton of whores soaked in water. His will be inside, with more drinks and louder music. Joseph's house is huge. No one will complain because he doesn't have neighbors close by."

"You, on the other hand," Izzy said, pointing at him and laughing, "...live next door to Kimmy who has a mother that nags and bitches for no fucking reason."

Riley shook his head. "You are both idiots. My party is going to be the shit. Everyone is coming." He stood up straight. "If you aren't there, consider yourself lame."

I shrugged and gave Izzy a knowing look. She laughed, and I said, "We'll take our chances." When he stepped back, I pulled off, swerving as he yelled something rude after us.

"What a dickhead!" Izzy chimed, lowering the visor mirror and checking her glossed lips. She fluffed her black hair and then looked at me with bright, green eyes. "So, what are we *really* doing? Joseph's last party was totally fucking lame." She clapped her hands, suddenly having a bright idea. "Oh! I know! Let's go to L.A. Frankie's mom has an apartment there. We can invite some friends, and I can get Marco to buy us some drinks. We can get wasted and then do the same again tomorrow night."

I glanced at her before focusing on the road again. Izzy was still my best friend, but I don't know what made her want to drink and smoke more often. She was becoming this untamed party animal, thirsty for attention. I guess I couldn't blame her for it, though.

It all started when she lost her virginity to Justin, this preppy rugby player that was a class higher than us. To make a long story short, Justin dumped Izzy when he realized he only had two weeks left before going off to college. My guess is he figured college pussy would be better and more convenient for him than a twelfth grader's.

I felt for Izzy, and I wanted to kick Justin's balls up to his throat, but like a champ, she recovered, moving on to Marco. She met him at a bar in L.A. when she was supposed to be helping her mom bake.

"That doesn't sound like a fun start of the summer." I scrunched my nose with disinterest. "Didn't your dad say your mom was throwing a cupcake party tonight anyway?"

She scoffed. "Yeah, but no thank you! I'm not in the mood to taste every cake she bakes." Her eyes rolled again.

"Your mom makes the best cupcakes! Are you kidding?"

"I'm pretty sure she'd rather me not show up. She knows I don't participate. My dad talks too much. I don't know why he even brought it up the other night. He just did it to make conversation with you. He knows I never show to Mom's baking parties." She looked me over through the corner of her eye when I stopped at a stoplight. "It's like he can never shut up when you're around. He goes on and on and on."

I blinked fast, unsure of what to say. There were times when Mr. Black could never shut up. Like when I turned seventeen and finally grew boobs big enough to have all the guys stare at. My hips had rounded out, and softball helped me maintain a slender waist and a flat stomach. My thighs had filled out as well, toned from workouts. Even my face had become smoother, free of acne and blemishes.

I'd learned how to do my hair at a young age, so flat-ironing it or even leaving it curly when I'd wash it was simple. I wasn't exactly a woman, but I was close enough. And although I was kind of insecure about my body, I knew there were girls that would have died to have it, so I didn't complain much. Perhaps he was just comfortable with chatting with me, spilling all the family secrets.

We arrived in Primrose in no time. I went home to change out of my uniform and into a black and yellow sundress and sandals. When I jogged down the stairs, I heard the echo of my father's deep voice. I hadn't even realized he was home. He must have parked in the garage.

I entered the kitchen, spotting him with his phone glued to his ear. He turned around to the sound of my footsteps and put on a gentle smile when his identical, hazel eyes met mine. I exchanged a smile, and then he held up a quick finger, silently telling me to wait a second.

Going for the bar stools at the island counter, I took a seat and picked up a banana. I was done eating it by the time Dad was off the phone.

"I swear they're trying to kill me," he muttered, placing his phone on the counter. He shut the screen off, and I smiled. I knew he had work to do, but, like always, he gave me some time out of his busy schedule. "So, I have your graduation date marked on my calendar. I know I've missed a ton of stuff this year, baby girl, but I won't be missing that. You have my word."

I grinned. "Okay. I believe you."

"What do you say to some lunch tomorrow? Ice cream afterwards maybe? We can hit that old ice cream shack we used to go to right by the beach."

"That sounds great. But... wait." I squished my brows together. "You don't have to work?"

He shrugged. "I can work around it. I'm proud of you. My baby girl is about to graduate high school! Soon, she'll be off to college." He sighed, almost in disbelief. "Where has the time gone?" Smiling, Dad came around the counter, pinched my cheek, and then kissed my forehead. He started to say something else, but his phone buzzed on the marble counter again. Cursing beneath his breath, he went back for it, checked the name on the screen, and then shook his head, his shoulders going into a defeated slump. "Sorry, Chloe. Gotta take this. Plans tonight?"

"Yeah. With Izzy. Last day of school." I hopped off the stool.

"Oh okay. Well be safe. Call me or your mom sometime tonight so we know you're still alive." He answered the phone call and started for the mouth of the kitchen. Before he disappeared, he quickly whispered, "I love you!" and then he was up the stairs, most likely on his way to his office.

Sighing, I tossed the peel of my banana in the garbage can, grabbed my cell phone, and then went over to Izzy's, walking right in. I no longer needed to knock. The Blacks trusted me.

When I walked in, Izzy was coming down the stairs in a tight purple dress. "Oh, Chloe! Hey, can you zip me up please?" She whirled around, bringing her hair over her shoulder.

"Who do you think is gonna show in L.A.?" I zipped the back of her dress, and she turned around, her green eyes meeting my hazel.

"Marco will show, and I'm sure Joey is ditching Riley's party. He always has pot, too. And he is so fucking into you." She whispered the last sentence, and just as she did, the sound of a motorcycle's engine hummed from the driveway. I stiffened. Izzy's eyes went wide like a deer caught in headlights. "Holy shit! Let me go get a cardigan or something. My dad will flip shit! And don't tell him where we're going!" she shouted as she ran up the stairs.

I straightened my back, listening as she scrambled through her closet. She wasn't the only one nervous about his appearance. I looked down at the seams of my dress, smoothing out the wrinkles with flat palms. My heart picked up speed, and I sighed. *What is it with me? Why am I so nervous to see him? I see him almost every day.*

It took a while for him to come in. I fidgeted on my feet, glancing at the couch. I could have taken a seat, but I didn't want to. I wanted him to see me, maybe compliment me on something I was wearing like he always did.

I loved this dress. I'd just bought it. Maybe he would compliment it.

So many crazy thoughts ran through my mind, but they all made sure to shut the hell up as the door creaked open and Mr. Black walked into the house, going through the mail in his hand and, soon, kicking the door shut behind him. When he spotted me, his eyes connected with mine, expanding. "Oh, Chloe." He put on a smile. "What's going on, Little Knight?"

"Hi, Mr. Black."

"Theo," he corrected.

I laughed. "I feel really weird calling you by your first name."

"We're all adults now, right?" he shrugged. "Calling me *Mr. Black* makes me feel old as hell."

"But you're not. You look great—I mean you shouldn't consider yourself old—" I sealed my lips, heat blazing in my cheeks. "I just mean... you're not old."

"Ha." He laughed softly, head tilted. He dropped the stack of mail on the table, walking forward. "That's nice to know." He studied my attire, smiling softly. "Cool dress."

"Thanks." I beamed inside, bursting with rays of sunlight—or maybe it was moonlight. It felt cool to have his compliment—like the moon—not hot and blazing like the sun. I fought hard to ward off my blush, looking towards the open window above Mrs. Black's favorite red, leather recliner.

"You two coming to Janet's shindig tonight?" he asked.

I whipped my head. "Um... I'm not sure. We're going to go to the mall. Izzy is going to help me pick out a dress for graduation day." I gave an innocent shrug and press of my lips. "It's right around the corner, after all."

"Really? I believe Izzy has had hers picked out since winter." He folded his arms across his broad chest, a crooked smile taking over his lips. I hadn't realized before, but he only had on a black muscle tank. His muscles flexed as his arms crossed, the detailed ink making my heart spasm a little.

Fuck, Izzy's dad was hot. With his goatee and hair styled the same ever since the day I met him. Classy and casual. Why couldn't guys my age look like him?

"Well, I'll let Janet know." He walked past me, and I caught a whiff of his scent. There was a smidgen of cologne, but it'd most likely faded from a long day at work. His natural scent was inviting. Delicious. My body hummed inside, familiar with his smell. "She might be a little disappointed, though."

"I'm sorry," I apologized. "If I find a dress in time, we'll try to make it."

Izzy trotted down the stairs with a small tote bag, greeting her dad as she wrapped her arms over his shoulders. "Hey, Dad."

"Izzy Bear, heard you weren't coming to your mom's party tonight?"

"Oh..." She pretended to care, pouting her bottom lip as she pulled away. "I was going to, but Chloe has been asking me to help her buy a dress for weeks now." That was the lie we agreed to use if our parents asked our whereabouts.

He looked at me briefly before focusing on her again. "Sure, kiddo." He gave her a sarcastic, *full-of-shit* look. "Come on, now. You don't have to lie to me. Just be safe and be sure to call me tonight. I won't hound you unless I feel I have to." He looked at each of us. "You're smart girls. And I trust you around Chloe. That's the only reason I'm letting you go out tonight."

My lips spread when his eyes bounced from hers to mine. They sparked a little, the brown pools gentle and confident. Unable to conceal the grin and the blush that ran over my face, I dropped my head, pretending I didn't notice the spark in his eye. Sometimes I wondered if Mr. Black was flirting with me or if he was just a really nice guy.

There were certain looks he gave me, looks that only boys that were into me provided. Like how he winked at me every time he saw me, and even when he stood only a few inches away, watching as I spoke to him and filled him in on the latest school gossip. He watched how my lips moved, and even noted how my eyes always rolled when I mentioned Riley. He wasn't pretending to be interested in what I had to say. He actually responded and even gave me advice.

It was... strange. But, for some reason, I liked it. He was the only one that actually listened to me. Not even Izzy indulged in my concerns fully. Most times, she was too busy talking about herself or something she got into, and if she wasn't, she'd be on her cellphone, texting or tweeting away while I quietly explained my reasons for being upset, happy, etcetera. She cared, of course, but she didn't listen quite as well as Mr. Black.

Izzy kissed his cheek. "I'll be safe, Dad. Don't worry," she promised. Then, she picked up her bag from the corner, gesturing for me to come on with a hurried swoop of her eyes. She was out the door in a second, and I followed after her, but before walking out, I took a glance over my shoulder. Mr. Black waved a hand, wordlessly saying, *"See you later."*

It was hard ignoring the heat that slid through me as he sat on the arm of the sofa, arms folded again, brown eyes hot and smoldering. "See you later, Mr. Black."

"Later, Chloe." *Chlo-ee.* I shut the door, but trust me, the way he sang my name replayed in my head all day and all night long.

Even as Izzy got completely drunk and puffed on marijuana, I thought about him. I imagined him, and then I remembered that, ever since I was twelve, I had always admired him.

He kept himself in great shape. He was nice to me. Sweet. And it seemed when he was younger, he was a complete badass, but Mrs. Black whipped him into decent shape and made him sort of good. I knew there was some darkness in him, and that alone intrigued me.

When I was a little older, spending endless hours at Izzy's and growing into my mature, girly ways, I wondered how he was in bed. I'm a little ashamed to admit that I heard him and Mrs. Black one night.

I'd slept over with Izzy, and it was nearing two in the morning. I could hear them when I went to use the bathroom. She sounded like she was in ultimate pleasure—like she never wanted it to end—and he groaned, gently banging the headboard against the wall.

I could vividly imagine him.

Eyes shut.

Body tense, ready to release.

I was sixteen. I was pathetic.

And crushing on my bestie's dad.

Hard.

Around 1:45 AM, Izzy's cellphone rang, buzzing on the nightstand. It was a constant ring. On and off. Maybe it was urgent. "Izzy," I groaned. "Your phone." She snored. When her phone stopped, mine decided to ring, and I picked up, answering groggily.

"Hello?"

"Chloe!" Mr. Black's voice came through the line, frantic and on edge. I perked up, eyebrows stitched.

"Mr. Black?"

"I—fuck. I need—where is Izzy? Where are you?"

"We're... at Frankie's. Why? What's going on?"

"Is she sleeping?" His voice sounded strained.

"Yes."

"I need you to wake her up... please."

"Mr. Black... what's going on?"

"It's Janet..." His voice broke. "I'm at the hospital and Janet... she—there was an accident."

"An accident?" I gasped. "What do you mean? What happened?" I hopped off the sofa, rushing to where Izzy had passed out on the floor. She groaned.

Mr. Black continued. "On her way home from the bakery she stopped at some—some run down gas station. Got robbed and mauled by some low-life motherfuckers. I swear to God if they find them I'll fucking *kill* them."

"Is she alright?" I asked.

"She... tried to fight back. Broke her jaw. Broke some ribs, and..." He swallowed hard, and his voice was unclear. "Because she fought back, they stabbed her eight times. She would have bled to death if someone hadn't found her, heard her cries for help." He sniffled. My heart cracked.

"Oh my god," I whispered.

"They don't know if she's going to make it."

I shook Izzy harder, and she sat up, eyes broad and confused. "What the fuck, Chloe?"

"Izzy, I—we have to go." I stuttered, keeping the phone glued to my ear. "What hospital?" I asked into the phone. Mr. Black told me where, and as soon as I was dressed and helped Izzy back into her dress, I grabbed her keys and rushed down the stairs, meeting at the car.

Izzy groaned, calling after me. "I'm so lost," she whined "I don't get what's going on. Why are we leaving in the middle of the night? Did Marco try to come onto you? I swear I'll fucking kill him."

I slammed the car door behind me, and when she was inside, I turned to face her, gripping her shoulder caps. "Izzy, I seriously need you to get out of your high and hung-over stupor and listen to me."

She frowned, forehead creasing. "Sheesh. Okay...?"

"Your mom was... robbed and stabbed eight times on her way home tonight."

"What!?" She gasped, frantic. Her entire body perked up, eyes growing wide. That was all she needed to hear to snap out of it. It almost seemed she didn't believe me with the look of utter disbelief masking her face.

"She's in the hospital," I went on, and I hated to see the relief in her eyes because I wasn't finished. "But they don't know if she's going to make it."

She cupped her mouth, eyes wide and watery. "Oh my god," she whispered. Then she waved her hands, tears spilling as she motioned for me to start the car and hurry up. "Well fucking go, Chloe! Go! Oh my god!"

I started the car and pulled off, unsure of what to feel... how to react. I felt numb for both Izzy and Mr. Black. I wasn't sure how to accept it either. If Izzy lost her mother, she would regret not showing up for the baking party.

She would hate herself.

I couldn't believe this was happening. Even as we reached the hospital, storming inside and finding Mr. Black in the waiting room, it still hadn't hit me yet. It hit Izzy of course. She sobbed hard into her father's chest, her body racking. Mr. Black tried remaining strong, but he couldn't fight the tears.

I lingered silently, my head down, purposely avoiding their eyes.

We sat in the waiting room for three hours. They were performing surgery, but the surgery turned out to be nothing more than another complication.

A doctor appeared in the waiting room. "Mr. Black?" he called, eyes sullen.

Izzy and Mr. Black jumped out of their seats, rushing for him. They had optimism in their eyes, but I could tell that was about to be crushed. Mrs. Black was already gone, and they didn't even know it.

Deep down, I knew it.

I knew she'd lost the battle. She was a petite woman, and to be stabbed eight times... I couldn't even imagine. This wasn't 50 Cent's survival story. There was no fantasy bullshit—no coming out of this.

This was real.

Raw.

And insanely depressing.

The doctor spoke, and immediately, Izzy broke down, clutching herself, eyes sealed tight as she wept. Mr. Black caught her as she threw her body into his arms, reeling her in, and swallowing hard as he did his best to nod his head and take heed of his emotions. Patting Mr. Black's shoulder, the doctor turned and walked away, leaving us in a muggy shower of gloom.

They stood there... well, *he* stood there. Holding Izzy. He was in a frozen state of mind, listening to his daughter weep, calming her by rubbing her back. It would have seemed warm and affectionate on his behalf, but those weren't his intentions. It was a habit he was accustomed to—soothing his daughter whenever she was in need. The act he was pulling now... it was confusing as hell. His eyes were too focused on the blank wall ahead of him. He was too stiff.

Too cold.

Too... wrapped up in disbelief.

Finally he moved. He spoke—did something to prove he was okay... for the time being anyway.

"Chloe," Mr. Black murmured, turning only a fraction of the way. I stood. His face was as white as a sheet of snow. "Take Izzy home, please. Make sure she's okay."

I nodded, immediately reaching for a torn up Izzy and making my way to the exit. Before I departed, I looked back. Mr. Black pinched the bridge of his nose, trying his hardest to fight off the tears. Only, it didn't work. And though I wanted to be there for Izzy, I also wanted to be there for him.

He had been ripped apart, raw emotion pouring out as he sat in one of the chairs, body shuddering. Tears threatened me, but I kept it together, cooing to Izzy as I made my way to the car. As she sobbed in the passenger seat, I sat still for a moment, gripping the wheel.

I wondered how it would have been if one of my parents had died. *Would I cry this hard? Would I care this much?* They were hardly around, even while retired, but I loved them to death. It was scary to imagine them no longer on this earth.

I looked at Izzy, watching as she swiped at the never-ending flow of tears. She hid her face in the sleeves of her cardigan, and her sobs stopped for what felt like forever. Her body went absolutely still, and my eyes widened because, from where I sat, it looked like she'd passed right out. Her eyes were shut. Her body was motionless. I couldn't even hear her breathing.

But seconds later, the loudest sob I'd heard from her all night was unleashed in the small space of her car, and I startled in my seat, swallowing the big pill of emotion.

"God, Mom!" she wailed, and then she fell forward, burying her face in the cup of her hands. I rubbed her back, silence overcoming me. Nothing I could have said would calm her grief.

For Izzy, it was too much to handle. No longer having a mother. No longer being able to share her life or future with the woman that birthed her and made so many sacrifices for her.

I can't imagine...

"Let's get you home," I whispered, starting the car and driving slowly, blank the entire way back to Primrose Way.

Mr. Black got home about two hours after we did. Sliding the curtain aside, I watched as he parked his bike and kicked the kickstand with the side of his leather boot. I waited for him to get off—waited for him to make a move—but he didn't.

The sun was just rising, a few rays shining down through the leaves of the towering palm trees surrounding him. None of the rays touched him, though. It seemed a higher power knew he was hurting, that his soul had been cloaked in darkness and anguish, and was cutting him some slack.

He sat on his bike for several minutes, and then he finally took action. Hopping off the leather seat, he opened the garage and as soon as he was inside, he picked up a few personal items, tossing them all out. Toolbox after toolbox came flying out, metal clanking and rattling as it slammed onto the concrete.

A sharp gasp passed by me, and I went for my jacket, rushing down the stairs, shutting off the alarm, and quietly slinking out the balcony door so my parents wouldn't hear me. After rounding the side of the house, I rushed across the street and up the Black's driveway.

"Mr. Black!" I called as he lifted a hammer in the air above his head. He was standing right above his old 2000 Harley. It was a classic, still in great shape. I only saw him ride it once. He wanted to save mileage... at least that's what he told us.

His head whipped to the side, and he looked at me, eyes red-rimmed, his face still pale. His nostrils flared, the anger present. The pain clear. His hurt cutting deep.

I lifted my hands in the air as I entered the garage cautiously, eyes hot. My throat dried out, lips parted as I tried formulating words. But what could I say? Other than saying I was sorry for his loss nothing felt like the right thing to tell him.

"Theo," I whispered, and his back straightened, his arms dropping with sluggish feat. "I know you're upset," I said. "I know this isn't what you wanted. Mrs. Black shouldn't be gone... she didn't deserve what happened to her—"

"I know she didn't." His voice was gruff as he cut my sentence in half. I'd never heard it that way before. Dry and scratchy and deep. It was the first time I ever felt unwelcomed by him.

"Destroying the home you two worked so hard for won't make you feel any better." I pointed towards my house, taking a few more steps ahead. "Izzy needs a safe place to come back to..."

He didn't say anything. Just stared at me, motionless. Then, before I knew it, the hammer was no longer in the air. His arms dropped, and it slipped out of his hands, hitting the ground with a heart-rattling *thunk*.

I didn't feel so safe while in the garage with him, but like someone trying to tame a wild beast, I kept moving forward. I didn't know what

Mr. Black was capable of. I didn't know if I could trust him while he was so angry. I didn't know the Theodore Black that thrived way before I ever existed. I didn't know his backstory, but I assumed he had an immoral temper.

I understood he was a good man and that he would never harm the people he loved, but I wasn't sure if I fit into that group. As someone he cared about... someone he *loved*.

After spending seven years around this man, he never could be placed in that "fatherly" category. He acted as more of a friend than a role model to me. Like he wanted to be my age again, living a free and reckless life.

Sluggishly, Mr. Black stepped back towards the door that led into the house, his face tightening. "I should have waited," he said, voice breaking. "Instead of going home early, I should have been there, following her home." He lowered to a squat, pressing his elbows on his thighs and folding his fingers in front of his mouth. "I was complaining about a damn headache, and she was good enough to understand. I should have just manned the fuck up. I should have stayed there. If I had, it never would have fucking happened."

"No, no, no," I cooed. Marching forward, I squatted in front of him, holding onto his forearms. "No, don't say that. You didn't know this would happen. Mrs. Black takes the same route home every night. Things happen that are out of our control."

"I should have just rode to fucking L.A. with her. This is the exact fucking reason we left from that fucked up city. Ignorant, stupid moth-erfuckers can never keep their hands to themselves. I swear to God if I find them, I'll fucking kill them. All of them. There was more than one."

I blinked my tears away, watching his run free. He didn't dare swipe them, and he didn't even try to hide. He no longer cared how he looked or how emotional he was. He was... comfortable with me. At least he was talking, not bottling it all up.

"She's fucking gone, Chloe. Isn't that some shit?" He scoffed, giving a smile that contained no trace of happiness. "Her, of all people... my fucking *wife* of thirteen fucking years. Dead." He shook and dropped his head. A few stray tendrils fell down on his forehead, eyelashes touching his cheekbones. I tucked the loose strands back. He looked up, and our eyes connected and barred for just a small moment.

"It doesn't seem real," I murmured. "It seems she could come home at any minute. Pull up in the driveway and greet everyone."

"Yeah..." His eyes held mine, the brown pools darker but softer. He studied my face, the small stretch of sunlight allowing him the opportunity.

Eyes connected.

Skin tingled.

Heartbeats quickened... my heartbeat.

Swallowing thickly, he stood to his feet, bringing me up with him. When he held my hands, it caused my skin to buzz, eliciting a fire within me. I controlled my reaction, taking a step back as he raked his fingers through his hair. He looked at me hesitantly, like he felt the same thing but couldn't speak on it—wouldn't dare speak on it. Breaking the silence, he said, "I'm going to go hit the shower. Catch some sleep if I can."

"Okay." I nodded. "When Izzy's up, I'll let her know you're here."

His face grew pained, almost like he didn't want to face his daughter. There was fear, fear that he might break down once he saw traces of his wife in his baby girl. Like her green eyes and small nose. Her wild personality. "Okay," he finally said.

He stepped back, looking me over before turning around and entering the house. I watched him go inside, the door shutting behind him. I stood in the garage for a moment, recapping all that'd just happened.

He was hurt.

He was devastated.

He couldn't believe he was the one suffering.

He, of all people.

Losing his wife.

Losing half of himself.

Losing what probably felt like *everything* to him.

I can tell you that Mr. Black was never the same again. I can tell you that he hardly ever showed up at home, and if he did, it was to shower and change clothes, maybe work on his bike late at night.

I can also tell you that he was angry, like the world and his life had gone to full-blown shit and that it could never be restored. He was always at work. Always busy, trying to steer his mind from reality, working to will away the broken life he hated even existed.

But for Izzy, he did his best. He survived. He attended graduation and even saw her off to college. She left a week and a half before I had to go, and during that week, I watched him from across the street, peeping out of my bedroom window. I watched as he worked on several different bikes, blasted rock music he'd never listened to before, and got so drunk in his garage that he'd pass out. Music like that, metal-rock, made most people hostile and angry.

I was certain that was his goal—to be angry with any and everything. To have an excuse and something to back him up if things went awry. He was being immature and taking his grief out in all the wrong ways.

When he'd pass out, I'd walk across the street to help him. I'd carry his weight up their two flights of stairs, nearly dragging him into his bedroom and laying him on his bed. This happened three nights in a row without a single issue.

Not even Izzy was taking it *this* hard. Yes, the pain still cut her deep, but she was healing from her loss, ready to start fresh elsewhere. I guess it was different for Mr. Black because he loved Mrs. Black in a completely different way. He lived in a home they shared and slept in a bed that I'm sure reminded him of her every single day and night.

One night—the fourth night I helped him—changed our relationship in its entirety.

He passed out in the garage again around midnight.

Sighing, I walked across the street and helped him up, going through the same routine, draping his large body on mine. He was damp with sweat, and grease marks soiled his shirt. I tossed him on the bed, and he chuckled then sighed.

He reeked of gin this time. I shook my head. Knowing he'd hate himself if he ruined his sheets with his dirty boots, I bent down, untying the strings and pulling one of them off.

Mr. Black kicked the other foot as if he was trying to get rid of me, like he had no clue I was helping. "Mr. Black," I said, struggling to catch his foot. "Please stay still. I'm trying to take off your shoe."

"Mr. Black?" he repeated, voice sluggish. It took him a while to sit up straight just to find me in the dark. The bathroom light was on, but the door was cracked. Only a sliver of light showed, revealing part of his face. His glassy eyes caught mine, his supple lips separating as he said, "I like it better when you call me *Theo*."

"Well, *Theo*, please be still so I can take your other shoe off. Don't want to ruin your sheets, right?"

"Yes ma'am." He grinned, teeth white and glistening. I ignored the drumming of my heartbeat, pulling off his other boot and then standing, placing it aside.

"There. I'll put some water and aspirin by your bed. You should take it in the morning." It was weird talking to him now. Normally he'd pass right out once he hit the sheets, but not this time.

No, this time he stared at me as if he wanted something—something he knew he shouldn't have. His eyes roamed my body, up and down, breathing heavy. Words were begging to be spoken, but instead he kept quiet, allowing his actions to speak for him.

Standing from the bed, he leisurely walked towards me, but I stumbled away, my back hitting a wall, preventing escape. I wasn't afraid of him, though. No, in fact, as his smoldering brown eyes pierced mine and he stood before me in nothing but a grey muscle tank, I couldn't help but falter.

He was such a beautifully damaged man. So much pain and chaos and hurt in his eyes, but it didn't mask his good looks. I wanted to make him better with the only way I knew how.

Affection.

Hugs.

And sweet, tender kisses.

But hugging and kissing Mr. Black would have been wrong... *right?*

"I don't want you to leave," he admitted. "You've taken care of me and Izzy..." He met up to me and cupped one of my cheeks. I expected a rough hand touching smooth flesh, but it was gentle, his hands free of callouses and blisters, courtesy of the gloves he often wore while working. "I appreciate you so much for that. Taking care of me.

Watching out for me. I know I can get crazy—do some really childish shit." He stroked behind my ear, running his tongue over his bottom lip. "God, you have no idea how beautiful you are, do you?" My heart pounded.

I couldn't speak. I didn't need to.

"I know you like me, Chloe."

"Mr. Black, I—"

"Theo... please," he begged, eyes shutting briefly before opening again, "...just call me Theo. Call me by my first name. It sounds so good coming out of your mouth." The pad of his thumb ran across my lips, feathery-light. My core heated, a gush of warmth flowing to my sacred area.

"Theo," I whispered, pressing a hand against his chest.

"Yes?" He got a thrill out of me saying his name. I saw it in his eyes, how they lit up and sparked like a shower of meteors.

I tried creating words—lyrics I'd rehearsed—but the way he looked at me and how close he was to me, I'd never felt this before. Not with any kind of man. No man had ever made me feel this way—ready to pounce on top of him, smother his lips, and take him whole. Just Theo.

"W-what do you wanna do to me?" I tempted, my wavering voice barely heard. I was being bad. Naughty. I knew better.

Theo's face became hard like the metal he worked with, the light emphasizing his chiseled features. Locking eyes with me, he gripped my waist, reeling me into him, and breathing deep as his nose ran down the angle of mine.

Before I knew it, he'd yanked my spandex shorts down, his mouth angled above mine. He paused for what felt like an eternity, testing me. Teasing me. Playing with my mind and body.

But, instantly, he spoiled me, mouth crushing mine, his tongue thrusting between my lips. He groaned, and I defenselessly fell into his touch, his hands on my waist, picking up one of my legs as he turned for the bed.

My back hit the soft padding, my left leg pushed up to my chest as he sank against me. Theo lifted up and yanked off his belt. Then, he undid his pants, grasping my hips, nearly bruising my waist as he brought me closer. His arm shot out towards the nightstand, and he dug in the drawer, pulling out a small, square, gold packet. A condom. As he tore it with his teeth and took the time to slide it on, I could have wriggled out from under him... but I didn't. I just lay there, wanting it.

Craving it.

In that moment, I was his for the taking. My lower half exposed, hips tilted up in the angle he desired. He could've stopped—I could tell he was debating whether to keep going or call it quits—but he proceeded, the confliction in his eyes rapidly subsiding. I was so glad he didn't give out.

His cock sank deep inside me, and I was consumed by a hot, welcoming rush with each slow stretch. He stilled, shutting his eyes tightly and groaning, the veins bulging under the ink on his arms and neck. God, he was so thick and long, everything I ever imagined. Quite possibly more.

I adjusted around his size, whimpering for him to stroke, move— do something. "Fuck," he cursed under his breath as he finally started. "So fucking tight." He looked down at me, and I thought he would stop once he realized exactly what was happening, but he didn't. He moved slowly, his cock filling me up, bringing me over the edge. Bringing me higher. "Damn, Chloe. You're so fucking *wet* for me."

His mouth came down on mine again, our tongues colliding, warm bodies greedy for each other. We'd wanted this to happen for quite some time now. The both of us. From the moment Mr. Black noticed the changes that had taken place in my body, I was sure he thought some pretty naughty things about me—things he'd never share with anyone else. But back then, he was a married man and I was underage. It was bad.

Wrong.

Dirty.

But now, I was nineteen, on my way to college to start a new life. He was a widowed, gorgeous man with needs that needed fulfilling and a dark, cluttered mind that needed clearing.

As I lay on the bed, watching this gorgeous man take me, thrusting hard and deep, bringing my legs to my chest and pumping just enough to reach my g-spot, I couldn't bring myself to care about anything else outside of this. Not even the fact that I was losing my *virginity* to him.

There was pain, and even an odd stretching sensation that I couldn't ignore, but once that passed, it was the greatest thing I ever endured. True pleasure taking over my body, letting out noises within me that I never knew existed. I was sure he was too drunk to notice, or maybe he was too drunk to care. I wasn't saving myself for anyone. I just never felt like any of the other guys were worthy enough. But for Theo, it was astonishing what I would do for him—what I would give just to be close. Damn. I wasn't sure if it was sickening or delightful.

I needed to get it out of my system, and so did he. We needed to get it over with, forget about whatever feelings we held back on because it was obvious we would never be able to be together, even if Izzy wasn't my best friend and his wife was long gone.

Our age played a huge, scary part.

It would be oddly accepted in this world.

Theo's body locked, his hands on either side of my head, eyes bolted with mine. Only his hips drilled, the definition of his muscles exposed. "Your pussy is so tight and wet for me, Chloe. My *Little Knight*." He leaned forward, his lips coming to the shell of my ear. "You've saved me so many times." He slammed, and I cried out, my fingernails biting into the smooth flesh on his muscled back. "I owe you this much. I owe it to you to make you feel good—comfort *you* this time. Show you what a real man can do. I know you've wanted it," he breathed. "Trust me. I know. I see the desire in your eyes *every single fucking day*, and it kills me."

And then it happened. His deep, orgasmic voice. His large, toned body on mine. The heat thick in the air, his hand cupping the back of my neck, the possessive hold he had on me and how he repeatedly pressed on a g-spot that had never been triggered... god, I came. I came so hard. *So fucking hard.*

My body shook violently, out of control. I'd never felt such a thing. It was magical and intense and fucking amazing. I screamed, sighed, and then moaned his name.

"That's right," he breathed, still tipping me over. "Cum for me.

Cum all over my fucking cock, Chloe. You've wanted this. Fucking *claim* it."

I shuddered, and he groaned, dropping his face into the crook of my neck. "Goddamn." His voice was heavy and gruff as he came next, crashing into me three more times before collapsing and panting wildly.

He was still buried within as I lay there, staring up at the ceiling. I felt wonderful for a split second. Utterly amazing. I listened to my heart beating fast like the wings of a humming bird. Absorbed the feeling of his warm breath drifting past my damp skin. I was drunk on the way his sweat mixed with mine, his chest heaving. For the briefest of moments, I felt like I belonged there... but I knew I didn't.

My face straightened, and I immediately came back to the sobering reality. *Oh my god.* I couldn't believe it. I'd just fucked Mr. Black, the man across the street. My neighbor and my best friend's dad. A man that was twenty years older than I was...

And I couldn't take it back.

I lifted up, and he rolled onto his back, sighing as he shut his eyes. I watched his relaxed position, how he sighed again as if he'd been waiting on that to happen for years. Something bad settled in the pit of my stomach, gutting me. I so badly wanted to cry.

Climbing off the bed, I walked forward, picking up my shorts, sliding them on and then tucking my hair behind my ear. Theo touched his crotch, and when he felt something wet, his brows puckered, his hand shooting up above his face.

He sprang up, looking from the redness on his fingertips to me. "Chloe... oh shit." He blinked in my direction, shocked. "Chloe—why didn't you tell me?" he whispered. His speech was still a slurred mess. I figured it best not to get into it. It didn't matter. It was done. There was no taking it back—or dare I say *giving* it back.

"I—I should go, Mr. Black."

I had a feeling he didn't quite understand what'd just happened—the true depth of this situation. It would take him a few hours of recouping and getting sober to realize the act of sin we'd just committed. "Wait—Chloe... hold on. Did I just... did I just take—" He was unable to get it out, still stunned. Still drunk. Still at a loss for words and on the verge of passing out.

I opened the door. "I think this will be the last time I help you when you pass out, Mr. Black."

"Chloe?" he was still confused, struggling to come to a stand.

"Please be careful, Theo. Have a good night." I shut the door and hurried home, feeling like the entire neighborhood had heard me—or at least watched me through x-ray goggles or some shit. It didn't help that Ms. Rhodes's stupid dog barked, bringing attention to the night. I quietly entered my house, tiptoed upstairs to my bedroom, took a quick shower, and then got into bed.

My head fell to the left, my cellphone sitting on the nightstand. I picked it up. The only person I was concerned about was Izzy. I wanted to tell her that I'd made a mistake—that we'd made a mistake.

But I knew if I did, she'd never forgive it or look at me the same, no matter what he was going through. She'd blame me for getting close to him in his hour of need. She'd blame me for everything and sympathize with her father. She was the only true friend I had. I never kept secrets from Izzy, but this was one I was taking to the grave.

So I dropped my phone, looked towards the window, and figured it was best not to *ever* let her know. I tossed and turned all night, remembering just how he took me, claimed me. His mouth on mine, tongue desperate and needy. His masculine body close, bringing me to absolute euphoria. I never thought I'd feel so much my first time.

I sighed because I'd never felt so amazing and so horrible all at once. This would change the way Theo saw me, especially the whole popping of the cherry thing, so I prepared myself for the worst. I prepared to be ignored by him, never to be looked at in the same, innocent way.

I told my emotions not to get involved because, after all, it was just sex. I made him feel just a little better and that was what I wanted. For him to forget his pain for a little while. To feel normal again... at least a tad bit happier, even if there was a cost on my behalf.

But I was only fooling myself.

It was much more than that to me. *Just sex.* No matter how hard I tried, my feelings for Theo only became stronger. I became attached to the idea of him. Weak and vulnerable for him. I couldn't stand it. I couldn't stand myself for giving in. Falling victim to my fantasies. My desires. I knew better. We, as adults, knew better.

Theo had no care for right or wrong the moment he lost his wife.

His well-being became polluted with misunderstanding. Rotten from prolonged anguish.

His soul was tainted black, and there was no going back.

"Fuck," I thought. *"Where do we go from here?"*

THREE

THEO

WHAT THE FUCK IS WRONG WITH ME?!

Chloe... *fucking Chloe!* The girl from across the street. The girl that just so happens to be my daughter's best friend. I watched her grow from this oddly proportionate twelve-year-old to a nineteen-year-old woman with a huge rack she couldn't conceal, full lips that moved fluidly when she spoke, and a perky round ass I couldn't help but occasionally stare at whenever she was around.

She had it all, the full package, and to top it all off, she was book smart. She never missed a day of school—never missed a class assignment or forgot her homework. Shit, I wished Isabelle could be like her —about the books and school, I mean.

When I came to, realizing what'd just happened—the blood on my fingertips, the way she ran out of here—I sprang up, but the bedroom door was already shut, light footsteps scampering down the staircase. "Chloe!" I called after her, shooting for the door. Unfortunately, my fucking pants were still around my ankles, cock limp.

Stumbling ahead, I landed face-forward on the carpet, groaning as I created a loud *thud*. My palms burned the carpet, head swirling.

God damn it.

I was so fucking drunk and so fucking stupid.

Pulling my shit together as much as I could, I walked towards the window and saw her enter her home, a place that felt so far away from me. A place I knew I could never enter without permission.

It took several minutes for her bedroom lights to flicker on, but when they did, I saw her standing still for a moment. Her sheer curtains always showed where she was. She was looking into the mirror, most likely trying to figure out what in the hell just happened.

I swallowed hard as she moved away from the glass. I didn't see her anymore after that. "So fucking stupid," I scolded myself, sitting on the edge of the bed. My fingers roughly raked through my sweat-dampened hair, a soreness already migrating to my head.

Why couldn't I pull it together? Even my own daughter had swept up the pieces of her heart, ready to start fresh. I still couldn't wrap my mind around it. Janet... she was fucking gone.

My wife was gone.

Dead.

Just like that, within the blink of an eye.

I loved her to death. She was half of me—the reason I kept breathing so long ago. She was part of the reason I still stood on this earth, her and my daughter.

I slowly spiraled that night, considering myself a complete fuck-up. A low-life. A fucking idiot.

Only idiot thirty-eight-year olds fucked nineteen year olds.

Only fuck-ups spiraled so hard and so fast that they saw nothing but a blur and soon ended up passing out in the garage.

Only a low-life would have the audacity to come onto such a sweet, innocent girl, a girl who so clearly wanted to help me get through this pain. This harsh, unbearable pain. Only a fool would end up taking something that sacred away from her, like it didn't even matter.

But it mattered a lot.

The ache that I had was there, but the crazy thing about it was I lost sight of all losses while she was around. All the pain, all the suffering, and all the hurt just seemed to disappear. While I was buried deep in that tight, mind-blowing pussy, all agony faded. While I held that sweet, young girl close, feeling as she accepted me—took me whole, inch by savory fucking inch—it was gone. All gone.

She had wanted me for years. I could tell when someone was interested, but the thing about her was she didn't put it on display for everyone to see. Hell, I don't even know how I figured it out.

Chloe had always had a thing for me, and perhaps my bantering and teasing her as she grew didn't help get rid of those feelings. If anything, I'd only enhanced them, making her wonder. Making her dream... question.

I was trying to play it cool, but I never had to become someone else while she was around. She accepted us. She understood us. She understood *me*. She was an amazing person, but just like that, I'd stolen her innocence and filled her with guilt and a spill of my own darkness.

It was a curse, the darkness. It always snuck up on me somehow. Right when I thought I was doing well, it would show up, stealing all the goodness away from me. The blackness would seep through me, ruining my life, turning me into someone I couldn't stand to look at.

"Fuck!" I barked, rising to my feet. I watched the mirror, how my chest heaved and my body dripped with prohibited sweat. I couldn't stand what I saw. The dark circles around my eyes from weeks of depression, the way my eerie reflection stared back at me, almost taunting. Laughing. Mocking.

Growling, I rushed forward and punched the mirror on the wall. The glass shattered, pieces falling apart and dropping just like my heart did the night Janet died. Trickles of blood formed from deep cuts on my balled fists. It sucked because I felt nothing, and all I wanted to do was feel—feel something. Feel *anything*. Feel her... the sweet, beautiful girl.

But Chloe... *no*.

My head shook as I glared at my scattered reflection, eyes dark and lips thin. I couldn't touch her again, no matter how hard it would be. This would change everything between us—all we'd established. The bond we'd created over the years. All of it was now gone. Flushed away like it never existed.

Although she may have wanted it, Chloe wasn't the type to come running to me, begging for more. She was the type to sit around and wait for me to speak up and make a move no matter how awkward she felt about previous actions. And she was too smart to inform Izzy... *fuck*, Izzy. I hoped she never found out.

She liked me, and I liked how she made me feel like I wasn't a total fucking loser. As badly as I would have loved to keep going, make her mine by taking her over and over again in every possible way, I just couldn't do that to her. I should have paid attention. I should've taken notice of the pain that ran across her face when I first entered, how she held me tight, nails biting flesh.

She deserved better than having to deal with my brokenness, a man with no self-control—no guidance. A man with a dark past and an even darker heart. That was my mistake, leading her on like that, taking from her what so clearly didn't justify being mine.

Sad, I couldn't even hold it in anymore. My cock throbbed hard when I saw it was her head that was between my legs, pulling my boots from my feet in a gesture not even meant to spark lust. He'd been begging me more and more to make a move whenever she made an appearance. The first few nights, I did pretty well, controlling my raging hormones, but that fourth, fateful night took a turn on us.

She wanted me. She knew better, but she *wanted* me to take her raw on that bed. Help me forget for just a little while. Allow me to remember that there were still options. I felt horrible fucking Chloe on the bed I shared with a wife that hadn't even been dead for a year, but I couldn't help myself.

I had to claim it. I had to show her that she wasn't the only one feeling those urges, wondering about the *maybes* and the *what ifs*. She needed to know that I, Theo Black, was far from a saint, and that I constantly had some wicked thoughts about her.

She needed to know... I just wanted to *show* her... that's understand-able, right? *Right?*

Fucking moron, my heart whispered.

Fucking champ, my cock chanted.

I don't even fucking know, my helpless mind murmured.

Shit. I had no clue what to think anymore.

FOUR

CHLOE

THEO DIDN'T COME HOME the following night. No loud, angry music. No metal tools clanking around. No empty glasses slamming on the concrete. Just peace and quiet. It felt strange.

I didn't like it.

I wondered where he was, what he was doing, or worse—if he was still alive.

The question of him being alive was shortly answered when I heard the grumble of his motorcycle. The growl came to a hush, engine shutting off, and I dropped my book, uncrossed my legs, and narrowed my eyes as I walked towards the window.

Looking out, I watched as he stumbled towards the door, pulling out his key and struggling to stick it into the lock. My window was cracked, so I heard him curse beneath his breath as he tried getting it in. I rolled my eyes. At least he hadn't passed out again. He'd gone elsewhere to get drunk. Maybe he did understand me last night.

Finally, he was inside, and I was relieved. I shut my window and locked it, walking back to my leather recliner in the corner and returning to my book. I was curious about what he was doing, though.

Thinking about him distracted me from devouring the romance novel I'd just bought.

I shut the book, blowing out a heavy puff of breath as I climbed out of the recliner and entered my bathroom. I took a long shower, tossed on a large black T-shirt, and climbed into bed, shutting the lamp off.

Moments later, as I lay in darkness, my phone buzzed on the nightstand. It was a text from Izzy.

Izzy: My dad isn't answering his phone. Is he okay?

I responded quickly.

Me: He's fine. Just saw him getting home. I'm sure he'll call.

Izzy: Ok. Good. I was a little worried. Keep an eye on him, will u?

I struggled between a true laugh and a scoff. *Yeah*, I thought. *I've been doing that all damn summer.*

Me: I will.

Izzy: Thanks, Chlo. Ur the best.

I started to ask her how the college life was going, but my mind changed within the same moment. I wasn't up for chatting, not after feeling like I'd betrayed her. I couldn't believe I still hadn't told her what was going on. She deserved the truth, even if that meant losing her.

I just couldn't imagine her reaction.

I'd seen Izzy angry, sad, depressed, happy, content, and even confused, but I wasn't sure what I'd get if word got out that I'd messed around with her dad. Ignoring my guilt, I shut my eyes and curled up beneath the blanket, drifting off to sleep.

The next day, around dusk, I went for a jog at the neighborhood park. Stress had been eating away at me. I was done packing for school and tired of being cooped up in the house. With Izzy gone, I had no one to hang with, so I slid into some jogging pants and a tank, tied my hair up, and was out of the door in seconds, my earphones wedged in my ears.

I started a light jog to the park, waving at a few of the neighbors. All of them were so full of shit. All stuck up and rude, but I was the type that liked to play nice when I had to. The manners Dad taught me, I suppose.

Finally reaching the park, I picked up my pace, hitting the trail and then meeting at the track, running it four times while catchy tunes filled my head. The running distracted my clustered mind for at least fifteen minutes, the air filling my working lungs, the wind nipping my damp skin. I felt great when I finished. I even sang along to some of the music, stretching on the park bench before heading back home.

But that momentary feeling of peace vanished when I saw a shirt-less Theo Black running along the same trail. He had on headphones, muscles glistening, and his body art standing out more than ever.

He caught me bending in front of the fountain and slowed down just a little. His gaze matched mine, uncertain, but immediately, he picked up his pace, rushing through a thick line of trees and down a different trail, a rockier one that was harder to traverse.

I shouldn't have felt so angry, but watching him disappear and act like I didn't even exist had me heated. And it was a shame because I swore I wouldn't let the emotion take over me. Lies. All lies.

There was something about the way he looked at me—so many unanswered questions in his eyes. So much confusion, guilt, but most of all, a recognizable lust. Perhaps that was the reason he took off.

I stopped my stretching, took a sip from the fountain, and then turned to jog back home. I didn't make it to the exit of the park though because there he was again. He appeared on the trail I took, panting heavy, eyes hard on mine. I stopped in my tracks, forehead creased, eyebrows stitched.

"Chloe," he said after catching his breath. He snatched off his headphones and stood up straight, sweat enhancing his rock-solid body, streaming down his chest. "Can we talk... please?"

I shook my head. "We don't have to. It's no biggie." I ran around him like I wasn't just deep in my feelings. He caught my elbow before I could flee, twirling my body his way. It was effortless, his grip light.

His line of sight automatically fell to my lips, and his parted. I knew what *that* look meant. I swallowed hard as he spoke, trying to preserve control. "Look, I know you might think I'm some kind of perverted motherfucker for coming onto you so strong, but... *shit*." He blew a breath, head shaking. "Look, I'm sorry about what happened. I swear it wasn't supposed to go down that way."

I was speechless. I was sorry as well, but then again, I wasn't. I'd lived out a fantasy. Something I'd wanted to happen for a very long time. Why regret so much? "I don't think you're a pervert." I paused, unsure if I should share the rest of my thoughts out loud. "You weren't the only one that wanted it to happen. I... tempted you."

He swallowed hard, ignoring my previous statements. "You can't tell Izzy about this," he told me, face scrambled. He didn't know if I'd told her or not.

I frowned, narrowing my eyes up at him. "I would *never* tell her." It felt weird even saying it aloud.

"I know but..." His lips twisted as he released my arm, observing my anger. "Fuck—don't look at me like that."

"Like what?" I blinked rapidly.

He stepped forward, head slightly tilted. "When you're upset, it shows. And it's hard to ignore because you're hardly ever upset. I just want to fix it... make you smile again. Make you feel better." His hand ran down my cheek. My breath collected in my throat.

I wanted to back away as he drew me in—run like hell—but I couldn't. *Damn it, I couldn't.* He smelled so good, his natural scent along with a light spritz of cologne made my insides prickle. And don't even get me started on his slender body, the V that sank deep into his basketball shorts. Theo held me close, one hand gently traveling down the curve of my hip.

"Don't do this," I whispered. "Please," I begged, but I didn't mean it. I didn't mean a single damn word of it. Finding the strength to pull away, I shook my head and started to run, but he caught me.

His face was hard, eyes darker when I looked at him again. Instantly, he gripped my hand, rushed through a line of trees, and shoved branches and leaves out of the way. In a matter of seconds, he brought me before him, spinning me around until my back hit rigid bark.

He pressed against me, his mouth claiming, his tongue gradually sliding through and dancing with mine. I moaned and sighed, pushing against him, wanting him to stop and go all at once. I wanted him away from me—off of me—but I also wanted him to *never* let go. To hold me close.

My eyes burned because I wanted to cry, but the tears never fell. This was happening. This was happening to me all over again. To us.

Wow. The second time in less than forty-eight hours.

My fucking goodness.

Theo picked me up, and my legs instinctively latched around his waist. He then walked forward, and my backside landed on a soft patch of sweet smelling grass. My eyes cracked open, spotting white daisies surrounding us. The sunlight made his skin sparkle, enhancing his devilish beauty.

I yanked off his shorts as his lips pressed on my cheek. His groan was deep, his sweat-dampened body rubbing against mine. He had my pants off, legs bent, and in no time, he was taking me.

Right there.

On the grass.

In the park where people passed by us only a few feet away.

Some people walked or jogged. I could spot their shadows zooming by, oblivious to the sinful act taking place.

Unable to control my cries of pleasure, he cupped my mouth and shushed me. His gaze penetrated mine beneath the setting sun, sweaty forehead creased and nostrils flaring as if he were angry and concentrated at once. He was taking out his aggressions on me, fucking me ever so softly. As badly as I didn't want it happening that way, it was. And I wasn't stopping it.

"Why didn't you tell me?" he asked gruffly.

"Tell you what?"

"That you were still a virgin."

"It didn't matter," I admitted.

His eyes squeezed shut, and I gasped as he hit a tender spot that made my back go into a slight bend. "It does matter."

"Why?"

He crushed his lips together. "Knowing that I was the one to take you first will make me want to fuck you every time I set eyes on you now."

I shook my head.

"I'm serious. But all you have to do is tell me to stop. Tell me to stop," he whispered. He was half-stroke. "And I will. I will never touch you again, Chloe."

I could have, but deep down, I didn't want him to. I never wanted him to stop. *This* to stop. *Us* to stop. "No," I mustered, hooking my arms around his neck. A smile twitched at his lips, but his eyes were just as hard as before. Unreadable and dark.

He pounded deep, swiveling in slow, torturous circles. Cupping my face, I allowed his tongue to swirl with mine again, feeling as he inhaled my moans. He didn't want me completely quiet, just quiet enough. He wanted to hear me... wanted to listen to me breathe his name.

I wasn't sure how no one heard the grass rustling, the grunts, groaning, and sighing. I mean, I honestly didn't care as long as they didn't ruin this moment. This perfectly imperfect moment.

Theo was above me, thick arms planted outside my head, stroking deep, leaning forward, and placing damp kisses on my neck and chest. I turned my head away, fighting the inevitable, but he stole kisses from me, proving I could go nowhere. That he would always get his way.

I hated it

I loved it.

I couldn't do this anymore.

But I wanted *so* much more.

My back curved, eyes shutting. My walls constricted around his massive length, juicing. Soaking. *Milking*. Tipping my head forward again, he forced me to focus on his eyes, our foreheads meshed. His entire body tensed moments later, and soon he bared teeth.

No longer able to hold it in, he let go, bringing his mouth to the crook of my neck and sucking me there, sucking until it stung—my fingernails biting into his skin. Pleasure and pain.

"Fuck, baby," he groaned, unable to control his volume. My body jolted as he stilled and then whipped back, pulling his cock out and having no choice but to cum on top of the grass. On me, it would have left a mess, but inside me would have caused true chaos.

I was grateful.

My mind swirled into a daze. The sky seemed to spin above. The line of trees staring down at me, mocking me with their leaves flapping in the wind, shaking like they were almost laughing. I felt embarrassed, but then Theo looked at me and I felt like a goddess.

I couldn't believe it'd happened *again*.

A second time.

How the fuck did I let it happen so easily this time?

Theo sighed, standing and yanking his shorts up. He looked down at me, and a flash of pain crossed his face. I sat up, pulling my pants up as well. We were quiet for a moment, adjusting ourselves. I felt warmth oozing between my legs, and something sparked within me. I ached, longing for him to take me all over again.

His lips parted, and I expected positive words, but I'd deliberately received the opposite. "We... we shouldn't do this anymore, Chloe." He ran his hands over his face. "Fuck—I... I don't even know how we keep getting here. I was wrong. So fucking wrong."

My eyes became hot, thick with unshed tears. Only moments ago he asked me if I wanted him to stop. He was confusing me. I didn't get him. What was it that he wanted from me?

"You're so young," he went on. "So inexperienced and so innocent. I can't keep taking that from you." He looked away, guilt-ridden, and then focused on me again, awaiting a response.

I stood, looking him deep in the eyes for a brief, intense moment. I saw the confusion. The trouble I was causing his emotions. My heart snagged. My head dropped. I walked around him, hugging myself as I rushed through the line of trees he'd dragged me through only minutes ago. I left out of the park in a hurry, jogging back home, biting back on emotion. Fortunately, I won. No tears on the way there.

Theo was nowhere in sight as I entered my house. I figured he meant it this time. And it was good because he was right. We couldn't do this anymore. It wasn't okay. We both were doing it for very bad reasons.

While I was showering the scent of him away, allowing it to seep down the drain, he must have made his way back home. His bedroom light was on. I peeked through the curtain, expecting him to be in his garage or even inside the house, but instead he was on the porch, looking right at my bedroom window.

I gasped, taking a step back, but I could still see him. I was sure he knew I was still watching.

He had a beer in hand. His lips were pressed thin, eyes full of regret and curiosity. I bet he was wondering the same thing I was. Why did we feel so good together? How in the hell did we let it happen twice? Why couldn't we deny this lust? What was it that made us get so lost in each other that we completely forgot just who we were? The wrongs and rights? The pain and suffering? The fucking age difference? Fucking Izzy?

It was confusing... and so very hard to fight.

Perhaps it was the thrill...

Or maybe it was the off-limits thing? Human beings loved taking advantage of what they knew they couldn't have.

Maybe he did it because he hadn't had any in a while and I just did it because—well, because I'd had a crush on Mr. Black for many, many years. I dreamt about him. Thought about him almost every single day without even realizing it before.

Maybe it was because, deep down, we'd wanted each other. We had a connection—an undeniable one. I could read him, and he liked that. He didn't have to speak, didn't have to tell me what was wrong, because I already knew.

His pain? I wanted to be the one to take that away.

His conflicts? I wanted to be the one to settle them.

But I was only dreaming. I had to stop. Dreaming never got me anywhere before. Why would it now?

Knowing this, I moved away from the curtain, stepping back slowly, and looked into the mirror of my vanity. I was sure someone could have spotted the hickey he left on my neck from a mile away.

I tried covering the shame with my hands, but I quickly moved them away. Seeing the mark made me tingle below, my core clenching. Running my fingertip across my lip, I imagined him kissing me again.

Holding.

Smoldering.

Looking me deep in the eyes.

His kiss. His touch.

His smell.

Him.

I didn't get it. How could I want more? How could I do this to myself, knowing it would result to nothing?

Why did I care?

Why did it feel so incredible, but oh so painful?

How was I supposed to forget about my first time with a man that wasn't even supposed to take it?

Why did it seem my morals went flying out the window whenever he made an appearance? I was a good girl. I'd always been a good girl, but he'd brought the dark little Chloe Knight right out of me.

Shit. Why couldn't I just forget about Theodore Black?

———

Two days later, my car was packed up, my keys clutched in hand. "I'm sorry we can't drive you there, sweetie," Mom said, adjusting her skirt. "I know how big this is for you."

"Don't worry about it. Dad needs you in San Fran. You know he can't do it all by himself." She rolled her eyes, and I sighed, deciding to quickly change the subject. I didn't even want to get her started on the man that she now thought was *soo annoying*. "I'm excited about USC. It'll be fun. A great experience."

"Well, I'd hope so with how much money we're paying for tuition." She laughed with an edge of sarcasm, tucking her curly brown hair behind her ear. "Just be safe." A kiss on my cheek. "Call me as soon as you make it there."

I nodded, rounding the car. "I will. Love you, Mom."

"Love you too, sweetie."

I jumped in the car and started it. I hated that Dad wasn't here, but when work called, he always went running. Even while being retired, it seemed he worked more now than ever before. He wasn't getting paid to be one of the greatest accountants in Cali, but people loved him and he wasn't dead yet, so they were going to use him up until he was a no-good, withered-up, forgetful man. I couldn't blame him. He wanted the best for us, especially me. If there was one thing I knew about my dad, it was that he feared going broke. He was without money before, unable to provide for himself before he got to college and received inheritance from my greedy grandfather.

It sucked he couldn't even see his own daughter off to college, but he did keep his promise about coming to graduation. He showed up on time and even found me afterwards to fly me in a private jet and spend a night in San Francisco.

I shrugged it off and started to wave at Mom again, but her phone was now in her hand and soon to her ear. She talked quickly as she turned her back to me, entering the house several seconds later.

I sat in the driveway for a while, eyes damp, my heart slowly drumming in my chest. Whatever. It was seriously whatever. Finally fed up with being put last, I rapidly blinked the tears away and drew in a deep breath. I connected my Bluetooth to the car because I needed music. Lots of it if I was going to make it through the drive. Alone.

I pulled out of the driveway, silently telling my home goodbye. Putting the car in drive, I allowed my foot to hover above the gas just as I so happened to look to my right.

Standing in the garage with a wrench in hand was Mr. Black. His nostrils were flared, lips pinched tight with his gaze pointed right at me. I assumed he was thinking negative things. *Not even a goodbye? Farewell? See you soon?*

A wave of dread passed through me as I watched his lonely eyes. I wanted to jump out and hug him—tell him so many kind things—but I didn't. Theo needed to know that we would never be the same—that I would soon be over him once I was in college.

I wasn't planning on coming back home anytime soon. It was like coming back to nothing. My parents always acted too busy for me, my best friend was miles away, and her father was just across the street, normally strutting with a tank top or no shirt on at all. I was weak for that man, the sight of him making me wetter than a river. If I had stayed, I would have been his for sure. In a way, he owned me, but if I left, it wouldn't be that way.

I needed escape. I needed a fresh start. I needed someone my age. Someone new. Let's just say Primrose was not the place to be, so instead of lingering, I drove off just as he was coming down the driveway to try and speak to me. I purposely broke our connected line of sight and hurried out of the neighborhood, away from Primrose, my parents, and Theodore Black.

As soon as I was out of the neighborhood, a thousand weights lifted off my shoulders... off my chest. I could breathe. I could fly. I felt momentarily free.

But, I admit, I was going to miss them. My parents. The neighborhood and all the bitchy, self-worshipping occupants—them, because they showed me that I actually had some good within me. And *him*...

Man, especially him.

FIVE

THEO

WHAT DID I EXPECT?

For her to get out, kiss, and then hug me goodbye? I knew she was leaving, off to college. I hurt her, told her straight to her face that we couldn't be. It fucking twisted me up inside watching her run out of the park as if I'd broken what was left of her heart—demolished every trace of feeling she ever had for me.

She remained in the middle of the road, her eyes locked with mine, glued for a while. I had the urge to go, to make a move and beg her forgiveness.

But she pulled off.

My heart felt like it'd been ripped in two, but it wasn't a brokenness that I felt. My heart had been torn apart and flushed away for many months. I was simply devastated. With her gone, I'd have no one to look after me, no one to look forward to seeing. No one to talk to... no one to fucking *understand* me.

Alone. That's what I would be. The thought of it terrified me. That night, several hours after I settled with the idea that she was most likely gone for good, I got drunk again. Why? Because I didn't want to be alone, and if getting drunk until I felt numb could help, then so be it.

I faded away in my garage but left the gate open. That small ray of hope that always kept its place in the back of my mind thought she'd show up again, help me upstairs, and give me a chance to apologize. Ha. I was only fooling myself.

She wasn't coming back. She was moving on, something I couldn't make happen just yet. It was all in my drunken mind, hoping she'd return. She knew better. She knew it the moment she pulled out of Primrose.

She was gone, and it would have been foolish of her to come back and give it all up for someone like me.

SIX

CHLOE

THREE YEARS Later – 22 Years Old

USC was a dream—more like a fast-paced, colorful blur.

After two years, I had only been home once. That one time was because Izzy wanted to visit her mother's grave. Afterwards, we took off, catching waves at the welcoming beach of Ventura. Luckily, Mr. Black didn't show up during that one visit. I was scot-free, glad I didn't have to face him.

During my time away, I'd gotten really close with my roommate, Mariah. She could be nice, but she was a huge party animal. At first I didn't like her. She came off a bit stuck up and selfish, but after getting to know her, I settled with the understanding that she only seemed that way because she kept it real.

She was genuine and honest, and she didn't sugarcoat a damn thing. Unlike Izzy, where she'd make up excuses about a certain dress I bought, beating around the bush about its fit, Mariah would tell me straight to my face that the dress I wore wasn't a good color on me or a good fit—whatever it just so happened to be.

I didn't like it at first. I had a weird taste in fashion, so I assumed she didn't grasp where I was coming from whenever I wore certain things, but after a while, it came in handy.

During freshman year, I hardly partied. I went to *one* party, and it was the lamest thing I'd ever attended. Because of it, I vowed never to go to another. I was only fooling myself.

Sophomore year was fantastic. That's when Mariah and I became closer. She took me to the *real* parties where even the smartest of students, like myself, got wild and let loose. I was afraid of becoming that, but I had to live. Start fresh. This was the best way to start. No regrets. Just fun.

I never got too wasted to the point where I'd vomit over the staircase or balcony of a frat house like some of the girls did. I only got drunk enough to where I felt good—enough to the point where I was able to still control my actions but wouldn't dare set foot behind the wheel of a car.

During my college life, I did my best to forget about the small things, but of course those "small" things happened to cross my mind every single fucking day. Those "small" things were the reason I'd rushed to a clinic to get birth control as soon as I was settled in my dorm room on the first day. He'd made me a woman, and with that, came responsibility. I hated the shot, but I also knew I wouldn't keep up with the pills. Whatever was best, right?

In class, when my psychology professor would drone on about brain waves and REM, I thought of Theo. I couldn't help myself. I doodled pictures of the tattoos I could remember and even wrote short stories full of fantasy shit that he would never say in person.

I wondered every day if he was okay, and at one point, I had even considered calling to check on him. But I knew better. Plus, Izzy's daily phone call to me would prove he was. There was never a call where she wouldn't mention her *hot-as-sin* father.

She told me lots of times he was unhappy. Still hurting... but also that he had a girl toy on his arm only four months after I left. The *girl toy* part made me jealous. I wished then that he had a *Facebook* or

Twitter so I could see her face, but I forgot he was a forty year old man. He didn't need social media—didn't thrive on it like leeches or check it first thing in the morning like it was the newspaper as we did.

I wondered if she was blonde or brunette. If her body was better than mine? If her butt was bigger? What color her eyes were? Or if he had a nickname created just for her... like he did for me?

I'd contemplated calling him so many times. Izzy would never know, and we'd vowed to keep whatever happened years ago between us. Ugh. Jealousy was an ugly trait, and I hated that I even carried it.

For a while, I was upset that I left without saying goodbye—leaving us open-ended—that is until the party at the beach happened. Everyone had just finished finals. Mariah and I were looking for something to do to pass time before our summer break started, so we took up the invitation.

That night, through heavy drinking and slurred sentences, I met Axel. Axel was exactly how he sounded. A jock. A cocky son of a bitch. Built with a wavy buzz cut and smooth chocolate skin, almost like my father's. He was handsome and, sadly, a football player.

There was just something about football players that lured me in but turned me off all at once. Like an idiot, I invited Axel to come spend summer break with us while highly intoxicated. I wished I hadn't. I had to share my bed with him, sleep with him. Talk to him. He had a terrible vocabulary. It was obvious he'd only gotten into USC because he had an athletic scholarship. And I only said yes because he had a nice body and a pretty smile.

When he spoke, I wanted to gag.

When he flexed his muscles, kissing his biceps, I wanted to spit up in my mouth.

When he didn't speak, though, he was a gorgeous being. Far from smart, but I dealt with him because there were times when my needs got the best of me. I was desperate, but not even the cocky, arrogant Axel could fulfill them.

I knew who I needed.

Who I *wanted*.

And exactly how I wanted it.

But that was a no-no. It would never happen again, especially now.

I was sure he realized he'd made a mistake with me. It'd been two and a half years. He'd obviously let go if he had a new girl around.

Other than constantly thinking about Theo, the college life was great. But the third year happened to be the worst.

Due to all of his working out of retirement, my father became too old and too sick. He almost worked himself to death.

Mom... *fucking Mom*. She hired a caregiver to watch and help Dad while she spent her many days and nights traveling the world. And not only that, she had a boyfriend. A fucking boyfriend! How was that even okay if she was still married?

I was angry at her, mainly because she was the one that was supposed to be by his side, caring for him, providing, loving, but I knew Mom had given up on her marriage a long time ago. It was clear she was only around for the money. Don't get me wrong, she honestly loved my father at one point. I saw it, bright as day. And she also loved me with her whole heart, but when it came to herself, that's who she loved most.

So, instead of spending my summer with friends, I drove home to spend it with my father. He was already in the early stages of Alzheimer's while I was in school. The disease was the very reason he felt it was time to retire. He didn't want to be the blame for forgetting something—messing up numbers.

Over the course of those three years, though, his disease had progressed. To make matters worse, he'd had a stroke while grocery shopping by himself. Mom normally did the shopping or sent someone out to do it. I was glad I wasn't a witness to such a tragedy.

I wanted to be there for my father, and I also took it as an opportunity to focus on my next semester, take up some reading for my English degree. I wanted to become a second grade teacher, spread creativity, and help develop young minds the right way. It had always been a dream of mine.

I drove home the day after I finished exams. I could check my scores online. In that moment, family was more important. It took me an hour and a half to get home. As soon as I did, I called Izzy before getting out of the car.

She answered, her tone chipper.

"Izzy, you didn't text me back earlier."

"Sorry, Chlo. I got caught up with unpacking, and Dylan wouldn't leave me the hell alone." She groaned. "But I suck because I totally forgot to tell you that I can't even come home this summer. I may be on a bit of an academic probation."

I gasped. "What the hell? How?"

"All that partying." I knew she was shrugging while putting on an innocent face. "It gets the best of you. But I swear, I'm going to get it together. I have to. My dad will kill me if he finds out. Hey, do me a favor and don't bring up the summer school thing. I kind of told him that I volunteered to help for a summer camp for teens."

"I... won't. What makes you think I'll even get the chance to talk to him?"

"I don't know. You guys always talk. He asks about you all the fucking time like I'm supposed to know how you're doing when you're two hours away from me. I'm like, 'Dad. We don't go to the same school. I don't know what Chloe's doing.'" She laughed.

My heart stuttered, and I looked through the rearview mirror, spotting the familiar home that belonged to the Blacks. *He asks about me?* That was the first time I'd heard that one.

"Anyway, I'm sorry Chlo. I think summer school ends like two weeks before the fall semester begins, and if so, I'll come see you. I don't know. We'll see. But until then, hang in there and update me on Papa Knight. I can't believe your mom, by the way. Total bitch move."

I scoffed, rolling my eyes. "You're telling me. I'll call you or something soon. Make sure you focus, alright? Tell Dylan to get lost. Books before boys!"

"Always has been!"

"Always will be." I smiled, Izzy laughed, and I hung up, blowing a sigh as I stared at the home ahead of me. My home. It felt so unfamiliar to me now.

My sick father was in there. Fortunately, there was a certified nurse also looking after him so I wouldn't be completely on my own, but this was frightening. What if he forgot my name? Or the fact that he even had a daughter? The last thing I needed was my parents forgetting I existed.

Picking up my tote bag and slinging it over my shoulder, I pushed out of the car and shut the door behind me, adjusting my wool fedora hat and then my shorts. It was humid outside, the air thick with the California heat. My clothes automatically clung to my skin. I needed to get inside.

I walked to the door, pulling out my house key. I couldn't believe it felt so strange to be home. And worse? Right across the street from the man I had constant fantasies about. Before entering the house, I glanced back. The garage gate was closed, the driveway empty. Lights out.

No one was home—well, *he* wasn't home.

Work, possibly? I don't know. His schedule was foreign to me now, but I used to know it like the palm of my hand.

I twisted my lips, walking inside and shutting the door behind me. The AC was strong, cooling the hidden parts of me that were hard to keep at a decent climate. I took off my hat and placed it on the wooden rectangular table by the door, calling for anyone to appear.

Several seconds later, a short Hispanic woman with curly brown hair appeared. Her cheeks were chubby, as well as her fingers. She was at least four inches shorter than me, but her smile was way bigger than mine could ever be. It was weird. She didn't look like how I pictured her when we were on the phone a week ago. I expected a younger woman wearing loose clothing and her hair pinned up. But her hair flowed to her shoulders, her floral blouse and khaki's proving she was exactly how she dressed. Simple.

Still beautiful, nonetheless.

"Hi!" the caregiver chimed as she came rushing my way. She extended her arm, and I shook her hand. "You must be Chloe!"

"In the flesh." I smiled.

"Wow," she gasped. "You look so much like your father." She placed a hand on her hip.

"I get that a lot."

"Well, welcome home! It's so good to meet you. Margie, by the way. You know, just in case you may have forgotten."

"I didn't forget," I laughed.

"Great!" She walked past me, entering the kitchen. "I was just coming down for your father's soup and crackers. He has a bit of a head cold, but other than that, he seems fine today."

"Today? What do you mean today?" I walked in the kitchen after her, head tilted.

Her eyes met mine briefly before she focused on the bowl she was placing on a tray. "Your dad has his days... some where he'll know exactly who and where he is and some where he won't even know why there's a portrait of him with two strange girls on the wall beside him." She looked up at me again, waving a hand. "The strange girls being you and your mother."

"Oh." I looked away, folding my arms. Margie walked around the island counter and went up the stairs. I was hesitant on following her up, but when she glanced back and caught my uncertainty, she quickly gestured for me to follow.

"Come on up! He's been anxious to see his baby girl."

I smiled, nodding as I took the stairs with her. For a heavyset woman, she moved fast. I loved it. It was just what my dad needed after living such a fast-paced life. Taking the stairs by twos, I followed Margie into my parents' master bedroom. The room was much colder than the rest of the house, the way my father always liked it. The walls were no longer a pale shade of blue but more of an indigo. It suited him. A tranquil color. My father was never the type to be on edge. He was a laid-back guy, way easier to talk to than my mom... whenever he was around anyway.

A king-sized bed stretched across the center of the room, a TV mounted right across from it, and on the bed was my father. He was sitting upright, the blue blanket I knit for him while I was in summer camp in eighth grade spread out across his lap. Pill bottles were lined up on the dresser on the east wall. There were at least ten little orange and white containers.

Entering the room, my eyebrows glued together as I stared at him. It seemed he hadn't eaten in weeks. He was skinnier with dark circles beneath his eyes, lips a shade whiter. His dark skin was still smooth, though. A nice chocolaty-brown complexion.

I stared from the bedroom door, wanting so badly to cry for him.

He looked lonely, but I knew my father. He would never show it, and he damn sure wouldn't admit it.

"Daddy?"

Dad whipped his head to the right, eyes immediately turning bright as he looked from the quiet game of golf on the TV screen to me. "Baby girl!" He opened his arms, and when he did, I rushed forward, sinking into them as I sat on the edge of the mattress. "How's my ladybug doing?" he asked, kissing the top of my head.

My eyes burned even more, bottom lip quivering. I pulled my shit together and said, "Never better." Then I gently removed myself from his embrace, meeting his sad hazel eyes. "How are you? Margie tells me you have a cold?"

"Ehh." He waved a hand, dismissing the idea. "No cold. Just a runny nose."

"Hmm. You sound a little sick to me."

He laughed and then held up his forefinger and thumb like he was about to pinch something. "Maybe just a little." He looked me over, proud to see I was still holding my own. "You look great. How's school? Your grades?"

"You know my grades are great. School is nice. Finally got along with my roommate," I informed him.

His eyes expanded. "Good. I know how hard it is for you to make friends. Speaking of, where's the little girl? You know, the one you grew up with from across the street?"

"Izzy?"

"Yeah, her!"

"Izzy is spending her summer at a camp. She volunteered to help some kids near her school."

"Oh. How nice of her." He placed his hand on my forearm, shaking his head. "You know you didn't have to come watch over me. That's what I have Margie for."

"No, Dad," I said as his lips pressed. I squeezed the hand that was on my arm. "I *needed* to come back. It's been a while. Plus, I missed you." I took a swift look around the room. "I missed being home."

"And you know I missed you." His smile was genuine.

I scrunched my nose and looked at the TV while Margie placed the tray on his lap. "Since when did you start watching golf?"

"You kidding? I watch golf all the time? You remember when you used to come to the golf courses with Uncle Clay and me? You loved it!"

"That was so long ago," I laughed. "And you didn't watch golf back then unless it was in person."

"Same thing. But you remember, right?"

"Of course I do." I was surprised he could.

"See." His eyes lit up as he picked up his spoon.

My face stiffened as I watched him try to eat his soup with the handle instead of the ladle of the spoon itself. And what hurt most to watch was him thinking he was doing it correctly, struggling to slurp tiny droplets. I glanced at Margie who stood in the corner, ready to come to his aid, but I shook my head, grabbing the spoon and fixing it for him.

He didn't say anything. I was surprised he allowed the assistance. I guess he was tired of struggling to eat. After catching up with him a little further, I let Dad eat the rest of his soup in peace. I told him I was going to my room to take a quick shower.

That quick shower turned into two hours of moping in my bedroom and checking my laptop for final grades. I refreshed the page frequently, but nothing appeared on the portal.

Before I knew it, darkness had fallen, and when I went back to check on Dad, he was sound asleep. Margie informed me that she would be downstairs tidying up. After cleaning, I heard the TV turn on in the living room. Then, an hour and a half later, I heard her come back up, check on my father, and then enter the guest room. This was obviously the usual routine. She could hear if my dad needed her through the monitor she carried.

It saddened me to see him this way—almost like a helpless child. It made my heart ache. I wanted to weep for him, but Dad hated tears. He hated to see his girls down. I sucked it up, turning off my lamp and lying flat on my back, gazing up at the glowing stars on my ceiling.

I remembered the day Izzy and I put them up there, bouncing on the bed with our palms flat, sticky side of the stars up. I was a little taller, so I got more up than she did. Now that I think about it, I'm pretty sure she only got three of the ten up there. There are stars on her ceiling too. We shared the package.

Headlights flashed across my wall, and my thoughts were interrupted. I sat up, my heart catching speed, knowing the lights usually only came from one direction.

The Blacks' house.

Walking towards the window, I placed a single finger behind the curtain and peeked out. A black *Dodge Charger* with matte black rims and LED headlights parked in the Blacks' driveway. With my curiosity getting the best of me, I continued watching. I'd never seen the car before.

Another new toy of his?

Finally, the passenger door opened, and a young girl that looked about two or three years older than me stepped out, fluffing her blonde hair. She said something as she ducked down and looked inside the car again.

I frowned. From where I stood, she was beautiful. Her makeup flawless, the streetlights reflecting off her nose ring. Her lips were full, body slender in a gold club type dress. Her wavy blonde hair swam to the middle of her back, her high heels making her appear way taller than she was. She walked around the car, and the driver door swung open. And out stepped none other than Mr. Black.

So... that was his girl toy, huh?

All of my questions were answered in that single moment.

She had blonde hair.

No, her butt wasn't bigger than mine, but she definitely did a daily routine of squats.

I wouldn't say she was prettier than me, but we were kind of on the same scale. She just wore more make up, so she could have been less attractive beneath the layers.

Her legs looked better, though.

And her hair was obviously styled by an expensive hairstylist.

She reminded me of a knock-off Mrs. Black. It was depressing to think he'd searched for someone that reminded him of his deceased wife.

Theo stumbled out of the car in a drunken manner, shutting and locking the car behind him and then following after the girl to get to the house. Before they made it inside, his arms draped around her waist from behind and his lips pressed on the bend of her neck. His laughter was loud, but she was clearly irritated with the state he was in.

I felt somewhat sorry for her because I knew exactly what she was dealing with—only, I didn't think it was *that* bad dealing with a drunk Theo Black. She treated him like a child, brushing him aside, scolding him, and demanding him to get it together. He wasn't obnoxious, but he could get annoying when you attempted to help him.

They entered the house, and the door shut behind them. My eyes remained glued on the house, watching a few lights turn on. Shadows passed by the windows, their silhouettes getting higher as they made it up the stairs.

The bedroom lights were the last to flicker on. Their silhouettes stumbled in front of the window, lips glued. My heart pounded in my chest, my eyes unfortunately wet. I swallowed the thick lump in my throat, trying to force myself to look away, but I couldn't.

I felt pieces of my heart snapping off, my insecurities increasing. How could I feel like this? Why did it hurt so much to see? It had been so long, but apparently time couldn't even take away my feelings for him.

They made out for quite some time. And I don't know why the hell I couldn't pull away. It was like watching a train wreck. It was heartbreaking, but I couldn't help but look. She was clearly over her bitching and whining, divulging in Theo's embrace, hot kisses, and hard, delicious body. It was easy to look over the way he acted once you caught sight of him.

Finally, they stumbled away from the window, shadows disappearing. I was over the edge, nervous, waiting for something to happen. I wanted her to argue, back out of the make-out session. Leave the house. Take the *Charger* and go. Leave him alone. Something *bad* needed to happen. Right now.

And it finally did.

Only, it wasn't bad for them.

It was bad for *me*.

The lights turned off, and it was obvious what was about to go down. He was staking his claim. He was doing the very thing I hoped he wouldn't.

Making her, *his*.

I stepped away from the window, my heart barely beating. Why it hurt me so much to see after so many months without him, I do not know. I mean, after all, I was the one that left him hanging in the driveway before I went to school. I was the one that avoided him and didn't bother trying to speak to him for three years. I was the one that fucked up, so why be upset? Why let knowing he'd moved on hurt me?

I shrunk in my bed, staring at the wall across from me. It took a while to fall asleep, but I managed, and of course, it was just my luck that after what felt like months, I dreamt of Theo Black again.

All of his masculine glory.

All of his tattoos.

His beautiful smile.

His thick, sensual cock.

The patch of grass he fucked me on a few days before I left for school. The way he shushed me, begging me to stay quiet but also wanting me so badly to scream to the sky. I dreamt of all of him. Every single thing about him.

Then I woke up, facing reality at five in the morning.

I felt defeated. And stupid. And... weird about all of this. What the hell was I thinking, coming back to this place?

Fucking Primrose. It never failed to let me down.

SEVEN

CHLOE

THE NEXT MORNING, I smelled the crisp, salty scent of bacon. It'd been years since I smelled anything cooking in the mornings. Sitting up, I pushed out of bed and lumbered my way to my bedroom door, cracking it open. The aroma was much stronger as I peeked out. I inhaled, and then my stomach growled.

I felt severely hung over after witnessing Mr. Black with his *toy*. Something fatty, greasy, and unhealthy was definitely needed to cure me. Brushing my teeth and washing up a bit, I tossed on a pair of sweatpants, tied my hair up, and then hurried downstairs, barefoot. The soles of my feet landed on the wooden floorboards as I met downstairs.

Rounding the corner, I spotted Margie in the kitchen, my father at the bar counter. He sat there, almost lifeless. I came to a halt, watching as he tampered with the edges of the newspaper spread out in front of him.

When I was younger, during the times when he would actually be around, the paper would be in one hand, the other occupied with a piping hot cup of expensive Colombian coffee. But today, both hands were vacant, his stare empty.

Margie spotted me and hurried my way after placing the hot plate of bacon on the counter. "I'm guessing today is one of the bad days?" I asked quietly.

Margie looked at me, eyes full of sorrow. "I'm sorry. Hopefully he comes around. He took his pills. They should help."

I blinked my tears away, nodding and then sighing as I walked ahead. I took the stool beside him, picking up the box of Cheerios and dumping them into the empty bowl on the counter. "Morning, Dad. How you feeling?"

His head turned vastly, eyes boring into mine. "Dad? I'm not your father." He blinked, confused. "Hey, lady!" he hollered at Margie, who rushed to his side. "Who is this girl? Why is she calling me her dad?"

"You are her father, Mr. Knight. This is Chloe, your daughter. The one in the pictures on your nightstand."

He looked around the kitchen. After studying his surroundings for nearly ten seconds, leaving us in an uncomfortable silence, he asked, "Where am I?"

My heart snagged, emotions running wild. I swallowed hard, suddenly in no mood to eat. I started to reach for him, but he quickly jerked his hand away. My eyes instantly burned. I knew I couldn't take it personally, but how was that humanly possible when the man that helped bring me into this world couldn't even remember my name? Better yet, his own?

"Uh, Chloe, sweetie," Margie called, gesturing for me to meet her in the corner in front of the breakfast nook. I slid off my stool, walking her way. "He most likely won't eat anything crunchy. I made the bacon for you, so feel free to eat it. I was just going to run off to the store for some yogurt and oats. He loves that during days like this. Do you think you can watch him?"

I looked from Margie to my father who was staring at us strangely, almost like he didn't trust us. His eyes were wide, lips pressed thin, brows knitted. I hugged myself, feeling way too uncomfortable in my own home.

"Or would you rather run the errand for me? I didn't want to bother you too much—"

"No, no. Please," I said quickly. "I can go. What kind of yogurt?"

"Any brand is fine as long as it's vanilla. Any type of oats, preferably honey." She smiled, but it didn't touch her eyes. "We could tag along with you..."

"No, it's okay. He should probably stay here." I forced a smile, backing away and giving my dad one final glance. Margie nodded, tending to my sick father again. Rushing out of the kitchen and up the stairs, I shut my door behind me and stood there for a moment, leaning against it.

Tears wanted to be set free, no doubt, but I kept my shit together. Talking to him felt like many bullets were being shot straight into my heart. It hurt. But I had to suck it up. This was what I signed up for this summer. He was still my dad, whether he remembered me or not.

I changed clothes, clutched my keys, and zoomed downstairs, purposely avoiding having to go into the kitchen again. I made a mental note of the yogurt and oats and jumped into my car, driving straight to the market.

Once inside, I searched through the aisles, coming across the oats. I snagged two bags just in case, and then started for the dairy section. Making the turn, I ended up on aisle nine, and standing in front of the line of milk in the cold box, nearly perplexed as he looked for his brand, was Theodore Black.

I came to a screeching halt, eyes expanded. Out of everyone I could have run into in Bristle Wave, it was Theo. I started to turn back, but he looked up while scratching the scruff on his chin. When he caught sight of me, I could sum up every emotion that most likely flooded his veins. His heart.

Joy.

Sorrow.

Anger.

Confusion.

I stood still for a moment, unable to form words. Speaking wasn't going to happen on my end... at least, not right away. Theo's throat worked up and down, and he stepped away from the milk, his head shifting into an angle as he released the cooler's door.

"Chloe." His voice was smooth and deep. Like warm honey drizzling throughout my entire body. Delightful. Delicious. "Uh," he scratched his head. I began to turn, but he called after me, causing me to stop in my tracks. I heard the heavy crunch of his boots swiftly coming in my direction, and in no time, he was standing before me, a precarious smile hidden beneath his goatee. "Damn... how long's it been?"

"Three years." My voice was dry. I stepped back.

"I... can't even believe it." His eyes roamed my body but, surprisingly, it wasn't in a sexual manner. "Man, you look great. What brings you back to Bristle this summer?"

"My dad is sick." I shrugged. "Just here to help him." I hated that I was being so informal, so rude. But the image of him sleeping with someone else was seared into my brain. I couldn't get rid of it. It haunted me. I hated him for it. Petty, I know.

Theo's smile dropped, brows puckering. "Sick? What happened? Is he alright?"

"He has Alzheimer's and he had a stroke not too long ago. His nurse says he has his days, but I'm sure he'll be fine." That was a lie. It was obvious he wasn't going to be okay. Not for long.

"Damn. I'm sorry." He seemed really sincere. I used to tell him all about my parents... way before... well, you know. His lips did that thing. The twisty kind of thing that made him appear so innocent, like he wouldn't hurt a fly. There was something different about him. His eyes were still sad, but he held his head a little higher, his back straighter. He seemed to be doing okay, but just *okay*. Not great. Not wonderful. Just okay, taking each day one at a time.

"Listen, we should catch up, have some lunch sometime at my place? I bought a grill! Hardly even use the damn thing. Could whip up some burgers, hotdogs, steaks—whatever you want. I can get whatever we need right now, while I'm here." He looked around the grocery store, smiling a little.

I couldn't help but stare at him. Why? Why was he acting like we were okay? Like we hadn't laid our hands on each other? And let's not forget the fact that I still hadn't told Izzy? We were taking this to the grave, but he was acting like I was nothing? Like I was a mistake and he wanted to start over—start fresh and get rid of the imprinted memories.

I did my best not to appear upset. "Mr. Black, I should finish shopping. I have to get back to my dad."

"Oh." His smile faded, fingers slipping into the front pockets of his loose jeans. He'd added more tattoos to his arms and even his neck. He wore a tight, white V-neck shirt that revealed most of his upper chest, and—*wait, hold on*. What was that poking through the chest of his shirt? Was that a *nipple ring?* My goodness. How was I supposed to pretend to be upset with him if he kept making himself even hotter? "Right. I'll let you go then." He stepped aside, lips pulling upward in a tight, forced smile.

I did the same, stepping around him and completely forgetting about the yogurt. It was on that aisle, but like a selfish little girl, I wasn't going to get it until he was gone.

Like an idiot, I walked around the store, waiting until I saw Theo check out up front. He looked around the store while pulling out his wallet. He was most likely looking for me, but I stayed hidden on aisle three with my arms full of yogurt, waiting until he was out the door before going to check out myself.

When my items were bagged, I exited the market, relieved to escape the memories of Theo Black on aisle nine, but low and behold, there he stood.

He was casually propped against the front of his car with his arms crossed. Most of the ink on his biceps was on display. His sleeve was a work of art, each intricate piece a symbol of what he stood for. The bow and arrow for bravery. The skulls for the darkness within him. Even the tribal signs for his wild, primal side.

I started to stop, but a car honked at me, forcing me to keep going. Theo pushed off of his car with a small gleam in his eyes, one that I didn't quite understand. To me it read, *I'm up to something*, while also saying, *I'm going to get you to talk to me! I don't care if it's the last thing I do, Chloe!*

I popped the trunk, tossing the bags inside. Through my peripheral, I saw him coming closer, his white shirt appearing brighter beneath the blazing sun. I opened my door, started to close it, but he caught it just in time, pulling it open.

"Alright," he sighed, arms folding again. "What's the deal here, Little Knight?"

Little Knight.

Ugh.

That name made me want to spasm around him countless times.

"What are you talking about?" I asked instead, maintaining my standoffish behavior.

"I know when you're upset about something. Shit, if anyone has the right to be upset it should be me." He cocked a brow. "So why are *you* upset with *me*? I haven't spoken to you in three whole years. Please tell me what I did—why you're hanging onto a grudge with me."

"You didn't do anything."

He leaned forward, his cologne brushing past my nose. "Sure about that?"

"Positive." *Lies.*

He chuckled, eyes locking with mine. "If nothing's wrong, what's a harmless grilling out at my place going to do?"

"You know damn well why I can't come over there."

"We have a lot to discuss."

"Yeah, like your new girlfriend," I scoffed, looking away.

"Oh, so *that's* what it is." He was amused by my response, lips quirked. "But what about you, huh? I heard all about your football playing boyfriend." His amusement faded. He seemed agitated with the fact that I actually had someone else around after him. I guess we were on the same boat, but I would never admit to it.

"He's not my boyfriend anymore." I looked up.

"And she's not my girlfriend."

I rolled my eyes, starting my car. "Whatever you say, Mr. Black." His brown eyes were hard. He hated when I called him that. It reminded him of the old days, back when everything was okay—way before he ever took my virginity. Gripping the wheel, I focused ahead on the parking lot full of cars. Knowing he wasn't going to leave until he received a response, I calmly said, "I can't come."

"Why not?"

"I just... can't."

Theo straightened his back, blowing out a breath. Then, he shut my door, and I frowned, watching as he walked away. I thought he'd surely had enough, but I was wrong. He marched around the back of my car, met at my passenger door, opened it, and slid into my coupe, a grin on his lips, one that eerily reminded me of Izzy when she was up to no good.

"You have no excuse. You're home. You don't have any homework or tests to hold you back. You obviously have a nurse or someone that can watch over your dad, otherwise he'd be here with you, so come tomorrow night. I'll have everything ready. Drinks on me." He flashed a crooked, boyish smile. "I learned how to make frozen margaritas."

I shook my head. "No."

"I won't get out of this car until you say yes."

I laughed. "I think you're forgetting that I live a house away from you."

He wiggled his brows. "And while you go inside, I'll still be sitting in the car. I won't leave."

"Sounds stalkerish." He chuckled. It was nice to see it actually touch his eyes. I sighed. I didn't want to give in. I couldn't. No way. I looked forward again.

"Listen," he murmured, "I get why you don't want to come, but I promise I won't behave the same way I did three years ago. It'll be... better. I'm not the same sad man you had to take care of back then. I'm better now, and I got a little help."

"Hmm."

"What?" He lifted his hands in the air innocently, that crooked grin still present. "I'm serious. I won't."

I looked him in the eyes briefly before dropping my line of sight. Inhaling and then exhaling, I finally agreed, but I was still a bit reluctant. "Alright, Theo. But I'm only coming for the food and drinks you promised. Nothing more."

"Food and drinks. You got it." The laugh lines around his eyes formed again, his eyes chinking up. Grabbing the handle, he pushed the door open and stepped out of the car, but before taking off, he bent down to look at me. "Tomorrow night. Come around six. No need to knock." And with that, I was left with a wink and his heart-stuttering smile before he took off, hopped into his Charger, and drove away.

Collecting the emotions that'd easily gone astray, I finally pulled out of the parking lot and drove home, unable to fight the smile that lingered on my lips. I shouldn't have agreed, but "yes" was the only answer I could give. When a man like Theo looks you in the eyes, pleads, and begs, and then offers food and drinks, you can't say no. Only a fool would decline.

It worried me that we would get carried away with the drinking, become too comfortable and end up like we were before. But this time, I knew better. I was older, and he said he sought help, which was great. He was in need of it back then, especially when I was no longer able to assist him.

He seemed better, like his head was back on straight again. He seemed content with his life for the most part, but there was some part of him that would always be missing.

Sadly, I wasn't sure if it was Mrs. Black he was missing or the girl that helped him up to his bedroom during those lonely, drunken nights. Theo confused me, but we were much older now, and I was sure if he could put the past behind him, so could I.

It would be one night of harmless eating and drinking. And then I'd be back home, and soon off to college never to deal with Mr. Black again. One night I could give... right?

EIGHT

THEO

THE LAST PERSON I ever thought I'd see again was *her*.

Chloe. Little Chloe Knight. *That* girl. The one that made me do unspeakable things. The girl that, somehow, set my soul on fire. The girl that made me feel good and pure and safe, but at the same time bad, dirty, and wrong. There was just something about her.

Despite the age difference and the fact that I'd taken advantage of her innocence, she truly made me feel things I never thought possible. What's crazy is she made me feel things that I never felt with Janet, and with her, I thought I'd felt it all.

She still looked the same—no, actually she looked better. He wild curls made her look purposely untamable. The sun made her perfect olive skin shine. She had an urban/hippy way of dressing now. Short blue jeans, ripped at the hems. Round sunglasses tucked in the collar of her shirt, feather-like earrings and a ton of bracelets on her wrists. It suited her. She reminded me of young Norah Jones. A girl of sweet melody. A woman of beauty, pain, and bliss.

I don't know how I managed to still lose my breath around her. So beautiful and still carrying small hints of innocence. She hadn't changed a bit. She'd matured, all signs of a good thing.

I'd made a promise to myself a long time ago that I would curse her out, grab her roughly, and shake her by the shoulders, demanding an answer as to why she didn't tell me goodbye. I, of all people in her life, deserved a farewell. Yes, I can admit that three years before I'd gone off the deep end. I was losing my shit, losing my fucking way, but I still deserved a little regard.

I guess none of that mattered. Everything I said I would do when I saw her again, didn't dare happen. Just the mere sight of her made my heart do cartwheels, my cock pulse.

Her body had matured too. She was blessed in all the right ways. The chime of her laughter was beautiful, riding straight to my crotch. She still laughed the same. I remembered that, and also the way she moaned. How she cried and even how she whispered my name. I remembered *everything* as soon as I laid eyes on her in that grocery store.

But she pretended I was nothing—like none of what we did mattered anymore. I feared that maybe she'd gotten over me, or worse —that she was going to rat me out. I needed to know if she'd changed, so dinner was the motive.

She denied.

I refused to take no for an answer, so I waited in the parking lot, the sun beaming down on me. She tried to hide; I saw her ducking in the aisle. I got a kick out of it, laughing as I saw her coming out, shocked to see me standing right there, only a few yards away from her car.

She was a smart girl, but she knew how I was. I was persistent. I didn't give up, and when she finally agreed to dinner, I'd never felt more relieved. In that moment, I knew she'd still kept that secret to herself.

Come on. It was Chloe for Christ's sake. She held all of my secrets, and I held hers. I told no one about what happened between us. Those were moments that only we could talk about, moments that meant so much.

I felt horrible for hurting her, but it was time to make it right.

I thought I was past this girl, but I was so damn wrong.

Seeing her brought me right back to where we started, wanting to reel her in. Make her feel better, because the pain, hurt, and sorrow was all too clear. I needed to make up for my mistakes.

I wanted to make her feel like a virgin all over again—only this time, I'd know better. I would take my time, handle her correctly, like a virgin is supposed to be treated. With kindness. Gentleness. Care.

I would make her grateful that it was me who popped her sweet, delicate cherry, and I bet she would never leave without saying goodbye again.

NINE

CHLOE

THE FOLLOWING DAY WAS TERRIFYING. Not only was Dad worse, but he was also running a high fever and refusing to take his medicine. Without his memory, he was a mad man. Margie and I spent three relentless hours trying to calm him. She ended up crushing one of the pills and dumping it in his yogurt. The pill soothed him a lot.

By six that evening, he was in bed, numb as he watched a game of golf. I felt bad for him. I hated that we had to trick him into getting calm, tell him who we were and that we were there to help him not hurt him. He didn't trust us.

Not only was Dad's behavior taking a toll on my mind, but someone else's dad was as well—Izzy's. I planned on going over around 7:30, even though he said 6:00. It would be a late dinner and a late round of drinks, but it would give me an excuse to leave as soon as possible, you know, since it would already be kind of late? I planned on staying for about an hour.

Yeah, that was the plan anyway.

It took me a while to find something to wear. I was about to put on a dress, but then I realized how easy it would be for him to sneak a hand beneath. Shorts would have been too revealing, but it was really hot. I refused to put on jeans or look like an idiot by wearing sweatpants during the middle of summer.

So, I tugged on some self-made jean shorts and a white blouse with the sleeves cut off, fixed my curly mane, and applied an Indian-styled headband, and then I was out of the door.

The walk took less than a minute, but as I walked across, it felt like it'd taken a lifetime. The garage gate was open, and Theo was just walking out, opening the deep freezer. He took out a pack of unthawed steaks (I'm guessing he was keeping them cool), and when he heard my footsteps, he looked up. I threw up a quick wave, unable to hide my smile as I spotted him. He looked... amazing. And I was sure he hadn't even tried.

It was simple, really. Cargo shorts, a black T-shirt that hugged his firm body, and a pair of black Nikes. His hair looked like it'd just been trimmed, washed, and styled. It wasn't this way yesterday. Did he do this for me, or was it that time of month for a routine haircut? Either way, his attire was effortless, his entire appearance mouthwatering.

"Little Knight!" he chimed, holding his hands out. I walked into the garage, past his bike that had greasy tools surrounding it. "Didn't think you'd show." He held up the pack of steak, taking a quick glance at it before looking at me again. "I was just about to season these T-bones and toss them on the grill."

"Sounds great." Turning, he opened the door and held it open, allowing me inside. It'd been a while since I last set foot in this home. The last time was that night... the night that changed *everything*.

I walked in ahead of him, slipping out of my sandals and then walking to the kitchen. There were empty margarita glasses set up on the island counter. The house looked different, more modern than the upscale look Mrs. Black tried to uphold.

He'd changed the black appliances to silver, and there were now two ovens in the wall across from me. The flat stovetop was built on top of the island counter that took up the center of the spacious kitchen. Theo walked in after me, barefoot now. I supposed the Japanese tradition was the only thing he hung on to.

"Why'd you think I wouldn't show?" I asked as I sat at one of the cushioned barstools at the island.

Theo walked on the opposite side, drawing out a butcher's knife and cutting through the plastic that was wrapped around the steaks. While pulling out the T-bones, he shrugged and said, "It's nearing eight o'clock. Dinner is usually served somewhere between five and seven." One of his cheeks tugged up, forming a crooked grin.

"My... dad isn't doing so well." I looked away. "I was at the store yesterday because all he'll eat is vanilla yogurt during his bad days. Bought a ton."

"Man." He shook his head. "Can't believe what he's going through. Now that you finally get to spend time with him, he's—" His words quickly stopped flowing when he realized where he was headed and how much it would pain me to hear.

The thing about Theo was he kind of had no filter. He spoke his mind. He didn't care if feelings happened to get hurt. Izzy used to hate when he'd blast her in front of our friends or during sleepovers. He was a real man, one that didn't sugarcoat shit, not even his own feelings.

He turned and walked to the sink to rinse the steaks off, putting an end to that conversation. After doing so, he glanced over his shoulder, smiling again. "Come here." He gestured for me to come with a cock of his head.

"For...?"

"I took up some culinary classes. Wanna show you something." One shoulder lifted in a shrug, as if he didn't want his pride for cooking to show. "Lots of time on my hands now. You know how to cook?"

"If Ramen noodles and PB&J sandwiches count, then I guess so."

He laughed, watching as I slid off the stool and walked his way. He pulled out the wet steak and then took a step to his left, placing them on a cutting board. Grabbing the meat hammer from a case containing various kitchen appliances, he tore off a sheet of plastic cling wrap and then set them aside. "That doesn't count," he chuckled, eyes bright. "But I'll teach you a little something." He pointed to something next to me. "Grab those seasonings, will you?"

I reached for the bowls of seasonings and started to give them to him, but he held up his hands. "Nah!"

"What?" I asked.

"This is all you."

"Oh no," I shook my head, shoving them against his chest. "The meat will be so salty. It'd be better if the *professional* did it."

Smiling, he grabbed the seasonings and placed them on the counter. "Fine. But you're pounding." He picked up the hammer, handed it to me, and then placed the plastic sheet on top of the steaks. "Come on."

My eyes flickered up at him, uneasy. "What if I fuck it up?"

"Well, now." His eyes were slightly expanded, still warm. Comforting. "Someone grew a potty mouth while they were away, huh?"

"Sorry," I apologized as he stepped aside.

"Don't even worry about it. You should hear Izzy. I think she forgets she's actually speaking to her dad when we're on the phone sometimes."

"Yeah," I released a breathy laugh. When he noticed he mentioned his daughter, a draft of seriousness passed by us. It was so easy to talk to him, so easy to fall for such a beautiful, easy-going person. But it helped that he'd brought her up. It made me realize instantly that I wasn't here to play nice or even play house. I was here for dinner and drinks.

Dinner and drinks.

Drinks and dinner.

Whatever.

"Alright," he held his hands out, pointing towards the steak and quickly getting off the subject of his daughter. "Have at it. Beat it 'til it's blue."

Laughing, I lifted the hammer and slammed it onto the red meat. Theo walked away, pushing the doors open that led to the deck. He checked the temperature of the grill, and I couldn't help my wandering eyes.

He moved swiftly, fluidly. There was something about him now. He walked lighter, head higher, but there was still a small cloud of darkness hovering above his head—one that would never go away. Not until he came to peace with his past. Or, better yet, stopped blaming himself for things he couldn't control.

When he was back inside, he dusted his hands and walked my way. The closer he got, the tenser I became. It was then that I realized he had a spritz of cologne on. It was an earthy scent, drifting past my nose, the smell of the seasonings long gone as he met at my side. His arm brushed mine, his hand reaching over me to grab the flavorings.

"Okay. I think we're good," he said as I slammed the hammer down once more. He grabbed a few pinches of the garlic, pepper, and a mix of salts he'd put together, smearing them on the steaks with his fingers. "I'm gonna toss these babies on the grill now. I'll whip us up some margaritas while they cook." He picked up a pan, placed the T-bones inside, and walked to the deck, winking before stepping outside.

"Sounds good." I sighed, ignoring the flutters that thrashed in my belly. Theo placed the steaks on the grill, and I walked out with an inquisitive gaze, watching as he flipped them back and forth in peace.

Taking notice of my stare, he briefly looked at me with a hint of amusement on his face. "Something on your mind?"

"I'm just... curious about something."

"Yeah? What's that?"

"I don't know," I hummed, sitting on the bench a few inches away from the grill. I folded my legs, looked up, and caught him staring at them, running his gaze up and down. He avoided my eyes as he looked away, pretending to focus on the grilled meat. I pretended I didn't notice him looking. "You seem much better now, Mr. Black."

He huffed a laugh, placing his fork down. "Alright, there you go with that *Mr. Black* thing. Chloe," he murmured, turning my way and stepping closer. "You can call me Theo. I realize there's a big elephant in the room—one we should probably address. If you want, we can talk it out. Hopefully that'll get you to ease up. You seem... tense. See, I wanted to wait to talk about that, but if you insist."

"No—it's not that," I quickly responded. "I just... have a lot on my plate. And if it really makes you feel better, I will call you Theo. Not Mr. Black."

"Good. I'd appreciate that." He picked up the silver fork again. "As for that elephant in the room, how about we just let him go, pretend he was never here."

"Is that what you want?" I questioned.

His eyes met mine. "Is that what *you* want?"

"I think it'd be best," I admitted, but there was a little lie behind that statement.

"Whatever you want, Little Knight." I'm not sure he noticed, but a faint smile touched his lips, one I was sure he meant to hide. He knew there was still something sparking here, something really, really hard to ignore. Fireworks popped. Electricity zinged and zapped, shooting straight to my core.

Inhaling deeply, I stood and watched as he flipped the steaks once more and then took them off the grill. "Looks good!" I said.

"Think so?"

"Yes. I've been dying for a really good steak lately."

"Well it's a good thing you're in town, huh?" He revealed one of his dimples, and I followed him inside. Once the pan was out of his hands, he went for the fridge, pulling out a jug of lime margarita juice and then some ice from the freezer. He went for the blender and asked, "So, school is good? Liking USC?"

"Oh, I love it! I mean at first I didn't like my roommate, but she's cool now. I get her."

"You were never the type to really make friends," he said.

"Yeah, my dad said the same thing."

"That's not necessarily a bad thing. Sometimes having too many friends leads to trouble... and stress. Trust me, it took me a very long time to come to terms with that conclusion."

"Yeah, I've only seen one friend come over. Wasn't his name Mr. Brant or something? Cool guy."

"Yeah... about that..." He looked away, dumping ice into the blender. "Mr. Brant only wanted one thing. Had to let him go."

My lips twisted. "What do you mean?"

"Money..." His eyebrows pulled together. "When he found out about what happened to Janet, he showed up more often. Found out he was only taking advantage of my situation, getting closer to me for the few checks I'd receive due to her loss."

"What?" I gasped. "Seriously?"

He nodded.

"What an asshole."

"Agreed." He turned on the blender, crushing the crushed ice even further, filling the room with a loud *whirring* noise. I toyed with the cotton edges of the placemat in front of me, focusing on the horizontal prints.

"I would never do that to anyone. It seems so... wrong," I said over the noise.

"Well, I could give him the benefit of the doubt by saying his mom had finally kicked him out and he had just been fired from a well-paying truck-driving job, but I won't. He's an adult. I was going through a hard time, and to try and take advantage of me at my weakest point is pretty fucked up. I understand not having money, but all he had to do was ask. I always look out for the people I care about. He knows this. Instead, he tried to steal it, going through my papers to see if he could find a pin number to my accounts. I caught him in my office one night." His head shook, the disappointment unmistakable. "But, it is what it is." The blender came to a hush, and he poured two glasses, one for himself and one for me. After digging in the drawer in front of him, he pulled out a purple straw and tossed it into one of the glasses, sliding it across the counter.

"Favorite color." He beamed.

"Look at you," I teased. "You still remember." I accepted the drink, deciding it was best to stop talking about his deceitful friends and his deceased wife. I took a quick sip, my taste buds going into a heavenly rage, flooded with tangy lime. "Wow! This is really good."

"I added a little something to the margarita mix before you got here. Can you taste it?"

"No." I shook my head. "But it's great. What is it?"

"That would be spoiling it."

"Just tell me," I laughed.

He took a sip of his and placed the glass on the marble countertop, folding his arms. "Just a few drops of cherry flavor."

"Wow... never would've guessed that one. I was thinking strawberry or raspberry."

"Close." He walked to the fridge, pulling out a glass bowl with potato salad inside.

"So, cooking, huh?" I inquired, lifting my brows as I smiled at him. "It's what you do to pass the time now?"

"It... helps." He put the bowl down and then grabbed two plates from the cabinet above. "See, I went to therapy because my mom thought I could use it. I don't believe in therapy, and, luckily my therapist understood that, so he told me to find something to do that can distract my mind, ease my discomfort. An outlet."

"When did you go into therapy?"

He was hesitant, avoiding my eyes. "About three months after you left." *And only a month before you met your girl toy.* "I started to... spiral. Instead of going to work, I'd go to the bar. My mom dropped by one day to check on me, saw me looking and feeling like utter shit, and signed me up, refusing to argue with me about it." He sighed. "I'm grateful. Mom always knows best, right?"

"Hmm... most moms."

"Speaking of, where is yours? Never see her car parked up front anymore."

"Well, my mom decided to be a bitch and turn into a travel-happy cougar."

He busted out laughing. "Cougar? Really? Young guy? I can't picture it."

"Really? 'Cause I can. He can't be too much older than I am." I cringed. "Kinda... weird after seeing her with my dad all my life."

"So she just flaked out... left your dad here to take care of himself?"

"She got Margie for him, and luckily we can trust her. She's a really sweet woman. Her number one concern is my dad, so that's good I guess."

"Yeah." He placed his palms on the counter, his muscles flexing without effort. I looked away from his arms, but then my eyes met his. *Damn it, wrong place.* I was supposed to look down or to my left, even to my right. But, no. I looked up, trapping myself.

Our eyes fastened—clinked. And when they did, it was hard to look away.

Man, he was truly a beautiful sight to see—a sight for sore eyes as they say. His gaze traveled down to my lips, lingering there for just a moment before he tore them away, picking up his margarita and turning for the potato salad again.

"Well, how about we eat and forget about reality for just a little while. I was told food is a good way to comfort the soul."

I agreed with a nod. "Sure. Let me go wash my hands really quick. I'll be back, I swear." His eyebrows rose, amused by my last remark. I was out of the kitchen, mentally cursing at myself for the last thing I said. "You'll be back?" I muttered under my breath once entering the bathroom. What the hell did I even mean? *Where else are you gonna go?*

I gripped the edges of the cool porcelain counter, staring at myself in the mirror. Familiar hazel eyes sparkled from the lighting above, the pit of my belly still fluttering.

I felt... different. Relieved? Perky? I don't know. I just know I felt totally different here than I did in my own house. Like all of my worries had vanished for a while and nothing mattered but the food, drinks, and... *Theo.*

Just Theo.

Always Theo.

Duh, Theo!

Shaking my head swiftly, I turned the knobs and stuck my hands beneath the stream of water. I then brought my wet hands to my face, rubbing beneath my eyes and looking at myself again.

It's just dinner, Chloe. It's just dinner. Get over yourself.

Shutting off the water, I dried my hands and then walked out again. Theo wasn't in the kitchen when I returned. Frowning, I called his name, and he responded from the deck, his voice a short distance away. It was then that I noticed our drinks weren't at the counter. Nor were our plates or the food. I walked out, my bare feet landing on the smooth wood.

He sat at the round table in the corner, the food set up with two China plates across from each other.

"Figured we could eat out here. Feels good tonight."

I looked from him to the stars in the sky, gripping the door handle. The wind bristled by me, flowing through my hair, wrapping me up in its comforting breeze. It was a very good night to eat outside, so I walked ahead, taking the seat across from him.

He had a smile on his lips, observing me as I got comfortable. "What?" I laughed.

"Nothing." He pressed his lips, picked up a fork, and stuck it into one of the steaks, placing it on my plate. "Help yourself to whatever."

I browsed my selection, eyes moving from the potato salad to the green beans and then the yellow rice. I helped myself to the rice and green beans, deciding to eat the potato salad last.

"Actually," Theo said, and when I looked up he was still peering at me, gaze inquisitive. I straightened my back, becoming insecure as he scanned me. "I just wanted to let you know that you look great tonight. Really great. I'm digging this modern hippie thing you have going on."

"Oh." I bit a smile, digging my fork into the green beans. "Uh, thank you." See, I knew someone would love it. Mariah hated how I dressed, and Izzy didn't understand the choices I made whenever we shopped, but Theo liked it. My heart went wild.

He nodded and cut into his steak. Our talking during dinner was minimal. Other than the music he had playing from the sound system in the living room, we hardly spoke.

We did chat about little things, like other meals he'd learned how to make, how he now had more than enough employees at his shop to run it, and how he didn't even have to work at the shop himself anymore. He was very proud about that. He'd finally made it to a position in life where he could do what he wanted all day long and still make money. I was proud of him for it. It was all he ever used to talk about. His shop. His dreams. It was great.

After dinner, we went to the kitchen for another round of margaritas, and I even had a slice of key lime pie he'd prepared. It was delicious. That cooking hobby of his worked out wonderfully.

I finally checked the time on my cell phone when our glasses were empty and our pies half-eaten. It was nearing 11 PM. I couldn't believe how quickly time had passed. Although it was a little awkward at first and, yes, there was an oversized elephant in the room, I had a great time. I refused to speak on said elephant. Speaking on it was a risk, one I didn't want to take. I didn't want to ruin such a great night.

"Wow," I breathed. "It's getting late. I should get going. Check on my dad."

"Right—shit, yeah." I was sure he meant to sound enthusiastic, but his tone was far from it. It was somewhat deflated. I detected the defeat in his eyes, how my absence would soon bring back loneliness. I hated it, but this was no excuse. Although Margie was there, I wanted to check on Dad myself. She needed a break, some sleep after dealing with him all day long.

"I can... maybe swing by sometime later this week? Bring some pizza or something. I won't attempt trying to cook," I laughed.

He rubbed his forehead as he followed me to the garage door. "Yeah, sure. Just let me know. My schedule is pretty clear now. Don't do too much these days."

I stepped into my sandals and then walked out. The light was now off in the garage. I stepped into the night, but I could still see him from the lights shining from the kitchen and hallway.

"I will definitely let you know." I took a step back, almost stumbling on my own two feet. He caught me before I hit the shelf next to me, holding onto my elbow. "Careful," he murmured.

My breath caught in my throat, the proximity depleted. He was standing right in front of me, his hand still on my arm, now working its way down. It was unintentional, I was sure, but it didn't prevent my body from heating up, my core from constricting.

He looked at my lips again, wanting so badly to steal a taste, but before I knew it, his hand was no longer on my arm and he'd taken a step back. His eyes were still soft, mellow, and full of a soft, blazing fire. His pink lips moved, fixing in a way that was all too familiar to me. I don't think he could help it anymore. He wanted to do what was going to happen next ever since he set eyes on me in the market.

It truly was unexpected.

He leaned forward and placed a smooth, slightly damp kiss on my cheek.

"I'll see you soon, Chloe." His voice was deep, humming right to my panties, his mouth only a few millimeters away from my ear.

"See you, Theo," I whispered, my hazel irises interlocked with his brown. Finally, I tore them away and turned around, stumbling out of the garage and hurrying across the street before I did something drastic. I took a glance back when I met at my front door.

He was still there, standing inside, only a few inches away from the garage door. From the streetlights, I could see him smiling beneath that well-trimmed goatee. One of his hands was in his pocket, the other on the wall in front of him where the switch was.

I said goodbye with a small wave, opened my front door, and before I could shut it, I heard his garage gate close, guarding me from his presence.

I didn't see him the next day.

But I did see him the day after that... and he wasn't alone. All the giddiness I felt from the dinner we shared to that small peck on my cheek immediately disappeared when I saw the same blonde girl pull up to his house in a white Honda with pink rims.

I stood at my window, staring out, waiting to see what would happen next. They came back out of the house together, hopping into his Charger and taking off. They left around seven that night and didn't come back until midnight.

When they arrived, I heard his car pull up. I frantically climbed out of bed, watching as he kissed the girl goodbye through her car window. She pulled out of the driveway, leaving Primrose, though I was sure it was just for the night.

This time, my curtains had been pulled aside, and I may have purposely kept them that way to see when he'd return. I continued my watch. He entered the house, a few lights flashed on, and then the bedroom light came on.

What I did not expect was for his blinds to open and him to be standing right there. Right at the window, looking right at mine. Gasping, I backed away, pressing my back to the wall.

Did he see me? Know I was watching?

I didn't know.

I dared another look, and saw him still standing there, his head in the tilt he normally held it in. Innocent. Curious. He'd gone without a shirt, the jeans he wore hanging low on his hips, showcasing two slices of a delicious V.

My brows knitted. I wasn't sure if he could see me. He left the window, and I waited. Seconds later, my phone buzzed on the nightstand. I looked towards it, heart slamming still. Walking back, I picked it up but went back to the window. He was there again, the phone to his ear.

And then it hit me. I looked down at the person's name that flashed on my screen. *Mr. Black.* Surprised, my heart caught speed, and I answered, my voice soft. "Mr. Black?"

"Hey Chloe."

"Everything okay?"

"I don't know," he said, voice low. "You tell me."

"What do you mean?"

"You just gonna stay in your room and watch me, or are you gonna come over and actually talk to me?"

I huffed a laugh, looking up, heat bombarding my cheeks. Being embarrassed would have been an understatement. "I'm—I don't know what you mean."

"Turn on your lamp," he demanded.

"Why?"

"I want to see you."

I looked towards my lamp, hesitating. He was quiet, waiting for me to follow through. I blew a breath, going for my lamp. Then I met at the window again, and he was still there. His expression had changed though. He was smiling now. It was gentle. Sweet.

"Damn. Is there ever a time you don't look good?"

"Please," I laughed, tugging on the hem of my tank. It was then that I realized I had no bra on. I covered my chest with my arm.

"Don't do that."

"Do what?"

"Cover up. Just stand there... let me look at you."

Slowly dropping my hand, I stared ahead, allowing Mr. Black to get an eye-full. I was in my most natural state—hair up in a bun, shorts low, revealing too much leg, and sporting a white camisole that exposed firm, brown nipples.

"What are we doing?" I asked, voice barely heard.

He was quiet for a moment, his face serious now. "Picking up where we left off."

"I don't know if we should…"

"I don't know if we should either." I saw him fidget and look down. "You know I never stopped thinking about you, Chloe." He lifted his head. "You haven't even been here a week, and I already want you back."

"What about the girl that just left?"

"She's… a friend."

"That you kiss and sleep with?" I retorted, voice full of sarcasm.

"I can easily drop her. It's nothing."

I scoffed.

He was quiet for a moment. "I'll definitely drop her if you let this be…"

"What do you mean *let it be*?"

"I know you still keep up with Izzy. I know you feel guilty about it. Shit, I do too. She'd hate me if she knew I ever placed a hand on you in that way…"

"But?"

"But, I feel better around you. Like your soul is filling me up, providing positive energy. I don't think I should deny that feeling. It feels too good—it's almost like a high."

I was quiet for a moment, meeting his eyes as he held a full smile. "I've felt empty for a while now—well, ever since leaving Primrose."

"So have I. You know that night when you helped me to my room?"

I knew exactly which night. "Yeah."

"I'd never felt more alive, Chloe. I was afraid of going too far with you—I mean you're young and you hardly knew a damn thing back then—but I couldn't stop myself. I couldn't control the urge you gave me. I wanted to caress every part of you. I wanted to hold your face in my hands, stare you in the eyes all night as I made the sweetest love to you. You may have thought I considered it a quick fuck—easy pussy." He shook his head. "Nah. Trust me. It meant way more to me than that. Like most of my worries had faded in that one single moment. Like I could… *live* and not feel so fucking blue."

His words lit my soul on fire. I battled a grin with a straight face. "I figured you did it just to feel something... release some steam, ya know?"

"No..." His head moved side to side with disapproval. "Can't believe I'm even saying this, but you know damn well I've felt something for you for a long time. I know to others it seems fucking perverted and maybe like I'm fucked up in the head, but you're a good girl.

"Other than Janet, you're the only person that knows me. I connect with you. I don't even have to speak and you already know what's wrong. I feel good around you. Content. And when you left, it hurt like hell. Watching you go but knowing I couldn't stop you because you *weren't* mine. I'd considered you mine for years," he laughed. "In some crazy way, I made you mine and wanted you for myself and nobody else. It hurt to let that go."

"Really?"

"Yes. For years I've always felt the unnecessary need to protect you. Perhaps that need merged into deeper places, places that I can't control or stay away from, no matter how hard I try or how much it may burn." He was quiet for a moment. We stared at each other. "Just give me the summer, Chloe. Let this summer happen for us. I know you've been curious. I know you've been craving me. Know how I know?"

"How?" I whispered.

"Because I crave that tight, sweet pussy every fucking day." He flashed a smile. I clenched in my panties, sinking my teeth into my bottom lip. Great. Now I was fully turned on. "Just the summer."

I dropped my head, focusing on my toes. "Theo... I—I don't know. It just seems so bad because of Izzy and how quickly it happened after Mrs. Black passed—"

"I know," he whispered, cutting me off. "I know. And I understand." I peered up. We looked at each other for several seconds, brown matching hazel, breath bated, until he pressed his palm on the glass and said, "Just... let it be. I'll try if you try."

"I'll take it into consideration."

One of his cheeks lifted, a half-smile on display. "Dream about me."

I pressed my hand on the cool glass, a warm sensation flourishing from my throat to my chest. It burned in the sweetest way possible. I felt soaking wet below, in dire need for him to take me—satisfy me like none of those selfish college boys could.

I needed a man, but not just *any* man. I wanted the beautiful, glorious man that stood only yards away from me, craving similar temptations. "Goodnight, Mr. Black."

He chuckled, and the hum of it made my stomach swirl with heated desire. "Goodnight, Miss Knight."

TEN

CHLOE

SOMETHING VIBRATED on the hard surface beside me.

I groaned, my eyelids heavy. Through thin slit eyes, I took a peek at the alarm clock. *7:15.* Way too early for any type of meaningful conversation. I shut my eyes, flopping onto my stomach, but my phone vibrated again.

"Seriously?" I muttered, snatching my cellphone from the nightstand. **Wild Child** appeared on the screen, and I shook my head, answering groggily. "Mariah you better have a damn good reason for calling me this early."

"Oh, I do!" Her tone was chipper and confident. "Guess what I'm doing?"

I sat up, raking my fingers through my hair and asking "What?" with a sigh.

"I'm riding with Tiny to Bristle Wave."

My eyes popped open, all tiredness subsiding. "Bristle Wave?" I asked. "What? Why?"

"Well, shit, Chloe, all you ever did was brag about it. I looked into it some more and liked what I saw. Even got my dad to rent us a boat."

She was so full of herself, like she'd had everything going according to plan. Only, she didn't. I was there to watch over my dad. The fun had to wait.

"Mariah, I told you I can't leave from home much this summer."

"Oh, come on. It's just one night! We have nothing else better to do right now so why not have a few drinks on the boat. I heard there was a club there that everyone loves. Good drinks, good music. Know the name?"

"Brix," I sighed. I knew all about Brix. It was the club all the college students hung out at when school was over and they were back at home. It was a way to get through the night in BW, drown in cheap drinks, and dance the night away. Izzy and I went once, and I hated it. There were a lot of older guys that reminded me of wolves hunting innocent sheep, half-dressed waitresses, and boys that refused to leave you alone until you gave them a dance. "You sure you wanna go there? There are way better clubs in L.A."

"I thought about that, but you should be as close to home as possible, C. Come on I'm not *that* self-absorbed."

"Yeah," I laughed at that statement. Mariah was one of the most inconsiderate people I knew. She only cared about herself, never thought about how someone else would feel if she took the wrong action.

"Anyway, we have a hotel so you don't have to worry about us popping up, but I would love it if you came out with me tonight. It'll be fun, I swear. And the first two rounds of drinks are on me."

I blew out a breath, my bangs flapping with the puff of air. "I will let you know. It really depends on how my dad acts today..." *And if Theo decides he wants to hang out.*

"Ugh." She smacked her teeth. "Fine. Just let me know. Talk later!" She hung up, and I dropped my phone, staring at the sky-blue wall across from me. I sat there for a moment, realizing I had no plans for the day. I had planned to spend it out on the deck in front of the pool, catching up on a steamy novel by Maya Banks.

"Mr. Knight you have to get in the shower!" Margie's voice cut through the silence.

"No!"

"Please, Mr. Knight!" she hollered. "It's been three days."

I frowned towards the doorway and hopped out of bed, rushing to his bedroom. He was standing in the bathroom, Margie blocking the doorway so he couldn't escape. He tried pushing past her, but she was a strong little woman, holding her ground.

"What's going on?" I asked her.

"I heard him through the monitor and came to check on him. He's kinda smelly so I told him he needed a shower. At first he agreed, but now he's putting up a fight. It's been three days, Chloe. You would think the man would want to shower."

"Three days, Dad? Seriously?" I stepped behind Margie, looking over her shoulder at him. He was now sitting on the edge of the tub, the shower running in the far corner. "You're wasting water." I maneuvered under Margie's arm, going towards him. When I was directly in front of him, I lowered to a squat.

"You're still here, little girl? Stop calling me your dad. I'm not your dad."

"Yes you are." I remained patient. His words didn't hurt as much. I knew he didn't mean them. "I'm your daughter, Chloe. I am twenty-two years old. I am your only child, and you smell absolutely horrible right now."

He fought a smile, folding his arms and looking away. The amusement was faint on his face. He wanted to laugh. I could see it in his eyes. Dad was still in there somewhere. "I do not," he mumbled.

"Yes, very badly. I think it's best if you listen to Margie and jump in the shower. Wash your man parts. We won't look. We promise."

His head turned, eyes meeting mine. I put a genuine smile on, but he only stared at me. "Fine," he grumbled, uncrossing his arms. "But you two have to get the hell out. I need privacy."

"Do you know which is the soap and which is the shampoo?" Margie asked, removing her guard.

"Yes. I can read!" he snipped.

I stood, going towards Margie and bobbing my head, gesturing for her to give him some space. "I'll stay in the room," I told her. I shut the bathroom door behind me, and she sighed. She still had on a lavender nightgown, half of her hair still in rollers. She looked exhausted. "You should go catch a few more hours of sleep. I think I can take over for a while."

"Oh my goodness," she sighed. "Are you sure? This is my job—it's what I get paid for—"

"I know," I said, interrupting her. "But everyone deserves a little break here and there." I shrugged. "I can handle it."

She capped my shoulders with her hands, her gratefulness on full display. "You are a lifesaver." Releasing my shoulders, she turned for the door and said, "Let me know when you need me. I swear I'll only sleep for one hour."

I waved a hand. "Don't worry about it, Margie. It's all good."

She gave me one more thankful smile and then walked out of the bedroom. I heard her door shut behind her and when it did, I looked at the TV. He was watching the news today. Walking towards the bathroom door, I knocked softly. "Dad, you okay?"

"Fine."

"Let me know when you need me."

"I won't."

I laughed, twisting on my heels and then climbing on top of his bed. Crossing my legs Indian-style, I grabbed his remote and flipped through the channels. I ended up on the cooking channel and immediately thought of Theo. Just the mere thought of him made my belly thrash with tiny butterflies. There was a swarm of them, fluttering around, proving just how much I, indeed, cared for him.

Just let it be. Just let it be? I was still unsure. I mean, it would have been wrong to never tell my best friend, but then again, some things just... happened.

The right thing to do would have been to inform her, but I loved her too much to create such drama in her life. I cared for her, and she was still a little unstable about her mother passing away. Knowing that her father had slept with me only six weeks after her death would cause all hell to break loose.

But I liked Theo... a lot.

And I also loved Izzy. She was like a sister to me. I could talk to her about any and everything—everything but *this* anyway. Maybe it was best to make the sacrifice, forget about Theo and avoid him so I could keep my friendship with her on the right track.

I sighed, and seconds later, Dad walked out of the bathroom with a blue, cotton robe on. He glanced my way uncomfortably, walking to his closet. "How'd it go in there?" I asked, fighting a laugh.

He grumbled something beneath his breath, cracking the closet door behind him. Almost ten minutes later, he walked back out. I expected comfortable clothes, but instead he had on a pair of khaki shorts with an argyle shirt that matched his socks. His leather shoes were tied tight, and in his hand was a navy-blue flat cap.

"Dad..." I climbed off the bed, brows furrowed. "What's happening here?" I pointed between us, doing a small, sarcastic spin action with my finger.

"I want to go golfing today." He walked towards the window and looked out, observing the neighborhood. "It's a nice day."

"How are you feeling?"

He shrugged. "Not too forgetful. Still have my good swing."

"Did you take your meds?"

"Yeah," he huffed. "Nurse practically shoved them down my throat."

"Oh." I placed a hand on my hip. "Well, okay. But I'm going to drive you. Margie told me the doctor said you couldn't get behind the wheel."

"Man," he frowned, head shaking, "that woman tells you every-thing, huh?"

"That's a good thing. The keys are hidden, so don't go trying to look for them."

"Women," he mumbled as I trotted out of the door.

I laughed, walking down the hallway and entering my bedroom. I took a five-minute shower and then got dressed in a pair of shorts and a blue polo and gathered all my hair into a low ponytail. Placing the black baseball cap over my head, I snatched up my keys, my cellphone, and my wallet, and then walked back to Dad's room. I was surprised he was still in there. I guess he really was feeling himself today. Good.

"Ready?"

He looked up, standing. "Was ready almost thirty minutes ago, baby girl."

Yep. This was Dad. The one that called me "baby girl". The one that actually knew who I was. I smiled as I followed him down the staircase, and after we ate a light breakfast—yogurt, walnuts, and bananas—we were in the car, on our way to the golf club.

While Dad golfed and I was practically his caddy, slugging heavy clubs around the green fields, I'd received a few text messages from Izzy.

Izzy: *I'm bored.*
Izzy: *Chloe?*
Izzy: *Is papa Knight ok?*
Izzy: *CHLOEEEE!!!!*

I sighed before responding. Such an impatient being she was.

Me: *Papa Knight is fine. At Bayroots with him now.*
Izzy: *The golf club?*
Me: *Yep.*
Izzy: *I feel so bad for you right now.*

Tell me about it.

I looked up, watching as Dad steadied the club in his hand, the golf ball ready to be struck. He drew back twice, steadied his hand again, and then jerked back once more before completing his swing. The metal club hit the ball with a loud *thwack,* and we both watched it soar, landing on a patch of grass only a few yards away from the planted flag.

Someone let out a deep whistle from a few feet away, and when I turned to look, I was unfortunate to see Riley, my ex from high school, and his obnoxious dad. *Oh, God.*

"You have one hell of an arm on you!" Mr. Hunt yelled to my dad, walking in his direction. Of course, that left Riley to come my way as Mr. Hunt continued talking, leaving me stuck in an awkward situation.

I couldn't leave because Dad needed me, but on the other hand, if I had left, it would have spared me from Riley's ignorance.

"Well, damn," Riley said, eyes running up and down my legs. "You still have those softball player legs on you." I thinned my eyes, picking up the bag of clubs and following after Dad and Mr. Hunt. Riley caught up to me, a smirk on his lips. "It's been so long, huh, Chloe? You go to USC, right?"

"Yep."

"Shit, you know we trashed them during the championships. Fucking murdered their asses."

"Good for you," I sarcastically noted.

"So what's up?" he asked, running his fingers through his thick bed of curly reddish-brown hair. He'd grown it out, and he had developed more acne too. Weird. I always thought acne was supposed to disappear the older you got, not worsen.

"What do you mean?"

"What are you in town for? USC's only like a few minutes away right."

"An hour and a half actually." I tried not to roll my eyes. "And I came for my dad."

"Yeah, figured it was something. I remember you saying you would never come back once you left."

"Yeah, well..." I shrugged, dropping the bag as Dad came to a halt. "Shit happens. Sometimes you need to surround yourself with family."

He scoffed. "Bullshit. Only reason I'm here is 'cause my uncle Joe died. Funeral was yesterday."

"Oh." I pressed my lips, turning the screen of my phone back on.

> **Me:** *OMG. You won't believe who just showed up.*
> **Izzy:** *Who?!?*
> **Me:** *Riley Hunt.*
> **Izzy:** *Ew. Wtf? I thought you were going to say someone hot.*
> **Me:** *He won't stop staring at my legs.*

I looked up, and his eyes were focused on my thighs, yet again.

Normally, it was the butt or the boobs, but since I had neither on full display, it was the legs. Ugh, he was so fucking weird.

"You know I'm in town until tomorrow afternoon. We should hang out tonight or something."

"What makes you think I want to do that?"

"I don't know. You're obviously bored as fuck if you're hanging around Bayroots and watching your dad play golf." He laughed hard, proud of his inside joke.

This time, I didn't prevent my eye roll. He was a complete jackass. I turned my back to him and looked towards my dad again. He was still watching Mr. Hunt talk. He seemed a little confused.

"Know what I mean?" Riley asked, moving forward and licking his lips. "Have fun together... alone. Just like old times."

Ew. I cringed and moved away, feeling bile building up in the back of my throat. Dad turned to look at me, and I took advantage of the opportunity, walking ahead with the clubs and getting far away from my really unappealing ex-boyfriend.

"Everything okay?" I asked.

"Yeah, yeah. Just need a different club."

"Oh." I pulled the bag around, and Mr. Hunt told us to hold on one second, rushing towards Riley again and demanding his cellphone from the bag. Yeah, now I see where Riley got his *everybody owes me* attitude.

Dad scratched his head after accepting the club. "I feel like I've seen that man before, but I have no clue who the hell he is."

I laughed. "That's Mr. Hunt. His first name is Jake. You volunteered to go on a field trip with him one time—a long time ago."

"Oh. The boy knows you?" he inquired.

"We... used to date."

Dad's face was full of disgust, nose scrunched, forehead creased. "Him!?"

I glanced back. "I know..." I turned forward again, looking down at the grass. "I don't know what I was thinking."

Dad chuckled. "Don't sweat it." Then he tipped my chin back up. "We all fall for pimply, odd-statured people with arrogant attitudes."

I giggled. "You're crazy. Go swing!"

He put on a smile, walking forward and getting into position.

When he tipped the ball into the hole with the flat edge, he went to take it out, and I jotted his score down.

"I'm guessing he isn't your type then, huh?" Dad looked at me as we started towards the golf cart. I peered up at him, my hat shielding my face from the sun. There was gentleness in his eyes, his curiosity burning. I guess I didn't expect him to know anything about this—my relationship life, that is. I never talked about boys with my father. Like, ever.

"He's... way too simple-minded for me." I glanced back, watching the Hunts struggle with which club to start with.

"Yeah, that I can see. You're a smart girl. You need someone on your level—or even a little higher."

"Mm-hmm."

"So what is it that piques your interest?"

"Ya know..." I hesitated, unsure as I started the cart and drove to the next course. "I don't really have a type, but for some reason I always end up with a football player at my side. I don't get it."

"Hot bods," he mused, grinning.

I choked on a laugh, twisting my lips and putting the cart in park. "It feels weird talking to you about this."

"You might as well get it out now. I'm sure I won't be able to remember it by tomorrow... maybe even tonight."

I swallowed thickly, but Dad acted as if his comment wasn't meant to be damaging. For some reason, that comment brought me right back to reality. The fact that he had Alzheimer's. The fact that he most likely wouldn't remember my first name by the following morning, maybe even the same evening.

Hopping out of the cart, Dad pulled out one of the tees and stuck it in the grass. I stepped out and dropped the bag, watching as he stood there for a while with the golf ball in hand and a confused expression now on his face.

I realized what was happening before he could ask, "Where'd I get this ball from?"

Picking up the bag of clubs, I walked towards him and took the ball away, pulling out the tee from the grass. "We've been out her for about two hours now, Dad. I think we should head back home."

"Uh... yeah. I guess." He said nothing more as I collected the clubs and tossed them in the back of the cart. Dad climbed inside, sitting forward, eyes ahead. He was disappointed. I pretended his forgetfulness didn't bother me by mentioning how great his swing was—how he still had it. It made him feel somewhat better, but not entirely.

The car ride was quiet on the way back home. We arrived in fifteen minutes, catching Margie in the kitchen, whipping up some lunch. "Well, look who's back!" she chimed, turning around with a pink apron tied at her waist. "How was it?" she asked as I shut the garage door behind me.

"A disaster," Dad grumbled.

"Was not," I argued. "It was great, Margie. He still has his swing."

"That's wonderful!" Her chubby cheeks spread as she looked from me to my dad. "Are you hungry, Mr. Knight?"

"No, no." He waved a hand. "I just want to rest." He said this while he was already walking out of the kitchen. Margie quickly turned the stove off, following after him but giving me a wink before disappearing. She had it from here.

Blowing out a deep breath, I sat at the counter and ran my fingers across my face. It was getting worse for him. I didn't know how much more I could handle.

Slipping off the stool, I tiptoed upstairs and took a shower, ridding myself of the ninety-degree heat. Once I finished, I got dressed and heard my phone buzz in the pocket of my shorts.

I figured it was Izzy or even Mariah. I was wrong.

It was Theo.

Theo: *Plans tonight?*

Me: *...not sure yet.*

Theo: *Can we meet?*

Me: *What if I end up having plans?*

Theo: *I asked first.*

Me: Actually, no. Someone already beat you to the punch.
I just haven't confirmed or anything yet.

Theo: *A guy??*

I frowned, but then I smiled, pleased to know he even cared.

Me: No. My roommate is coming to Bristle.
Wants me to hang with her.

Theo: *A specific place?*

Me: At stupid Brix.
Me: I'll be free after the club...

Theo: *Well if u get bored u should come to Dane's.*
Only a block away from Brix.
Drinks on me if you decide to come, LK. No pressure.

Little Knight.

My cheeks blazed like a furnace. If Theo was coming to the city, that meant I needed to dress accordingly—look too hot to touch. I called Mariah and told her I'd show. She was beyond thrilled.

After setting a time, I relaxed during the rest of my day, taking up the idea of reading a book by the pool and wondering just how I would make it through a night that ended with Theo Black. I didn't confirm with him on purpose. I didn't need him thinking I was too eager to see him, even though I was.

I thought of every bad scenario—someone knowing he was Izzy's dad, seeing us put on a display of affection in public or quite possibly catching us making googly eyes at one another. That person would then inform Izzy or someone that knew her, leaving us both fucked and left to drown.

But then I thought of the good.

I could drink with him... again.

I could have a good time with him beneath dim lights. Dane's, a place where no one worried about what anyone else was doing. A place where alcoholics could drink without limits and women didn't have to worry about being harassed because the alcoholics cared more for the bottles than various amounts of ass flouncing around.

I could smell him again... taste him again... hold him again.

There were way too many possibilities, and although I had those bad scenarios in the back of my mind, nothing could top the excitement I felt coursing through me when I thought of him.

I was ready. I needed to see Theo.

And I needed him immediately, in every way possible.

ELEVEN

THEO

DANE'S WAS JUST like how it used to be during my worst times—dim lights, a weird peanut smell, and annoying alternative music that was, fortunately, easy to ignore with the flat screens plastered on every cement wall, streaming ESPN. The waitresses still dressed like they had no mother to raise them. Short leather skirts or short black shorts and tank tops that showcased a large pair of tits.

I picked up the whiskey Marcel slid across the bar, giving him a quick bob of my head as I lifted the glass to my lips. He returned the gesture before turning his back to me with a rag and a wet glass in hand, clearing it of soap and droplets.

After taking a long sip, allowing the burn to further relax me, I flicked my wrist, checking the time. It was nearing midnight. I thought for sure she'd make an appearance before now, but I guess I was wrong.

My leg bounced, my shoe pressing into the metal bar of the chair.

I looked around, thinking maybe she was somewhere else. Maybe looking for me? Shit, who was I kidding?

She knew better.

Maybe it was a good thing she didn't show.

We needed to get over each other. Though I hated rejection and being stood up, I could understand a no-show. And the worst part? I couldn't be upset about it. She was young. I was twenty years older than her. She was in college with her whole life ahead of her, and I'd already established mine. I owned a car shop and had settled my party-going ways a long time ago.

I finished off my third whiskey, and Marcel turned, one of his bushy eyebrows arching. "'Nother round?"

"Nah." I pulled the wallet out of my back pocket with the chain attached and flipped it open, sliding two twenties across the counter. "I'm good for the night. Gotta drive. Appreciate it though."

Marcel accepted the change. "Mmmhmm."

Standing from the stool, I turned for the exit, the bright neon lights burning my eyes as I staggered toward the door. Before I could reach the handle, the door had already swung open, and a young girl with the ends of her hair dyed pink dashed in, laughing so hard I swear she was about to pop a lung.

"Oh my gosh! This place fucking sucks!" she yelled, loud enough for Marcel to hear. I glanced back. Marcel's line of sight shifted from the TV screen above him to the girl. He then looked at me. I shrugged, looking forward again. "Damn it, Chloe! Why'd you drag us here?"

Chloe? I wasn't sure how I made out that name, considering the girl's speech was horribly slurred. My back straightened, breathing turning shallow as I focused on the other girl that walked through the door. And my fucking god, she looked amazing. Good enough to fucking eat, but maybe just a little too hot to devour right away.

In this moment, as she walked inside with a halter dress that hugged her body, strappy heels, and her hair pinned up, it seemed she was on fucking fire. And for only a millisecond, I couldn't breathe. I liked this fiery side of her.

Blazing.

Burning.

Untouchable.

If I got too close, I knew she'd burn me. But, like a child, I was mesmerized, dying to cop a feel. Unable to stop staring. Wanting so badly to play with that raging blaze.

Fuck.

Her eyes caught mine when she made it through the door, a guy following behind her. My fists automatically clenched as he pressed his palm on the small of her back and said something to her, but then he hurried for the pink-haired girl. I realized he wasn't Chloe's date. He was the crazy girl's.

Pink Hair and her date went to the bar, ordering a round of drinks from an irritated Marcel. He was never the type to kick anyone out, especially if the kids looked wealthy and ready to drink the night away, and that was exactly what they looked like. Ready to party. Ready to get wasted. Ready to blow all their money on overpriced drinks.

I turned forward again, watching as Chloe stood there, a light smile on her face. Her hazel eyes bolted with mine, the sound of a lock clinking in my head, verifying that I would no longer be able to look away from her for the rest of the night.

Her skin looked as smooth as satin beneath the dim lights, her hair probably as soft as silk. It was actually tamed tonight. No wild curls. No hippie style to go along with it. It suited her as well. She had a versatile appeal.

"Hi, Theo," she murmured, taking a step towards me. "Sorry I'm so late."

"Nah... it's all good." I took a step with her. "Didn't think you'd show though."

"Good... that's exactly what I wanted." Her cheeks stretched.

"Oh really? And why is that?"

"I wanted to see how long you'd wait."

I shrugged. "Playing the hard to get game, huh?"

"No not at all," she teased.

"I just figured you'd made up your mind... chose a different path."

Her brows narrowed. "What do you mean by that?"

"You know what I mean." Her eyes moved quickly from mine, avoiding the subject at all costs. Sighing, she looked from me to the bar, shaking her head at her friends. "Those must be the friends that beat me to the punch, I presume?" I decided to forget about the subject too.

"Yep."

"Wild," I chuckled.

"Her name in my phone is actually 'Wild Child'. What a coincidence!"

I glanced over my shoulder. "I can see why."

She continued a smile, rocking on her heels. To avoid awkwardness, I pointed back with my thumb, gesturing towards the counter. "How about we join them? I owe you a drink, right?"

"Oh—no!" She waved a hand. "You don't have to. I'm DD."

"DD?" I frowned, confused.

She giggled. "Designated driver."

"Ohh." I cracked a half-smile. "I knew that. Shit, one drink won't kill you. Come on!"

She looked at me and then at the bar. I guess all of the aligned bottles on the shelves felt welcoming because she finally moved forward. "Fine, but sheesh," Chloe laughed, walking past me and meeting at the far end of the bar. "Come on Mr. Black, you aren't *that* old. You should know what 'DD' means."

I watched her hips swing, throbbing when my last name ran off her lips. I controlled myself, keeping my voice even as I said, "Your generation is a little different than mine." I followed her to the bar, taking a seat.

"How so?" she questioned.

"Just is. Some of the shit I hear kids say now confuses the fuck out of me."

Chloe laughed, her eyes shimmering from the dim lighting above. "Like *YOLO*, *thot*, and *Bye, Felicia*?"

"Exactly! What do those even mean?" I gestured for Marcel to come my way and after ordering another drink for myself and allowing her to order her own, she responded.

"*YOLO* means 'you only live once'. A *thot* is a girl that apparently is a whore, or someone that will sleep with anyone for attention. And *Bye, Felicia* pretty much means 'get the fuck out of here with your bullshit'."

My eyes expanded, and I couldn't help the laugh that spewed out of me. "Wow... see! Like I said. This generation comes up with some pretty wild shit."

She shook her head, still fighting that cute little grin. Her arm happened to brush mine, a bolt of electricity lighting my core. As if she felt that same spark, she looked up at me, but she didn't dare move away. The smoothness of her skin on mine, the flesh on flesh, was all too familiar, and I refused to kill this moment by pulling away. I couldn't be a pussy, pretend nothing was here when there was clearly so much.

So many unanswered questions.

So many unshared moments.

So many times I've wanted to make her mine repeatedly, take her in every position, hear her whisper and then cry my name, hold me close as our lips molded, our breathing entwined, deep in passionate trances.

I placed my hand on top of the one she had resting on her lap. Moments later and the wild girl appeared over Chloe's shoulder, her drink sloshing all over the countertop, interrupting our connected gazes. Chloe turned quickly to take the drink from her and placed it on the counter before she could spill it on our clothes.

"Chloe," the girl whined. "Can we pleeaaassseee go back to Brix? I was having so much fun there!"

"I know, but you swore we could come to Dane's at twelve, Mariah." Chloe frowned.

"Yah... I know, but...ugh." She looked around in revulsion. "We're not having fun here." She pouted her bottom lip, placing her elbow on the edge of the counter. She then zoned in on me, her hooded eyes narrowing. "Oh my gosh... you are so fucking hot!"

I pressed my lips, nodding in appreciation.

"No seriously..." The Mariah girl stood up straight. "Is he why you wanted to come here? My *fucking* goodness he's beautiful."

Chloe's cheeks burned, and she purposely avoided my eyes.

"He looks sooo familiar though..." Her lips twisted as she walked around Chloe to get a closer look at me. When it finally registered, she said, "Oh! I know! He totally looks like your friend Izzy! You know, the one we hung out with for spring break last year?"

In an instant, my face went strict, jaw ticking. Reality, like a whirl-wind, hit me and I turned forward, looking up at the screen and pulling my hand far away from Chloe's. I pretended not to notice Marcel looking at me from his end of the bar. I was sure he'd been wondering why I was hanging around my daughter's friends at a bar... buying them drinks. Snooting it up with her *best friend*.

Swallowing thickly, I picked up my drink and finished it. When I finally looked at Chloe, she was speechless as well, like she, too, had forgotten about reality. Her head dropped, pulling from our connected line of sight. "How about I take you guys back to Brix?" I offered, sliding off my stool.

"It's okay. You don't have to." She downed her cranberry-vodka and then slammed the empty glass on the counter. "I can take them back."

"You sure?"

"Yeah," Mariah butted in. "That was her first drink of the night. So fucking lame, right?" Her laugh came out like more of a cackle, causing her date to join in on the laughter with her. Man, they were annoying little shits. How could she deal with this all night? I'm almost certain that, when I was their age, I wasn't that obnoxious.

"Come on, Tiny!" Mariah waved for the lanky boy at the bar to follow her outside. When they were long gone, Marcel blew a sigh and picked up their glasses, wiping their area clean. Chloe remained seated, looking at me for a brief moment before dropping her head.

"She doesn't know who you are," she murmured, "...if that's what you're thinking."

"Yeah, I know." I scratched my chin. "Sure you don't want me to drop you off?"

She stood from the stool, looking into my eyes as she neared me. My pounding heart caught speed as she placed a hand on top of my shoulder. "I was actually thinking about dropping them off and meeting you... if that's okay?"

"Shit... yeah. More than okay."

"Where should we meet?"

I thought of it, and when I pictured the perfect place, I told her, "I'll text you the address."

She nodded. "Okay." Then, she walked past me, her round ass

bouncing, heels clicking across the wooden floorboards. Glancing over her shoulder, lips full and supple, she sarcastically asked, "Just try and make it a little public, will you?"

She had no idea. The place I had in mind was more private than a secluded hotel room reserved for a celebrity. With a half-smile on my lips, I watched as she left the bar, her words running back and forth in my head. I leaned my elbows on the counter, sighing as I pulled out my cell phone. Marcel still stood at the bar, clearing his throat.

When I turned around to look at him, his brows were stitched, lips pressed thin. He was a buff guy with a shiny, bald head and a hoop earring in his left ear. His reddish goatee had grown out since the last time I saw him, his grey t-shirt stained with sweat. "Mind telling me what the hell that was?"

"What do you mean?" I pretended I didn't know what he was talking about.

"The girl," he gestured towards the door, "...the one that's about half your age that just walked out of here. Isn't that little Chloe?"

I glanced down, running my tongue over my teeth. I could have explained it to him, but I just didn't know how. "Look, Marcel, just pretend you didn't even see her here."

He grunted and it just so happened to be the sound of his laughter. "I see plenty of shit going on around here. Trust me, this isn't the worst of it. Ain't my business but... be careful, man. And be wise."

He, of all people, knew what he was talking about. He knew my daughter. I talked about her at least once every time I made an appearance here. Considering he had a daughter himself, I could only imagine what he was thinking.

Did he consider me a pervert?

A dipshit?

An idiot that overpaid for drinks?

As all of that clicked in my brain, I started to think... what if an older man came onto my daughter? A man that I thought I could trust? A man that was supposed to look out for her, not fuck her brains out?

Fuck no. I couldn't even fucking imagine a man my age touching my daughter. My child. My fucking *life*.

Dropping another wad of bills on the counter for Chloe's forgetful friends and myself, I marched for the exit and hopped into my car, cranking it and driving to the one place I should have been all along.

Home.

Away from the fantasies.

Away from what wasn't meant to be.

Away from Chloe.

TWELVE

CHLOE

HE DIDN'T TEXT ME.

Or respond to the text I sent him. Not even a phone call. At first I was worried, thinking he may have gotten into an accident or maybe caught up with something, but when I saw him casually entering his home with a box of tools the following night, I knew he was avoiding me.

I tried thinking of what may have happened between the time I left him and now. Other than Mariah blabber-mouthing about how he looked like Izzy, I couldn't think of much. Maybe the mere mention of his daughter's name was enough to make him realize that he was getting off track—that he couldn't go back to what we were before.

It couldn't be that way. He couldn't hurt her, and he also couldn't hurt me. Distance was understandable, but all he had to do was *tell* me. What was all that talk about sharing just one summer? Did he not think of her then? Or was he too far gone in his thoughts and thinking with his dick?

I considered it him thinking with his other nonsensical head.

It whipped at my emotions, but I had to put myself in his shoes. I was tired of beating around the bush, dying for this man to touch me, feel me—do *anything* that would make me feel *something*. I just wanted to go back to school, forget I ever came here and saw him again.

Ugh. Men.

Speaking of, my father had trapped himself in his bedroom, refusing his meds again, which eventually resulted in a tough day for us. He called us strangers (as he always did) and even threw one of his trophies at us when we came to bring him lunch.

My day was stressful. Margie had way more patience than I could ever uphold. I wasn't sure how much more of this I could handle—the confusion from Theo and the stress I endured while putting up with my father. I was a strong girl, but there was only so much I could handle right now.

I sat on my bed a few minutes after I saw Theo entering his home, knees drawn to my chest, tears shedding. A knock sounded on my door seconds later, and Margie walked in with a basket of my folded laundry. Seriously, she was too much. Freaking wonderful. When she caught sight of the tears on my face, she quickly apologized and hurried back out, but I called for her to come back in.

"It's okay," I whispered.

"Are you sure sweetie? I don't want to be a bother."

"No bother at all." I swiped my face, clearing my eyes as she placed the basket in front of my closet. "What's going on?"

"I washed most of your clothes. Thought you could use a little help." Her smile was complacent. "I also wanted to let you know your father is finally asleep. He ate a little bit of yogurt and some of his banana, so hopefully that'll hold him over for the night."

"Oh, okay." I nodded. "Thank you so much, Margie."

"Of course, dear." She started to turn, but then changed her mind, looking at me again. "I—well, I just wanted to ask you about something."

"Yeah?"

Stepping forward, she twisted her fingers in front of her and hesitated for a few seconds. "It's none of my business at all, and you don't have to answer, but... I saw you coming from across the street the other night? The man kissing you on the cheek?" She blinked, an ounce of overprotectiveness in her eyes. "Is he the reason you're upset?"

"Oh, god, no!" I slid to the edge of the bed, and she pressed a hand to her chest, relieved. "No. The man across the street is a really good guy. He invited me over for dinner. I've known him since I was twelve."

"Oh. How nice. Does he have children?"

I looked away. "Just one. A daughter."

"Oh." Margie's eyes maneuvered to the picture on my nightstand. The black and white photo of me and Izzy standing right in front of their house across the street. "I'm going to take a wild guess and assume that's her?"

I glanced up. Margie's head was slanted. When I didn't say anything, she walked forward and sat beside me. "Sweetie, you don't have to talk, but I just want you to know that whenever you think you need to, I'm here. I know your mom isn't around and your dad isn't in the very best state of mind to take in your problems on top of his own, so if you need an ear, I'm always here." Her chubby cheeks spread, grey irises full of kindness.

"Thank you, Margie. I appreciate that." She nodded but remained seated as if she knew there was more. Surprisingly, I continued our chat. "I mean, don't get me wrong, I have been thinking about Theo—"

"That's his name?" She pointed towards my window.

"Yes..."

"Ahh. You call him by his first name. I see my eyes weren't deceiving me. There's much more to that kiss on the cheek, huh?"

I huffed a laugh. "A lot more. How can you tell?"

"Let's just say I may have dealt with a situation like the one you're in. Goodness, it was so long ago, but I can remember everything." Silence fell between us. I assumed she was thinking of whomever the man was, remembering every single detail like I did every single damn day.

"He isn't the reason I'm upset, though," I murmured.

"No?"

"No. It's just Dad. I feel so awful for him. For Mom not being here, him being alone. It kinda sucks, you know?"

"Oh, honey, your dad will be okay. Trust me, he's a strong man. Just very stubborn on the days he can't remember much."

"Is it supposed to be that way?"

She shrugged and sighed. "It could be worse."

"I bet you hate your job now, huh?" I laughed, teasing.

"You know... it's actually not so bad. Mr. Knight is a good guy on his good days, and I was fortunate enough to meet his sweet daughter. I swear I thought I was going to have to deal with two stubborn people when I heard you were coming home. I was kind of scared."

I snickered. "Nah... I hear I can be pretty laid back like him."

"You have a lot his traits, but when it comes to love..." Her eyes softened. "I think you get that from your mom. The testing of boundaries, wanting what you know you shouldn't have. What you *don't* need. Trust me, I know."

I wanted to frown, but I was too stuck on how spot-on she was. She knew so much about us. It was strange. I felt like I'd met her before, a very, very long time ago. Way before my memory could ever be established. "Did you—did you know my mom personally?" I squinted my eyes in her direction.

Margie stood, looking down at me with a faint upward curve on her lips. "Your mom was my roommate in college. We used to hang out a lot even after you were born, but... certain things set us apart." She sighed. "She chose me to watch over your dad because she trusted me —knew I wanted to be a caregiver and nurse."

"Wow... it's kind of like she had this all planned out."

"Well, I don't mean to bash your mother or anything, but when it comes to life, she lives it and refuses to have anything holding her back. I'm pretty sure when she heard about your father's Alzheimer's, she was already planning how to get out of the situation but still keep the money in her pocket. Why do you think she only has one child? Because she didn't need more holding her back, but she also wanted to have that experience in her back pocket to talk about whenever the conversations arose with other mothers. Why do you think you're so distant from her? Why she only gave you an hour of her day when you were young? Why she isn't here right now?"

"She gave more than Dad could. He was hardly around."

"Your father worked very hard to provide for you, Chloe. He—" She froze. I could tell she wanted to say more but had to rapidly stop the flow of her words, swallowing hard and holding back. "Anyway, remember what I told you. Anytime you need to talk, I'm here." Margie moved towards the door, but I hopped off the bed.

"Wait—Margie!"

She glanced back as I stood in the middle of my bedroom. "Mom wasn't all bad, you know?"

"I know, sweetie."

"And about Theo... well, I'm just a little confused right now, is all. I'm sure I'll figure that out soon."

She put on a genuine smile, gripping the doorknob. "That, I'm sure about too, lovely. But I'm also sure you won't be figuring it out anytime soon."

I stared at her, unsure of what else to say. This was the most I had ever spoken about boys to anyone older than me. Margie seemed to hold wisdom and understanding. She was a patient woman, and I could use that in my life.

Honestly, it kind of scared me to think about opening up to a woman I'd just gotten to know, but it also thrilled me to know I could come home to someone that would listen and understand. Someone that wouldn't judge me or think I was insane or selfish for my actions. Someone that understood exactly what I was going through.

We swapped smiles. "Goodnight, Margie."

"Goodnight, *bella*."

When the door shut behind her, I blew out a breath, sitting in the chair in front of my computer. Headlights crossed my window, and an immediate frown took over. Hopping from the chair, I rushed to the window, watching as Theo's *Charger* pulled in the driveway backwards. He climbed out, and out of the passenger door came the girl with the blonde hair.

I blinked hard, biting hot tears. They walked to the door, her ahead of him. When they were inside, I could no longer look. I knew what was about to happen. Izzy didn't call her his "girl toy" for no reason. She only came over when he was in need... when he was desperate to get off.

My head shook hard, and unfortunately, the tears fell. If he didn't think he was hurting me, he was wrong. He was *killing* me, and being here in Primrose was making me spiral and lose myself all over again.

I felt just like I did right before I left.

Like scum, a piece of gum on the bottom of someone's shoe.

Worthless. Pointless. In the way.

Switching the lamp off, I slipped beneath my blanket. I fell asleep, and luckily, I couldn't remember my dreams. I just slept, but when I awoke, my head was pounding. I checked my alarm clock. 12:18 PM.

"Ughhh." I groaned, sitting up. My head pounded even more. I'd slept a little too long. Climbing out of bed, I went to the bathroom to freshen up and then put on a pair of shorts and a tank top.

After informing Margie that I was going for an afternoon run, I was out of the door with my earphones plugged in my ears. I ran around Primrose twice and then entered the park, the park that held so many memories.

As I neared the fountain, I helplessly looked to my right and spotted the line of trees Theo had taken me through once before. I knew that patch of grass was still there, the daises and sunflowers.

I picked up my pace, running faster, zooming through the park and hitting the track. I ran it five times, until I became too tired and too out of breath. Bending forward, my palms on my thighs, I inhaled much needed oxygen, trying desperately to rid myself of all memories of him. It was impossible. They'd been seared into the core of my brain. They were permanent. There was no getting rid of him.

The sun beamed down on me, heating my skin even more and making sweat spill down my face. Footsteps sounded behind me after several seconds had passed. Glancing over my shoulder, I spotted *him* running in my direction. I was sure he couldn't see me. I was standing by the fence, out of his line of sight.

I should have stayed bent over, perhaps then, he wouldn't have seen me, but I stood up straight, watching him come nearer, and his eyes moved to the right, face going stiff. I couldn't believe he still ran this track every day. I thought he'd killed that habit a long time ago, but it explained how he was still in great shape.

Sweat glistened on his forehead, beads spilling down his defined chest and over his eight abs. He slowed his pace, meeting my eyes. We stared at each other, me confused and him remorseful. Lips parted, he began to speak—explain himself—but I quickly turned, dashing off and regaining all the energy I'd lost only moments ago.

"Chloe!" he yelled after me.

I ignored him, continuing my run to the gap in the fence. When I made it through, I hit the trail and jogged without looking back. Heavy steps crushed the gravel behind me, and I gasped, finally peering over my shoulder, spotting Theo getting closer.

I picked up my pace, but I was no match for him, the man that used to play soccer when he was in high school. The man in such fine, sculpted shape. *That* man, period. His hand wrapped around my wrist when he made it by my side, spinning me in his direction.

I instantly protested, struggling to yank away. "Theo! I'm done! Why can't you just leave me alone!?"

His eyes glistened, full of an unexplainable ache. Nostrils flared, he watched as I clawed and scratched at his hand, tears threatening to spill from my eyes. "You don't feel bad about this?" he asked angrily, brows furrowed

"About what!?"

"About this! *This*, Chloe!"

My fighting came to a cease, confusion taking anger's place. Then, I realized what he meant. As he stepped forward, brought a hand to my waist, and tugged me in, I figured it all out. This, as in the foundation we lived on. The reason we'd met in the first place.

The guilt.

The shame.

The bad.

The good that felt so horribly wrong.

He watched me with intense brown eyes. My bottom lip trembled, and when he noticed, he reached up, pressing the pad of his forefinger on the center of my mouth to stop it. Then, before I knew it, his face inched forward, and his mouth found mine. A groan rumbled deep in his throat as his lips collided with mine.

My body reacted way differently than it should have. Instead of fighting—instead of protesting and shoving him away—I sank into his arms, and he picked me up. My legs hooked around his waist, hands cupping his smooth cheek. The scruff on his unshaven face rubbed across the smoothness of my palms, his damp lips consuming me. He stumbled into the shade. My back bumped against a tree, but his mouth didn't dare pull away from mine.

His cock grinded between my legs, his arousal making me crave every solid inch of him all over again. I moaned, my mind begging me to tell him to stop but my body refusing, falling deep into this lust. Into his clutches.

In that moment, I felt like we couldn't be stopped, like years of avoidance and disregard had finally caught up to us—like life was telling us we would never forget about each other. But then, in just the same amount of time, I remembered last night and the pain I felt when I saw him walk into that house with the girl.

"Stop, Theo." I shoved his face away.

His head traveled down, lips pressing on the crook of my neck. "I don't know what it is about this fucking park," he growled. "Maybe it's the way the sunlight bounces off your skin when you run through the trail." His head lifted, gaze matching mine. "Or maybe it's because when it comes to this place, we aren't restrained. And no one can see. No one cares. It's *our* place..." His finger came to my chin, tilting it up. His lips then landed on my cheek, and he kissed me tenderly, blinking slowly before his eyes dropped. He then placed my feet on the ground, running his fingers through his damp, raven hair.

I felt like I'd been ripped right away from him. I wanted him to stop, to listen, but I didn't want him away from me. I moved forward, placing my hand on his chest. "Why didn't you text me?" I whispered. He struggled with words, eyes avoiding mine. I caught his face in my hands, forcing him to look at me. "Why?"

"You know why, Chloe."

"You thought of Izzy?"

"I thought of *you*."

I frowned. "No. You didn't think of me."

Confusion made his face warp.

"If you had thought about me, we wouldn't be here. You would have known that I was actually looking forward to that text—a location. A place to meet."

"I can't fucking hurt you, Chloe. Don't you understand that the only thing that comes out of this is pain? Someone will get hurt in the end..."

"Don't you think I know that? Yes, it's a risk—"

"A risk we shouldn't even try to take."

I sighed, mildly agitated. "If we don't, we'll keep ending up like this —in this fucking park, fighting hard not to touch each other." His lips pressed, but I continued. "If we don't do anything about it, every time we see each other, it will result in a situation like this."

He looked down. "Fucking you in the park..."

"You touching me," I added.

"Unable to fight my feelings..."

"Me craving every single part of you... never forgetting what we did."

Theo stepped forward, looking down at me, jaw locked. His smoldering brown eyes bolted with mine. With slow, cautious action, he lifted his arm, bringing his hand to my face. He cupped my cheek, and his head lifted as he studied my face, breath bated.

My breath caught as well, the air between us impenetrable. The air surrounding us was hot and thick, weighing us down. Holding us in this moment. Using the pad of his thumb, he stroked my cheek, pressing his forehead to mine.

"I can't stay away from you," he said, voice low and deep. My core hummed in recognition of *this* voice, the deep and husky one that made my pulse accelerate and my insides overheat. "I try so hard to fight it, but it's clear now." He held my face tighter. "It's so fucking clear now, Chloe. Avoiding you is damn near impossible."

"So... what do we do?" My voice was faint.

He looked me over, and in that moment, it seemed he thought of every possible thing that could go wrong—every disaster that could happen. But when it came down to the wire, he had the same thought in mind as I did. "We hope this is just a phase and try to get over each other."

"Just this summer?"

His eyes became soft. "Just one summer." After he said that, his head moved down, and his mouth found the lips he'd been dying to get a taste of. This time, I didn't fight him. I didn't ward him off or push away. I fell deep into Theo's black sea because it'd been so long since I felt this. It wasn't scary, and it wasn't sticky or dark. I... liked it. The dark, clashing waves he created within me, the feeling of floating, drifting—so far gone while with him.

I'd wanted this to happen for years now. Theo Black in front of me, on top of me, *taking* me. Making me his. Owning me like he did the very first night we attempted this crazy, fucked-up relationship.

In no time, we became antsy. Hands all over, bodies grinding, hearts pounding. His hands became greedy, tearing at my shorts and then yanking my tank top over my head. I tore at his shorts, and when his cock sprung free, I gripped it, grinning behind our kiss.

His groan was ferocious, body in need of more. Hungrily, he kissed me while my legs snaked around his hips, and he sank into me. A sharp gasp brushed by parted lips, my mind no longer crowded but focused on this solitary moment. His strokes were slow and rigid, our breathing heavy. Our foreheads were touching, my arms laced around his neck, and our lips only a breadth away.

His face turned as hard as stone as he watched me, as if it'd been years since he wanted this and now that he had it, he couldn't fuck it up. He wanted to take it slow, but I could tell he wanted to fuck me until I couldn't take anymore.

"Talk to me, baby," he breathed in my ear. "Tell me how long you've waited for this."

"Too long," I breathed, tugging him closer.

"You didn't come home..." He stroked faster, panting deep. "You avoided me for three years, Little Knight. Such a bad girl, making me suffer like that."

"I... I didn't know how to face you—what to say."

Reaching up, he gripped my face and forced my eyes on his. "You face me like this," he growled, nostrils flaring. "With my dick deep inside you and your eyes right on mine. Like this, Chloe," he grunted, slamming into me. "Like you've always wanted."

My chin dropped, and a loud moan shot to the treetops. This time, he didn't bother covering my mouth. He wanted to hear me, and he didn't give a fuck who else could.

Theo released my face, his palms going to the thick trunk of the tree. He took me mercilessly, grunting and growling, his body going stiff as my teeth sank into his bottom lip. Cupping my ass, he walked away from the tree and lowered my back to the grass, stroking harder, faster, drilling so hard a clapping noise echoed through the small forest.

"You feel so fucking good, baby. Still so fucking wet for me." His brown eyes roamed my body. I started to writhe, gripping the arms that were planted on either side of my head, watching as only his hips moved up and down, side to side. My eyes rolled to the back of my head, and I clenched repeatedly, soaking the length of his massive cock.

He didn't stop.

In fact, he picked up his pace, his name a forbidden exclamation spilling from my lips. He conjured a yelp so shrill it made birds scatter. He scanned the area, and when he saw our surroundings were clear, he craned his head, bringing his mouth down.

Holding one side of my face with one hand, he used the other to grip my thigh, stroking repeatedly in the same, deep, relentless stroke, until he let out a heavy groan and came, eyes sealing, body jolting.

"Oh fuck, Chloe." His voice was full of disbelief, as if he didn't expect to cum so hard and so soon. He stilled in his position above, falling from his high, head dropping, and eyes landing on me.

He panted.

We panted, staring into one another's eyes. Leaning forward, his lips brushed my cheek before moving over to my mouth. "Your pussy is perfect, you know that?" His upper lip curved, and the top row of his pearly whites was revealed.

"Stop it," I murmured, fighting a smile. He moved aside, allowing me to sit up. He watched me for a few seconds, and then he leaned forward, lifting a hand to pluck something out of my hair.

"I like this park and all, but we can't keep making shit happen here." He laughed, flicking the piece of grass away.

I giggled. "It just... happens, I guess."

"I guess... but you deserve better. A room. A nice place." His gaze softened. "With me."

The longer he looked at me, the more my smile happened to collapse. Every bad thought flashed in my brain like hazard lights, along with one of the very reasons I was upset with him to begin with. "Last night," I said, voice breathy. "I saw you."

His head tilted. "Saw me what?"

I dropped my head plucking a piece of grass.

"With Trixie?" he answered for me.

"That's her name?" I tried not to laugh but couldn't help the smile.

"Sounds stripper-ish, right?" he chuckled.

"Uh, yeah!"

"She only stopped by to pick up her clothes. Nothing happened. I promise."

"How do I know you're not lying? She is your *girl toy*, after all."

"We aren't really going to make things happen anymore..."

My brows narrowed. "Why not?"

"She's moving to Las Vegas. I already don't trust her here. I damn sure wouldn't trust her there."

"Oh my god," I laughed, "*Is* she a stripper?"

"Nah... but she works at Dane's. It's pretty much the same thing."

"That's where you met her?"

He stood up and tugged his shorts up to his waist, then he went for my shirt and shorts on the ground. After helping me up and handing my clothes to me, he said, "Yep. Kind of just... happened."

"Hmm. Like we did?"

He scoffed. "Definitely nothing like that."

"Do you love her?" I avoided his eyes after asking the question, afraid of his response. I focused on adjusting my panties and putting on my shorts, staring at the ground, but he tilted my chin, head shaking as our eyes met.

"I don't love her, Chloe. She was just someone that... distracted me when you left and helped me forget about certain things." He paused, dragging his eyes down my five-foot-seven frame and then bringing them back up to mine again. "But now that you're back, well"—he shrugged—"I guess I realized she isn't exactly the type of woman I want running around in my life."

"No? So what kind of woman are you looking for?"

He moved forward, a boyish smile on display. Stroking my cheek, he quietly answered me. "I want a woman with brains, but also one that knows how to have fun. A woman with dreams. Goals. A woman that knows what she wants, even though she knows it may be bad for her. A woman that doesn't mind taking risks in order to be happy."

I inhaled a wisp of air, looking away. All those things I could relate to, but there were plenty of other women out there that could also relate—women that had no sort of relationship with his only child.

"Hmm."

When I was all dressed, he hooked an arm across my shoulders and led the way back to the trail. "What are you doing tonight?" he asked.

"I'm not sure. Why?" I looked up, meeting the brown irises that were already on me.

"Come with me to my boat."

"Your boat?" My eyes expanded, brows rising. "I didn't even know you had a boat!"

"Bought it a few months ago. It's not huge or anything, just something to get me from point A to point B. It's where I was going to take you after Dane's." He stopped walking, turning me in his direction, the palms of his hands curling around my upper arms. "Forgive me for not sending you a location the other night," he begged, eyes full of remorse. "I was just... really fucked in the head. I don't know what was going on with me. I had this small chat with Marcel, and it sort of fucked with me."

"Oh." I paused. "I have one question..."

He pulled away, looking at me oddly, almost like he already knew the question I was going to ask. "What's that?"

I fiddled with my fingers, focusing on the ground. "Do you really think this will last all summer?"

Relief washed over him, and he drew in a thick amount of breath, nodding. "Let's make the deal right now. All summer, no thoughts of the past. No thoughts of our lives or who it may be that ties us." His face changed when he said his last sentence. He hated owning up to the betrayal as well. The thought of his baby girl finding out about us would kill her and possibly damage their bond. Our bond. "Let's promise to pretend that we're two strangers. Like we've never met before and are only looking for a good time. You could use it. I could use it."

"But... what if more comes out of this?"

His face changed, his attitude no longer carefree. "We agree now that nothing more comes out of this." His face was stern, eyes like steel. Gripping my shoulders, he said, "Promise me, Chloe. We can't take this farther than it is right now... okay?"

I swallowed hard. "Okay." My voice was defeated. He noticed.

"Fuck..."

"What?" I asked as he roughly raked his fingers through his hair.

"Maybe we shouldn't do this... I shouldn't do that to you—make you think this is just me wanting to get my dick wet." He pulled me into him, watching me with a gentle stare. "I don't want you thinking I don't care about you. I care about you a lot. You're a good girl, and you know me just as well as I know you. It's just—well, if we still want to be in each other's lives, as well as Izzy's, we have to settle on some terms and keep some things out of the way."

"Like love?" I whispered.

His throat worked hard to swallow the lump that'd been lodged deep inside. "Love... will get in the way. To protect ourselves—to protect Izzy—let's settle on this. Trust me, we'll still have a good time. We'll make this one of the best summers of our lives. And when it's all over, we'll still be at an understanding." He dropped his head to catch my eyes. When he did, he asked, "Is that okay with you? We don't have to. I understand you not wanting to. The risk involved—I just need to know if this risk is one you will take with me. If I'm worth it to you. I'm sick of pretending I don't want you."

I struggled with a smile, unsure, but as he looked at me, so child-like, his face handsome, eyes full of want, need, and the same hunger I'd clung to for years, I knew I couldn't say no, no matter what feelings came out of this arrangement.

"Just the summer," I told him, smiling. "I think you're worth the risk, Theo." Then I kissed his cheek, and he nodded with a smug smile, following me out of the neighborhood park.

We were hand-in-hand until we reached the exit, then we went our separate ways, never losing sight of each other, even as we walked on opposite sides of the street. Not even as cars passed by us, quick blurs that meant nothing right now.

When we made it to our houses, entering our front doors, we took one final glance and finally lost sight of one another. Even while he was gone, I knew he still thought of me. Probably just as much as I thought of him.

Knowing it thrilled every single part of me.

Later that afternoon, after hitting the shower and helping Margie clean up the kitchen, I was at the diner on the pier of Bristle Wave with Theo. Like most men would, he ordered a double cheeseburger with extra bacon and cheese and a side order of fries. I helped myself to the honey-glazed salmon, a side of broccoli, and a sweet potato.

"You eat like a girl," he teased, poking at my fish with his unused fork.

I gave him the evil eye, chewing thoroughly before speaking. "I'm sorry I'm not a brute like you, ordering extra meat and fries."

"Yeah... I'm pretty sure I'm going to end up on the toilet later on tonight."

"Oh my gosh!" I gasped. "I'm trying to eat here!"

He busted out in a laugh. "See. Like a true little girl."

"Whatever." I sipped my sweet tea. As I placed my glass down, I felt a pair of eyes on me. I'd felt the heavy gaze on me ever since we entered the diner. It was really starting to bug me. I couldn't *not* look anymore.

Turning my head a fraction, I spotted a woman sitting in the corner, magazine in hand, and a half-eaten slice of cherry pie on the plate in front of her. She caught me watching her stare at Theo. She looked at me for a brief second before rapidly snatching her gaze away, focusing on her magazine again.

"Do you know her?" I asked. I gestured to my left, and Theo glanced over.

"Not at all."

"She's been staring at us since we walked through the doors."

"She's most likely curious..."

I thinned my eyes at him. "About what?"

"Us."

I frowned. "What do you mean?"

Theo's eyes bounced from mine to the woman again. She was pretending we didn't exist now, scanning her magazine with swift eyes. "Well, look at us, Chloe. We don't exactly look like we belong together. I'm much older than you are, and she isn't going to assume we're related with how much I've been absentmindedly touching you." He flashed a smile. "I bet she's been wondering why we've been playing footsies for the past thirty minutes." With quirked eyebrows, Theo's leg brushed mine, and goosebumps crawled along my skin. Reaching across the table, Theo picked up my free hand, curled it into a fist, and then brought my knuckles to his lips.

A hot flood ran down my throat, sinking deep and pooling in my panties. I blushed ridiculously as he kissed each knuckle while his eyes moved to his right, staring right at the woman that was watching us again.

As if she were shocked, she gathered her wallet, tossed a few bills on the table, and then rushed out of the restaurant, taking one more glance at us before slipping out of the door.

Theo and I laughed out loud, catching the attention of a few guests in the restaurant. Fortunately, they disregarded our silliness, returning to their meals and small chats.

"So, I've been meaning to tell you." Theo straightened up in his seat, his face getting serious.

"What is it?" I aligned my back as well.

He capped one of his fists, his elbows on the table, and hands now on his chin. "I've been thinking about putting the house up for sale."

Shocked, my eyes widened, and I dropped my fork. "For sale? Wow... are you sure?"

"I think it's time. I mean, I'm hardly ever home, but there's a reason behind that."

"And what is it?"

His brows drew together, lips twitching. "It... reminds me too much of Janet." The sentence came out rushed. His voice was strained, eyes no longer on mine as he scratched his head.

"Oh." I focused on the wooden tabletop.

"Not that I want to forget about her or anything, it's just when I go there, I always end up thinking about her. Standing or sitting in certain places, putting on makeup in the mirror in the bathroom, or even cooking her disgusting ravioli in the kitchen." His laugh seemed to cause him pain. "I thought getting the kitchen upgraded and remodeled, rearranging the bedroom, and even changing the paint in the house would help, but it didn't. I still feel her. I still think of her. I know you don't want to hear all of this but—"

"No. Stop. It's okay," I assured him. "You can talk about her with me. I cared for Mrs. Black, too."

He was relieved. It showed all over his face, his eyes sparking.

"You want my honest opinion?" I asked.

"Please?"

"I don't think you are ever going to be able to stop thinking about her, no matter where you live or how hard you're trying to move forward in life. It's natural. I mean, I still think of my Granny Joan sometimes. She was the fun grandma."

"That's true, but at least I'll know that the place I move to wasn't shared with her. Sort of like starting fresh." He hesitated for a moment, dropping his hands and running his palms across his jeans. "I know you don't want to hear it, but we shared a lot of good times in that house, and I hate that I used to have Trixie walking back and forth in there. I feel guilty in there—like I shouldn't be living freely. Like I still owe a debt to someone that isn't even alive." He sighed. "I see her red recliner in the corner of the living room, and I can't seem to get rid of it. Isabelle doesn't want it, and I refuse to just throw it out. Janet loved that chair. She'd flip in her grave if she saw it was in a dumpster somewhere."

"I understand," I murmured. I looked towards the ocean, allowing an idea to sink in. "Hmm... maybe I can take it off your hands. I could use a chair for my dorm at school."

His eyes lit up. "You'd do that?"

"Sure." I waved a hand. "Why not?"

Appreciative, he grabbed my hand again. "You know, you don't have to do stuff just to please me. You don't have to always be so generous."

"I don't mine, Theo. I swear."

His head shook, not negatively, but more in a *she-is-too-good-to-me* kind of shake. "Thank you, Little Knight." He smiled. I returned one. "So... you think I should move out?"

"I think if that's what you think will make you happy, then go for it." I squeezed his hand. "But I will miss not seeing you across the street whenever I happen to be in Primrose."

His smile was sweet and innocent. "You can always come visit me."

"Yeah..." My lips twisted. "That all depends on when you plan on moving."

"Well, see, that's the thing." He smirked. "I already found a place. I can move into it in two weeks."

"Two weeks?!"

One of his cheeks quirked up as he played innocent "Yeah... crazy, huh?"

"So why'd you ask for my opinion if you'd already made a choice?" I laughed.

"Just wanted to see what you'd think. I needed someone to talk to... hear me out and maybe back me up if Izzy throws a fit about me moving to a smaller place."

"Wait—you haven't told her yet?"

"Nope. You're the first person I've told."

"Really?" I lit up inside, grinning like a giddy idiot.

"Yes. I'll let her know when I'm all moved in..."

"Where is the apartment?"

He pointed somewhere behind me. I looked out of the window, spotting a small tower in the corner. "The condos right over there. They were just built right in front of the coast. It's convenient. Close to my job. Right down the street from the market and only a short walk to my boat... speaking of..." he smirked.

I laughed. "What?"

"You still haven't answered me about the boat thing?"

"What exactly will we be doing on this boat?"

His eyes focused on mine. "Do you really care for the answer to that question?" His leg brushed my calf, but something else was there —his hand. It ran up my thighs, nearing my heat. I clenched as he got closer but purposely kept his hand in the center, feeling weak as I help-lessly let my legs fall apart.

"I don't," I breathed. "I'm just curious."

"So many questions, huh?"

"Tons..."

"Let me answer them out there," he pointed towards the water. "Out at sea where no one can watch us. No one can hear us. No one will matter outside of us." I watched as his tongue ran over his lips, his hand moving higher.

He was right there, provoking me, expecting an answer. "You think we should jump right into this?"

He shrugged. "I told you, Chloe. Don't think. Don't wonder too much. Just let it be."

I inhaled and then exhaled deeply, reaching under the table and holding his hand. His brown irises sparked from the sunset, shim-mering as he looked me over. The sun made them appear to be an amber color, as clear as whiskey.

He looked at me as if he wanted to take me right there on that table. But he knew better. He was a wise man with a lot of self-control. That came in handy when it came to my desires.

"Okay," I finally responded. "Fine. I won't think. I won't wonder." I leaned over the table, and he did the same. Our lips touched, but instead of kissing him, I sank my teeth into his bottom lip and sucked.

"Fuck," he groaned, eyes hooded, fixated on my mouth as I pulled away.

"I'll just let it be." My voice was breathy, full of seduction.

"Damn right," he groaned. He tossed some money on the table and grabbed my hand. Within seconds we were out of the restaurant, me with my heart racing and him with a hard cock that he tried so hard to conceal. I couldn't believe I had this effect on him. I mean it was Mr.

Black. We knew each other well, but who would have thought we'd be where we were now?

Kissing.

Grinding.

Holding.

Hugging.

Touching.

Caressing like lovers, right before fucking like wild animals.

God, this man did so much to me. To my body and mind and even my spirit. But it wasn't bad. It was good. Theo allowed me to forget reality, which was what I needed that summer.

I needed to forget.

To let go.

To get exactly what I'd been dying for all those years.

Him all over again.

THIRTEEN

THEO

SHE DIDN'T WANT to go home yet, which was more than okay with me. She'd complained about her dad causing her stress and said something about a caregiver that she knew would actually look out for him.

Instead of driving back to Primrose, I took her to the beach, hoping it would clear her mind. We walked the shore, her arm linked through mine, a soft smile touching her lips.

"What are you smiling at?" I asked, glancing down at her.

She peered up at me before pointing her gaze to the ocean. The waves clashed with gentle force, the sun causing the blue water to shimmer. "I'm just thinking..."

"About what?"

"Well, tomorrow, on your boat." She looked up at me again, stopping mid-step as her lips twisted. The face she made was cute. Confused and childlike. "Is it an all afternoon thing or...?"

"Ahh." I smiled as she did, knowing exactly what she was getting at. Turning in her direction and placing my hands on her waist, I stepped in closer, my mouth pressing on her forehead. "Do you want it to be an all-day thing?"

"I think at least four hours would work best. Food, music, and drinks included of course. Does the boat have a deck?"

"A pretty big one," I assured her.

She clapped her hands ecstatically, bouncing on top of the sand. "Good! Maybe I'll bring my bathing suit to tan a little. I haven't been able to all summer."

"You kidding? You don't need a tan." I tugged her slim body into mine again, and she blushed as my nose skimmed her jawline. When my lips found the shell of her ear, I murmured, "You're perfect, baby."

I felt goose bumps crawl along her skin, her lips parting as she slightly gawked.

I couldn't help my laugh. This girl had no clue what I was capable of. She was accustomed to young men, boys that were impatient and too eager to bust a quick nut. But for me, I was patient. I wanted my lover to achieve ultimate bliss and satisfaction, and then I'd go for the kill.

Drilling.

Pounding.

Screwing.

Grinding.

Even licking.

The pussy would surely be mine. I'd leave her thinking for days, wondering what more I could do to make her mind and body feel truly amazing.

"What are you thinking?" Chloe questioned, brows piqued.

I fought a grin, shaking my head and grabbing her hand, continuing our walk. "Oh, nothing, Little Knight."

We stopped and faced the ocean. Chloe released a long sigh, as if she'd been in need of a relaxing moment like this for a long time. I drew her in tighter, and her hand pressed on my chest as she leaned into me.

"So, no more Trixie?" she asked.

"Nope. No more."

"Was she upset about you breaking it off with her?"

"Not too much. I mean, we weren't exactly dating. I'd set the rules a long time ago."

"Just sex," she whispered, voice defeated as she dropped her head.

I turned, cradling her face in my hands. "That's all it was. Nothing more. I swear." I struggled with what to say next. I didn't know if I wanted to share deeper feelings, but when her hazel eyes connected with mine, I had no choice. She expected answers, expected to know why I'd replaced Trixie with her again. "She... didn't exactly fill the hole I felt inside. It was kind of pointless, to be honest."

Her frown was faint. "Is that how you feel about me?"

I stepped back, folding my arms. "Did you really just ask me that question?"

"Yes, I did." She stepped forward, limiting the gap between us. "I want to know, Theo." Her hand ran down my arm, her finger tracing the outline of the lion tattoo I got when I was thirty-two. "Do you consider me someone like Trixie? A quick fix? Someone you know won't deny you?"

Her hand continued traveling down, meeting at my belt buckle. She tugged on the metal that secured it, vaguely running her tongue across her lips as the buckle clinked. Then her hand dropped, and she softly ran it across the bulge in my pants, the bulge that was now hard as a rock.

My breathing stifled, my hormones getting the best of me. Reeling her in, I listened to the soft gasp that soared with the salty breeze, and when my fingers slid through her shorts and beneath her panties, she panted, but her hand still remained on my cock. "You know damn well you aren't just a quick fix to me. We have history. Chemistry. You think I had this with Trixie?" I looked between us, my fingers delving deeper. When she didn't respond, I said, "Answer me, Chloe. Talk to me."

"No," she whispered, pressing her forehead against my arm. "No, I'm sure you didn't."

"No is correct. I know you can deny me. You've done it before. I also know I can trust you, which says a lot because I don't trust just anyone." My mouth hovered above hers. She wanted a taste, just a small one if nothing at all, but I held back, listening to her breath hitch and then return to normal, feeling as she tried hard not to make her knees buckle.

Her eyes sealed tight as I circled her clit in slow, torturous circles.

"Oh, God. Theo... you have to... stop." Her voice broke each time my finger sank deep, returning to normal when it was shallow. "I'm going to cum if you keep doing that."

I leaned forward, whispering in her ear. "That's the plan, baby. I want you to cum. No one's around. No one will hear you. Just think of me. Just feel me. You don't have to rush it. Trust me, I can do this all fucking night."

I suppose it was the sound of my voice, how it hummed in her ear, shooting straight to her core. Or maybe I'd just hit the trigger spot. Whatever it was, it came quickly. Her fingernails sank into the flesh on my arm, her mouth parting as she moaned. She hung onto me as if her life depended on it, and I studied every reaction—the flutter of her eyes, the whimper that caught in the middle her throat—my cock throbbing as her other hand now gripped my crotch.

"So fucking beautiful, Chloe," I murmured as her body finally settled. I tipped her chin, my mouth coming down on hers, our tongues colliding. She clung to me, her body unbalanced from the aftermath. "You know that?" She blushed, but she didn't look away. She stared back into my eyes, bashful. Gorgeous. "So, so beautiful."

Her grin was contagious. I picked her up in my arms, placing her back on the soft sand and centering my lower between her legs. As badly as I wanted to take her, and as much as she wanted me to dive deep and fuck her on that beach, I didn't.

I was eager, but I could wait. I *needed* to wait because I had big plans for the next evening. I had so much to teach my Little Knight. My young queen. There were things she needed to experience, and I wanted to be the one she shared all those things with.

Now that I had her back, I wasn't letting go. Not until this summer was over. And even when it was over, I was sure I'd still think of her, hoping we could do the same thing the following summer.

So, on Palm Beach, I only kissed her 'til the sun sank. I grinded my hard cock between her legs and fingered her mercilessly until her body wracked beneath me, shuddering, shaking, quaking. Trust me, it was hard keeping myself in check, but the bigger picture would happen tomorrow.

On my boat. Just the two of us. No one to watch. No one to hear.

No one to interrupt. Just the mere thought of that was more than enough to run with.

This girl was mine. Her pussy? *Mine*. Her entire body—all for me to explore, indulge in, and be greedy with. Everything about her was going to be mine, and I would have been damned if I allowed anything to take her away.

FOURTEEN

CHLOE

IT'D BEEN a while since I woke up happy.

You know, the feeling you get when your heart beats madly. A stream of morning sunlight beams down on you and you can't help but feel wonderful because sunlight means brightness and happiness, and everyone in this world could use a dose. I wasn't just content, I was moving forward with my life and taking it one minute at a time. There was depth in my exhilaration.

There was a smile on my face, light in my eyes as I looked into the mirror in my bathroom. With my towel draped around me, I watched as water spilled down my chest from the tips of my wet hair. I had no clue why I had even washed it. It was going to be messed up by tonight. I suppose that didn't matter. I wanted to look great for Theo. Fan-fucking-tastic.

So, after blow-drying and flat-ironing my messy mane, I hurried out of the bathroom, taking out one of my favorite bathing suits. It was a red one-piece with one shoulder strap, the waist and the back of it cut out in the shape of an oval. Yeah, I admit it showed a lot of skin, but it was perfect for this evening.

I checked the time on my alarm clock in the corner. 12:14. I had an hour and a half to finish getting ready. Just as I reached for my cover-up dress, Margie knocked on the door, calling my name.

"Come in!" I called, sliding the dress over my bathing suit. Margie was inside before I could tug the entire thing down. When she spotted the flash of red, a slight frown etched her face.

"You're leaving already?" she asked.

"Yeah. I have plans with..." I paused. I didn't want to tell her who I was spending my day with. Her eyes were inquisitive, no judgment present. "Theo wants to show me his boat."

"Oh, I see." I expected her to say something about it, but she didn't. "Well, I wanted to tell you that your father and I most likely won't be home until later tonight. He has an appointment at four, and after that I have to go meet my son for his band concert at eight."

I gasped. "What?! Margie, you didn't tell me you had a son!"

Her cheeks turned a soft shade of red. She shrugged in a bashful, adorable way. "I was afraid that if I brought him up, he would be all I talked about. I didn't want to ruin your summer with stories about him."

"Yeah right! That's amazing. How old is he?"

"Only a few years older than you. Twenty-nine." She beamed, clearly proud.

"Wow. That's really great. I bet you're an amazing mother."

She laughed, her cheeks still rosy. "I did my best to raise him. He's a very good boy."

"I bet."

I dropped my gaze. Speaking of moms made me a feel a little ill. I had no clue where my mother was. It was like, after I went off to college, I no longer mattered to her. I guess she figured I'd be okay without her, which happens to be true, but the least she could do was check in, email me during her travels at least.

"Well, have fun on your boat trip." Margie's voice cut through my thoughts. "I hope you and Theo have a blast. You deserve it after the hell your father put us through this week."

"Yeah." I blew a breath, tucking my hair behind my ear. "Dad can be a little wild."

Her face was gentle as she stepped back, giving my room a look around before grabbing the door handle. "Just be careful, *mi amor*," she said softly. "Have fun, but be careful." Margie was out of the room before I could even blink.

When she was long gone, I turned and faced the full-length mirror hanging on my closet door. My expression hinted of confusion. Margie had experienced this before. She probably knew exactly how I felt— ecstatic, ready to see a man of another generation and spend my day with him.

She most likely knew how it felt to wake up happy and feel like all worries were gone. I bet she never wanted it to end, the same feeling I carried with the mere thought of Theo.

Sighing, I walked to my closet and pulled out a small tote bag. After putting a few necessities inside, I went back to my bathroom and applied a light coat of makeup to my face. Then, I examined my reflection, pleased with the finished product. It wasn't too much, but it certainly wasn't basic.

I smiled.

I went back to my tote bag, strapped it over my shoulder, and hurried downstairs. Fortunately, Margie was in my dad's bedroom, helping him get dressed. I spent nearly thirty minutes in the kitchen, pacing back and forth, waiting for time to pass me by.

When it came to him, I was very impatient.

I waltzed to the living room, peeking through the blinds, spotting Theo's Harley parked in the driveway next to the Charger. I hadn't seen his bike out in a while. I didn't hear it come or leave from Primrose.

Flicking my wrist, I checked my watch once more. I still had fifteen minutes to go before going to his place at the time we had planned. Walking into the kitchen, I placed my bag on the countertop and opened it, giving it one last check.

Snacks? Check.

Cell phone? Check.

Sunscreen and tanning oil? Check.

I headed for the living room again, walking in small circles beneath the twirling ceiling fan.

Alright. That's it.

Sadly, I could no longer wait. I picked up my tote bag from the kitchen and hurried out the front door, locking it behind me.

In no time I was in Theo's driveway, walking past his red, silver, and black bike. My finger ran across the rubber handles, my other hand drifting across the smooth leather of the seat.

"Can you believe it's still the same bike?" Theo's deep voice sounded behind me. It was close, and when I turned, he was only a few feet away, smiling with a bag slugged over his shoulder.

"This is the same one?" My eyes broadened. "The one you were about to..." I cut my sentence short. I refused to bring up the night he almost destroyed this "toy" of his.

"Yep." Grinning, he walked around me, placing his bag inside one of the leather saddlebags attached to the sides. "I like to keep up with my toys."

"Wait." I held my hands up, looking from him to the bike and then him again. "We're taking Ol' Charlie?"

"Hell yeah!" He swung his left leg over the seat and sat, the bottom of his boots landing on the concrete. He grabbed the helmets hooked on the handlebars and put his on before handing me a solid black one. When I accepted it, he steadied the bike and gripped the handles. Then he looked my way, saying, "Come on, Little Knight. Boat's waiting."

I stood, wide-eyed for a several seconds, as I held the helmet to my chest. Never had I ridden on Theo's motorcycle. When Izzy and I were younger, he refused to take us on a ride until we were sixteen or older, but when we turned sixteen, we were no longer interested in taking a ride on his bike—well, let me rephrase that. Izzy was no longer interested in riding her dad's bike, but I would have been willing and ready if the conversation of a bike ride with Theo Black ever arose.

Theo patted the spot behind him, his brown eyes warm and welcoming. Unable to prevent my toothy, child-like grin, I strapped on the helmet and hopped on.

I made sure my tote bag was secure between us, and then I snaked my arms around his solid waist. When I was settled, he brought the engine to life. At first I thought his body was vibrating from the rumble of the bike, but it turned out he was laughing, glancing over his shoulder as he reversed the bike down the driveway and the wheels touched the street.

"Ready?" he asked, peering over his shoulder.

"A little nervous," I admitted.

"Don't be. I've been doing this bike riding thing for years." He caressed the back of my hand for a short second and then pulled away, gripping the handlebars again. I looked to my left, at my house.

Margie and Dad were walking out the front door. She assisted him, most likely telling him to be careful. Dad had no clue what was going on, following her lead.

Margie looked up, eyes averting from me to Theo in less than two seconds. Theo happened to look as well. "Caregiver?" he asked over the deep grumble of the engine.

"Yes. She's nice. Don't worry."

"Hmm." He smiled at her. She returned a wary one. I gave Margie an assuring grin, and when Theo asked if I was all good, I excitedly nodded my head, and he took off, leaving Primrose and Margie's line of sight.

Something about that little stare of hers made my stomach churn. It was almost like this woman could read the future, but if she could only understand that this was just a temporary thing, she wouldn't have been so worried.

I figured I knew what I was doing, and I knew Theo would be okay with me leaving once this was all over. I was riding it out, taking each day as it came. I wanted to talk with Margie more about this, but until then, I decided to forget about it.

I pressed my cheek to Theo's back, the wind causing my flat-ironed hair to flap wildly. A wave of comfort washed through me as I felt his muscles tense and then relax when he made a turn or came to a stop.

Theo was a natural at this, owning this bike of many years. He rode through Bristle Wave casually, passing by cars, large trucks, and even pedestrians, some who may have secretly envied us.

I could get used to this. I really could.

It took about fifteen minutes to reach the docks. Theo parked his bike in the lot a short distance away and then kicked the kick stand out. Once he helped me off, he opened the compartment and pulled out his bag. I stepped back, my legs like Jell-O, but the rest of my body completely relaxed.

"Liked the bike ride?" he asked, grabbing my hand and leading the way to the docks.

I looked up at him. "It was surprisingly fun."

It didn't take too long to get to his boat. We crossed two paths of wooden decks, and a white boat with black sails appeared. On the hull, in red print, were the words *Dirty Black*. Fitting.

"This is *yours?*" I asked, astonished as we stepped aboard. The boat swayed with the added weight.

Theo stepped onto the boat with poise, his cheek quirked up as he met my gaze. "All mine."

I looked from him to the wooden two-top table in the corner. "You said it was something simple—something to get you from point A to B."

"It is!" he laughed.

"No." I shook my head. "This is a damn party boat." And really, it was. It was massive. The polished wooden deck was ahead; I could spot it from a mile away. Big enough for a college crowd. There was a table and a cozy, cushioned bench in the corner, suitable to seat at least four.

"It's a cruising boat. Got it for a steal from Old Dane."

"Who used to work at Dane's? Didn't know you still kept up with him."

"Yep." His eyes lit up. "Wanna check out the inside?"

"Sure."

Theo walked around his bag and led the way down four stairs in the center. When the soles of my sandals landed on polished wood, I was completely mesmerized. It was perfect.

A curved sofa, black leather with glossy wood grain trim, hugged the wall. Sunlight filtered in from a rectangular window above it. A brown table was in front of the sofa with a short booth in the near corner. *Dirty Black* even had a small kitchen behind the lounging area, equipped with a small black mini fridge, a microwave, and marble countertops. This thing had to have cost him an arm and a leg.

"Sound system is over there." He pointed to my left. I spotted the glass case, a black music player in the cubby. "Used to have a TV, but it messed up."

"What happened to it?"

He shrugged. "No clue. The screen just went blank while I was watching the World Cup a few weeks ago."

"Damn. I bet that sucked."

He walked towards me. "It was hell. It took me thirty minutes just to get back home. By the time I made it, the game was over." He pressed his lips. "You win some, you lose some."

"What exactly do you do on this boat?"

He looked around. "Chill and think." He paused. "I spend a lot of quality time with myself here. Used to watch games but... well, you know." He held his hands out, giving me one of his usual *shit happens* gestures.

"Is it always just... you on here?"

He blinked, confused by what I meant at first, but his expression changed when it registered. "Oh." He scratched the scruff on his chin. "No. You're the first woman to be on my boat—the first person really." His forced out an uneasy laugh.

"Wow..." I was impressed. And pleased. But I couldn't help wondering if Theo was lying just to keep me happy like all men did. Honestly, he had no reason to lie to me. He had no reason to keep me around when this was only temporary. And if he did lie, I couldn't be upset about it. It's not like we were going far anyway.

"Ready to get the hell out of here?" he asked as he walked in my direction, running his palm across my shoulder.

"Yeah. I'd love that."

Theo's head slanted downward, and for a second he watched my eyes. His gaze drifted down to my nose, going further down until he stopped at my lips. Then his mouth fully consumed mine. The kiss was sweet like candy, savory like a chocolate cupcake a girl on a diet finally had the chance to eat on cheat day. It was warm and only a little damp.

When he started to pull away, I smiled behind his lips. He focused on mine, blinking slow, reluctant to move. But in order for us to truly be spending time alone and together with no worries, he had to get the boat going.

"Fuck," he breathed, his breath warm as it drifted down the line of my neck. "You're gonna be the death of me, Little Knight." His hand moved down my waist, rounding my ass and squeezing tight. I yelped as he spanked me, and because I wore nothing but a cover up over a bathing suit, I felt the sting.

It excited me even more, and when he pulled away, I wanted to drag him back in and devour him whole. *We have to go, Chloe*, I told myself. *You can get all you want as soon as we're at sea. Just make sure to be extra greedy.* So I let him go and sat on the sofa, laughing about my internal thoughts.

It was hard *not* to be happy around him. With Theo, I felt like the only girl in the world. Around him, I felt like I was floating on cloud nine, wrapped in a high that didn't go away until we were apart. But even while we were apart, I'd still think of him, and although thinking of him wasn't as magnificent as being in his presence, I still felt a draft of that high.

It was damn near impossible to believe that, at the end of this, we could never be. I didn't even want to think of how much damage we actually were to each other. We weren't a normal fling. We were unusual, rare and, sadly, the unusualness—the reality—was what stood in the way of complete happiness between us.

After Theo sailed the sea with me by his side, the breeze running through my tresses, he finally came to a stop. As he did, I scoped the area. I saw nothing but water. I glanced to my left. I could barely see Bristle Wave from here. The peaks of the hotels, homes, and towers were all I could make out. Other than that, we were completely alone.

In the middle of the ocean.

Just Theo and me.

The definition of screwed up perfection.

"Theo," I breathed after he picked up the anchor in the corner and dropped it in the water. "This is amazing." I met in front of him as he twisted around. His large hands capped the top of my shoulders, head in an angle. His face was handsome and meek. The black scruff on his jaw and around his mouth made his lips appear so full and kissable.

"Glad you like it, Knight." His tongue ran over his bottom lip, and once he released me, he turned for his bag in the corner. "We have all day," he sighed, digging through it and pulling out a glass bottle of Hennessy. My eyes popped as I studied the brown liquor. He shrugged, as if he'd just read my mind. "It's five o' clock somewhere."

Placing the bottle on the tabletop, Theo reached for the hem of his shirt, tugging it over his head. A toned, slender set of abs was exposed. There was proof that he kept up with himself, worked out hard every day and perfected his routine. As he tossed the shirt aside, looking me straight in the eyes, I knew the bottle of brown would be necessary. I had never been alone with Theo like this, in the middle of the ocean, secluded and away from the crazy world we lived in.

While we were out at sea, it was like being on our own private island, with booze, music, and an overabundance of ogling and making out. I didn't mind. I'd wanted this to happen for so long. Now that I had the chance, I wasn't going to ruin it. Quite frankly, nothing could ruin or disturb us. I checked my cellphone and had absolutely no service. I suppose that was a good thing.

Theo poured us drinks on ice, but I started with a bottle of water from the fridge. On the deck, we played a game of chess and then a game of UNO at the table. I whooped him in UNO, but he killed me in chess. Three times.

His laughter was contagious, his aura welcoming. We sat across from each other, most times gazing into each other's eyes, wondering what the other was thinking but other times truly having a good time —laughing, touching, grinning, and all.

It was nearing four in the afternoon. We had all day, but I knew sooner or later, one of us would get tired of this boat thing and want to go back for some grub or even some sleep. We indulged in snacks—cheese crackers, honey buns, and potato chips—but it wouldn't be enough for long.

Picking up my glass of cognac, I took a small sip. The liquid burned as it slid down my throat, but I continued to drink. I felt wonderful around Theo while sober, but with the benefit of this drink, I knew I would feel incredible. I drank until my short glass was empty, and when Theo came back down the stairs, he looked right at me.

He noticed something was different. Quickly, his brown eyes moved to the empty glass in front of me, and when he realized what had happened, his smile couldn't be prevented.

"My naughty Knight," he said, voice deep as he walked towards me. He stepped in front of me, still without a shirt. My eyes traveled down the length of his body, stopping right on the deep lines leading to his shorts. Reaching down, he gripped my hands and brought me to a stand. I didn't dare stop him.

With stifled breath, I watched as he observed me, his hand gliding down my back, landing right on my plump ass. "I've been dying to know what's beneath this dress." His voice was low now. With ease, his fingers curled around the bottom of my white cover-up dress.

Bringing it higher, he gradually exposed the curve of my ass, my waist, and then my bosom. I lifted my hands, helping him get the dress off. He placed it on top of the table, but those smoldering brown eyes never left me. They roamed my slim body, a hunger present now.

"My fucking goodness." I absorbed the growl, his deep tone. He fought to hold onto restraint, keeping his hands steady as they pressed on the small of my back, right above my hips.

"What?" I whispered, voice faint. I no longer felt wonderful. I felt incredible. The drink had hit me. Hard. Ugh, I was such a lightweight.

"Tell me something," he said, the tip of his nose skidding across my cheek, lips so close to my ear I could feel the heat of them. "Did you wear this for me or were you really planning to tan on my deck?"

"I wanted to tan," I said, feeling his mouth move to the crook of my neck. "Then I realized I forgot sunscreen. But I can't lie," I murmured. "This may have also been for you."

Theo chuckled, finding my response humorous. "I don't think you're gonna get around to tanning today, baby. The sun will be long gone by the time I'm done with you."

He leaned back, and the restraint he'd just had went flying out of

Dirty Black's window. His hands clutched my waist, and he swooped me up, my back hitting the plush cushion of the sofa.

My patience failed me. I stuck my hands downward and unbuttoned his jeans, feeling as he searched for the clasp that kept my bathing suit bound at the top. Once he snagged the strap, my breasts bounced, on full display. He focused on them for a brief moment, eyes hooded. His thumb fiddled with my right nipple, and I sighed. Then, greedily, he sucked, his mouth going around my nipple and tugging with a gentle graze of his teeth until the flesh hardened. My moan was heavy as he moved to the other, licking and lapping his tongue around it, mouth sealing to capture a full taste.

Once they were just the way he wanted them to be—solid, pointed, and erect—his head came up, and he towered above me. He watched as I slid his jeans down, hovering above my full breasts, eyes blazing.

"This won't be quick, Chloe," he said, lowering his face. In my ear, he breathed, "I'm taking my time with you while I have you out here." Fingers slid across the slit between my legs. My body jolted, and a faint smile touched his lips as he went on. "You can moan as loud as you want. Scream, if that's what you wanna do. But what you will not do is hold back." He gripped my face in his hands, brown eyes hard. "Understand, baby?"

My teeth sank into my bottom lip, a mix of a sigh and a groan filling my throat, and instead of speaking, I nodded. But I wanted to shout "Yes!" to the rooftops repeatedly.

Pleased with my response, Theo flashed a crooked smile, and his body started to lower, trailing down, damp kisses dropping on my skin. He took my bathing suit down with him, lifting my hips with ease and sliding the one-piece down my legs.

I was completely naked before him when the suit was gone. He looked me over, studying the pink opening between my thighs. He observed it for a while, and I realized he'd never seen me in the light, so up close and personal with nothing to hold him back.

No time to limit us.

No one to bother.

He liked what he saw.

I may have purposely shaved for him the night before, knowing what was in store for later.

I could tell he didn't want to look away. See, the thing I knew about Theo was that he was good at this. I was sure he'd done this hundreds of times, but I had no clue what to expect. In a way, he was my professor and I was his student, eager and ready to learn. He was teaching me everything I needed to know, teaching me things about my body that I didn't even know I would be capable of.

Spreading my legs apart, Theo brought me to the edge of the sofa. His knees hit the floor, and he bent over in front of me, head between my knees. A soft kiss was placed on my pubic bone. I shuddered, feeling his warm breath slither through the damp opening.

He looked up, brown eyes focusing on me. Then, one of his thick fingers slid in, diving deep. A sharp breath passed by my parted lips, and I adjusted my hips, moving closer to his face. He didn't budge. He fingered deeper, producing soft moans.

I swallowed hard, shutting my eyes, seizing each feel so I could remember later on.

"Don't look away from me, Chloe," Theo commanded, eyes trained on me as he shifted. "I need you to look at me while I taste you—while I eat this glorious, wet pussy like it's my only meal of the day. Can you do that?" I nodded, my eyes popping open again. "Answer me, baby. *Speak.*" His voice still held an edge of demand. "You know I love hearing you."

"Yes," I breathed.

His finger came out and ran up to my clit. He pressed on it, and I bucked a little. He chuckled. "I've been dying to taste this sweet pussy for years, you know that?" His question was rhetorical. With hungry, fierce eyes, Theo watched me as I writhed around two fingers now. His nose ran up my thigh, and when he adjusted himself, his nostrils flared. "I hate stalling."

And then he devoured, his tongue pressing on my delicate nub. He circled it with no manners at all, fingers driving deeper, curling just enough for me to feel him inside and out.

"Oh my god," I cried. I could surely feel him. His satin-like tongue ran over my clit, his thick fingers running in and out, producing moisture, tampering with my g-spot. His eyes never left mine, and I feared looking away. I knew he'd stop if I did.

So I watched him—watched as his mouth sealed around my clit and his elbow moved forward and backwards. He tunneled to my core, my mind on the edge of a cliff. I was about to tip over and land in hot lava, and Theo was right behind me, pushing me right over that cliff, sparking every single fiber within me.

I shuddered as I let out a cry, and since I was no longer able to control myself, I squeezed my eyes shut, breathing, "Theo, Theo... oh, God, *Theo!*" as his mouth lingered.

He groaned in response but refused to pull away even though I'd cum recklessly, my essences all over his mouth and chin. Gradually, his fingers drew out, and after providing another kiss to my sacred area, right between the lips, he pressed his palm to my thigh, running his tongue across his mouth.

He licked away the remainder of my sweet nectar, eyes intense. And then he stood, and before me was the longest, thickest erection I had ever seen in my life. I wasn't quite sure when he'd gotten rid of his briefs, but it didn't matter. His cock pointed right at me, as if it had chosen me itself, demanding me to come forth and accept him.

Using his right hand, Theo stroked the hard flesh between his legs, moving closer. "Damn, baby," he murmured, his left hand going to the back of my head. "You came so hard for me." He palmed the back of my head, but there was no need. I wanted to taste him, swallow every last inch of him, along with the hot liquid that would soon follow.

I pressed my palms to his waist, my face moving forward. Dropping my chin, lips parted, I ran my tongue from the head to his shaft, and he stiffened. When I glanced up, his nostrils were red from flaring. His head went into a slight angle, and he brought my head forward again, leaving me no choice but to take his entire cock into my mouth.

"This isn't just about pleasing me," Theo told me. "Play with yourself. Show me what you like."

I paused, drawing back. "I've... never actually done that in front of anyone before."

He leaned down, and with a deep, core-clenching rumble next to my ear, he said, "Let me be your first again."

I blinked as he stood up straight. This was new, very new, but with him I wanted to be brave. I wanted him to know I wasn't just some little girl with no skill. I wanted to experience it all with him, learn new things, and figure out exactly what it was that pleased both him and myself.

So, I dropped to my knees, and Theo moved back half an inch, watching as my finger came to my sex. Wrapping my lips around his smooth tip, I thrust my finger in deep and then brought it out again while drawing him further into my mouth. His hardened flesh touched the back of my throat, and I gagged. He palmed the back of my head again, refusing for me to move away.

"You look good gagging around my cock, baby." He stroked deeper, and I gagged once more before he eased up, smirking down at me. Those brown eyes were hard to ignore. So demanding and full of lust and need.

His hips swiveled. I moaned as salty liquid crept down my throat. I worked hard, fingering myself and bringing my other hand up to stroke and suck at the same time. He was pleased to see this. He released the back of my head, and his fell back, a sigh tunneling out of him as I pumped rapidly, the sucking so loud it created a wet noise.

I listened to waves crash outside the boat, remembering just where we were and that nothing could interrupt us.

It was me and Theo.

Fucking and sucking.

Moaning and groaning.

Getting however much we wanted out of each other without the fear of reality cutting through.

Knowing this, I came around my finger again. I made a noise around his cock, one that hummed and gargled, and he looked down at me. I felt him get harder, and knew right away that he was about to cum, but he yanked out of my mouth, gripped my wrist to bring me to a stand, and then bent me over the sofa. My ass was pointed in the air, face down, and he was behind me, his massive cock sliding in from behind.

My sex showed no resistance to this beautiful man's member. My girl accepted him, knowing he'd been there before. Knowing his cock was the one that made her become a woman.

Theo sighed and then moaned as he slammed, grasping my thin waist and pounding.

Pounding.

Pounding.

"This. Fucking. Pussy," he growled. I could hear him reaching his brink. "Is. So. Fucking. Good." He couldn't hold off much longer, no matter how much he wanted to keep going in order to please me.

He let out a gratified roar, squeezing my waist tighter as I squealed. His hands went to my thick hair, gripping tight and tugging back. My eyes shot up to the ceiling, and I hadn't realized before that there was a mirror above us.

My word. I could see everything. His hard body behind me, owning every limb, dominating with every inch stroking in and out. Watching us go at it like this sent heat traveling through me. I felt all of him. I saw how focused he was, his attention fixed on the back of my head. His face, as well as mine, oozed with ultimate, undeniable pleasure. His mouth hung open, and he went deeper each time, as if he couldn't get deep enough.

In that moment, I could read Theo Black as clear as day. He loved being inside me. He loved fucking me. He loved owning, dominating, and penetrating me 'til my eyes rolled to the back of my skull.

And that was exactly what happened. Only, he was no longer behind me. He was on top now, thrusting hard, one of my legs in the air and his thumb pressing down on my clit, circling with steady rhythm until I quaked and shuddered. He drove harsher, deeper, and then he slowed down, wanting me to feel everything.

With my back arched, I cried his name again, his power twisting his name from me in an entranced wail. He grunted in response, fell forward, and came with his mouth around my nipple, his thumb still pressed on my swollen nub.

"Damn, baby." His voice was loud, cock pulsating. I whimpered, but not out of defeat. I whimpered because, shockingly, I wanted more. So much more. We were far from finished.

"The sun is still up," I told him, teasing.

He looked up, laughing hard, forehead damp with sweat. His hair was glued to his face. The sunlight beaming in struck the glistening sweat on his neck, illuminating the tattoo on his neck—*Fearless*. It was tatted in Latin. He told me the meaning of it a long time ago, back when I was fifteen. I had no idea how I remembered the meaning.

I traced the pad of my finger across the black script. This piece of inked real estate was his trophy after winning some brawl at a motorcycle club. When he told me about that, I knew instantly that Theo had a wicked and dark side to him.

Sitting up, he raked his fingers through his hair, looking down at me with half a smile. "I know the sun's still up," he responded. "But we both needed to get that quick fix in."

I sat up on my elbows. "I agree." I tugged on his arm, bringing him back down. His landing was soft as he dropped on top of me. His eyes softened as I cupped his face and then slowly kissed him. My hips worked on their own, thrusting against the warm flesh that dangled between his thighs. I wanted him to feel everything—all of me. The tender neediness in my kiss, the ache centered in my body. I needed filling... lots of filling.

He didn't stop me. He returned the affection, working up his own thrust. I knew how men worked. It would take a few minutes for him to be fully restored and ready, but I just couldn't wait. I was an eager, horny, little girl.

"Patience, babe," Theo murmured between kisses. "The sun may still be up, but we aren't leaving anytime soon." His lips met my cheek, hooded eyes hooked on mine.

"Promise?" I whispered, placing another kiss to the corner of his mouth.

He did the same. "I promise." I drew his bottom lip between my teeth, gently grazing. He laughed behind the tiny bite. "Naughty Little Knight," he exhaled before consuming me. We kissed passionately, tongues twisted, until his cock became rock-solid again. With our focus on nothing but each other, he slid in, taking me raw beneath the streaming sunlight.

The boat swayed. The waves crashed. The sun was bright,

expecting and beckoning for me to make an appearance. Although it would have been great to take the sun up on that tan, no amount of summer bronze could compare to my lifelong crush and my *first* officially making me his Little Knight.

Absolutely nothing.

FIFTEEN

THEO

FUNNY, she thought I was fucking around about making her mine 'til the sun went down.

I watched as she passed by me, connecting her phone to the stereo system. Her hips swayed as she hummed to a song stuck in her head, and once the music filled the room, her back straightened, and she turned my way.

The only piece of clothing she wore was the white dress that covered that sexy ass bathing suit. The bathing suit had been put aside a long time ago. The sun was now setting, and she started a slow dance to *Own It* by Drake.

The tune was fitting, slow at first and then it would pick up. Lifting my hand, I gestured for her to come to me with my forefinger. With a coy smile sweeping across her lips, she strode my way, breasts bouncing beneath the see-through dress with each slow yet deliberate step.

Stepping between my legs, she climbed on my lap, adjusting her perfectly round ass on the center. She swung her hair aside and her arms hooked over my shoulders, fingers entwining behind my neck.

"Can I show you something?"

She bit her bottom lip, and my cock twitched. "Show me what?" she murmured.

Without minimal thought, I reached down and pulled her dress over her head. Her arms lifted to make it easier, and once it was gone, I had full sight of her tits. My mouth ached for a taste, but I remained patient, lifting my hips and pulling my briefs off.

Chloe's hand ran down my chest, her skin soft and smooth as she sat back and wrapped that same hand around my cock. Her eyes then flickered up, watching mine, breath bated. "Show me what?" she breathed again.

I glanced down, pulsing as she stroked me. Her thumb skimmed over my tip, and I groaned quietly, shutting my eyes for a brief moment. I had to collect myself. This girl—she made me so fucking impatient. I wanted to tear her pussy up, make her sore for days.

But I had to remember, she was just a girl that was still learning, and I was a man who knew exactly what he liked. So, I stopped her from stroking and gripped her waist to lift her a few inches. Her mouth fell open as I slowly slid her on top of my cock. She was right on the head, but the fullness had obviously consumed her. Her eyes closed, and her chest heaved with deep breaths.

"Look at me, Chloe."

Her eyes fluttered open. I brought her down a little more, and a sharp breath passed by my ear as she leaned into me.

"Watch me," I demanded. "Feel me, baby." I watched her face drip with pleasure. "You feel me, Chloe?"

"Yes," she breathed. "I feel you."

I dropped her down, completing the slide, and she gasped. Sitting her upright on my cock, I studied her, loving the expression she put on when every last inch of me was buried deep inside her. I was balls-deep, the sensation of her warm, wet pussy enveloping me whole. I wanted so badly to cum, but I kept it together.

"Ride me." She looked down at me, collecting all of her hair on one side of her face. She was unsure, a minor look of fear present. I palmed her ass, comforting her and drawing her in closer. "Here," I murmured, squeezing her ass-cheeks in my hands, "let me show you what a *real man* likes." My hand slid across her smooth skin, stopping at her waist, moving her hips forward and backwards. Her pussy swiveled on my cock, and she panted as she grinded with me.

When she finally got the hang of it, knowing exactly what I liked, she moved my hands away and straddled me, dipping low, her breath snagging as she sank. Damn. I swear it was better than I ever thought possible.

Her slender body moved up and down, bounced, and rotated. I sucked on her nipples to prevent myself from fully focusing on the sensations she brought my cock, groaning around them, and then she lifted my head, her warm breath skimming across my lips. Our mouths barely touched, and something about that made fucking her even sexier.

Sparks flew, beads of sweat collecting and spilling down her chest the faster and longer she went. I cupped her delicate face in my hands, needing a taste of her, wanting to feel her full lips on mine. The quick rush I felt as I kissed her deep, watching her ride me like her life depended on it, made no damn sense. How could she make me feel this way? Like I was a teenager again, fucking my new girlfriend for the first time?

With Chloe, I felt confident. I felt like I could take over the world. There was someone that accepted me other than my deceased wife. Chloe, this amazing girl, had no idea how great she made me feel.

Skin slapped with the sound of crashing waves.

Moans and groans became louder, heat thickening the space around us, crowding the cabin.

Her tight pussy surrounded me whole, squeezing and then releasing with a slight bounce. *Oh, shit.* If she kept doing that, I was going to cum for damn sure. As if she knew that was the trigger, she rode faster, her palms on my chest, forcing my back against the sofa. Her gaze fixed on only me, her teeth biting in her bottom lip.

"Ohh." She let out a breathy moan, knocking her head back as she continued.

I cupped her ass. "You look so good, baby," I told her, pressing my chest to her abdomen. "Look at you. Look at the mirror." I kissed her chin, meeting her hooded eyes through the reflection on the ceiling. "Look how fucking sexy you look on top of me, baby. Riding me.

Fucking me. Taking control." I brought her face down, gluing her mouth to mine as I caught her cry of pleasure, swirling my tongue around hers, stealing every delighted sound right away.

Her body became rigid, stiffening as she bucked forward. Her pussy still squeezed tight around me—gripping and holding—but when she came... *my fucking god*, she grew even tighter, and my eyes sealed. I had no clue she could get so tight around me, but the clutch was real. No longer able to hold it all in, I released, coming harder than I did the first four times.

"Fuck, baby." A deep grunt filled the gap between us. I squeezed her perfect ass in my hand, sucking on the bend of her neck. She allowed me, tilting her head back, pulsing hard and shuddering just enough for me to feel. Once I collected enough breath, I laughed. "Now, *that's* how you ride a man, Chloe. Goddamn." She giggled as I kissed her cheek, then she hooked her arms around my neck. "You looked like you already knew what you were doing up there."

She shrugged, her forehead dropping on my shoulder. "I may have learned on my own."

Frowning, I asked, "How?" My face went stiff as I lifted her head.

She laughed. "Theo, really?" she teased. "It's not what you think. I just so happen to read a lot of books with some *amazing* sex scenes in them."

My face softened. I felt foolish. "Oh." I swiped my forehead as she climbed off my lap and collected her dress. "So books are like porn to you?"

"Yep. Ever heard of E.L. James? Sylvia Day? Maya Banks?" She tugged the cover up down, concealing her terrific body.

"Nah," I admitted, huffing a laugh.

"Well, a woman can learn so much from reading their books. Look at it this way: you have the Internet, I have the library," her lips twisted, "... and bookstores. It really does come in handy." She grinned, revealing beautiful, pearly teeth. "If you ever wanna do something to make me happy, buy me books. I will love you forever." She flashed her gorgeous smile again.

I chuckled, standing and pulling up my briefs. "Yeah, I bet, Little Knight."

She stepped back, pointing her thumb towards the fridge. "Want me to get a water?"

I watched as she twirled but kept her eyes on me as she glanced over her shoulder. "Sure. Grab us some drinks. I'll meet you on the deck. There's still a little sun out."

She scoffed. "Not enough for me to tan with, sir."

I laughed, collecting her towel and then walking up the stairs to get mine off the back of the chair. I spread the towels on the deck, and Chloe came out several seconds later with two, cold, bottled waters in hand. She extended a bottle to me, and I thanked her and sat.

Tugging on her arm, I brought her to my lap, and she yelped, laughing in the process. God, I loved the sound of her laughter, the high and low chimes. The way my chest grew hot when I realized it was pure joy I gave her. I had no idea how I made her so happy. I didn't know what it was about me that she liked so much.

My lips pressed to the shell of her ear, and I held her close, my arms wrapping around her middle. She smelled good, like creamy coconut. It was refreshing, and it definitely fit her. "What is it about me?" I asked calmly.

"What do you mean?" She sat up.

"I mean, what is it about me that intrigues you?"

She gripped my hand and shrugged her shoulders. "I... don't know. There are a lot of things about you that I find interesting. Intriguing. But if we're being honest right now, I have to tell you that I have been interested ever since the day I met you."

"Really?" I was surprised... and amused.

"Yeah."

"Why?"

"I don't know." She let out a small sigh, one that made her seem like a hopeless romantic. "There was just something about the way you rode into Primrose on that bike... and how you sat there so casually, like nothing in the world bothered you. Normally, I can read people like a book, but I couldn't tell what it was about you. I knew that day that I needed to meet you—the entire Black family. I could read Mrs. Black like a book. She was a busy woman that liked things to go her way and sometimes stressed herself out over the little things."

Shit. She was spot on. "And Izzy was just like me. Not old enough to fully give a damn about boys. Focused more on her books and movies and new shoes or dresses. But you... I don't know." She looked really unsure, like she was picturing the day all over again. "You just sat there with so many unanswered questions surrounding you. And I watched, hoping I would soon get some answers, but I got none. Let's just say you were really cool, *really* hot, and that really spiked my interest." She laughed.

"Hold on—*were* cool?" I teased.

"Still are, silly man." I chuckled, and she picked up her bottle of water, taking a quick sip before sighing. "Why can't every day be like this?"

I pressed my lips, my chin resting on her shoulder. I watched the water move, the waves shimmering from the sunset. The sky was filled with scattered rays, a shade of pink and orange blended with warm yellow. "I don't know," I replied.

She twisted a little to look at me. "Do you wish it could always be like this? With me and you, I mean."

Her eyes were filled with emotion. I swallowed hard, dropping my head. "If you're asking me if things could be different, then yes." I squeezed her, placing a soft kiss to her temple. "I do wish there were ways we could make this work." Her eyelids sealed blissfully, pleased with my response.

Reality.

It always caught up to us somehow. Though she was satisfied with my answer, I knew it was dumb to say. Even if we wanted more, we couldn't have it. There were some things I couldn't claim, and me claiming Chloe as my own was one of them.

But I didn't tell her that. I didn't tell her because, even while I held her close and we watched the ocean and the seagulls pass by with distant caws, I knew I couldn't ruin this moment right now.

This peace.

This bliss.

This beautiful girl between my legs, allowing me to kiss her. Allowing someone as myself to hold and protect her. She trusted me. She cared about me. I couldn't break or demolish that.

But plenty of other things definitely could.

My phone vibrated on the table. I glanced back, brows drawing together. Placing a quick kiss on Chloe's cheek before releasing her, I stood and walked to the table to pick up my cellphone. The name on the screen shattered all bliss. All peace.

Izzy.

Chloe walked towards me. "What is it?"

I swallowed hard, and when I turned to look at her, she immediately spotted the guilt in my eyes. Her entire demeanor changed. She no longer smiled. She couldn't even look at me.

Instead, she turned around, gripping the silver railing and looking towards the sunset. I looked from her backside to my phone. I'd missed the call, but I knew I had to get home and call my daughter.

Guilt-ridden, I walked towards her and wrapped my arms around her from behind. She sighed, and when I turned her around to face me, her eyes were damp. "No, Chloe," I whispered, pleading. "Please, baby. Don't cry."

"I—" Her mouth clamped shut in an instant. My heart ached, watching her struggle with words.

"Look at me." I picked her face up in my hands, and when our eyes met, her tears fell, skidding down her cheeks. With the pad of my thumb, I swiped them away. "It's okay. It's just a phone call. We can still spend time together, but we have to get back. I don't have good service out here, and I should call her back before she gets worried."

Damn. When I actually listened to myself, it seemed like I was having an affair, not that I was speaking of my daughter.

She nodded, swiping her face. "I understand... this is just crazy, ya know?"

A soft laugh blew out. "Trust me. I know."

"Well—" She stood up straight, removing her face from my hands. With a kind smile, she said, "We should get out of here then. I should probably go shower too." Her nose scrunched, a soft smile on her twisted lips. There she was, the Little Knight that understood me. The one that knew this whole ordeal was what it was and there would be no changing it.

So, after helping her collect her things, I went to the wheel and sailed back to the docks. I drove Ol' Charlie back to Primrose, but Chloe was quiet during the ride. When we were in my garage, I kicked the kickstand and helped her off. She forced a smile, placing the strap of her tote bag on her shoulder.

I sat on the seat, unsure of where to begin.

Luckily, I didn't have to. She started for me, face gentle. "I had fun today, Theo."

"Yeah," I sighed. "Me too. We should do it again." She thought on it, trying to figure out when exactly that would happen. I saw her conflict, how her eyes gave the internal debate away. "Anyway I'll text you." I hopped off my bike, stepping in front of her.

She nodded. "Okay."

We stared at each other for a moment through the darkness. Nothing but the streetlights gave leeway for our vision. I could read her like a book. She was clearly upset, but was trying hard to hold onto contentment.

Stepping forward, I cupped one of her cheeks, and my mouth came above hers, but I didn't kiss her. I lingered, and her hand came to my waist, body closer. We were like magnets, unwilling to break apart unless the cause was distance. "This doesn't change anything," I said. "You're still my Knight."

Her cheeks tugged up, eyes falling. "Go call Izzy," she teased, but the remorse was clear in her voice.

I brought my head down, and our lips molded. She released a sigh, her arms draping over my shoulders, fingers curling in my hair. I stumbled forward until her back hit the wall, but I didn't dare stop kissing her.

She needed to know that we were okay. That nothing would change and we could still let this summer be.

She was still my girl.

My Little Knight.

My baby.

My air.

My beautiful savior. I say "savior" because if it wasn't for her, I don't think I would have wanted to keep living after Janet passed.

If it wasn't for her coming to check on me and helping me during the darkest, most desperate times, I wouldn't have been there. I would have been gone a long time ago, drowning in sorrow or most likely dead.

My hands held her face, my groan deep. I didn't want to stop kissing her—I could have all fucking night—but when my phone buzzed in my back pocket, I pulled back, cursing beneath my breath.

Her eyes sparkled as she ran her tongue over her swollen mouth. Pulling away, she tucked her hair behind her ears and then stepped aside. "You should get that."

I debated on going for another kiss and calling Izzy when I was done, or getting it now and watching her leave me with sullenness she didn't need.

But I knew if I kissed her again, there would be no stopping. It would have gone further, and I would have taken her inside, going for another round. It would happen because I could never get enough of this amazing woman.

"Shit," I hissed, yanking out my cellphone. I answered, but my eyes never left Chloe's. I held up a finger, begging her not to leave just yet.

"Dad!" Izzy shouted.

"Yes, Isabelle. What is it?"

"Where the hell have you been?! I've been calling you for an hour straight!"

I glanced at Chloe who stood in the corner, her head down. I'm sure she was listening. "I was working, Izzy. What is it?"

"I got into an accident." It was then that I realized her voice was thick. She was crying.

I frowned, turning away from Chloe. "What?! What the hell happened? Are you okay?"

"Yeah I'm fine. I don't know. Some stupid SUV ran into the back of my car, and I lost control and ended up going over the curb. It's fucking raining here, and I couldn't see shit. God, my car is so fucked up! I need you to come here—call the insurance company or something!"

"Alright, alright. Calm down. Breathe." I inhaled and then exhaled deeply, turning in Chloe's direction again. She was no longer looking down. She was a step closer, concern written all over her face. "Let me call the insurance company, and I'll call you right back."

"Okay. Hurry, Dad." She hung up, and I dropped the phone, clutching it in hand.

"What happened?" Chloe asked.

"Izzy... she got into a car accident. She says she's fine, but the car is apparently fucked up."

Relief flooded her hazel eyes. "Was it her fault?" Her eyes were wider as she probed for more.

"No. She said an SUV ran into her." I hesitated. "She'll probably need me to go to Nois." Nois was where Izzy went to school.

"Oh. Okay." She held up her hands. "Okay," she breathed. "You should go handle everything. Just call me when you have it all situated. And if you have to go, well, just go. I understand."

I stepped forward with a nod. "Okay. But I promise to call you." I stroked her cheek. "Will you wait for me?"

Her smile was full, but I could still spot her guilt. Her silence was deafening, her mouth opening and then clamping shut as if he couldn't find the right words to say. "I feel like this is all my fault," she finally murmured.

I frowned. "No. If anything, it's mine. I'm the one that didn't have my phone around."

"Yeah, but I was totally distracting you." Her smile faltered.

I shook my head then kissed her cheek. "Don't blame yourself. Like you told me once before, it's life. Things happen that are out of our control."

Her eyes shot up. "Wow. I can't believe you remember that."

I flashed a smile. "I remember everything when it comes to you, Chloe."

After placing one last kiss on her lips for reassurance, I let her go, watching her cross the street and walk through her front door. On her way across, she looked back once, a faint trace of a smile present. I returned the same expression, waving once.

When she made it safely inside her home, I blew out a heavy breath, picking up my phone and calling the insurance company. My status with Chloe was puzzling, but when it came to my daughter, I had to see she was safe.

I felt terrible as hell for not answering sooner. I could have lost her too. Fortunately, a higher power had their eyes on her.

Not sure what the fuck I would have done if I'd lost my Izzy Bear too.

I wouldn't blame Chloe for a damn thing, but I would blame myself over and over again, going through the same struggle as once before, and that would jeopardize everything she and I ever stood for.

SIXTEEN

CHLOE

HIS GARAGE GATE was closed when I awoke, no cars or bikes in the driveway. He'd gone to Nois for Izzy. He called me right before leaving that morning.

"I'll be back as soon as everything is handled."

"Okay," I murmured, but I felt somewhat disappointed—not with him, but with myself. He was going to see Izzy. I could have tagged along, but I didn't quite trust myself with Theo around. I would have been self-conscious of every little thing, like if she noticed me staring or if she saw how he looked at me, or maybe even caught him standing too close. I missed the hell out of her, but I was going to have to wait to see her... alone. No hot daddy around to distract me.

Anything could have gone wrong, so I kept my distance. "Tell her that I'm glad she's okay. I mean I called her last night to check in, and she said she was fine and all, but I'm sure she'd love to hear it in person."

"I will." Theo was quiet for a moment. At first I thought he was thinking negatively— reconsidering all we'd done only hours ago on his boat. But that

thought quickly vanished as he sighed. "When I get back, it's you and me. I'm packing everything up. Think you can drop by and help?"

I laughed, crossing my legs on top of my comforter. "Duh. You know I will. Just make sure you keep the chair aside. I'm really taking it."

"Of course." I heard the smile in his voice. "Gonna miss you, Chloe." His voice was gentle, maybe the softest I'd ever heard it.

"I'll miss you too, Theo."

"Mmm," he groaned.

Giggling, I asked, "What?"

"I love it when you call me by my first name."

"Theodore," I said, rolling his name off my tongue. "Theodore Benjamin Black."

He chuckled. "You know way too much about me, Knight."

I smirked on my end. "Not my fault you're a blabbermouth around me."

"Take it as a good thing, babe. Not many get to know me like you do."

I paused. "You say that like you're a bad person."

He was silent for a moment, allowing my words to sink in. Finally, he said, "You'd be surprised. There's shit about me that only Janet and my mom know about. Shit that... I can't exactly take back. Sometimes I think my last name mocks me because of how dark my past was."

"What do you mean? What happened?"

"Long story, sweetheart." I heard his keys jingle. "But when I'm back, I'll be sure to fill you in. Pun intended."

I laughed out loud. "Whatever. I'll talk to you soon."

I heard a door shut on his end. He didn't respond, so I waited on the line, assuming he hadn't heard me. "Come to your window," he commanded lightly.

I stared ahead, listening to his car honk when unlocking. Gradually, I climbed off the bed, walking towards my window. I hesitated for a moment but quickly realized I had no reason to hold back. Pulling the curtain aside, I saw him standing right in the driveway, looking straight up at my window.

"There's my girl." He put on a beautiful smile, those light lines forming around his eyes. Those lines were the only things that gave his age away. Other than that, he was absolute perfection. With the phone glued to his ear, he lifted his left hand and waved, like he was just some regular, normal neighbor.

Blushing, I waved back, and then pressed my palm to the cool windowpane. "Get some rest, Little Knight."

"Have a safe drive, Mr. Black."

I saw him laugh silently, pulling his car door open. Then, I pulled the phone away from my ear, watching as he did the same, slipping into the driver's seat.

The car cranked, and he reversed his way out of the driveway, pulled onto the main road, and then drove away but not before looking up at me once more and winking.

I missed him already, and it'd only been four hours. I know, I sounded needy and desperate, but I seriously couldn't wait until he got back. I had many questions I wanted to ask him. I knew there was a darker side to Theo; I'd just never truly witnessed it. Other than watching him almost destroy Ol' Charlie with a hammer after Mrs. Black died, I'd never seen him spiral deeper. The desire to destroy something he loved seemed logical, considering he'd just lost the love of his life.

But I wondered about him—wondered what he could do and how he did it. I wondered if I could trust his darker side, a side that I'm sure not even Izzy had witnessed. If she had, she would have told me all about it.

I blew a breath, pushing out of bed and going towards my window for the second time that day. I looked at his home, and when it occurred to me that he would no longer be living there after two weeks, I had the urge to cry. I couldn't imagine not having him there. I couldn't picture another family in that home because, to me, that was the *Blacks'* home.

The first real, genuine people I met. A family that accepted me— took me in with welcoming arms and put a smile on my face every single day. They were my friends. My life wouldn't have been as much fun without them.

I hated change.

No matter how awful I felt or how heavy my heart would get when I thought of Izzy, I missed her like crazy. I felt awful about the wreck. It was my fault Theo didn't pick up the first few times. He was too busy trying to secure time with me, considering her phone call just another weekly conversation that could wait.

I called her immediately, and when I did, I spent almost an hour with her on the phone. Luckily, Theo had just left to handle some car business, which left her lounging in her dorm room on her twin-sized mattress. I remembered how her dorm looked: pink everywhere. Pink sheets, pink rugs, pink pillows, a pink lamp, even pink magnets to go on her mini fridge. Izzy loved pink just as much as I loved purple.

"But seriously. Are you okay, Iz? I got your pic of the car. That thing is totaled. You're lucky you made it out alive, girl."

"I'm fineeee. Trust me. Even though the accident was totally not my fault, they're trying to pin it on me. That guy hit *me*!"

"Yeah, but at least you made it out safely. That's all that matters."

"You sound like a parent," she laughed.

"Because I care?"

"Ehh." She made a *pfft* noise through the phone, as if she were exasperated. "So, I'm not sure about this whole summer relationship thing anymore. Dylan is starting to get clingy," Izzy said out of the blue.

"Why do you say that? Because he kisses you and actually cares unlike Marco did?"

She scoffed. "Oh my god, Chloe! Did you really just go there? The Marco card? What a bitch."

I laughed. "You know it's true. If a guy doesn't treat you like shit, you get bored. A terrible thing to want, Iz."

"Yeah, but even though Marco was a total dick, he made up for it... with his beautifully big dick." She busted out in a laugh, and someone in the background shouted something. "Oh, bite me, Jessie," Izzy spat.

"Holy shit! Jessie the Prude is still your roommate?" I was rolling with laughter now. Jessie went to Bradshaw with us. The biggest geek of all. There was nothing wrong with being a geek, but when you're a geek that snitches and lies... well... it's simple. You get shunned.

"Yes! And she's so fucking annoying!"

"Right here!" Jessie shouted in the background.

"Duh, Prude, I see you." Izzy snickered.

I shook my head. "You are so mean to her."

"Well, maybe she should find another roommate. She's lucky I agreed. She's still a liar. I don't know why I still put up with her. Why are you even here? Why aren't you home for the summer with your family or something?!" All of her questions to Jessie were rhetorical, and I was dying on my end, as in laughing my ass off. Izzy groaned. "Let me stop before she snitches on me. Anyway, back to Dylan... I don't know. He's always calling and texting, and when he's around I have, like, no space to fucking breathe. Yesterday morning, I asked him to buy me a donut and an iced latte from Dunkin Donuts, and he bought me a whole dozen. I was grateful, I really was, but then he spent the whole day in my dorm after I specifically told him it was my *girl* time and I wasn't up for cuddling. God, Chlo, you know how I get around this time of the month. Bitchin' it out to the max."

"Yeah," I snuffed, "I know. Trust me."

She sighed. "He just doesn't get me."

"Sooo why are you still with him? Why waste your time? His time?"

"Shit, I may get annoyed, but he has something to make me forget his clinginess! That magical mouth of his—now he can munch on pussy like it's dinner." This time, my laugh felt like it could shake the walls. Izzy joined in on the laugh as I clutched my sides and then swiped joyful tears from the corners of my eyes. "He does this thing—this circle motion with his tongue. Oh my gosh, Chloe. How could any woman ever get rid of that? An expert pussy eater." She continued her sniggling. "I love it, I swear. Maybe I'll get over him being so clingy if you get a boyfriend too. That way, we can both bitch and complain. Then we can do double dates and someone can distract him with sports talk or something when we go out. Yeah, totally do that, Chlo. Find a guy before I finish summer school so we can set up a date!"

"Yeah, I don't think I'm gonna force a relationship just so your clingy boo can be distracted."

"Boooooo," Izzy droned. "Fine. Your loss. How has summer been, though? Besides Papa Knight, is everything else good? Is Bristle Wave still a fucking bore?"

"Bristle is still quite boring, but I can't complain about the scenery. Dad seems to be doing better—oh, and I didn't even tell you that Mariah and Tiny came here last week!"

"What!?" she exclaimed.

"Yep. We went for dinner and ice cream first. We were supposed to be on a boat, but Mariah's dad never rented it out. But later that night we went to Brix, and guess who was there?"

"Who?" she indulged. I knew she was glued to the phone.

"Fucking Riley Hunt... again! He saw me, but I had to pretend Tiny was my date for the night just so he wouldn't bother me. But the dickwad just turned to Mariah like I wasn't even there. I swear, boys are just stupid. Tiny got so pissed and was about to pick a fight, but I spared Riley by dragging Tiny's lanky ass out of there and dragging them to Dane's."

"Oh my God! Are you serious?"

"Yes. Tiny was so mad the whole ride. They were wasted, Izzy."

"Ugh! See! I should be there. I'm so jealous."

"Please don't be," I said. "Trust me, you aren't missing much. Mariah and Tiny coming here was probably the most fun I've had so far." *And Theo*, the voice in the back of my mind whispered.

Izzy groaned. "Well, keep being bored until I can come home. Hopefully I can get a chance over the weekend. If I could leave now, I would, but some of my classes are on stupid campus."

"I know. I understand. I'm fine, Iz. You just worry about school. Bristle will always be here."

"I know. It's just so fucking boring on campus when no one is here. I have no choice but to focus." She laughed and then sighed as if all her stress had faded. "Man, I needed this talk. I swear you are my cure for a shitty, shitty day."

"Aww," I cooed, teasing her. "Don't be so melodramatic."

"Dude, I'm not. I'm serious. Other than my dad, you are the only person I can really trust and talk to about anything. You know me. I hate people sometimes, but I have never come close to hating you."

My smile dropped, as well as my beating heart. She said this, but little did she know that we both were breaking that trust day by day. I wanted to cry, get rid of the ball of pain building up around my heart. God, I just wanted to tell her, but I didn't want her to hate me. I didn't want her to change—us to change. I didn't want to lose my best friend. I refused.

Fuck, I was selfish. So very selfish.

"I love you, Chlo. Fa'sho."

I laughed, but the line of my eyes burned, thick with unshed tears. "That is still the corniest line I've ever heard."

Her giggle was comforting. "Whatever! I still think it's cool. And it fits. Now say it back before you break my heart!"

With a steady voice, a gentle smile, and a tear I knew she couldn't see trailing down my cheek, I finished our little rhyme, ignoring the thickness in my throat. "I love you too, Izzy Boo."

"See!" she busted out in a laugh just as I did, swiping my face. "Now, that's corny."

God, I loved these chats with her. The mindless, careless conversations I could share with her about any and everything. I missed the hell out of my friend, and it was still hard to wrap my head around the fact that I was holding one of the biggest secrets of my life from her.

After saying goodbye, I hung up. My head lifted, and I looked towards the collage of us pinned to my bulletin board. The photo of us on prom night was my favorite. We were flawless, and we didn't need dates because we were our own dates.

All the girls at Bradshaw envied us, our friendship most of all. They treated us like Regina and Caydee from *Mean Girls*, only we weren't mean and our friendship wasn't fake... and we didn't only wear pink on Wednesdays, especially Izzy. Everyone adored and hated us at the same time. They wanted to be us, which was weird because we sometimes didn't like being us.

Like now. I wished I wasn't myself. I wished I hadn't become so close to Izzy's father. I wished he was someone else—someone I could actually be with without the fear of losing someone else close and dear to my heart.

Downstairs, Margie and Dad were sitting on the living room sofa, watching a movie about vampires. I stepped around the corner, blinking as Dad actually sat there and watched the flick, eyes intense as he ran his hands over his peppery hair.

I entered the living room, snickering while folding my arms, and they both looked my way. "You guys are really watching this?"

Margie gave a helpless shrug, and Dad nodded. "I've always wondered what you liked so much about it." He scratched his head. "Gotta tell you, baby girl. I still don't get it. The whole glittery thing, the heavy breathing, and the damn werewolves... I am so lost."

I laughed. "It's a girl thing. You have to read the book to understand."

"Ehh. Seems like soft vampire porn to me. I'll pass." Apparently, this was one of his good days. Weird, it seemed on and off now, switching sporadically.

Margie shook her head with a laugh, and then she stood from the sofa. I turned for the kitchen, and only seconds later, she appeared. "Um... Chloe?"

I spun around, meeting her warm grey eyes. "Yes?"

Tucking a piece of hair behind her ear, Margie came my way, brows puckered. Immediately, I noticed the look of worry on her face, the questions running rampant in her eyes. "The man across the street— the one you're interested in— how long have you known him again?"

"About ten years now."

"Ten. Wow." Her eyes expanded. "Was he married once before?"

"Yes." I crossed my arms, stepping towards her. "Why do you ask?"

"Just curious." She put on a smile. "I see why you fell for him. That's a handsome man."

I chewed on a smile, uncrossing my arms and going for the fridge. After pulling out a cup of strawberry yogurt, I turned for the table in front of the bay window and sat. "He is pretty good looking."

"Yeah," she sighed. Margie's fingers twisted in front of her. There was something wrong. She seemed nervous, like something was bothering her. Before I opened my yogurt, I dropped the cup and narrowed my brows in her direction. "Margie? What is it? What's wrong?"

She looked towards me, stepping forward. She was hesitant at first. "My son is..." She started but quickly waved a hand, dismissing the idea. "Never mind."

When she began to turn, I called for her, hopping out of my chair.

Glancing back, she looked from the countertops she'd wiped spotless to me. "Margie, you can talk to me," I assured her.

She inhaled, releasing a puff of breath as her shoulders visibly relaxed. "Okay... well, it's just my son. He wants to spend some time in Bristle with me. He said he'd get a hotel, but I would hate for him to go through the trouble. I know you aren't used to strangers and I would hate for you or even Mr. Knight to think I'm trying to take advantage of my stay here, but—"

I stepped forward, holding my hand up. Her words stopped flowing in an instant, eyes glossy. Damn, I don't know what it was about Margie, but this woman had deep-rooted issues. It seemed she was afraid of asking for things, like someone had punished her before for asking for anything at all. I was truly sympathetic for the humble woman, but I needed her to know that everything was fine. "Margie," I murmured. "It's okay. He can stay here. We have another guest room and he's more than welcome to use it. I don't mind at all."

"Oh, God." She cupped her mouth. I was about to consider her dramatic, until she continued. "Oh my goodness, Chloe, thank you! Last night was my first time seeing him in three years. I truly, honestly, need this."

Oh. I felt bad for my previous thought. Three years?! Wow.

I dropped my hands, watching as two stray tears fell down her cheeks. I went back for the roll of paper towels, ripping one off and handing it to her. She accepted it, wiping her face clean. "Three freaking years?! Margie! Why has it been so long?"

She shrugged. "He has been very busy with his life. He's an orchestrator for a high school in Arizona. He hardly ever comes home because he's so swamped. And me... well, I happen to move a lot too. By the time he can actually come visit me, I'm booked for another caregiving job or working late hours as a nurse. We still keep in touch —he calls every day—but it has been hard not seeing my only child. Mi *hijo.*" My son.

"Was he raised here?"

"We lived in L.A." she smiled. "I was born in Mexico but raised here in the U.S."

"Oh. How neat. It's insane for him not to see you for three years, though. As a teacher, there's really not that many excuses."

"He has his reasons. He wanted to stay away from California to grow as a person—escape certain... things. He called me last week, told me his band had entered the finals and was traveling to Bristle Wave High for a performance. He took that as a sign of God telling him he was ready to come back this way."

"That's great!" I beamed. "So when will he be here?"

"Tomorrow morning, if that is okay." She looked at me for reassurance, grey eyes bright. I nodded. Her happiness was contagious. How her son could abandon his sweet mother, I did not know. If my mom were anything like Margie, I would have come home more often.

"I was thinking of making a big breakfast, and I promise you I will still be giving Mr. Knight the best care. He will never leave my sight. Let's just hope that he cooperates with Sterling around. He isn't very fond of people he doesn't know."

I scoffed. "Yeah, he's always been that way. He doesn't like to get to know people unless he has to, but I'm sure Dad will be fine. He'll live. Breakfast sounds great! I'll be sure to come down for it and meet your son. He sounds like a nice guy."

"He is a great man. He's accomplished so much when I didn't think he would. He's made me one proud mama!"

"I bet."

"Margie, the remote please!" Dad called from the living room.

Margie glanced over her shoulder and then looked at me. Laughing, she said, "Let me go get that. Thank you again, lovely. I swear, you are the sweetest girl." She patted my arm and then turned around, hurrying out of the kitchen.

I went back to the table for my yogurt. Unlike Dad, I loved to meet new people. Margie was a great person, and I was sure her son would be too, so there would be no worries about leaving them home alone.

After going for a run, coming back home to shower, and eating lunch, I took a nap but wasn't quite sure when I'd fallen asleep. By the time I awoke, it was dark outside, nothing but the streetlights glowing outside my window.

I scrambled out of bed, going for my cellphone on the desk. I snatched it up, seeing two missed calls from Theo and one from Izzy. A text accompanied Izzy's call.

Izzy: *My dad is acting weird. He seems... happier....*

I blinked at her message. No smiley face. No big, fat LOL. No second text message, harassing me about what I was doing or why I wasn't replying (which was normally the case.)

Was she onto us? Onto *me*? He seemed happier how? Since when? So many questions ran through my mind. I felt my heart racing, palms becoming clammy.

I disregarded her message, plugging the thought in the back of my head to make sure I returned her text. I went to my call log and saw *Mr. Black(2)*. Two missed calls.

Walking towards my window, I saw that his driveway was empty, his home dark. Only the porch light illuminated. Picking my phone back up, I pressed the call button, and the phone rang twice before he responded. "Hello?" His voice was heavy, the way he sounded when he'd had a few drinks.

"Theo? Are you back?"

"Got back about two hours ago. What happened earlier? Called you twice. Wanted to see if you wanted to catch drinks with me somewhere?"

"I was asleep," I informed him. "I don't know when I fell asleep, but I was clearly exhausted." I looked towards my alarm clock. *10:18 P.M.*

"Where are you drinking at?"

"Rykes."

I frowned. "Ew. Rykes."

He laughed. "Come meet me."

"Rykes isn't really my scene." And it really wasn't. The place was full of bikers, their "old ladies", and random men that loved picking a fight. None of them had respect for outsiders. So imagine someone like *me*, walking right into a place like *that,* and then sitting with an *older* man that was clearly into me. The thought of it made my skin crawl.

"Shit, you're right. I'd hate to beat a motherfucker's ass for touching or looking at you the wrong way." He paused, and I don't know what it was about his voice—perhaps it was the protectiveness, or maybe the possessiveness—but it made my insides swirl. Warmth hit me like a soft wave, drifting throughout each part of me, making me weak.

"So where should we meet?" I asked. My voice faltered. It was feeble. He caught the flattery in my response, laughing.

"Wanna check out my new place?"

"You already have a key?"

"I'm not supposed to officially go in and check things out until next week, but I know the landlord. He trusts me. Gave me a key as soon as I signed the lease."

A smile touched my lips. "Sure. I can meet you there."

"Okay, Little Knight. I'll text you the address. See you in twenty?"

"Twenty it is."

I arrived at a complex called Remy Place.

Theo was already waiting for me at the front door, and as I pulled up and parked, he dangled a bottle of vodka in front of him, leaning against the wall. I shook my head and laughed, shutting my car off.

"Saved you a drink... or ten," he said, grinning. Oh, Lord. He was going to get a kick out of bringing alcohol around me now. I was sure he remembered me downing that cognac and then riding him like I had no care in the world.

Stepping out the car, I walked towards him, and he opened his arms. I sauntered right into his welcoming embrace, and he sighed, groaning as he held me tight. "Missed you, Knight."

I smiled against his chest, wrapping my arms around his neck and curling my fingers into the edges of his hair. When he slanted his head back, I kissed him first, like the desperate girl I always became when it came to him. He wasn't even gone a full day, but it felt like an eternity.

"I see you missed me too," he chuckled behind the kiss.

"I did," I mumbled. "So much." His smile disappeared when he looked down at me, pressing those smooth lips on mine again. The kiss was fervent, heated, and delightful. I sank deeper into his hard, masculine body, absorbing the taste of scotch on his tongue, attaching myself to his entire front half.

"Damn, baby," he breathed when our kiss finally broke. "I feel it."

"Feel what?" I asked, my voice just as breathy as his.

"How much you've missed me." His hand snaked down my waist and landed on my ass, spanking and then squeezing. Cocking a smooth brow, he asked, "You feel it?"

"Yeah," I giggled. "I feel it."

With a boyish grin, Theo released me but reached for my hand, turning for the door. We walked inside, the cool draft of the AC brushing my bare shoulders. He led the way to the elevator and once we were inside, he pressed the quarter-sized button with the number four on it.

We were in the elevator alone. I felt him looking at me. I turned his way, asking, "Why are you watching me?"

He moved closer, a gentle kiss landing in my curly hair. "Just missed you, babe. That's all."

"Yeah?" My arms went over his broad shoulders again, fingers connecting as I latched them around him. "How much?"

His upper lip twitched. "Probably a little too much if we're being honest."

"Hmm. That's a good thing, right?" The question was rhetorical. I didn't expect him to answer because in our case, no, it wasn't a good thing.

My mouth met his, drawing out another deep groan. His body juddered, chest tensing beneath mine. I loved the uncontrollable vibe I gave him, the satisfied feeling I developed when his body was near mine.

Before I knew it, the elevator chimed, and the doors slid open. I pulled away, but my eyes were still connected with his. He held my gaze, clinging to my hand, his grip soft. Then, he led the way out, walking down the hallway and going past three doors before reaching door 404.

Theo unlocked the door, and as soon as we were inside, he flipped a switch. A light flashed in the corner, lighting small parts of the vacant living room. I walked past Theo as he shut the door behind us, my gaze traveling from the living room to the kitchen. There was a fridge and stove already set up, the chrome matching well with the black marble on the counters.

I studied his place in awe, moving ahead. I checked out each bedroom. There were two, both equally spacious, especially the master. The bathroom was amazing—full of chrome, black marble, and white accent pieces. I wanted to make use of the glass shower in the corner, steam it up with both sweat and hot water streaming between our greedy bodies.

I stepped back out, meeting a quiet Theo in the living room. He studied me but didn't say much. He stood near the wall, head in a slight tilt.

I turned a fraction, stepping forward. There was an open, rectangular window straight across from me, and from this spot, I had full view of the ocean. I blinked slowly, completely mesmerized.

"Like it?" Theo's voice was deep and soft, a warm tremble, as he stepped behind me, arms going around my middle.

"Theo, this place is incredible."

He hugged me against his body, warm breath drifting down my chest. Snuggling his nose into the crook of my neck, he murmured, "I thought I was going to have to spend this night without you." A sliver of fire shot through me, burning the most sensitive parts of me.

I turned in his arms. "Does that explain you being at Rykes?"

He looked down, watching my eyes. My face. "I needed a cheap drink... and some entertainment. A fight breaks out at that place every night. There's always some beef."

I wanted to roll my eyes. *Men.* "Why didn't you go to Dane's?"

His lips pressed. "Trixie works on Friday nights."

My smile collapsed, my entire demeanor changing. "Oh."

I started to pull away, but he caught me, reeling me back in. "I avoided Dane's for you, Chloe."

"I appreciate that, but..." I chewed on my bottom lip. I hated when he mentioned her. I hated it even more that she still ran through his mind every so often. "I don't know." I shrugged, waving a hand and realizing I was overreacting. I couldn't overreact. I couldn't send him running away. I made a promise not to get too serious. I had to keep it. "Never mind. It's whatever."

He tipped my chin when I dropped my head, those warm brown eyes fixing on mine. "You don't like when I mention her." This was a statement, not a question. He already knew the answer. Cradling my face in his hands, Theo pulled me close to him, so close I could feel his chest rising and sinking, the bulge in his pants that so badly wanted to be set free. "Tell me, baby," he whispered, walking forward as I moved backwards. "What name is it that you want to hear from my mouth?"

"Mine," I whispered. Then my back hit the wall, the bump light.

"Yours." He dropped his head, planting sweet caresses on the crook of my neck. "Alright, Chloe." His voice changed, his actions instantaneous. He lifted up my dress, sliding my panties aside. His fingers plunged, one and then two. It caught me completely off guard.

My next breath was sharp, the back of my head landing on the wall as he picked up one of my legs and hooked it around his narrow waist. I kept still, and he picked me up, moving to the bar counter in front of the kitchen.

"Chloe, baby," he murmured in my ear. "Chloe. *Fuck, Chloe.*" He said my name like he wanted to marry it, running the syllables off his tongue, finger-fucking me until my back curved.

My ass landed on the cool countertop, and in only seconds, his fingers were gone. My panties were next to go missing, dropping to the floor, and without hesitation, his tongue replaced those magical fingers.

It dipped inside, and I moaned loudly, clutching handfuls of his T-shirt. "Chloe," he groaned, his growl deep. "My sexy Little Knight. You know you're all I want."

I panted, listening to his voice vibrate between my quaking thighs, bringing me straight to the edge. I willingly thrust around his tongue until he brought it up, sealing those beautiful pink lips around my swelling clit. He sucked, tugging light enough for me to feel, and then released, sliding a finger into my damp, eager pussy.

"Don't cum yet, baby," he said, just as I was about to reach the stars. He pulled away, running thick fingers from my entrance to my clit and pressing down. He watched me writhe, smirking as if he were pleased with how well I responded to his touch. Picking me up off the counter, Theo slid his jeans down to his ankles, his entire cock exposed. The tip glistened, the taste of him still familiar to me.

His scent was strong. Musky and manly. Every bit of a real man. Every inch of what I craved. Theo still had me in his arms, my legs bound around him, and I eased around his cock, sliding down until he was all in.

He stilled, letting out a heavy sigh, one that blew past my ear and down my spine. "The sweetest pussy." His words came out in a rumble as he lifted me up and down. Our foreheads met, and soon, my back hit the wall. I wrapped my arms over his shoulders, lifting up and down with him as much as possible, soaking up every inch of him.

Bouncing.

Gripping.

All with light spanks to my ass and quiet yelps filling the air.

Lips touched, tongues colliding. He accepted my moans through parted lips, telling me to be louder. Begging me to call his name.

"Oh, Theo," I breathed, feeling his solid body going stiff. "Yes. *Fuck* yes."

He grunted, mouth falling on my skin, moving from the crook of my neck to my cheek and then to my lips. He devoured them like he owned them, like he'd kissed them plenty of times and knew exactly what they longed for. "The only name I wanna hear you say when you're like this is mine." He trapped my face in his hands. "You hear me?"

"Yes." The response came out rapid and shrill as he pressed his palms on either side of my head, creating a bumping noise against the wall with his knees.

"No one will be able to make you feel like how I make you feel, Chloe. I know your body—everything you like. I know this pussy, and exactly what makes her tick. I know because you always get *so fucking wet* for me, wringing me out 'til I'm fucking dry." His nose skimmed my cheek. "Sweet pussy... always so fucking *tight* for me. And always. So. Fucking. Good."

Theo's voice strained with the last set of words. His brown irises shimmered, face harder than stone. He sank deeper and deeper, like he couldn't get deep enough, and I clenched around his long, thick member, clamping and shuddering, sighing loudly just as he did.

His lips divided, and I took the opportunity to kiss his partially open mouth, his body quaking until he was empty. He groaned, and his head rolled once before his forehead hit my shoulder, his body sagging as it pinned me to the wall.

"Never get enough," I heard him say beneath his breath right before he lifted his head and kissed me whole, cradling the frame of my face in his hands. His thumbs stroked the edges of my hair, cock still pulsing deep inside. His beard lightly grazed the outside of my mouth, and a soft whimper escaped me when his head fell again and he straightened. I felt so good—always so good with him.

Finally, he pulled out, placing me on my feet but giving me a swift kiss on my forehead before pulling his pants up and going for the bottle of vodka on the counter. "I'm thinking maybe I should save this for move-in day." He gripped the bottle.

I smiled, adjusting my dress. "Yeah, I think that might be better."

I caught the satisfaction on his face before he could turn. I started his way when I was fully situated, but when I was at his side, my stomach growled, and he heard it. My eyes went wide, embarrassment flaming my cheeks as he asked, "Damn, babe? You hungry?"

I nodded, realizing I hadn't eaten since waking up. I came straight to Theo, not even bothering to at least grab a snack to satisfy the hunger pang I knew I'd feel later. "Just a tad."

He pulled me in. "Well, I'm gonna have to take care of that too, huh?"

I looked up at him. "How so, Mr. Black?"

He twisted me around in his arms, pressing his chest to mine. With his fingers holding my chin, making sure my eyes were focused only on his, he said, "You forget I cook now. Come on. Gotta take care of my knight in shining armor, right?"

"Um... isn't it supposed to be the other way around?" I tease as he started a slow waltz with me on the open floor, our hands clasped together, eyes lax and glued.

"Maybe so, but I consider you mine."

A bolt of electricity struck me as he stopped dancing and lifted my right arm in the air to make my body go into a little twirl. He caught me in his arms after the spin, and I grinned like a fat kid with cake.

"Still have those moves, I see."

"They'll never die." He smirked, and when he released me I picked up my keys and followed him out the door, leaving his condo in Remy Place for his home in Primrose.

SEVENTEEN

THEO

SHE WASN'T A PICKY GIRL—ANOTHER thing I loved about her. Janet was the pickiest woman I'd ever known. But Chloe, she vowed to eat whatever I cooked, telling me to surprise her.

Odd, they were complete opposites. Janet could be so uptight I felt it whenever I slapped her ass, but Chloe was so laid back and relaxed. It seemed nearly impossible to make her angry.

I decided to go with what I had planned for myself the next evening—grilled pork chops smothered in mushrooms and creamy mushroom sauce sided with broccoli and brown rice. A lot of protein. She'd be full all night.

I watched as she took her first bite, how her lips slipped off the edges of the fork once the food had consumed her mouth. And she hummed, like it was the tastiest thing she'd ever eaten. She moaned like I was fucking her again. I'm sure my cock would have twitched, but I was way too concerned with her opinion.

"So? Good?" I asked as she cut another slice of pork chop and stuffed it into her mouth.

"Good. Theo—" her head shook a *this-is-a-damn-shame* kind of headshake—"this is freaking amazing." She moaned again, but this time, her eyes shut as she absorbed each flavor, most likely the garlic I put in to accompany the onion.

Pleased, I sat next to her, grinning. "I'm glad you like it."

"Here," she said, handing me the extra fork beside her. "Eat some, please. I won't be able to finish it all."

I shook my head. "It's all for you. Eat. Enjoy it."

Her lips twisted, and she put the fork down. After cutting a slice of the pork and smothering it in the sauce, she brought the utensil up to my mouth. "Fine. Then I'll feed you."

My upper lip curled up. "Chloe—"

"Nah-uh." She shook her head. "Here." Her little devious smile was cute, possibly on the borderline of sexy.

I shook with laughter, playing along. "Alright." Then, I dropped my chin, allowing her to feed me. She grinned like Isabelle used to when I would finally join her in her tea parties with stuffed pink animals, dry crackers, and of course, no tea.

I chewed the food, pleased with the flavors. "Damn. I did good."

She laughed, withdrawing the fork. "You seriously did. This is amazing. Really. You'll have to make it again sometime."

"Just for you, I will."

I allowed her to finish eating while I cleaned up, and once she was done, I walked her way, just as she sipped from her glass of water. "I'm pretty sure if I still lived in Primrose, I'd be as fat as a pig."

I busted out laughing, helping her come to a stand.

"Fat or small, baby, you'd still be beautiful."

"Yeah right." She bashfully lowered her gaze.

"No, seriously. You would. And don't let anyone ever tell you otherwise. You're a gorgeous girl with a big heart, Chloe. It... pains me to even think about someone else sweeping you off your feet."

Her head lifted without my aid, and her eyes bore into mine, on the borderline of tears. I swept my thumb across her nimble chin, half-smiling. "Don't talk like that." Her voice was faint. "I..." Her voice broke.

"Chloe," I murmured. "We can't deny the truth. It'll fuck us up if we do. I can't be the one to ruin your life. I want you happy, whether that's with or without me."

I watched her swallow hard, a habit she did when she was upset, nervous, or bothered by something. "You're right," she finally said. Then she met my eyes, switching the subject. "Do you think I can stay here tonight?"

"I don't see why not."

She was happy with my response, sinking into my arms. I held my knight snug in my arms. I didn't know how the hell I was going to let this go—end this once it was time for her to leave. The thought of it killed me.

It'd only been a few days, but I'd never had so much fun—never felt this much since Janet. Not even Trixie could provide this amount of comfort, a feeling of overwhelming bliss. This was close to how it was with Janet, just as wonderful. Yes, there were ups and downs, but those could be easily overlooked with her presence.

I was glad she wanted to stay. I led her upstairs, somehow entering my bedroom with her in my arms. I placed her down on the edge of the bed and pulled her dress over her head as she tugged on my belt buckle. Once my pants were gone, I leaned forward as she went back, my hands outside her head, face only inches away from hers.

I heard her breath hitch when she felt my hardened cock between her legs. Then I remembered... this was where I first took her. Right on this bed. Right above her. But unlike that first time, I was actually paying attention now. I wanted to know what she was thinking and how she felt. I wanted to make this time feel like her first all over again.

So I took my time, trailing soft caresses down her body with my lips, the smooth valleys of her skin running by mine. I continued down, meeting at her yellow panties. They were simple, not lacey, stringy, or extravagant. Just simple. Sometimes simplicity worked best, and right now, it was certainly working. It worked for me because it gave me the satisfaction that she wouldn't expect what was coming. She expected plain vanilla, but I was about to add a scoop of every flavor that ever existed along with a whopping helping of decadent, rich fudge and a cherry to top it off.

Lifting her hips, I tugged her panties down, pulling them from around her ankles once they'd made it down. I moved back up, and she gasped as I kissed between her thighs, back arching for more. I'd already tasted her less than two hours ago, but I was a giving person. She wanted more? She had it.

My tongue started at her clit this time, circling and suckling with small nips. "Ah, Theo," she breathed, and in the same moment, her back curved again.

"Hold still for me baby." I pressed my palm to her pubic bone, laying her flat again. "Let me taste you. I love eating this pussy." She shuddered beneath the warm breath skimming through her glistening, pink slit. "I want to see those eyes. Look at me. Watch me."

Her head lifted, and she glanced down. When she made eye contact with me, I claimed her pussy with my mouth, licking through and through, tongue gliding in and out, running up to the mount with need. She tasted divine. So fucking amazing.

Her mouth fell open, and the room filled with innocent cries of pleasure. Sounds that drove me fucking crazy. I wanted to feel her. So badly.

Drawing away, I pulled upward, hovering above her again. The look in her eyes was desperate, full of a want that may never be satisfied. I eased down after taking my boxers away, nervous about how to go about her. I'd fucked her roughly so many times before.... *shit*, this was crazy. I felt like it was *my* first time again, too. I'd never taken anyone's virginity before Chloe. Janet wasn't even a virgin when I met her.

The tip of my cock met at her wet entrance. Her body relaxed beneath me, corresponding with the thickness. "You didn't tell me you were a virgin when we first made this happen, Chloe," I murmured, lips skimming the shell of her ear. She trembled, goose bumps crawling along her skin. "So tonight, I'm taking you like it's the first time again." My cock inched in with the last word. "Gently. Carefully. Exactly how it should have been."

The pleasure was clear on her face. She loved when I talked to her. Perhaps there was something about my voice that heated her up enough to milk my cock. My voice alone drove her mad.

I inched in with gradual force, our eyes fastened, and she cupped my face, allowing our lips to meet to fulfill the sweet ache. She wanted me to go deeper, but I held back. Fingernails bit into my shoulders, silently begging me to follow through.

And I did.

Finally.

As soon as my pipe filled her in, she moaned my name, as if she'd been waiting all this time to say it. I caught her indulgence, crushing her lips with ravenous force. I thrust just a little harder, but my strokes were still slow and even. I wanted her to feel it—all of me, like it should have been that very first night.

Her nails went deeper in my skin, our lips still twisted together. We were hungry for each other. Greedy. Our bodies grinded, in sync. I thrust just a little harder, trying my damn best not to still or go rigid. I was on the verge of coming, her wet pussy devouring and juicing my cock, tightening at all the right moments.

"Fuck," I breathed. I was so close. So close. But I grew even closer when she brought those supple, pink lips up and swirled her tongue around my pierced nipple. Her tongue flicked the metal, and she sucked just enough to make it taut. "Shit, baby," I groaned.

She responded to my voice, back bowed, slipping right off the edge with me. And when she came, wailing, "Oh, God, yes!" I came with her, going completely empty in that tight, sweet, fucking pussy. A loud, deep groan volleyed on the walls, the loudest I'd ever heard myself get.

Fuck, she was so tight. And so *motherfucking good*.

I collapsed but made sure not to crush her while breathing deep, panting with my mouth on the crook of her neck. She sighed, her entire body going lax beneath me.

"I have something to tell you." She stroked the edges of my hair.

"What?" I asked.

"You're my best," she whispered in my ear. I heard the smile in her voice.

I pushed up on one elbow. "Your best?"

"Yep."

"See, it's words like that I love hearing from you." Her giggle was shrill as I kissed the base of her neck. I pulled out and helped her up, figuring she was in just as much need of a shower as I was.

So we showered together. I used the bar soap, helping her with her wash, running it between her full, perky breasts to the pussy she allowed me to own over and over again. She loved my hands on her and hated when my touch left her.

I still couldn't believe she wanted me so much. Me, a man that was twice her age. A man that she wasn't even supposed to touch her. She knew the consequence behind this affair, the hurt she'd feel once she was around Izzy again.

I was serious about her having a good heart, and I couldn't understand how she continued to sleep with me, treating me like a king. I was *Chloe's* king— an unruly one but still one she respected and cared for. But I was also unjust and extremely unfair to my beloved daughter.

So much wrong.

So much right.

So much light and darkness, a mixture of both.

There was so much about the way she looked at me, how she didn't look up to me or fear me. She accepted me entirely, as she did herself. A girl full of so much love and passion. A girl that shouldn't have been lying in my bed.

She fell asleep on my chest, breathing evenly, and I watched her. The purity was what killed me. She may not have thought she was innocent, but to me, she was. I was the one that started this, coming onto her when I was too drunk to care. I lead her on, but we both took this to deeper, darker places.

We ventured into the same blackness I couldn't seem to escape, sinking further and further into the sea. But being under this sea was different. We could breathe, so it was okay. We could feel and touch and move. Nothing held us back, and nothing saw us.

Just like the ocean, our black sea was full of wonders—full of uniqueness and secrecy. It was our place, this vast ocean we lived in. It was for us, and the only way it could have been ruined was if something intruded, messing up the fluidity and transforming it into a menacing typhoon.

Unfortunately, the ocean can also be disturbed and interrupted. Peace doesn't always linger. Happiness doesn't always stick. Freedom doesn't always ring.

Our ocean of black, our tainted mess, would be demolished by the end of summer and *nothing* would be able to repair it.

It'd been so long since I had anyone sleeping with me in my bed. Three and a half years to be exact. Not even Trixie stayed the night. I always made her go. Our rules.

It felt good waking up next to Chloe, but what was even greater was waking to her soft, familiar hand running across the tip of my cock.

I stirred out of my sleep, but she shushed me, placing her other hand on my chest and gently forcing me to lie back down. I eased back, eyes trained on her before I looked down and calmed myself. Yes, it had been a while since something like this happened so early.

Her hand moved under the comforter, lifting up and down, stroking slow and smooth. My groan was hoarse as she put small pecks on my chest with her petal-like lips. Each kiss further aroused me. My morning wood needed to be satisfied.

I could never control myself in the mornings. There was just something about them, perhaps the crisp feeling of the sunlight or knowing it was a new day. Or maybe my few hours of sleep recharged me, building me up for another release to happen soon.

"Damn," I groaned. "Yeah, keep doing that, baby." She dropped the sheet, her head went down, and her lips wrapped around my tip. She did what I did not expect. I thought I could hold it a little longer, but that simple act alone was enough to make me explode.

I splurged into her mouth, shooting down her throat, and she swallowed every last drop, eyes on me, not daring to pull those hazel irises away. I jolted even more, pressing my palm to the back of her head and making the moist walls of her mouth mold around my length. "Fuck."

She moaned around my cock, bringing her mouth up, swirling her tongue swiftly around my tip and across the slit between and then pulling away, causing my hips to buckle. Pulling up, she grinned and then rested her head on my chest. "I've always wanted to do that," she confessed.

"Shit, thanks for giving me the first shot at it," I laughed, planting a kiss on her forehead. Leaning on my elbow, I turned to face her, admiring her physique. She looked good in my T-shirt, her slender legs toned in all the right places, skin smooth. Her nipples were what I expected, erect, prodding through the white cotton.

I ran the back of my hand across her cheek, and she caught it, holding on. "I've always wanted to ask..." She paused for a moment, lips twisted. "How often do you think of Mrs. Black?"

Her question caught me off guard. I felt my heart come to a slight skid. It wasn't as intense as it used to be. Before, my heart would slam to a standstill from the mere thought of Janet. The wound was deep, but with time, it became easier to accept—easier to control the emotion that used to wreak havoc. "Every day," I responded.

"You miss her a lot, don't you?"

I huffed. "Severely."

Chloe's brows creased for a single moment, then her face softened. "We... never would have happened if she was still here, huh?"

I blinked. I wasn't quite sure how to respond to that question. Yeah, if Janet were still around, I would have kept my boundaries, maintained distance, and considered Chloe one of Izzy's hottest friends. I wouldn't have touched her—hell, I never would have gotten so fucking crazy if it weren't for the murder of my wife.

Instead of giving a direct answer, I said, "Wanna know how fucked up my life was before? Why I sometimes think I'm the one that should have died that day?" Her eyelashes batted at me, and she adjusted herself, pulling her hand away. Her eyes were full of questions. I answered them.

"When I was eleven, I lost my dad. Seems like a corny job, but he was a firefighter, and I always admired him for it. Saving lives. Working day and night to provide for us. Risking his life on a day to day basis. I always wondered 'Why him?' when he passed, and I guess since I never came to terms with him dying. It was even harder dealing with Janet's death. My therapist says it was because I wasn't expecting to lose anyone else. I had finally found safety with her—security—but lost it within the blink of an eye. When I lost my dad, I became rebellious. My mom couldn't control me for the life of her." I laughed. "I regret putting her through so much hell—with being suspended from school for picking fights and even setting off firecrackers in the boys' bathroom just for the hell of it." My head shook. "Shit, for a while I thought I wouldn't live to see this age. I didn't want to live, and for some reason, when he died... nothing changed. Nothing got better. Everything became worse." Chloe's face was serious as I stopped talking for a brief moment.

"Life got so much harder for me and my mom. My mom worked way too much in order to support me, which left me at home alone. So... one day I met this guy named Horris at a bike convention, and he introduced me to this gang of bad-asses. All we did was cause trouble and fuck shit up for no reason. Some of them killed for fun. Tormented members of other gangs and robbed from innocent civilians." I swallowed thickly. "I hate that I'm even telling you, but... I almost killed someone."

She gasped. "Who?"

I focused on the silver sheets. "Janet's dad."

As if that were a twist, she gasped even louder. "What!? How?"

"Her dad is an uptight asshole. You probably saw him at her funeral, how he didn't say a single fucking word to me. Well, before I ever met Janet, I used to hang out at this bar in L.A. They played poker there every fucking night. Her dad happened to be there one night, knowing damn well he wasn't supposed to be gambling. At a young age, I'd learned how to play poker and was pretty damn good at it. Let's just say her dad tried to cheat and that left me with no choice but to beat his ass."

"You had a choice—what do you mean you had no choice?"

"My gang was there, demanding me to do something about it. And I'm no pussy. I wanted to show them that I could hold my own —that they didn't need to worry about me. Shit, the whole gang thought I was a pushover for a while, but that was only because I was quiet and new. But when they saw me beat her dad until he was black and blue... well, let's just say I was highly respected. Maybe not by her dad, but by the gang. *The Union.* That's what they called themselves." I laughed, remembering those dark and somewhat exciting days.

"Wow," Chloe whispered. Her eyes moved down to the jagged "U" on my shoulder.

"I got it as soon as the gang let me in," I said in reference to the tattoo. "I wanted to prove my loyalty to them. But that's not even the best part. Janet worked at the bar, doing dishes in the back, and when she saw her dad getting pummeled, she jumped right in, breaking it up and then cursing me the fuck out, threatening me with the nearest object. That object happened to be a broken glass bottle." I chuckled.

"No way! Damn, Mrs. Black was badass."

"She really was. That was how I fell for her. Unlike the other girls, she wasn't afraid of me. She wasn't afraid to destroy or kill me and something about that zinged me. I couldn't pinpoint it, but I knew I had to make it up to her."

"And what did you do to make it up to her?"

I fought a smile. "I found out where she lived and showed up at her doorstep. Her dad answered and tried to slam the door in my face, but I caught it in time, and Janet appeared. She was upset of course, but I told her straight to her face that I was sorry, and that I'd gotten carried away because of one too many drinks and too much testosterone around me. I apologized to her father with sincerity, and then I apologized to her for ruining her night. Then, I offered to help her dad out until he healed. Turned out, I broke his arm... and his nose." I winced. She laughed.

"You are so bad!"

"Hey,"—I shrugged—"back then, I had no guidance, and after a while, Janet understood my struggle. Trust me, it was hard winning her over. Took me three months before she finally eased up. I don't regret that part of my life, though. I could but... I don't. It happened for a reason. I was lost, and she found me." My lips pushed together. "One year later, she ended up pregnant. We were twenty when she had Izzy. So young and dumb and lost. But... somehow, we made our way through all of it, despite the struggles and tears. I wanted to do better, not only for her, but for our daughter.

"I dropped out of that gang and focused on making my life better. For some reason, seeing Isabelle for the first time caused me to come to the conclusion that being a part of that so-called 'family' wasn't the life for me. I realized, then, that I didn't want to spend my days beating older men over a game of poker and ten measly dollars. I wanted to spend it treating someone kindly, showing them how good I could be and that I wasn't some dumb streetwalker. I'd always been good at cars, so I got into it and worked my ass off night and day to provide for them. Crazy, though. Her dad thinks I'm a part of her death. He thinks I was involved in something gang related and they came for her. Fucking jackass."

Chloe's eyes were sympathetic. Understanding.

"Know something?"

"What?" she asked.

"I think I was given a daughter for a reason—as somewhat of a punishment for hurting Janet and her family. Also to make me a little softer around the edges. I used to be a huge prick. Nothing seemed to please me. I cared for no one's feelings but my own... until I met Janet of course, but even with her I was still kind of a dick for a while."

She sighed. "Either way, Mrs. Black was one lucky woman."

I struggled with a smile, allowing a soothing wave of silence to pass through. "You know... I've... never actually talked about her with anyone. I haven't mentioned her with anyone since she died. Not like this. Not out loud."

Her face straightened. "Seriously? Not even with Izzy?"

"No 'cause I know how much it'll hurt to bring her mom up during a conversation. If I even mention the word 'mom', her eyes get all watery. Can't stand to see her cry."

Sadness washed over her face. "Why me?" she asked.

I shrugged. "There's something about you." I stroked her cheek and then her chin with gentle fingers. "I have never been able to pinpoint it. What you do to me, I will never know."

She slid in closer, resting her head on her folded arm. "Well," she grinned, "I'm glad I can make you feel so enamored." Her grin was contagious. "Speaking of, what happened with Izzy and the wreck?"

"Oh." I rubbed my jaw. "I'm letting her drive my Charger until I get her another. Told her she can get a new one." I cocked a stern brow. "Found out she lied about the summer camp shit."

She gasped, as if she had no clue about it. I could read her like a book, plus I was certain Izzy had already told her. "She did?"

"Don't play crazy, Chloe. I know she told you."

She sealed her lips, fighting a laugh. "Well, she's my friend Theo," she whined playfully, moving in closer. "I had to cover for her. Keep my promise."

I grunted, trying hard not to join in on the bubbly laugh she let out. "Mm-hmm. Anyway, the car is totaled, and by that I mean completely fucked up. Insurance went up about two-hundred bucks." I shook my head. "She's fucking crazy, but she's fine. I can sell the salvageable parts of her car, start saving from that."

"Good. And that's a good idea." Her hand wrapped around my waist, her crotch pushing into mine. "You know, she sent me a message about you last night. She said you seemed... happier. Any clue why she may have said something like that?"

I watched her face for a moment before rapidly snatching my gaze away. Through my peripheral, I spotted her trying to catch my eye, but I couldn't look. There was a reason Izzy may have told her that, but my excuse had *nothing* to do with Chloe.

"Theo?" She sat up, crossing her legs. "Any idea why she'd say that? I thought she was onto us at first."

I was quiet for a moment, meeting her soft hazel eyes. Fuck, I hated the hopefulness she held, her eagerness for my response on full display. I was going to crush that hope, and I didn't even want to. But I was no liar. She deserved the truth.

"I... may have told her that Trixie was still around." Her smile vanished into thin air, replaced with a lopsided frown. It was clear. She wasn't thrilled. This wasn't the pouty look she normally put on when she was upset. This was a full frown, anger rooted deep. "Shit, Chloe, I had to tell her something," I said, backing myself up. "She asked me if I was still seeing Trixie, and I said yes, just so she'd back off. She knows me well. She knows I'm not going to 'seem' happier unless there's a reason behind it."

"But... why Trixie? Why couldn't you just say you met someone else? Someone new?"

"Because she would have asked me who that person was. Chloe, she asked me if I'd seen you since you'd gotten back. I said yes, and somehow she went straight into telling me I was acting happier. I thought surely she had a clue—that's one sneaky, smart-ass girl—but I backed it up with the first thing that came to mind. Saying I was still with Trixie." I tried reaching for her, but she pulled away, leaning back. Climbing off the bed, her feet landed on the floor, and she stood tall with her eyes trained on me.

"Theo, I just can't believe..." Her sentence fell short. She didn't say anything more. There was much more she could have said. She knew I couldn't bring her name up around Izzy. That would have definitely had her thinking.

"Chloe." Her name came out in a groan as she backed away, going for her clothes. She slipped out of my T-shirt, picking up her dress and bra. After hooking the bra, she slid into her dress, and I sat up. "Chloe, what else was I supposed to say?"

"You didn't have to say *Trixie*," she muttered hurriedly, eyes avoiding mine as she picked up her bracelets off the nightstand.

"Well what the hell else was I supposed to say? I never told Izzy I was going to break it off with her."

"Okay." Her response was simple, and for some reason, it got under my skin. I hopped off the bed, yanking on my briefs. I stood before her, but she spun for the door while struggling to latch her bracelet around her wrist. I caught her before she could go, gripping her face in my hands.

"Chloe, stop."

"I need to get home." She still avoided my line of sight, clutching the bracelets in tight fists.

"Stay with me a little longer," I pleaded, and she finally looked up. I expected sympathy, understanding, but no. This clearly bothered her. More than I thought. So much that she started talking crazy—bringing shit up that had nothing to do with the previous debate.

Fucking women, I swear.

"Theo... are you kidding?" she scoffed. "Don't you see? I'm not even supposed to be here! I wasn't supposed to be sleeping with you in your bed. Trixie is supposed to be there, according to you and Izzy." She shook her head and wriggled out of my grip. "It's just... it's not fair. It not fair to me. All of this... it's just so fucking wrong." She backed away but looked at me once more. "We're supposed to be better than this."

My next argument, I couldn't help. The words ran right of me. "Chloe, what did we agree upon when this first started? Huh?" I demanded. "You're getting too emotional and unstable about this—"

I realized instantly that I shouldn't have said it. It pissed her off even more. Her cheeks tinged red, brows furrowed, and in less than three seconds, she was out the door, zooming down the stairs.

I hurried after her, calling her name, but she didn't dare stop. She slipped into her flip-flops and fled my home as if it were a crime scene, rushing across the street to safety.

I stopped at my porch. It was daytime. Neighbors were surely out, and all of them were nosey fucks. I couldn't be seen running after her like this—shirtless, in only my fucking briefs. "Fuck!" I barked before walking back inside and slamming the door behind me when she was no longer in sight.

Fuck me. Why would I say that shit to her face? As right as I was, it was wrong to rub it in like that. She obviously cared about me. She was sensitive, and I was supposed to be the one to make sure her emotions were never tampered with.

"Damn it," I growled beneath my breath. I gripped the edges of the marble counter when I entered the kitchen, staring forward at the sunlight that beamed through the patio door, sparking my polished floors.

I was right and wrong, like every man on the planet when it came to women.

Her dinner plate from last night sat in front of me. No trace of food was visible, but the white china reminded me of her. Her nakedness and the soul that ignited mine and turned it into a furious blaze all night long.

I was stupid, with only one thought playing ping-pong in mind.

I hope she comes back to me.

EIGHTEEN

CHLOE

I RUSHED across the street without so much as a glance back, barging through the door that led straight to my kitchen. I dropped my keys on the first counter I came across, pinching the bridge of my nose with blunt pressure.

Tears were coming.

I thought I could fight them.

I was wrong.

I covered my face with my hands, swiping aggravated wetness away before anyone came down and spotted me. I dropped my hands, but when I happened to look to my left, someone unfamiliar sat at the counter with a cup of coffee in hand.

He had a natural tan complexion, similar to mine, eyes just as soft as someone clearly related to him—grey and filled with curiosity. He looked tall, with a broad chest and wicked, chiseled features. Dark, curly hair that was cropped and cut perfectly around the edges. Professional. Clean. His looks were sort of intimidating, but there was a kindness that orbited around him, proving I couldn't judge on sight.

He was just about to take a quick sip of the brew, but I was sure my entrance caught his full attention. I gasped, pressing a hand to the heart of my chest. "Ohmygod." The words flew out my mouth like a torpedo. My face turned as red as a cherry.

He put on a smile that seemed genuine and somewhat titillated. He was concerned, but by the way his eyes roamed my body, he clearly liked what he saw. I ignored his ogling. I'd become used to it after spending three years in a college full of horny, young men.

This guy looked like he'd just graduated college, not the age of twenty-nine like Margie had mentioned. He must have landed his teaching job very young. Lucky man. He had a youthful yet attractive face. I pulled my shit together, clearing the remainder of tears from my face and waving in his direction.

"Hi," he said then mashed his lips together. He studied my wet eyes. The urge to ask what was wrong with me was most likely on the edge of his tongue, but I was glad he didn't bother.

"Uh. Hey. Sorry." I swallowed hard. "You must be Sterling."

"Yes. And you must be Chloe."

"Yep." I felt super awkward and really stupid.

"Hmm." He made a noise, almost like a small laugh. "Great to meet you, Chloe."

He started to stand from the bar stool with his hand stuck out, but I fidgeted and he came to a swift halt. I wasn't up for handshakes or touching. He caught the hint, taking his seat and picking up his coffee again. He looked away from me. "I should go up to my room, let you finish your breakfast."

"Oh yeah. Please, go ahead. Don't mind me." He encouraged me to go. I was glad he didn't make me feel any more pathetic. I collected myself, told Sterling it was nice to meet him, and then scampered out of the kitchen, hurrying up the stairs and into my bedroom. I could hear Margie in my dad's room, arguing with him about getting dressed.

I didn't have the time or patience to deal with that right now. I decided it was best to allow Margie to handle her job alone. After all, it was her job. Even if the son she hadn't seen in three years was drinking coffee alone downstairs, most likely awaiting her presence.

Poor boy.

I felt sorry that he had to witness my outrage as well as listen to my father's stubbornness. I had no doubt he wondered where Mom was. I wouldn't have been surprised if he'd considered the Knight family a little dysfunctional.

Entering my room, I shut and locked my door behind me but hurried to the window, almost tripping over my blue rug just to make it across. His window was open, the curtains pulled aside, but he was nowhere in sight.

God, he was a jerk.

I couldn't believe he'd said that to me. Me? The girl that made him feel everything. I didn't mean to boast, but he made me feel alive too. And to say that right to my face? And then use Trixie's hoe-ass as his excuse?

No. I just couldn't deal.

Why did it have to be this way? Why couldn't things just be simple and easy? Why couldn't I just have them both? I could have told Izzy that I was sleeping with her dad, but there was a large risk of losing her. She wouldn't have respected that or tolerated it. Plus, Izzy spoke her mind a lot, a trait she clearly got from her father.

She wouldn't have sugarcoated anything. Not her feelings. Not how stupid we may have looked together. Not even how our friendship would surely be over.

We loved to talk boys, but it would have been weird as hell to talk about her dad. There would be boundaries. Everything would change. Izzy and I had this plan of moving in together once school was over. She'd be my roommate until we were in our thirties and engaged with great careers to back us up.

None of that would happen though if she found out about Theo and me. Not only that, I would have hated for Theo to ruin the solid relationship he had with his daughter because he was too busy sleeping with her best friend. I couldn't be the blurred line that stood between them. I was closest to her. She trusted me to never hurt her. The love we had for one another was immense, so it was easy to hurt one another.

It was bad. And dirty. And wrong.

And I wasn't bad or dirty or wrong unless I was around him.

Shit. Some things needed to change.

This was my wake up call.

Stop now, or you never will.

Three long and boring days went by, and I spent every single one of them at home. I didn't even bother going for my daily jogs. I knew, if I did, I would run into him. So I took up swimming a few laps in our pool.

I would have enjoyed it more, but I always felt someone watching me. The weight would be heavy, pressing into my back, and when I'd turn or look towards my house as I climbed out the pool, I'd see the guestroom curtains drawn and Sterling Martinez standing only inches away from the window.

He'd smile, but I wouldn't bother. I'd pick up my towel, watching him as I walked away until I could no longer see him. I swear, there was something about him that weirded me about. Yes, he was sweet and he clearly loved his mother by the way he kissed her on the cheek every morning, but he stared way too much.

No, it wasn't a stare of admiration or even interest. It was a deep stare, like he knew many secrets about me that I'd never told anyone.

Each day, I'd pass Sterling in the living room or the kitchen. When I was making lunch after my swims, he would walk in, wave lightly with a suave greeting, and then step behind me to get to the fridge. He'd purposely step by me, and the hairs would prick the length of my spine. The feeling was... bizarre. Yes, it crept me out, but it also gave me a cool, comforting chill.

"Sterling." I'd greet him in the flattest way possible, as if I'd known him for years and simply tolerated his presence. Like I said, weird.

On another note, during those three days I'd received constant calls and texts from Theo. I didn't respond to any of them. In order for me to keep myself in check, I had to keep my distance. Trust me, I wanted to give in infinite times, call back after he left a voicemail, begging me to return to his call.

The third night, I received the maximum number of calls from him. Six. Maybe I wasn't as desperate as I thought. We were obviously on the same level. I may have overreacted the other day, but he knew the reason why.

And he also knew it was wrong to continue this fucking charade. Pretending not to care. Pretending this wasn't more than what we both knew it was. We'd taken it too far in only one week. Imagine how far we'd have gone in two months.

That night, I lay in bed, staring up at the stars on my ceiling again. I felt hopeless, ending it like that. Were we over? Would he give up on the calls? Stop texting me or even bother with me once he came to the realization that I was right about trying to let it go? I say "trying" because I wasn't ready.

I couldn't stop thinking about him. Or the last night I spent with him. How I slept with him, cuddled up the entire night and inhaling his unique, manly scent. He got so hard for me the next morning, coming because it was me that made it happen.

I sighed, rolling over. It was nearing midnight. I stared ahead at the neon green numbers on the alarm clock across from me. I wasn't sleepy. Sleep would be nearly impossible with a mind this overcrowded.

Minutes passed. I forced my eyes shut. It didn't help.

My phone buzzed on the bed beside me. "Mr. Black" appeared once again, and for a split second, I started to answer, but quickly changed my mind, muting the buzz and placing it beside the clock.

The screen went black, but something rapped on my glass as soon as it did. Gasping, I sat up, looking towards the window and spotting a shadow behind it. The knocking broke the silence again, and I shot to a stand, rushing to the window because I knew exactly who it was.

I pulled the curtains aside, and there he stood—Mr. Black, sporting all black. A baseball cap was fitted on his head, his dark brown eyes pinned on me. I opened my window in a hurry, whisper-hissing, "What the hell are you doing up here?!"

He ignored my question, climbing through the window and landing with a gentle thud. I stepped back as he stood tall, turning and shutting the window. He didn't lock it, which was a good sign. He would be leaving soon.

"Theo, what the hell are you doing up here? Why would you climb through my window?"

He shrugged one shoulder. "It's obviously the only way I can see you." His eyes flickered beneath his cap. "Got me acting like a sixteen year old boy again."

I tried hard not to smile, and it worked. Inside, however, I was beaming. Folding my arms across my chest, I took another step away, one eyebrow cocked in his direction. I could see part of his face from the streetlight filtering in through the slit between my curtains.

He looked fucking amazing. If I wasn't so upset and working so hard to maintain my composure, I would have salivated at the mere sight of him.

A solid, black T-shirt hugged his body, black basketball shorts around his waist, and black Nikes to match. His tattoos were definitely a bonus, the ink beautifully sketched along his toned arms. As he stood there, I wondered how I stayed away for three whole days. Three days just seemed way too long to be away from Theo Black.

His body was solid, chest clearly defined beneath that shirt. And the bulge in his middle gave a clear idea of what a woman should have expected—and what I knew—when she made the decision to get into bed with him.

Stepping forward, Theo asked, "Why have you been ignoring me?" His voice wasn't sweet or earnest, like how I pictured his unanswered messages to be. It was slightly irritated. "I've called you for days, trying hard to fucking explain myself, but you won't allow me the chance."

I straightened my back. "Like you said, I was being too emotional. I realized it and backed off. What you wanted, right?"

"Did I ever say that?" His voice was dark. He stepped forward again, nostrils flaring with a mild edge of frustration.

"You didn't have to say it."

He frowned. I expected him to say more, but instead, he finished his long awaited walk to me, pulling me in and leading the way to my full-sized bed. "Listen to me, baby," he murmured, lips touching my ear. I shivered but listened, deciding a protest was pointless. "I've thought long and hard the past few days, and you know what I came up with?"

I pretended to ignore him, avoiding the panty-melting kisses he placed on my face and the center of my chest when he softly laid me down.

His head tipped up, eyes meeting mine. "How much I enjoy being around you," he continued. "And how, even though you may not think so, I care about you. Shit, I *love you*, Chloe. And if you can't see that, then I don't know what the fuck to tell you."

His smile was slanted, but my eyes were intense on his. He... he *loved* me? Theodore Black loved me? I never thought I'd hear those words come out of his mouth. We weren't supposed to love... or even care too much.

"No, this shit didn't happen overnight or even this past week," he explained. "I have loved you for nearly ten years now. Back then, it was a simple kind of love. The kind you'd give anyone you spent so much time around. But that day in the park, when you allowed me to take you for the second time and looked at me as if I was the perfect and greatest man on earth, I fell, Chloe. I fell so fucking hard, and all these years I've been trying to pretend I didn't because it happened too soon —too soon after Janet's death and in the midst of my grief. I thought surely it was my grief and abandonment that made me feel that way about you." His head shook as he sat up. "But no... that feeling was real. And it has been mutual. We said love couldn't come into this but, *fuck*, it's been here all along, Knight."

My heart stumbled over its beats, trying to grasp and cling to every word. "You... love me?" I whispered, sitting up with him. I looked him straight in the eye and kind of hoped he'd look away, falter—anything to show he didn't truly mean it, but he didn't. He stared right back at me with eyes so full and brown my tummy fluttered.

"A lot." His smile was boyish. Innocent.

I don't know what it was, but it set me on fucking fire. I stared at him in awe, and before my mind could comprehend my actions, I pounced forward, wrapping my arms around his neck and clashing into him.

He fell on top of me as I tugged him toward me, returning the kiss with the same burning intensity I held. God, I felt like the best girl on earth. Those three days of loneliness meant nothing. His words, and the fact that I had considered him a true asshole, were easily replaced with his confession. All negativity and hurt vanished, and my heart filled with a positivity that radiated to him.

I couldn't get enough. The bulge in his shorts prodded through, poking right at my sex. I assisted him with his shorts as he focused on mine. Our breaths mixed and mingled, lips brushing.

His cock was at my entrance, and he sighed before entering me, tensing as if three days was way too long not to have me.

I sank and rocked with his large frame, holding on tight as he quietly took me, mouth crushing mine, one hand cradling one side my face. Every part of me wanted to collide with this man, merge into one, because that was exactly what we were when alone. One.

Nothing could replace my feelings for Theo. I'd loved him since I was twelve, since I was a little girl. And he knew that, but he never took advantage of it until the timing was a combination of wrong and right.

I didn't blame him. I didn't even blame myself. This was never supposed to happen, but how could we fight it? It was extremely difficult to stay away from the predestined. This was bound to happen, and though it terrified me to think of its outcome, I just couldn't imagine my life without him in it.

But I also couldn't imagine it without Izzy.

I hated when she crashed through our moments. The urge to push him away was strong, but not as strong as my need to pull him close and never let go.

The thought of her was brushed aside, the guilt replaced with a large fill of this glorious man. His hips stroked evenly between my legs, and he continued the same, quick thrust for several seconds before releasing and groaning as quietly as he could. His head fell, and he kissed me where his mouth landed.

A deep sigh filled the room as he rested on my chest. Forcing his head up and meeting his mellow brown eyes, I whispered, "I love you too, Theo. I have loved you for so long." His arm tightened around me. "My love for you has been irreplaceable. No one has ever made me feel the way you do. I know it's wrong," I said, "and I know we shouldn't be sharing feelings like this, but it's all true. I hate lying to myself. I hate fighting it. I hate being without you."

He looked me over and then licked his lips, pulling out and moving up to my side. Gripping my chin with his thumb and forefinger, he tilted my head, allowing our mouths to press. I sighed as his tongue parted my lips, wrapping around mine, before he pulled away, grazing my bottom lip. "You are my little knight," he murmured. "My rock. My savior. I love you."

Those words repeated that entire night. He cuddled with me for an hour, and he joked about my anger, making me slap him playfully a couple times before leaving. He asked me to show up the next day to help him pack his things.

His landlord told him he could move in a few days early, and considering he had a ton of shit that needed packing, I agreed. After all, he wasn't going to be able to do it all on his own.

My anger subsided. Ecstasy raced through my veins, a feeling I developed only when he was around. I smiled like a child would on Christmas Eve night. With Theo, every day from that moment and forward, would be a gift.

"No thinking," he told me before leaving. He had already climbed through my window, his body supported by the thick branch of the tree. "No *what if's* and no *maybes*. We'll live. We'll have fun, and we'll hold onto our momentary happiness. We'll feel everything, and we'll fucking love it." He kissed me with so much passion it made my heart swell. "I love you, Chloe."

"I love you too," I replied. And I meant it. I really meant it, and it felt amazing to say out loud.

NINETEEN

THEO

LOVE IS A FUNNY THING, isn't it?

One minute you think everything is just so simple, and the next, you're whispering sweet lyrics to a girl you've always wanted as your own. Those three days were fucking insane.

I couldn't stop thinking about her, but what was worse was how the thought of *love* hit me like a clashing wave, the very thing that disturbed the black sea. Why else would I have been so concerned? Or wanting to spend every waking moment with her? Why else would I have called so many times, climbed up that skimpy tree, and then snuck through her window, just to tell her exactly how I felt?

It was wrong of me to say it knowing we couldn't take this thing too far, but I couldn't *not* tell her. This was Chloe, a girl I'd known for years. She grew up around me. She trusted me, and I trusted her. I had no reason to doubt it. She was way more mature than the average female her age. She was perfection, and every part of her I desperately *needed* to belong to only me.

But something deep in my core twisted and knotted, proving that she wouldn't be mine once this summer was over. She would be back at school, and she would most likely reconsider her love for me, or figure she needed someone her age. Most of all, she'd take Izzy into true consideration.

I didn't know what would happen, but until I was to find out, I was satisfied with where we stood. I walked across the street, tugging my baseball cap down until it was snug on my forehead. I met at the driveway, but to my surprise, a white Honda was parked there.

My forehead went tight, creasing with annoyance. I hustled forward, entering my unlocked door, stalking around the corner, and spotting Trixie sitting at the bar counter, her legs crossed. She wore a short red dress with spikey red pumps to match. Her hair was pinned up, but a smirk rested on her lips.

"You know, you shouldn't leave your door open this late, Daddy." Her voice was once a turn on, but it threw me off kilter, filling me with disgust.

"What the fuck are you doing here, Trixie?"

She climbed off her stool. "Well, I was coming to tell you that I found a job in L.A. Only a few minutes away from here. Which means I'm not going to Vegas. But"—she walked towards me, placing her palm on my chest and running it down as she circled me—"turns out someone has already moved on, huh?"

I grimaced. "What the hell are you talking about?"

She crossed her arms when she met in front of me again. "Why are you sneaking through windows, Theo? Hmm? Didn't you tell me once before that your daughter's best friend lived there? You were drunk and—" She went absolutely quiet, then her eyes became broad, a cunning smile taking over. "Oh my god." She laughed out loud. "Oh my fucking god. Wait—are you serious?" She was both shocked and humored.

I ignored her, walking to my front door as she followed after me. Pulling it open, I stepped back with my hand constricted around the handle and growled, "Get the hell out of my house. Now."

"Oh, I'm not leaving," she laughed. "No, I think I'll stay tonight."

My nostrils flared, and I did my best to control my temper.

"I saved your daughter's number when I went through your phone a long time ago. You know, just in case I ever had to fill her in on anything or if something were to happen to you. Hmm... maybe I'll give her a little call now." She met up to me, holding me around the waist. I went completely still, jaw flexed. "God, I've missed you, Theo. Take me upstairs?" she whined.

I moved out of her grasp and shut my door, gripping her face in my hands with blunt force as her back hit the wall. I made sure it was aggressive, but not too much to hurt her... *yet*. Trust me, I wanted to slap that devious smile right off her face, but I didn't hit women, no matter how much they tempted me to.

"What are you gonna do, Daddy?"

"Stop calling me that," I snapped.

"But I like it... and you loved it." She tried touching me. I jerked away.

With her face still fastened tight in my hand, I said, "Go home, Trixie. And don't come back. We're done. You know that."

"You left me for a girl that's, like, thirty years younger than you." Her brows pulled together, cheeks turning just a shade redder. Pulling her face away, she stabbed a finger at my chest and said, "I *dare you* to try and break it off with me now. Try it, Theo, and I'll run right across the street and bang on her window. I'll tell her we're still together, and I'm sure she'll believe me because she's a young, naïve, little girl who clearly doesn't have any common sense or decency if she's fucking around with *you*."

Her words gripped me like an anaconda, squeezing so hard it caused an excruciating pain in my chest. I stepped away, but my eyes never left hers. She knew she had me, and I knew she'd go to Chloe— or worse, go knocking on the door to cause a scene.

Trixie was the type of woman that thrived on drama. I don't know why I bothered spending three years around her trifling, immature ass. I knew what she was about the moment I met her, but her pussy hooked me. I was drunk, and she took advantage of that, riding my cock and then hopping down, allowing me to bust my load into her mouth.

She was nowhere near as great as Chloe, but still good. And she was easy... too fucking easy.

I used to sympathize, especially when she told me her dad abandoned her to further his career as mayor of a small city in Nevada and her mom was constantly in rehab for heroin, leaving her to take care of herself, but that night, I hated her with a passion.

I wanted to choke the life right out of her for even bothering to threaten my daughter and Chloe in any kind of way. She was fucking with my life—my love—and if this were the Theo Black from over twenty years ago—the one that dwelled during the Union—she'd already be dead.

But I wasn't him anymore.

I had changed.

And she had me right where she wanted.

Chloe would be coming to my home tomorrow, eager to see me, and if I didn't come up with a plan to get Trixie the fuck out of my house, I would lose my knight for good.

Damn.

I was fucking screwed

TWENTY

CHLOE

BEFORE GOING to Theo's to help pack, I spent a few hours with Margie and Dad. Margie made a load of pancakes, some scrambled eggs, and even bacon. I ate two of the pancakes and some eggs, and when I was almost finished, Sterling walked into the kitchen, rubbing his eyes.

He walked to his mom and told her *good morning* as he kissed her on the cheek. She smiled, asking if he wanted her to make him a plate. "Sure, Ma. That'd be great."

I figured he'd sit at the counter with Dad who was reading the newspaper, but instead, he came to the dining table, picking up the carafe of fresh coffee and pouring himself a mug. After mixing in some sugar and *Bailey's* Irish creamer—the same way I loved my coffee—he sat across from me, taking a long sip.

"Morning," he said when he placed his brown mug down.

"Good morning." I finished my slice of bacon, looking him over thoroughly. There were small bags beneath his eyes, his lids droopy. "You look like you haven't slept in days."

His brows shifted, and he fought a smile. "Long night."

"Doing what?"

He didn't respond right away. He took another sip of coffee first. "Catching up on a lot of files. Organizing music sheets... stuff like that."

"Oh."

He nodded, and Margie walked over, making it easy for the conversation to end. I picked up my empty plate and went to the sink to wash it. Of course, I felt the same familiar gaze on my back.

God, why did he always watch me?

Turning, I kissed Dad on the cheek and then I walked through the mouth of the kitchen, purposely avoiding Sterling's line of sight. I jogged upstairs and changed into one of my less appealing one-piece bathing suits, grabbed my goggles and a towel, and hurried back downstairs. I had to pass the kitchen to get to the deck, so I walked by with the towel around my waist. Thirty minutes had surely passed me by. I was good for a few laps.

"Going for a swim, Margie. Let me know if you need me."

"Take your time, sweetheart." Her voice was lighter. Cheerier. She was pleased about her weird son being around. I guess I didn't need to ruin that. Maybe he was being weird and watching me because he didn't trust me. Perhaps I scared him when I barged in that first day, causing him to lose all trust and safety in our home. Maybe this creeper approach of his was a way to keep his guard up, protect himself.

I rolled it off my shoulders, the bottoms of my feet landing on the warm, polished wood of the deck. I dropped my towel on one of the lounge chairs and went straight into swimming. I did three quick laps. I thought I heard the slam of a door, but I ignored it, assuming it was the neighbors.

When I surfaced, gripping the gravelly cement edge of the pool, I was so wrong. Standing right above me was Sterling, glowering right at me. I leapt back, water splashing with my startled reaction. "What the hell are you doing?" I lowered my upper half in the water, as if it would conceal my breasts. It didn't do much. Clear water, and all.

"Nice day. Thought I'd take a swim too."

"Um..." I paused, moving back, glad the water covered at least some of my frame. "I was just about to get out."

"No, you weren't." His face was straight. "You normally swim eight laps, right? You have five more to go."

Okay. Yeah. He was really, really starting to creep me the fuck out. I pulled out of the water as he jumped in, hiking towards my towel and snatching it up to cover myself as quickly as possible. "Why are you such a fucking weirdo," I muttered with my back to him and yanking off my goggles.

"I didn't realize I was bothering you so much." He looked at me beneath furrowed brows.

"Yeah," I scoffed. "You really are."

"Well, you know what bothered me?"

I turned when his deep voice got louder. "I don't really care."

He went on. "I wasn't up grading papers, you know? It was just really fucking hard to sleep with people talking and doing things they *shouldn't* have been doing so late at night." He dropped his arms in the water, starting a thoughtless float. "So, who was it that snuck through your window last night, Chloe?" My eyes expanded like never before. I stilled, staring down at the creep as my heart slammed in my chest. He continued. "I heard you two arguing... saw him leave about an hour later and go into the house across the street. Saw him this morning too, expecting a young boy but was definitely mistaken and surprised by who I saw. Older man?" He smirked, brow piqued. "I knew there was something different about you. Is that what you like?"

"What?" I said, my voice a gasp and a whisper. "Why were you even listening? Most people pretend things like that don't happen." More proof he was possibly a psycho with mommy issues.

He lifted his hands in the air innocently. "Kinda hard not to when I could hear everything. Including the noises of pleasure." He shuddered a little, as if a vivid image of Theo and me crossed his mind. I wanted to shudder too, die from complete embarrassment. "You're lucky my mom slept downstairs and your dad was drugged up in his bedroom. Just saying." He sank under the water and swam to the other end. When he came back up, I started to ask him what else he heard, but he went back under in the same amount of time, purposely ignoring me. He obviously didn't want to speak on it anymore, but it wasn't okay with me. He... heard me. *Oh, God, he heard me.* I needed to know what all he heard.

I huffed as I watched him swim back and forth without much need for air, and then I rushed to the door, yanking it open and storming through the kitchen. Dad and Margie were no longer there.

I wanted to tell Margie that Sterling couldn't stay here anymore, that he needed to be in a hotel, but she would have hated me for it. The last thing I wanted was to get on her bad side. It seemed hard to get on her bad side. She was too nice, and somewhat of a pushover, but something told me she didn't mess around when it came to her son.

I zoomed upstairs and into my bedroom, shutting and locking my door behind me. My phone was ringing on my bed, and I sped for it, momentarily putting the thought of Sterling's eavesdropping behind me.

Izzy's name appeared on the screen, and surprisingly, I was relieved to see her calling. I answered without a moment of hesitation. "Hey Izzy! Busy?"

"No. Chlo! Just going with the flow."

I laughed. That was our greeting. Something we picked up when we had finally gotten cellphones at fourteen. "What's up? How's summer school going?"

"It fucking sucks. I need a damn break already."

"It hasn't even been that long!" I laughed.

"Yeah, but... ugh, who cares? This is so pointless." She groaned. "I regret partying so hard now."

"Well, that's what happens, kiddo."

"So, how are things? How's your dad?"

"He's... taking it day by day. He has his days where I just want to break something, maybe punch a hole in my wall out of frustration, but he's fine. I think the new meds are helping. He seems to have more better days than bad ones now."

"Oh. Good. That's awesome."

"But there's this one fucking problem..."

She gasped, ready to indulge in my drama. That was a first. She must have been really, really bored. "What?"

"My caregiver, the sweet, amazing woman I told you about?"

"Uh-huh."

"Well, her son is staying here for a few days. Honestly, he's really hot, but Izzy, he's a freak. He scares the shit out of me, I swear."

"I stopped listening after you said he was hot," she teased. "Hold on, how is he a freak? What has he done to you? Do I need to bash his junk in?"

"Nah, he hasn't touched me or anything, but since he's been here, he's been watching me do my laps in the pool. I'll see the guestroom window wide open and he'll be standing there, just *watching* me. Then, today, when I was doing my laps, he just popped up at the edge of the pool. It scared the shit out of me."

"Seriously? Oh my gosh, he sounds fucking craaazzzy!" She sang the last word.

"I'm starting to think some psychological issues make him that way. But that's not even the freaky part." I sat down on the edge of my computer chair. "He said he wanted to join me on the swim, and I told him I was just getting out. Then, he said I wasn't, that I had five more laps to go. I had only done three laps. I normally do eight, but isn't it weird that he knows that? He's too observant. Fucking weird."

"Wow... Chloe, you better high tail it like hell. Tell my dad!" she giggled. "He'll set him straight."

I started to laugh until she mentioned Theo. I forced one just to pretend nothing had shifted, but I felt the shift deep inside me. My face turned sullen as I peered up at my window with the knowing he was only one house away, my chipper mood quickly seeping through the cracks. A heavy, remorseful feeling replaced it. I stopped smiling. "Right," I breathed, still forcing my laugh.

"Well, I just wanted to check in. I hope Papa Knight doesn't cause too much hell. And if that freak tries to lay a hand on you, let me know! I'll come straight to Bristle Wave and drown him in that pool."

"You're wild, Izzy. Text me later."

"Alright, chick. Will do."

I dropped my phone, running my fingers across my face before raking them through my damp, mangled curls. I couldn't think too much. Like Theo said, don't think, but shit, it was damn hard not to feel the bad.

I dropped my towel and entered my bathroom, hitting the shower and then stepping out, drying off and checking the mirror. I wasn't quite sure what time Theo needed me to come over and help him, but it was still early. I was ready to see him again, but I decided to take care of myself.

I plucked my brows with the tweezers on top of the porcelain bowl, wincing with each deep-rooted tug. I then shaved my legs, under my arms, and... down *there*. After all, a girl needed to be renewed after such a perfect night.

After taking care of specific feminine needs, I went to my closet, dressing in a black pair of spandex pants, a camisole, and a pair of sneakers. I wasn't sure what all he would need packed or how much moving he planned on doing in and out of the house, so dressing comfortably was best.

Too eager, but still holding onto my patience, I walked to my window, looking out for the first time today. The eagerness I carried quickly vanished. There was a familiar car in the driveway, a white Honda, and my heart sunk as well as my excitement. That was... that was *her* car. Trixie. What in the hell was her car doing there and how long had it been there?

I figured only one person would know the answer to that question, so I scampered downstairs, doing my best to control my fury. After all, it could have been a simple coincidence. Sterling walked into the kitchen with a towel hung behind his neck and over his shoulders. He used the ends to clear his ears, and then he looked at me, watching as I hurried in his direction.

"You said you saw him leave last night," I murmured, getting way too close for comfort. But I didn't care. I needed answers. "You saw him... was that car in his driveway all night long?"

"What? The white one?"

"Yes."

He looked me over, confused. "I think so. Pink rims, right?"

My heart nearly stopped beating. "Yes." Oh, God. She had been there all night. But where was he? I left Sterling standing in the kitchen with a perplexed expression and a sarcastic "You're welcome!" trailing after me.

I was in a haste to get upstairs. I walked into my bedroom and called Theo right away. My blood reached boiling point. How could he say he loved me only the night before but have her there waiting for him? There had to be a reason for this, but nothing seemed to add up other than him still wanting her around, perhaps to keep him company when I went away for school. The line of my eyes thickened as the phone rang and rang. He didn't answer.

I called again, moving towards my window to look out, and as I did, I saw Trixie walking out the front door, blowing a kiss before shutting it behind her. Her keys dangled in her hand. She moved casually, hips swinging. Her hair wasn't disheveled, which was a good sign, but it was still a bad thing that she was there at all.

Wasn't she supposed to be in Vegas? Why the hell was she still around? He didn't love her... he loved me... right? Too many questions. Too many irrational thoughts.

I watched the skank pull out of the driveway, but what made my heart ache deep in my chest was when she pulled out and looked up, right at my window, as if she knew I was watching.

And, I couldn't believe it, but the bitch waved at me, twinkling her fingers as if she were superior. She pulled off, her body shaking with laughter before exiting Primrose. My body shook violently, hands curled into fists. I breathed evenly through my nostrils. I was usually the calm girl, the one that never got too upset, but this? This had gone too far.

Theo Black had a lot of explaining to do, and I was going to figure everything out. Right. Fucking. *Now*.

I took the staircase with a trail of fire behind me, one that Sterling backed away from as soon as he saw me storming down. He didn't say anything. He still looked confused and slightly worried, but he stayed away, afraid of getting burned.

Out the front door I went, fuming as I crossed the street and went up Theo's driveway to get to his two-story house on the hill. I didn't bother knocking or ringing the doorbell. I barged right in, slamming the door shut behind me.

He appeared around the corner, brows stitched. "Chloe, I was just about to call you when I found—"

"No, Theo." My voice dripped with the red I carried deep inside. Pointing and standing square in front of him, I asked, "Why did Trixie just leave your house? How long has she been here?"

Theo held his hands up, silently begging me to calm down. "That's what I wanted to call you about. I just can't find my fucking phone. Bitch hid it somewhere so I couldn't call you."

I scoffed, shoving a hand onto my waist. "Do you really expect me to believe that?" I looked around the kitchen before looking behind me. I spotted his cellphone sitting right on top of the glass table beside the door. I went for it, snatched it up, and shoved it into his hands. He looked down at it as if he was staring at the devil himself.

"What the fuck—no, Chloe, she put it there before she left. I looked everywhere for it! She had it! You have to believe me!"

My head shook, tears threatening to spill, but I kept it together. "So much for feeling everything."

I twisted around and made sure I was out of his house before he could come after. Normally, he wouldn't chase after me, but this time, he did. He hurried out, shouting my name, and before I could hit the main street, he gripped my elbow, picked me up, tossed me over his shoulder, and then walked back for his house.

His body was hard, but I pounded and kicked, begging him to put me down. I knew he wouldn't. He no longer cared. There were neighbors out, all of them watching, flooding me with embarrassment.

I hated him. So much.

When he was inside the house, he placed me on the rug in his living room, and I immediately shoved him with my hands as soon as I was free. The tears had surely left me, trailing down flared cheeks. "You're a liar, Theo! That's all you are! A liar!" He flinched, but I knew I wasn't hurting him with my actions. I was killing him with my words. "You know how I feel about you," my voice cracked. "You know how much I love you, and you used that against me! I can't even stand to look at you! What am I to you? Huh? Just a quick lay? Easy pussy for the summer?"

My voice thickened, filled with a blistering heap of emotions. I hit him again and again, pounding, wanting to hurt him like he'd hurt me. He didn't speak, and it only increased my anger. I went in for one last blow with both hands, but he caught my wrists and a deep grunt filled the room as he crushed me against his large body.

My fighting didn't stop. It was weak and lame, but I didn't stop. "I hate you," I whispered. "I swear. I hate how you make me feel."

"You don't mean that," he murmured. His voice broke, cutting my heart up in a thousand ways. "You don't fucking mean that shit." He lifted my head, and when I didn't focus on his face, he gripped it in his hands, forcing me to look at him. "Come on, Chloe, you know me! You fucking know me! I wouldn't lie to you! Trixie saw me last night—she saw me climbing through your window. She waited for me to get home —said she found a better job in LA and wasn't going to Vegas—but she saw me. She is going to use this shit against me. She fucking threatened to go over and tell you, but I didn't want you to hear it from her. I wanted you to hear it from me—the truth. I'm a forty-two year old man. I have no fucking reason to lie to you. Those days when I used to play mind games with girls are over. A real man stands up to his demons. Trust me, baby," he murmured, swiping one of my tears away. "I'm not lying to you. I would never lie to you."

My sniffles calmed as his voice hummed through me, the tears slowly drying. What the hell? Was he serious?

"Look, I told her about you once before, and she remembered. She knows what you are to me... to Izzy. She has Izzy's number. She said she'd call her, Chloe. Fucking Izzy. She said she'd tell her everything. I fucking panicked, and I knew if I kicked her out, she'd call first thing and fuck up everything."

"W-what?" I gasped then jerked away, not because I didn't believe him, but because this was bad. Really bad.

"Wait—why would she threaten you? She wants you back?"

He didn't answer. He didn't need to. The drop of his head and how it hung in shame was proof enough.

"Theo, oh my God," I swiped my face. "This cannot be happening right now!"

"I was trying to tell you. She knows... she knows everything. She stayed last night, but I didn't sleep with her. I got her drunk and let her pass out on the couch." I could imagine it vividly. I was sure she tried to seduce him, touch him, and even offer to suck him off. She was a girl that thrived on sex. I despised her existence. "I thought I could get into her phone, delete Izzy's number, but it's locked." He scratched his head out of nervous habit. "I tried, Chloe. I swear I did, but until I get that number deleted or get her to leave me alone, I have to keep seeing her."

"Theo, no." I placed my hands on his shoulders, looking him in the eyes. "I'm sure she's going to write it down as soon as she gets the chance. She may seem dumb, but I have a feeling she's not. Why else would she threaten to snitch? She's gonna need a backup plan."

"Shit," he hissed.

I looked down, battling tears again. Silence surrounded us, and when it occurred to me what we would have to do, I wanted to cry. "There's... only one thing we can do." I stole a peek at him, and as if he had the same thought, his face went stone cold. He hated the idea, but deep down, he knew I was right. "We have to tell Izzy."

Theo stared at me for several seconds, then he walked past me, dropping on the sofa. "I—shit, we can't do that."

"What other choice do we have?" My voice was thick. I walked towards him, taking the spot on his left. "I've had this planned out in case she ever found out. I'll tell her that it was my fault. That I tempted you, and we got carried away."

He groaned, his face planted in his hands. "She'll never believe that. She knows how you are and how much you value your relationship with her. She'll know it was me." He dropped his hands. "Fuck, man, I'll lose her. I know I will. She won't forgive me, and if she does, she'll never look at me the same. She won't trust me... she won't come home." He looked down, brown eyes glossy. "She's all I have, man. Her and *you*. I can't afford to lose both. Because I know if she finds out, I won't just be losing her, I'll be losing you too. You'll regret it. You'll hate yourself for ruining your friendship with her, and that'll leave you no choice but to stay away from the person that intervened. Me. We can't, Chloe."

I watched his eyes and saw the loneliness within them. The gloom was clear. He knew we'd fucked up the moment we decided to touch each other. He knew his daughter, how stubborn she was. He also knew that she'd jump to conclusions about him, consider him a fuck-up husband to Mrs. Black because he had sex with me only six weeks after her death.

It wasn't nearly enough time to heal. She'd blame him and tell him straight to his face that he was a coward, that never loved his wife and was ready to move on. I knew because he told me she called him a pussy for not waiting for Mrs. Black after the bakery party. I knew Izzy just as well as I knew him. They were alike in ways, but when it came to acceptance, that was one trait Izzy was shy of.

She wouldn't understand; she wouldn't get it. She'd wonder about it for the rest of her life, most likely questioning our friendship. She'd try and say it was all bullshit, that I stuck around to get closer to Theo, but really it wasn't. I loved Izzy, but I broke her heart three years ago, and she didn't even know it.

"I'm so sorry for this mess," Theo apologized. He grabbed my hand, giving it a gentle squeeze. I stared down at our fingers, the silver band that he never took off now missing from his ring finger. The tan mark was no longer there. It blended in with the rest of his olive skin. "Look, how about I cook you some dinner? We can talk about this."

I dropped my head, and with a calmness that nowhere near justi-fied all I was feeling, I stood, releasing his hand. "No, I think I should go. You know neither of us can think when we're around each other. I'm nothing but a distraction for you."

He shot to a stand as I backed away to the door. "Don't say shit like that, Chloe." He marched forward, clasping my face in his hands and forcing me to look at him. "Don't say stupid shit to me—don't say shit you don't even believe. You aren't a distraction. You have never been a distraction for me."

"No? Then what am I?"

He released my face, watching my sullen eyes. "You are *everything* to me." He blinked, his hands capping my shoulders. With his lips on my forehead, he whispered. "Everything. I love you. Never think twice about that."

I swallowed thickly, but I allowed him to hold me. Why? Because I really needed to be held. Yes, we needed to talk this through, but it couldn't happen in that moment. In that moment, I was vulnerable, and all of my emotions had been put on display. I needed space—time to myself. I needed it to be just me.

So I left Theo with a swift kiss on the lips and then the cheek, and he watched me walk across the street and into my house. As I shut the door behind me, my eyes flashed to Sterling who was sitting on the sofa, flipping channels with the TV remote. When he saw it was me walking through the door, he perked up, asking, "What in the hell was that about?"

I ignored him, slightly rolling my eyes as I made my way up the staircase. My door slammed, and I flopped on my bed, face-first. The cool sheets smothered the visible shame, and unfortunately, I could still breathe.

I didn't deserve to breathe.

I didn't deserve this shitty lifestyle.

I didn't deserve to hide, suffer, or cry.

I deserved to be Chloe Knight.

Happy, carefree, and not so... guilty.

TWENTY-ONE

CHLOE

Two weeks.

That's how much time went by, each day inching by like a snail on a hot summer day.

In between sneaking in and out of his house and having to be updated on when Trixie was gone, we tried to work something out. Of course we tried over and over again to stop seeing each other—end it all cold turkey, no looking back—but it was damn near impossible.

I couldn't ignore him.

Not even when he moved. Luckily, Trixie didn't know where his new place was right away, so she didn't get the opportunity to show up like I could, but during the middle of our arrangements, she made an approach, demanding his address. I saw her show up at Theo's house, angry about the **For Sale** sign pitched in the yard.

I despised her. I wanted to bash her skull in plenty of times. I could have done it the day she stopped by, but that wasn't me. I was too good of a person, and at times, I considered myself a pushover. I had a backbone, but it was very fragile.

There was one day we had all to ourselves. An entire day and night since Trixie had a double shift. I got lucky, and Theo did something different. He took me to a tattoo parlor in L.A. He only trusted one person, some artist named Rob at Coast & Ink. The shop was neat. I'd never been in one before. Izzy and I always talked about getting matching tattoos but never got the chance to.

That day, I believe Theo was out of his damned mind. He got a tribal wave tattooed above his left collarbone, close to his neck. I instantly knew the meaning of it before he could explain.

"Why?" I whispered when we left the shop and met up to Ol' Charlie in the parking lot. "Why would you do that for me?"

"Because the ocean is our place," he murmured, his body close, his hand cupping the back of my neck. "The sea will always remind me of you."

Ink. Dark, beautiful, permanent ink would forever remind him of me. I wanted a copy for keepsake. I'd contemplated getting something similar one day, maybe when everything wasn't so intense. His artist was a good one, but he was very strict about his sketching. He didn't want anyone copying his work, and he had even signed the rough draft and final sketch of Theo's dark wave. Too bad Theo had signed a contract that clearly stated he couldn't get the drafts or the finals. His shop had some crazy rules, but their high quality made up for it.

I begged. Theo begged, but it didn't work. He told us the tattoo on his arm was all we needed—that he never gave his drafts or sketches away. He was just being a jackass. Theo said he'd get a copy for me— that the Blacks always got their way and Rob would regret not giving it to him the first time. It wasn't that serious, but to see his determination was sinfully delightful.

Maybe, after all this time, this was true love, or so I thought. Trixie called his cellphone later that night while we were tangled in the sheets. And before leaving, I lay on his chest, fighting the tears begging to be shed.

There wasn't anyone I could talk to about this other than Margie, so I filled her in on everything. She understood our situation more than I thought she would, but her only response was to try and let go. I didn't like the advice because we were trying. It was just too damn hard.

And to make matters, well... worse, I found her kissing my dad when I came home late one night from Theo's. It really must have been one of his good days, because he groped all of Margie's curves, holding tight, kissing like his life depended on it. I was shocked—never saw it coming.

I didn't interrupt though. In fact, I found it kind of cute. Apparently, Margie heard or saw me going past the bedroom because later on that night, she came into my room with one of my dad's robes on, her cheeks flushed.

I tried so hard not to snicker as she quietly shut the door behind her. "So... um... how long?"

She blushed, her face cherry red now. "A while now, sweetie. About a week after you came home."

"Wow," I breathed, stunned.

She walked my way, sitting on the bed beside me. "Believe it or not, I have loved your father for over thirty years."

My eyes expanded. "You've known him for that long?"

She nodded. "Back in college, I met Richard first. He was in one of my math classes. I'd always found him handsome, but I didn't think a guy like him would be interested in a chubby Spanish girl like me. But he was very intrigued, even agreed to come study with me every Wednesday night." She was tickled, grinning as she focused on my carpet. Then, her face straightened. "Your mother saw him during one of our study nights. I purposely scheduled on Wednesday nights in his dorm because I didn't want her to see him. Your mom is a... very envious person. There was one night when they were doing plumbing on Richard's hall and the library was closed due to reconstruction. We were left with no choice but to go back to my dorm room. Well, I had no choice. He kept begging me to see it, and I didn't want to keep telling him no. So, we got there... and Bonnie was laying right on the bed. I didn't expect her, but just like that"—she snapped her fingers —"she stole him away from me."

"Seriously? Why would she do that if she knew you were interested?" I was angry about that.

Margie shrugged. "Like I said, she was a very envious woman. She hated when I had something she didn't. She swore she was my friend, but whenever I got a new pair of shoes or met a guy that really liked me, she'd either rain on my parade or do something to get the guy to notice her."

I grimaced, not at Margie but at my mother's behavior. "Ew, Margie, why did you even stay friends with her?"

"It wasn't for her, sweetie. It was for Richard."

I blinked.

"See, I had never expressed myself to Richie the way I'd always wanted to. I dreamed of telling him how I felt and then having him tell me something just as great in return—maybe even better—but I was only dreaming. Richie fell for your mother, and she stuck around because she learned he had inheritance from grandparents he'd never met and would soon be taking over their accounting and banking business. Bonnie came from nothing, so she stuck with a man that could give her any and everything."

"Why didn't you ever say anything to Dad?"

She chewed on her bottom lip, perplexed as she zoned out. "Because... for a few years he was happy. And by the time I had the courage, it was already too late. They were getting married. Trust me, Bonnie always knew I loved your father, which is why she tried to string me along by having me take care of him during these rough times. She knew I wouldn't say no— she knew I would stick around because I love Richie. I care for him, and I know exactly what he needs and what he deserves. Basically, she handed me her leftovers. When I told you that your father worked hard and could hardly be there for you, that was because of Bonnie. She made him slave for her to have continual income, threatening divorce—something he didn't want. She made him take international jobs, not giving a damn if he was around to watch you grow up. I got his letters. His calls. He was always upset with Bonnie, and from what I saw, she didn't even care."

Margie crossed her arms, shaking her head.

I dropped mine, ashamed that I'd even come from such a woman. Not that I didn't already know she could be selfish, but I didn't think she'd land a blow that low—especially towards a woman so nice.

"You mom has her qualities. Like you said, she isn't all bad. But... like I said. She will always put herself first, even before her own child."

I was saddened to hear about Mom's true colors, and the more and more I thought on it, the more I realized how glad I was that Margie was around and my mother wasn't. Margie deserved my dad, and he deserved her. He deserved a woman that gave instead of someone that just took, snatched, and then ran with his heart and soul. Margie patiently swept up the pieces, restoring his happiness.

I talked to Margie a lot, more about myself and my situation with Theodore than anything else. Unfortunately, Sterling was still around when I filled Margie in on my hectic taboo ordeal. High school students were out for summer break, which gave him ample time to work from home. He worked a lot at the desk in the den, but I didn't realize that was his place of peace until I told Margie all about my complications. He was only a room away.

That night, about two hours after I asked her what I should do, Sterling came up to my room. He knocked first, which I was glad for. When he stepped in, I drew my knees to my chest, swallowing hard as he shut the door behind him. I was a little terrified of this guy. All I got from him the past two and a half weeks were odd stares and weird vibes.

Before he made it too far, he held his hands up in the air innocently. "You don't have to be scared of me, you know?"

"You weird me out," I admitted.

He laughed, finding my rapid response funny. "I... have a bad habit of not being able to express myself. I can be very... weird, as you put it."

Ya think?

I shrugged.

"Listen, um... I heard you talking to my mom in the kitchen. I know, I know, I shouldn't have been eavesdropping again,"—he held his hands up as I started to tell him off—"but I was in the den, and lately I've been a little worried about you."

"About me?" I narrowed my brows, releasing my legs. "Why would you be worried about me? You hardly even know me."

"Well, see, it's weird 'cause I feel like I know a lot about you. All my mom ever does is talk about you. She's always wanted a girl. You're good to her. Sweet to her. She loves that you don't act like the average female your age."

Something about the way he said that made a few parts of me soften. It could have been the kindness in his voice or how his mouth twitched to fight a smile. I realized then that Sterling was no creep. He was just a man that wasn't sure how to take me. He didn't understand me or why I did the things I did, but he never bothered bringing it up again.

When I thought of it, I actually appreciated him for not telling anyone about Theo coming through my window—especially Margie. Maybe he wasn't so much of a weirdo after all.

I eased up a little, shoulders dropping, but he stayed in the same place. I noticed then that he had a tattoo on his shoulder. It looked familiar, then I noticed it was an exact replica of the tattoo Theo had below his collarbone. A jagged looking U. *The Union.*

Holy... fucking... shit.

He saw where my eyes landed, and he covered it. "You know about this?"

I pretended I didn't. "Nah. What's it mean?" I asked, brows creased. I pushed off the bed, walking towards him.

His Adam's apple bobbed. "It stands for The Union. It was a... gang I was in when I was younger. I've changed."

"Yeah," I sighed. "I see that."

"You know, it kinda hurt my feelings when you called me a creep the other week," he teased, chuckling.

My mouth twitched, but I couldn't fight my smile. "I'm sorry... you were just really, really starting to weird me out. Why do you watch me swim?"

"I used to swim a lot."

I was surprised to hear that. Margie never mentioned he was a swimmer. "I took up the hobby after college. The water was soothing. I loved how it felt going through my hair, surrounding me." He shrugged. "Used to have a really bad temper. I'm ten times better than who I used to be. I don't swim as much now since I work so much, but when I get the chance, it's amazing."

"Swimming helps me relax too." I stepped back.

He blinked twice before looking me straight in the eyes. "Do you love that man over there?"

It was my turn to blink as if I were clueless. "Who? Theo?"

"I assume that's his name." Sterling smirked.

I sat back down, blowing a breath. "I... do. He means a lot to me."

"How long have you known him?"

"Since I was twelve."

Sterling's eyes went wide. "He's been hitting on you ever since you were twelve? Sounds like a fucking pervert."

"No, he was not hitting on me since I was twelve. I was nineteen when we actually... *did* something. But by that time, he was really spiraling, and he was no longer married." I remembered that night clearly. I would never forget it. I sighed.

"I guess I can't blame you. I know the feeling."

My face warped with confusion. "Of what?"

"Of falling in love with someone you know you can't have. Someone older... a generation or two ahead of you."

My heart pitter-pattered, the beats light, but blood whooshed in my ears. Sterling rubbed the back of his neck, eyes avoiding mine. And then I saw it... shit. All this time I thought Margie was the one that had fallen for an older man—a forbidden lover—but it was her son who'd fallen for the older lover. Sterling had obviously told his mother everything. No wonder she knew so much, and no wonder she could sympathize.

"Maybe now you can see why I've been kinda worried about you. I know how hard it is to let that go—to move on. It's hard to think about, especially when it's mutual. You know, my mom kinda told me the man was also your best friend's dad. She had no right to tell me, but it was one of those days where she couldn't stop talking... and I kinda forced it out of her."

Damn it, Margie! I snatched my gaze away.

Sterling stepped forward. "You don't have to feel ashamed, alright?" I looked up, and he was still watching me. "Trust me, I understand your struggle. I have no room to judge anyone on God's green earth."

"Hmm." I wasn't sure what else to say.

"Hey—can I tell you a story? I think you'd be interested. It's pretty similar to what you're going through." He put on a friendly smile, and surprisingly, the lopsided curve of his mouth intrigued me. I wanted to know his story. I wanted to know what he did to come out of his taboo affair.

"Sure." I scooted towards the edge of my bed.

Turning only a fraction, he grabbed my pink chair and pulled it to the center of the room, near my bed. He sat down, folding his fingers in front of him, his elbows on top of his thighs.

"So, when I was twenty, I joined this gang called The Union. The craziest, wildest time of my life... but that only lasted for a little while. They make you do some pretty crazy shit. A gang like that attracted naïve, young-minded men like me. Especially young men that had been abused, neglected, or abandoned. My dad used to hit me and my mom when—well, you know. I'm sure you can put two and two together." His smile was uneasy.

Wow. That explained so much, not only with him, but with Margie as well.

"Anyway, The Union doesn't believe in true love," he told me. "They think women were put on this earth for them to fuck and have their babies, but they don't think love is necessary to the life they live. I didn't understand why they didn't believe in love, and I hated they didn't because I was falling in love with someone. It was natural and real and extremely hard to ignore or avoid. I knew The Union would never understand or accept it, so I kept my love a secret. I never wanted them to find out." Sterling looked down, his breathing going heavy. "I... uh..." He struggled with a smile and a frown. "Shit, I don't even know why I feel so comfortable telling you this, but she was a great woman. I worked with her often. I was surprised she gave me a job. I guess she knew I needed it. And she was kind enough to give me a chance.

"She hated my lifestyle with a passion, but she was very sympathetic. Her compassion was overwhelming. It made me bloom, feel things I never thought possible. So, I started showing up for work more to make her happy and making less appearances with the gang of men that thought love was a stupid, made up word. With each day, I fell more and more in love with her, and after only a few weeks I couldn't stay away."

"Aw." I smiled. "She must have been really great if she could make you come out of the gang on your own."

"Ha. She was, trust me. I loved that woman with a passion. Everything about her made my heart pound. She loved me a lot. She'd work late for me, just so we could spend time together. When my car broke down, she would pick me up for work... but that was the mistake... her coming to my home."

His eyes swarmed with emotion as he cleared his throat. "The Union... they'd been watching me. They saw her. I never told them I wanted to drop out because, with my father gone and my mom always working, they were sort of my family—people to keep me company. But when they saw her picking me up, it caused all hell to break loose." He focused on the wall across from him. "I was doing so good, going to school for her. I wanted to make her proud. I'd always loved music, so I focused on making that my career and was lucky enough to graduate. But... just when I thought everything would get better, it got so much worse.

"During my graduation night, she was brutally robbed and stabbed. Her life was taken, and I didn't know it until two days after I graduated." I gasped sharply, the pieces of his stories all too familiar. My eyes were wide as hell, and the drumming of my heartbeat had come to a cease as I listened to Sterling's every single word. That story... *robbed and stabbed? Three years ago...* oh my god.

He continued, leaving me no window of time to butt in. "I was busy, so busy and moving forward with my life so much that I didn't even realize The Union had been watching my every move. They... envied me. They didn't believe in love. They didn't condone it. They saw I was falling hard for her, and they—they did something about it." His voice cracked in the middle of the last sentence. "I was supposed to be vice president of the gang, step up to the plate and soon take over, but I gave the position away. I think doing that made them suspicious."

His body shook with silent, painful laughter. "I don't like to think of her death as what separated us. There were many things that separated us—many things that stood in the way. Honestly, I don't think we ever would have been together, no matter how hard we loved one another or how much we wanted to be. The first thing that stood in the way was our age difference. She happened to be ten years older than me. The second thing, she had a child. A daughter. And the third and biggest thing, she didn't want to leave her husband, mainly because he had never wronged her... and because she still loved him."

Daughter?

HUSBAND?!

Oh my God.

My palms went clammy and cold, my mouth dry like it'd been stuffed with cotton balls. Sterling was... *Holy shit*... He was...

Sterling blew a puff of air that caught my attention again, and luckily for him, his tears didn't fall. It'd obviously become easier for him to talk about his loss, but his loss was what made me wonder.

It could have been a coincidence. Him being in the same gang that Theo was in. Residing in L.A. where the murder happened and where they used to live. After all, Theo got to love, and from my understanding, he wasn't as invested in the gang as Sterling was. Maybe they just didn't care for Theo and saw he could protect himself without them. I couldn't help but think there were way too many coincidences, all of which petrified me.

Sterling looked at my pale face, expecting questions, some kind of reaction, but I couldn't react. I couldn't do much but stare at him, speechless.

"Anyway, I wanted to tell you that I know what you're going through. Not being able to be with a person that is a generation or two ahead of you. Is he married? The girl with the pink rims? What is she to him? Kids?"

I nodded at the last question, but it was all I could do. Speaking was unlikely to happen. He took my speechlessness as something else —probably a disinterest in his past and his love life—so he slid out of his chair, placing it back in front of my computer.

"Shit. I apologize if my story disturbed you. I'll leave you alone now."

He went for the door and told me to have a good night, but before he could shut it, it finally occurred to me that there was *one* question I needed an answer to in order to know if my coincidences were just that —coincidences—or if they were hard, cold truths.

"The woman you loved, the woman that died," I said, my voice barely a whisper, "What—what was her name?"

A faint smile touched his lips, as if he would remember her name for the rest of his life. It was as if the thought of her name alone was enough to bring back the wonderful, temporary forevers he clung to. "It was Janet," he said. "Janet Black."

TWENTY-TWO

THEO

FOURTH OF JULY WEEKEND.

I used to love it years ago. I'd light the grill, ready to inhale the scent of sizzling meat while Janet whipped up some goodies for us to indulge in later. Now, my daughter was away, and well, Janet was gone.

This Fourth of July I was going to be spending alone in my condo. Chloe hadn't text me back since the previous night. Her reason could have been that she was working on keeping her distance. That's what was supposed to be happening anyway.

So much shit was going on. I wasn't happy about any of it. I stressed like a motherfucker, trying to keep Trixie on some level of contentment while also maintaining Chloe's happiness. I wouldn't kiss Trixie, I wouldn't hug her back, and I damn sure wouldn't fuck her. Someone else's name was written on my cock with permanent ink, and her name was Chloe Knight.

Trixie whined about every fucking thing. She threatened me repeatedly, leaving me no choice but to do something to make it up to her. I'd take her to Dane's where she could dance with her half-naked friends and I could drink until my rage wasn't fully consuming me.

Then, she'd leave with them but swore she'd return. And on the nights when she'd leave to go party, I'd call Chloe first thing. I hated the position I put her in. I never wanted her to think she came second. I loved that girl with my whole heart. She didn't deserve this, but I just wasn't ready to let go.

Perhaps she was ready now. She wasn't answering my calls or responding to my text messages. It'd been hours, and I needed my fix. I'd contemplated going to see her way too many times, finally giving into the temptation. I drove to Primrose, in hopes that she'd be somewhere visible where I could catch her attention.

Worry seized me, and when I entered the neighborhood and saw her car in the driveway, my heart fucking swelled. I drove closer with a faint smile on my lips, but when I caught sight of a familiar black car parked in the driveway, my exhilaration flew with the wind.

Oh. Shit. It wasn't just any black car.

It was a black Charger.

My fucking Charger.

I stopped in the middle of the road, bike grumbling louder than I ever thought possible. Or maybe it only sounded louder because I wasn't supposed to be there, and neither was Izzy.

I turned quickly and sped out of Primrose, heart racing as I rode home. I parked my bike just as my phone buzzed in my back pocket. Surprisingly, it wasn't Izzy, whom I expected to call and shout at me for selling the house. It was Chloe.

I answered. "Chloe?"

"Hey, Theo, um... Okay, so maybe the world and all its forces are just totally against us right now, but why in the hell is Izzy in town? Did she tell you she would be coming?"

"Hell no." I kicked the stand of my bike and hopped off. "Shit."

"She's going to her car right now to get her phone. I'm sure she's about to call you." Chloe breathed hard. "Damn it," she groaned. "I wasn't prepared for this at all."

"Me neither, babe. But listen, when she calls me, I'll tell her to come over. Just stay calm, alright?"

She sighed. "Okay. Okay," she said twice, but I heard the anxiety in her voice.

"Love you, Chloe. Call you when everything is situated."

She didn't tell me she loved me back. Instead, she said *okay* and then hung up. I dropped the phone, throat working hard to swallow. Moments later, as I stepped into my condo, I got the expected call from my daughter.

And I answered, telling her my new address after receiving some harsh, annoyed remarks about selling the house she practically grew up in. She told me she'd be on the way in twenty minutes and then she hung up.

Slouching on the sofa, I picked up my cellphone and shot Chloe a text.

Me: I'm so fucking sorry, Chloe. I don't want you to go through this.

She replied:

Chloe: It's fine. I have something really important to tell you. We need to find a place to meet so we can talk.

Me: I'll send you a time to meet me at the boat when Izzy is settled in.

Chloe: Okay. And I love you too, Theo.

Delight tickled the corners of my mouth, but the message about her needing to tell me something really important made me go back and wonder exactly what was so important she couldn't say it through text.

Other than Izzy being home, it was clearly bothering her. She could handle Izzy, I knew that, but there was something else bugging her that she could only keep secret for so long. Usually, Chloe was good at holding her tongue.

Maybe this was too much and she was ready to end it now, quit now while her best friend was face-to-face with her. Maybe she wanted to meet privately so she could give me one more touch, one last kiss, and maybe even one last round of passionate love making.

My heart wrenched, body going slack. I stared at the window across from me. The waves normally comforted me, but not today. They were just... *there*. Just like how I was.

Just surviving. Without her, I wouldn't have much of a purpose. I'd have Izzy, but soon Izzy would move forward with her life and not need her dad as much. And I'd be left alone... again.

All over again.

Izzy said twenty, but she arrived over an hour later, and by her side was... Chloe. She'd given me the heads up before arriving, so I was prepared when they showed together.

"Izzy Bear!"

"Dad!" Izzy ran into my arms, but as I held her and looked over her shoulder, my eyes locked on Chloe's. She stood a step away from the door, eyes holding mine. There was something wrong. She lifted a hand to chew on her fingernail, shifting her weight twice. A hand slapped my chest, and Izzy pulled away, looking up. "Why the hell didn't you tell me you were moving?! The house! It's empty!" Her eyes were wide and glossy. "Dad, all the stuff. Mom's stuff—"

"Is safe, Isabelle. Trust me."

Her shoulders sagged with relief. "Good." She clapped her hands and walked around me, taking the place in fully. "Well, at least it's nice here! And that view, oh my gosh!" She pranced around, running her fingers across the brown leather recliner and then passing by the dining area. "One of these bedrooms better be mine." She quirked a brow, walking towards the rooms.

"You already know it."

Grinning, she entered the first bedroom, her gasp audible. As she took her time, looking around the condo, I walked to the kitchen, gesturing with a flick of my fingers for Chloe to follow. She walked with hesitation, peering around the corner.

"What happened to keeping our shit together?" I teased, pulling down two empty glasses from the cabinet. I placed them on the counter, opened the fridge, and pulled out a pitcher of lemonade. After filling a glass with ice and sliding it across the counter, I said, "Drink this. It'll distract you. You look like you've seen a ghost. Calm down, okay? We're fine. It's fine. She's not onto us." *I think...*

"It's just weird that she showed up like this," Chloe whispered. "She usually calls ahead of time. Izzy never just pops up... not like this." Her eyes bounced over her shoulder, and then she looked at me again, saying, "Do you think Trixie got to her?"

"I've been watching Trixie. She hasn't done anything. Trust me." I wiped my forehead with slight aggression, sliding my empty glass away. "It's all good, Knight. We'll be okay."

"She's not done with summer school, you know?" She sipped her lemonade, using it as a true distraction. "She's just here for the Fourth."

After she said that, Izzy came around the corner, shouting, "Dad! We have to throw a cookout on that deck! Like, seriously! That thing's huge. Hey, why don't you invite your girlfriend?" She folded her arms and smiled at me. My heart dropped to my stomach for Chloe. "I think its due time to meet her, especially if she can convince you to move out and leave everything behind without even telling me first."

"I chose to move. Needed something smaller and cheaper but still nice. It's close to work. Convenient. I was going to tell you when summer school was over. Wanted you to focus, kid."

"Dad, I'm an adult now." She stepped to Chloe's side. "I think you forget that we can handle whatever." She wrapped her arm across Chloe's shoulder, and Chloe joined in on the laughter, but the smile didn't touch her eyes. "But, listen, I'm serious about this cookout. Tell Trixie to come, and Chloe can stay too! Dad, oh my gosh, she has this really hot and cool guy that's been staying at her house all summer." *What?* I stiffened behind the counter, hands balling into fists, but luckily, Izzy couldn't see them. She continued talking, but Chloe saw right through me like a wall of glass. "Chloe said he was a freak—that he was always watching her or whatever—but I don't think he is. I think he just has a crush on her."

Chloe dropped her head.

I did my best to seem uncaring, but deep inside, it was pissing me off. Why didn't she ever tell me there was another man staying with her? And that he was into her?

"Really?" I asked, pointing my gaze on Chloe. "What's the kid's name?"

"Sterling. So hot, and apparently they are on good terms now. I think they made out or something. She denies it,"—she nudged Chloe in the ribs—"but I just think she's not ready to fill me in yet," Izzy said. "Hey!" She looked at Chloe. "We should go back and tell him to join us for dinner. You'll grill out, right, Dad? Chloe and I can see if we can pick up some fireworks from somewhere or something."

I breathed as evenly as possible. "Sure. I have some steaks and hotdogs around. I'll see what I can whip up."

"Great! But please tell Trixie to come. I really need to see what this woman is about." Fuck. Izzy was setting us up to fail. With Trixie around, it would disturb Chloe, throttle her emotions to the fullest, and with that *boy* around, the one into her, it would piss me off, and I sucked at hiding my emotions.

"I'll see if she's available today. Kinda last minute, so don't get your hopes up about meeting her."

Izzy scoffed. "Dad, please. You're acting like you don't want me to meet the woman that has made you happy. All I care about is that you're happy now." She looked at Chloe. "Have you seen her or met her?"

Chloe looked from me to Izzy, responding quickly. "Yeah, I've seen her."

"Is she hot?"

Chloe pressed her lips. I knew the words she wanted to say. I was sure there were plenty of things on the tip of her tongue, ready to spew fire, but instead, she went with Izzy, playing along with her best friend. "Oh, so hot! Mr. Black would be insane to not bring her around, especially if that's what makes him *happy* and all."

My eyes hardened on hers, our gazes locked briefly while Izzy laughed out loud. "See, Dad," Izzy laughed, tucking her layered black hair behind her ear. "Now you have to bring her. If you don't, I'll go through your phone and call her myself." She gave me a playful evil eye. I nodded, gripping the edges of the counter.

"Go do what you have to do," I said, holding back on a clipped tone. "I'll get the grill started. Food should be ready by the time you two get back."

"You mean us three," Izzy butted in.

I blinked.

"Sterling, remember?" She held out a hand, giving me one of her usual *Duh, Dad, you should know this* kind of looks.

"Right."

"Come on, Chlo." She reached for Chloe and went for the door. While dragging her along the way, Chloe glanced back once, eyes glossing before Izzy caught her attention again and they hurried out of the condo.

When they left, I released the breath that had been trapped in my lungs. I spotted my phone on the counter, refusing to call Trixie. But Izzy... I knew my daughter. She'd sneak my phone and call Trixie up just to meet her. When she wanted something, she made a way to get it, no matter what.

I sent Trixie a dry text, informing her that Izzy was in town and that she should come over for the Fourth to meet her but only for an hour or so.

She responded quickly.

Trixie: *I'll be there, Daddy. Can't wait to meet your lover's best friend.*

I gripped the phone in my hand, the urge to throw it at the wall overshadowing every shred of common sense within me, but I held off, sliding it into my back pocket instead.

Tonight was going to be a fucking disaster.

TWENTY-THREE

CHLOE

"WHY ARE YOU DRIVING SO SLOW?" Izzy's voice sliced through my thoughts. We had just left the store, picking up some fruit and desserts as well as the cheap firecrackers that didn't do much but spark a little and make a ton of noise. Everything that could have gone wrong was happening all at once.

"I'm not. I'm going the speed limit," I said.

"What person our age goes the speed limit?" Izzy teased.

I forced a laugh. I think she noticed my off behavior, but before she could ask me what was up, her phone buzzed, and she answered it. It was Drake, her boyfriend. I knew she wouldn't be getting off the phone until we got back to Theo's condo... hopefully.

I was purposely driving like I was chauffeuring Miss Daisy, hoping to come up with any kind excuse to get out of this evening. First off, getting Sterling seemed so wrong with all I knew. He'd slept with Mrs. Black! Theo's wife! If Sterling saw pictures of her, he would surely speak on it. He'd ask questions. He'd lose the little trust he had in me for not saying anything beforehand.

When I pulled up to my home and he walked out, my face went stale. He was smiling, but that had quickly dissolved when he spotted my concern. "You sure you want to come?" I asked as I glanced back at Izzy who was too busy chatting on her phone to pay us any mind.

"Sure, why not?" He shrugged with a smile. "Figured you might need someone to distract your friend there." His eyes bounced in Izzy's direction.

"Yeah." Sighing, I turned for the car and hopped in. Sterling slid across the backseat, and when his door shut, I put the car in reverse, my nerves on end.

"Hey, I'm gonna call you back." Izzy hung up the phone once I was out of Primrose, peering over her shoulder at Sterling. "Hi, again, mister." She flirted with him, as she always did when a hot guy was around, boyfriend or not.

"Hey." I saw Sterling toss a light wave at her through the rearview mirror, and then he looked at me, catching my eye. I looked away, focusing on the road. He was probably thinking exactly what I dreaded. *"Your best friend is here and you're going to be around her dad—the man you love—all night long! What in the hell are you going to do?"*

My heart pounded hard in my chest when I slowly pulled into the Remy Place parking lot. Izzy was eager to get out, rushing to the trunk to grab the few bags of groceries. I took a bag from her, and Sterling took that bag from me. "I got it. You don't need any more weight on you right now."

I thanked him with my eyes, but Izzy looked at us, probing with thin eyes. "What is that supposed to mean?" she laughed.

Surprisingly, Sterling covered up for it quickly. "Oh, you know, her dad and the Alzheimer's and all. He's been giving her and my mom hell lately." He smoothed his curly brown hair back as we entered the building.

"Oh." Izzy's lips pressed, and when she walked ahead of us, Sterling gave me a look that said, *"I don't know how you're going to get through this night."*

He may have thought that because Izzy wasn't the type of person to hold her tongue. She talked a lot but asked questions even more, especially when she was confused about something. She was a firm believer in the saying "There is no such thing as a dumb question."

It was a good thing Sterling wanted to come. He could prevent any unwanted drama, quite possibly distract Izzy if something was said or done out of context between Theo and me. Izzy, after all, could be easily distracted.

We made it up to that familiar fourth floor, all with Izzy talking about how she'd hoped her dad grilled everything right and didn't burn it. I started to tell her that he wasn't going to mess it up because he'd gotten great at cooking, but I stopped myself. I had to be careful now. If Izzy didn't know something about Theo, I had to pretend I didn't either.

Opening the door, Izzy waltzed right in, going for the kitchen to place her grocery bag on the counter. Sterling followed in after me, murmuring, "Here we go," as he shut the door behind him.

I walked to the kitchen with Izzy. Theo was nowhere in sight. "Dad?" Izzy called. She walked out of the kitchen, and we all heard him return her call from the deck.

"Come on, Chlo," Izzy insisted. I went with her, stepping onto the deck. Theo was in the corner with his grill on, flipping burgers with an annoyed look on his face, and to his right, sitting on the brown chair was Trixie. She was fixing her makeup in her handheld mirror, but when she caught sight of us, she quickly stopped tampering with her reflection, releasing a gasp.

Theo noticed how she glared my way, pausing on grilling the food. She hopped to her feet, scampering towards us in six-inch heels. "Oh my gosh!" She hugged Izzy, and to my surprise, Izzy wasn't pleased about it.

I laughed. She was the one that wanted to meet her. I guess I should have mentioned that Trixie was only like two years older than us. "Hi," Izzy forced her greeting. "You must be... Trixie?"

"I am! And you must be Theo's little Isabelle. He talks about you all the time."

"Yep." Izzy's brows puckered, and she took a step back as she glanced from Trixie to her dad.

"And you," Trixie said, stepping around Izzy. "Why, you must be Chloe. Her best friend, right?" She pulled me in and hugged me too tight for comfort. It took every ounce of strength within me to remain calm and hug her back like a decent, innocent person would. I couldn't believe she was playing this game. Hadn't Theo told her to behave? He needed to put his bitch on a leash.

"Wow, you're really friendly," Izzy noted as she looked Trixie over in her white romper and red wedges. Her earrings were dangly and blue, matching the headband that kept her blond curls behind her ears. *Festive bitch.* She'd dyed her hair, giving it a red tint. Wow. Did she want to be Mrs. Black or what? She must've caught a picture of her somewhere. I shook my head.

"Yeah, well," Trixie sighed. "I like to make everyone feel like they can be themselves around me, you know?"

"Hmm." Izzy walked around Trixie and grabbed my hand. "Well, it's nice meeting you!" Izzy gave her dad a sharp look when Trixie pulled out her cellphone. "Chloe, come with me to change clothes?"

"Sure."

We walked back inside where Sterling sat on the sofa watching a game of soccer. "Wow, you made yourself right at home, huh?" Izzy giggled.

"I guess I did, huh?" Sterling held his hands in the air with an innocent lift of his shoulders.

"It's okay. My dad won't mind." *So she thought.* "Chloe," she hissed, turning me in her direction, "Why in the hell didn't you tell me she was like, twelve!?"

"I didn't know! From far away she doesn't look that young."

"Ugh." Izzy groaned. "I don't like her. She comes across as phony to me. I read people, and I know she's only with my dad because he makes good money. She's a grubby little bitch."

"Well, it's who your dad likes, Izzy." That hurt to say. I swallowed that bile down as quickly as it came back up. "If he thinks girls like her are what will make him happy, then you can't be mad at him."

She waved a hand. "Yeah, whatever. Now I see why he didn't want to invite her to dinner. God... I'm gonna go change and wipe this disappointment off my face." Izzy turned and walked down the hallway, entering one of the bedrooms.

I blew a breath, turning around. Sterling was still on the sofa, but his eyes were on me now, not the TV screen. "How'd it go out there?"

I gave him the evil-eye and sat in the recliner. "This is a fucking train wreck waiting to happen." He sympathized with me, sitting forward as if he were all ears. "That bitch," I whispered. "She actually had the nerve to hug me in front of Izzy."

"Why do you call her a bitch? What did she do to you?"

"She is coming between me and Theo. She said she'd snitch if he tried to leave her for me. She found out about us the same night you did. She saw him climbing out of my window."

"Really?" He was shocked to hear that.

"Yes." I slouched back, wishing it were Trixie's head on that soccer field on screen and me doing the kicking.

"Well, maybe it's a good thing she's here right now, Chloe. Just saying."

I whipped my head to look at him, brows going thin. "What do you mean?"

"I mean... maybe it's a good thing she's here tonight. You'll have no choice but to keep your distance from him."

"Fuck that," I muttered, glancing towards the balcony. "She doesn't even deserve him."

"And you do?"

I turned my gaze on Sterling again. I hated his smart mouth, his mellow face, but most of all, I hated that he was *right*. I hated that he knew so much and had gone through something similar to this himself. Speaking of...

"Hey, there's something I should tell you—" I started to speak, tell him all about Mrs. Black being Theo's wife and even about how Theo was once in The Union, but Theo came inside, shutting the balcony door behind him with a tray of burgers in hand. My mouth snapped shut when I looked back.

"Food is almost ready." He glared at Sterling.

Sterling stood, extending his arm. Theo accepted the handshake, but his brown eyes never drifted. "I'm Sterling. A friend of Chloe's."

Theo cocked a brow. "Just a friend?"

Sterling was hesitant, looking from him to me. "Stop it, Theo," I butted in. I stood up, and walked closer. "He knows everything about us. So just stop."

Releasing his grip, Theo stepped back, giving Sterling a once over. "Everything as in what?"

"Well, I know you two are a thing and also that you shouldn't be. I also know about the girl out there on the balcony, how she's trying to cause hell." Sterling ran his palms across the back of his jeans. "Just found that one out actually. You don't have to worry about me, though. I get it. No judgment here. I understand." Yeah, I bet he did.

"Mmm." Theo grunted, turning away from Sterling and looking at me. "Come with me to the kitchen," he said before walking away.

I waited a moment, giving Sterling a nod before going to the kitchen. "Need help?" I asked with bland enthusiasm.

"There's seafood pasta in the fridge. Take that out please." Theo's voice was clearly irritated. I turned for the fridge, pulling the door open and taking out the clear bowl.

"Can't believe she actually touched me," I grumbled, slamming the bowl on the counter. "Theo, I don't know if I'll be able to do this all night. I think I'm going to leave after we eat. Izzy will understand."

"Leave early with him?" He scowled in Sterling's direction. Sterling was oblivious. "Why didn't you tell me he was staying at your house?"

"What's the big deal? He's the caregiver's son. She wanted to see him after not seeing him for three whole years."

"I don't care. I don't like how he looks at you. And how the fuck does he know everything about us?" He puffed, slinging out a knife to cut some cucumber. "Did you tell him?"

"He heard us the night you snuck through my window. And... he also heard me asking for advice from Margie."

"Margie?" He looked confused.

"The caregiver."

He still looked lost.

I rolled my eyes. "His mom."

"Oh."

"Seriously, you have nothing to worry about with him. He's a good guy. But... he's also what I wanted to talk to you about."

He stopped cutting, dropping the knife on the cutting board. "What do you mean?" His face paled.

"I'll tell you when we meet at *Dirty Black*. I should go back out there. I shouldn't be seen too close to you." I began to turn, but Theo caught my arm, his head angled. "Do you... like him?"

His question was absurd. My face contorted, and I pulled my arm away, grimacing at him. "Are you serious?" I hissed, thinning my eyes. "I'm standing in *your* condo feeling like the worst woman and friend in the world because I love you, and you ask me if I like *him?*" I scoffed. "You're ridiculous, Theo. Seriously." I started to turn, but quickly caught myself, ready to add more fuel to the fire. "Oh, by the way, Izzy hates Trixie. Just a heads up. I'm pretty sure this night is about to get a whole lot worse."

He looked at me briefly before snatching his gaze away, jaw ticking, nostrils flaring.

I folded my arms. "Just like me, she can see right through her. You shouldn't have invited her."

"And you shouldn't have brought your friend over there."

"I had no choice. Izzy wanted him to join us."

"Yeah, well, neither did I."

Theo's nostrils flared again, his upper lip peeling back as he looked towards Sterling again. Sterling cheered over the game, and Theo's mouth twitched. What was the big deal? Sterling was a nice guy. The last thing I was worried about was him. I worried about Theo. Us. That whole damn night was going to have my nerves running wild.

The balcony door drew shut, and Trixie's heels clicked along the floor. I jerked back, fiddling with the plastic wrap covering the pasta. "Theo, baby, I think the hotdogs are done." She stepped into the kitchen, coming up on his side as he diced cucumber.

"They're not done. Told you to stay out there."

"Why? It's too hot out there."

Theo's jaw clenched. "Whatever, Trixie." He collected all the cucumber, put it on top of the prepared salad, and then grabbed a pan for the hotdogs. He was out of the kitchen, but not before looking at me with guilt running deep in those brown irises.

I watched him disappear around the corner, and from behind, Trixie cleared her throat. I turned, looking straight into her blue eyes. She stood with her arms folded, looking me over as if I was the ugliest thing she'd ever seen. "If you know what's best for you and Theo, I suggest you stay away from him tonight. Actually, stay away from him period."

My mouth fixed on a heated response, and I stepped forward, but a hand touched my shoulder. Sterling appeared at my side. "Hey, got anything to drink in here?"

Trixie was surprised to see him. She liked what she saw. That was obvious. "Oh, sure!" She went for the fridge, stepping in front of me and pulling it open. "I bought some of Theo's favorite beer and some wine coolers for myself... and the *girls*." There was venom in her voice when she referred to us... well, me. "Help yourself!"

"Thanks." Sterling took charge of the fridge, and Trixie sauntered past me, giving me one final lookover before leaving the kitchen and returning to the balcony. When she was gone, I uncurled the fists that I hadn't realized I'd made, pinching the bridge of my nose. "Alright?" Sterling asked.

"Fine," I muttered, leaving the kitchen. I went down the hallway and into the bathroom, shutting the door behind me and locking it. It was hard not to slam it, not to break everything in sight, but I kept my emotions stable.

Breathing evenly through flared nostrils, I stared into the mirror above the vanity, gripping the edge of the granite countertop. The tears had already started, and two slid down my cheeks. A knock sounded on the door seconds later.

"Chloe?" It was Izzy.

"Yeah." I cleared my face, but she heard the thickness in my voice.

"What's wrong?" She jiggled the doorknob, her voice sincere. "Come on. Open up."

I contemplated opening the door. I didn't want her to see me crying. Not only that, but I needed a lie to back the tears up.

So, like Sterling did, I knew I had to use the very thing that made me volunteer to spend my summer in Bristle Wave. Unlocking the door, I stepped back and sat on the edge of the tub. Izzy walked in, looking right at me with concerned eyes. "Chloe?"

"I'm okay. I swear."

"You don't look okay. See, I knew I wasn't crazy. Something seems so off about you today. I didn't want to say anything in case you were on your period or something, but now I see it's not that time of the month for you."

"Next week," I sighed.

"So what is it then?" She sat beside me. When I didn't speak right away, her face changed, and she justified herself. "Look, I know we don't see each other as much as we used to, but you're still my best friend, Chlo. You can talk to me about anything."

"I know." I cleared my face. "I know, Iz. I'm just so stressed out about my dad. I keep wondering why I tortured myself by coming back here." Lies.

"That's not torturing yourself. I was supposed to come but... college is a lot harder than I thought." She sighed. "We were supposed to hang out too, but... shit happens. Plus, you have a good heart. You did good by coming back to Bristle. He needed family around. Your mom didn't want to step up to the plate, so you did. No one can blame you for that. If anything, your mom should be to blame... leaving him alone like that. What kind of wife does that to her husband anyway?" Her face pinched.

I shrugged. "Selfish ones."

"Yeah," she scoffed. "Exactly. But you're not selfish. So calm down and come with me. Dad said the food should be ready in a bit. You can help me set up the table." I nodded, allowing her to pull me up to a stand. She playfully pinched my cheeks when I was upright, giggling as she then bumped my hip with hers. I couldn't ignore her silliness. I laughed, dropping my head as we exited the bathroom. From the hallway, the soccer game sounded louder. I heard Sterling hooting, cursing, and cheering for God knows what team.

Izzy went to the kitchen to pull down some Chinaware, and I went for the cupboard, pulling down four glasses. I purposely forgot the fifth one. Fuck Trixie. After setting up the table, Theo was inside with the rest of the food. I placed the salad down, and Sterling assisted Theo with the meat, placing it in the center of the table.

Then we took our seats.

And dinner was served— a really fucking awkward dinner.

Izzy, of course, talked as if the world revolved around her. She went on and on about summer school and even the wreck and how it all went down as if we hadn't heard that story a million times.

Sterling was nice enough to comment and chime in on her stories when Theo and I couldn't stand to. And Trixie glared at me the entire time as she nibbled on a hotdog without a bun. She downed three glasses of wine like it was a ritual, but she was afraid to eat a piece of bread? She was ridiculous.

She purposely leaned into Theo, whispering to him. He'd ignore her until Izzy would glance their way and force a smile at the weird couple. Despite the sick control Trixie had over our lives, I couldn't help but think she felt out of place. She finished off her glass of wine and took three wine coolers out of the fridge, making those alcoholic beverages her friends for the night.

Dinner was a wrap within twenty miserable, desolate minutes. I was ready to go. "I think I'm gonna hit the pool." Izzy looked out the window. "It's so nice out right now. Hey, Chloe, you wanna join me? Sterling?"

Sterling and I looked at each other. "Nah, Izzy, I think I should just get home. See how Dad's doing."

"Oh! Right." She nodded, and surprisingly, she didn't pout about it. She understood, especially after my fib about being stressed over him. "Well, what about you, Sterling?"

"I... should probably get home too."

"Aww." She whined this time. "But we haven't even lit the fireworks yet! I have a car too, you know? I can take you back if you want."

Sterling glanced my way for a brief moment. I remembered him saying how he hated passing up the opportunity to swim. I had no reason to hold him back, so I shrugged. "Okay. Sure," he agreed.

"Cool. I'll go change. I think my dad has some trunks you can borrow."

Once Izzy had given Sterling a pair of trunks and then changed into a gold and black two-piece bikini, they left the condo. I blew a breath as I collected the dirty plates from the table, bringing them to the kitchen where Theo stood. It was then that I noticed Trixie wasn't around.

"Where'd your girl toy?" I asked.

He walked around me, going to the table for the half-empty trays of grilled meat. "Drunk as fuck in the bathroom. Probably shoving a finger down her throat to get rid of the little bit of carbs she ate today."

"She acts worse than me." I helped him clean off the rest of the oak table, picking up the cups, beer cans, and the one wine glass that belonged to the trick. "She isn't staying the night, is she?"

Theo didn't answer. He dropped everything on the counter as I tossed the cans in the recycling bin and then the cups in the sink. When my hands were free, he pulled me into his arms, clutched my face in his hands, and devoured my lips whole. He crushed them but not too much to the point it caused pain. Just enough for me to feel it —to know that he'd wanted this to happen all day long.

Like always, our tongues did a slow dance, mingling and swirling, my body pressing into his. A moan filled the kitchen, one I couldn't hold in, and then I sighed as he groaned. I felt his cock hardening through the jean material, and when the kiss broke, his brown eyes were like hot coals, black and burning.

"No." He finally answered my question. "But I wish you could stay tonight."

"I can't," I moaned.

"I know. I guess tonight didn't turn out as bad as you thought," he murmured, planting a kiss on my cheek and another on my forehead.

"I guess not," I whispered.

He held my face in his hands, looking me over. "Alright. What's bothering you?"

I batted my lashes. "What do you mean?"

"I mean, other than Izzy and Trixie being here, there's something bothering you. What did you need to talk to me about with that Sterling kid? I've been wondering all day. I can tell when something's wrong with you."

"Oh... yeah..." I sighed. "There's something you should know about Mrs. Black... something I found out just yesterday night."

In an instant, Theo's body went stiff, his face going hard like stone. He didn't like me mentioning Mrs. Black... not when it involved something he may not have known about. "What are you talking about?" His question came out hurried and discouraged.

My throat worked harder than usual to swallow. He stared at me, and at first, I was willing to tell him, but when I spotted the raw concern—the cold, dead look—I didn't want to. I didn't want to be the one to break the bad news to him. I didn't want to be the one to ruin Mrs. Black's reputation as a good wife. He deserved to hold onto the goodness of her. Who was I to taint it with black?

"Chloe?" Theo demanded.

Just as his voice bellowed, the front door shot open, and Izzy rushed back in with Sterling trailing behind her. "Forgot my towel!" she said, but she was too buzzed to wonder why we were standing so close. I pulled away, tucking my hair behind my ear, and Sterling walked closer, brows raised as if it were a close call.

"Thanks for the heads up," I snipped at him.

"She was going too fast." He looked away. "I thought you were going home?"

"I am." I gave him a look, one that was plainly telling him to leave me alone. Theo had his eyes fixed on Sterling. His look was cold and cruel. Furious and heated. And then it hit me—the reason he'd gotten so livid. Sterling... he had no shirt on. He'd taken it off most likely when he was on his way to swim. He was oblivious... but only because he didn't know.

"Holy shit," I breathed, and Sterling heard me.

He looked confused. "What?"

He pointed his gaze on Theo next, but when he caught the fury in his eyes, he took a minor step back, one eyebrow furrowed. "What the hell is that?" Theo's voice boomed even louder than before. Storming out of the kitchen, he wasted no time gripping Sterling by his throat and pinning him to the nearest wall.

"Theo!" I shouted. "Stop!" I darted around the counter, grabbing his arm, but he pulled away.

"What the fuck is that on your shoulder!? Huh? You still with them? Did they send you to kill me!? Fuck with my life!? MY LOVE!"

In the heat of the moment, Theo turned my way and glared down. "Chloe! Who the fuck is he, huh?"

"That's what I wanted to tell you!" I wailed. "I was trying to explain!"

"Explain what?!" he barked.

Thick tears lined the rims of my eyes. God, I was so tired of holding it in. I hated all of these secrets—all the lying and holding back on how I truly felt, so I let go of everything. I put myself first, knowing deep down that I was truly selfish for doing such a thing. "You think Mrs. Black was innocent, but she wasn't who you thought she was!" I exclaimed. "She was cheating on you with Sterling!"

Theo blinked rapidly, eyes still broad as he released Sterling. Sterling clung to his throat, looking at me with wide, confused, grey eyes. "What?" he wheezed. "No—no I didn't even know she was your wi—"

"What did you just say?" Theo moved towards me, shutting Sterling up and acting as if he never even existed. His eyes were on me. The spotlight was on me, but I didn't want to shine. His hands went to my upper arms, and he held me. His grip was tight and rough, but he made sure he wasn't hurting me. "Chloe, don't fuck around with me! Don't make shit up about her! You didn't even know her like I did!"

"I'm not." My voice broke as I looked at his red-rimmed eyes. "That night, when Mrs. Black was murdered, it was because of The Union. Remember when you said there was more than one guy—well, there was. A whole gang. You never told me they didn't allow love, but Sterling did. He used to be a part of their gang, and as his punishment, they robbed him of his love, killing the woman he was in love with. He loved Mrs. Black, Theo. And she loved him. She was with him on those nights she'd work late. She stopped at that run-down gas station because she was most likely on her way to see Sterling."

The room—the entire condo—went absolutely still. If a pin dropped on the hard surface of the floor it would have caused all ears to rattle. Theo released me and staggered back, staring at me as if I had a demon on my shoulder. He shook his head back and forth, muttering the word "no" over and over again.

"No," he growled. "No. You're lying!"

"I wouldn't lie to you! Sterling!" I rushed for Sterling. "Tell him! Tell him what her name was."

"No, Chloe." He scowled in my direction. "He'll fucking kill me, damn it!"

"Just tell him! It's the only way he'll know this is true—that I'm not making this up."

Sterling's damp eyes turned on Theo. He dropped his hands from his throat and stood up straight. "Her name was Janet Black... but I swear I didn't know you were her husband when I came here. I knew she had a husband and a daughter, but I didn't know who you or Izzy were... not until now." He focused on me. "Chloe must've just been too afraid to tell me." He dropped his head. "Shit."

Theo looked both of us over with an incredulous expression, and in a matter of seconds, he spun around and barged through his bedroom door. He returned with a photo album in his hands, the same one that I'd gone through the first day they moved to Primrose. He flipped the pages, going to his most recent picture of Mrs. Black. Pointing a thick, angry finger, he gruffly asked, "Her? She was the one you slept with? This woman?"

Sterling looked down, and I could see the admiration quickly fill his eyes. I also witnessed the pain he held, how he'd constantly wanted to blame himself for her death. If he'd never met or fallen for her, she wouldn't have died.

"Yes," Sterling whispered. "Yeah, that's her. That's—that's Janet."

Theo watched Sterling's reaction, how guilt swarmed him and ate him up. He caught the anguish, the same pain he felt when he lost Mrs. Black. They had both lost a good woman, but both of them felt betrayed. By the way Sterling looked at Theo, I was sure he could see all the love Theo had for his dead wife. He saw that she was most likely happy to be with him, but that she'd also given half of her heart to him. She couldn't choose, so she kept both.

Seeing the two of them watch each other and not know what in the hell to do was hard to witness. I couldn't block my tears or prevent the sniffling that came along with it. I wasn't sure if they wanted to strangle each other or feel deep pity for one another.

"Is all that true?" Izzy's voice cut through the turmoil, and everyone turned to look at her. She stepped forward with a towel in hand, eyes glistening. "Is. That. True?" she asked Sterling.

He looked down. "Yes."

Theo started to lunge forward with the urge to attack Sterling, but something stopped him from doing so. Perhaps it was because he knew it wasn't his fault for loving Mrs. Black. Sterling fell for her because she accepted him entirely for who he was, just as she did Theo. In a way, Theo was only looking at a younger replica of himself. I could hear everyone's heartbeats, their minds racing with drama, chaos, and pain.

"Mom... cheated?" Izzy whispered. "That—she would never do that."

"Oh, sweetie, it's not like Theo really cares." Trixie appeared out of nowhere, wobbling as she met at Izzy's side. She was wasted, some of her makeup smeared, the edges of her hair frizzy as if she'd constantly put cold water on her face.

Izzy jerked away. "Get off of me!"

Trixie narrowed her eyes. "You know what?! Fuck this!" she yelled. "Fuck everyone in this fucking place! I am so *sick* and tired of the side eyes and the shit talking behind my back. You think I don't hear it, but I do, and you know what, screw all of you because none of you are perfect!" She stumbled forward, pointing one finger at me and one at Theo. And as she did, my heart jumped out of my chest and hit the floor because I knew what was coming. I knew she was truly, honestly done being around, holding in her juicy information. "Especially the two of you!" she seethed. "You sneaky little sons of bitches! You thought you were so good that no one would *ever* find out, but I did. And you both are fucking idiots!"

"Trixie!" Theo's voice was loud as he marched for her, grabbing her arm and pulling her away, but she jerked and twisted out of his grasp. She was quick, rushing in Izzy's direction.

"Hey, I bet you don't know that your dad and your best friend are fucking, do you?" Her voice, though slurred, was comprehensible, and it felt like the heart that was on the floor—my heart—was now being stomped on by a stampede of wild bulls.

My body seemed to do nothing, but I wanted to rush forward,

tackle Trixie to the ground, and tell Izzy it was all lies. But... but... I couldn't. I was stuck, not in a trance or a daze. Just stuck.

"W-what?" Izzy's forehead creased as she turned to face Trixie who was being hauled away by Theo. Theo's anger lit his face. He was red from head to toe, stalking towards the door and tossing her out.

"Yeah! She's fucking your dad! Some friend, huh!" she shouted before the door slammed in her face.

Theo didn't move once he'd slammed it. He just stood there, staring at the back of the glossy brown door.

I was just as motionless. Powerless.

In that moment, as Izzy's watery, depressed eyes met mine, I snapped out of my stupor and rushed for her. She backed away from me, holding her hands up and warding me off as if I had a contagious disease. "Izzy, I am so sorry," I whispered, head shaking. "It was never supposed to happen. It was really late, and he needed someone to help him so—"

Izzy held her hand up but said nothing, which was disturbingly rare. I wanted her to speak. Shout! Do anything. Curse me out if it made her feel better. But for nearly one whole minute, she was mute. Theo finally turned around, but he avoided his daughter's watery eyes, focusing on the floor. Sterling walked past him and out of the condo, leaving the three of us standing there with heavy minds and empty mouths.

"I can't fucking believe you." Izzy finally spoke, but the words were far from kind. They were sharp, deadly, and dripping with venom. "You fucking *skank*! You said you came here for you dad—to help him—but you were here fucking mine all along!?"

"Izzy, I swear it wasn't like that!"

"No? Really? Then what was it?"

"I did come here for my dad—we were—" I didn't know how to respond. My tongue was twisted, but my mind was filled with way too many responses. I had always wondered how this day would go if it ever happened. The "if" was what scared me, but when I thought of it, I had so much I could have said to back myself up, but it was much harder than I thought. Nothing felt right—nothing but telling her the shocking truth. The one thing I knew. It was all out of love. *Love!* That's what it was, but I couldn't spill that truth.

"Yeah," she breathed. "Exactly. Wow." She shook her head, huffing a laugh that didn't dare light her soul. "And Dad, you... *wow*." She was shocked, finding this information truly unbelievable. "I can't even fucking believe you would do something like this. With Chloe!? You're twice her age, Dad! You could be her fucking father! You're fucking *disgusting*! Is that what turns you on? Girls that can consider you their dad? Girls my age that don't know any fucking better?" She scoffed, snatching up her purse and storming for the door. Before she could get there, Theo caught her, spinning her around.

"You're not driving angry, Izzy. Stay here so we can explain."

She seemed to blow fire, yanking her arm away and backing up. I moved forward, eyes thick, full of tears and heavy with apologies. "Fuck you, Dad! Fuck you! Now I see why Mom cheated on you! You're a selfish prick who only thinks about himself! Did you even care to think about how *I* would feel about this? I'm your only child, and she is —no, *was* my only friend. And you..." She turned my way, looking at me directly.

"Izzy," I whimpered. "Please." *Please what, Chloe? Please what!? Say something, stupid! Anything!*

"You..." Her head shook, her upper lip curling as she disappointedly shook her head at me. Her voice cracked, and I was sure the ache she felt was all too real. I knew it was similar to the ache I felt... the hurt. The pain. It was hard to bare. "You aren't a good-hearted person," she grumbled. "You are a no-good, inconsiderate *bitch*. You've always had the hots for my dad. I always knew it. I just didn't think you'd take it *this* far. You knew staying around me would get you closer, didn't you? You are a little fucking *whore*, just like your mom! I knew some of her would rub off on you somewhere."

"Isabelle *fucking* Black!" Theo's voice roared. He was angry. Pissed the fuck off. His knuckles had whitened, nostrils flaring with a locked jaw and knitted brows.

Her words were like leather belts, whipping every sensitive part of me. I called her name repeatedly, begging forgiveness, but I wouldn't be forgiven. She wouldn't because she didn't understand... or maybe I didn't understand. I hurt Izzy. I'd had my heart broken before, but I was certain I'd broken hers that night. She was angry, yes, but she spoke out of raw anger because she trusted me. She loved me and felt like she could talk to me about any and everything.

I would have never taken advantage of my friend, but I couldn't say I had the right to fuck with Mr. Black. I had no right. And I clearly had no real respect because I went through with sleeping with him many, many times.

"Fuck you, Dad!" She fled.

I buckled when my best friend—ex best friend—stormed out of the condo. Theo was torn, unsure if he should go for me or for Izzy. He debated, peering my way and starting to come, but then he stepped back, looking towards the door.

He ran out the door, calling after his only child, and I fell, my knees hitting the hard floor, tears streaming. I'd cried before, plenty of times. But never like this. Never, ever like this. A gaping hole had formed in my chest. It would be hard to fill. I'd been picked apart, my heart cracking with each withered beat. It was a painful feeling. It hurt... it hurt so damn much. "I'm sorry," I cried to nobody. "I swear I didn't want it to happen like this..."

I died little by little.

I hurt.

I died some more.

Imagine blood seeping out of every pore, spilling right from the gash in your heart. Imagine not being able to prevent the bleeding. Can you imagine that pain? Not being able to control something that feels so close, yet something that is so deep inside you that you can't reach it unless you rip yourself wide open, clawing with raw loathing?

You suffer as you scratch, knowing that soon you will die inside and out because there's nothing you can do to stop it. You can't stop the drumming of an emotional, beautiful heart, not unless you stab a dagger of hatred right through the center.

Just imagine that, but bleeding out ten times faster than the average person. Imagine bleeding for lost love, broken hearts, and damaged souls. Imagine feeling nothingness—an unbearable ache that will never be fulfilled.

Can you imagine?

Can you feel it... that very ache that I had no choice but to feel?

I sat on Theo's floor for what felt like an eternity, folded over, my face buried in my hands. A door shut minutes later and heavy footsteps came my way. They stopped right beside me, and with a gentle grasp, I was pulled up.

I glanced up, and through blurred vision, I could tell it was Theo by his broad shoulders and straggled hair. "Couldn't make it to the elevator in time."

"You can't let her drive angry."

"She won't." He lifted up the key fob. "She forgot the keys."

I sniffled, dropping my chin. "Theo, I—I feel so bad." My throat dried and thickened, eyes welting again. "We never should have touched each other..."

His face saddened, tears collecting at the rims of his eyes. "I know, Chloe." He pulled me in and inhaled. His warm breath ran down my shoulders when he exhaled. "I'm so fucking sorry, Knight."

He held me, rocked with me for just a little while. "This can't be fixed," I whispered. "Can it?"

He didn't say anything. I didn't expect him to.

Pulling back and tilting my chin, he said, "Come with me to the docks. It should get you to relax... calm down for now. She'll come back. She has to. Let her take some time to cool off, and let's hope she doesn't do anything crazy."

"Should we go after her?"

He was perplexed. He wanted to, but he and I both knew Izzy would be hard to find, and if we did find her, we would get another ear full of hatred and shame. So he shook his head. "Nah. Let her come back to us."

She'd come back to him. But me... hmm. No. But I nodded anyway, and he brought his mouth down to kiss me. I expected to feel that same heat, that quick fire that always made me combust deep inside, but instead, I felt nothing. It didn't feel like how it felt once before.

It wasn't dirty or bad or wrong. It didn't even feel good. I didn't feel *anything*. I was numb to his touch, like my body had anesthetized itself, preventing me from feeling anymore pain, or hurt... even the love.

He noticed... I think. If he did, he didn't speak on it.

Theo grabbed his keys, and we were at his bike in no time. During the ride, I clung to him as if my life depended on it, but there was something about the position I was in. He was quiet, but I was quieter. I still cried, going over all the times he and I made love, how we secretly created a relationship that couldn't be understood. The foundation of our relationship was Izzy. If it weren't for being her friend, I never would have met or hung around Theo so much.

I was sure his mind was crowded, not only with how he was going to gain his daughter's forgiveness, but also with Mrs. Black. She'd cheated on him... with Sterling. She lied about a lot of things. All these years he thought she was only loyal to him—and for a while she was—but for the last few years of her life, she wasn't. She'd given half of her heart to a boy that had similarities to her first love.

That night, I was sure Theo's peace with her death had changed. He didn't know his wife like he thought he did. Hell, he hardly got to spend much time with her because she was always working, and by "working" I meant messing around with Sterling.

I held Theo that night, and as my tears dampened his T-shirt, I only had one thought in mind, a thought that cut me so deep and gutted me so much I felt like I was suffocating.

He was right about the guilt I would feel if Izzy ever found out about us—how it would eat me alive if I even dared to continue what I had with him. My heart still beat, but it was aching. My soul had been shattered and crushed. I had no desire to smile, no desire to be happy or to feel complete.

I'd lost my only friend—my sister.

I'd lost her.

Forever.

There was always the question of what it would be like if she ever found out, but now that she had, everything I knew about myself seemed so meaningless. If she were to forgive me, it would never be the same between us. A permanent awkwardness would surround us whenever we were together, pushing us further apart and making it that much harder to be happy.

My body racked, the sobs blending in with the wind that passed me by. I sobbed because I would never see Izzy again. I cried because, after that night, I would be someone else—someone without a partner in crime or with calls and texts to look forward to.

But I wept most because, after that night, I was never going to hold Theo like this again.

TWENTY-FOUR

THEO

THE WORLD I had restored after three lonely years came crashing down again. And this time, it was really, *really* fucked up.

My baby girl... my daughter. I couldn't believe myself. After raising her to be the woman she'd become, showing her the ropes in life, and teaching her the basics of how to survive in this crazy world, I'd sent her running away from me. I broke my baby's heart—actually I'd broken two hearts.

Her trust in me? Gone.

My Isabelle...

It's sad to think that I never thought I would get to that point—of her finding out about Chloe and me. I wanted her to stay oblivious to it. I wanted to keep my daughter in my life but also keep my little knight in shining armor.

Who was I kidding? I knew I couldn't have both—that I couldn't keep going on with Chloe like I did. Her words... they broke the little that was left of my heart, and when she spewed her anger at Chloe, I felt fucking terrible.

It wasn't her fault.

It was mine. I never should have touched her. I never should have relied on her to take care of me. I was a grown man. I shouldn't have needed saving by someone that hardly even knew better. I shouldn't have expected her to come running, picking up all my damaged pieces and restoring them.

But I did. I didn't regret it, though. As horrible as I felt, I didn't regret what Chloe and I created. I would never regret someone that made me feel alive again when I thought it would be damn near impossible to. I loved that girl—I loved her more than life itself, but I loved my daughter unconditionally. More that I can put into words.

I loved Janet dearly, but after finding out she'd lied to me, I went blank. She cheated on me, something I never would have done to her. She hardly knew that kid. She'd known me for fifteen years of her life but risked putting our relationship on the line for a kid that most likely considered her a good, easy lay.

Chloe said he loved her, but I didn't believe it. I didn't believe it because he didn't love Janet the way I did. Wholly. Fiercely. Passionately. Undeniably. Fuck, I couldn't believe I'd spent so many years with her, and in the end, it turned out she wasn't happy with me.

Where did I go wrong?

What did I do?

Did I not love hard enough?

Did I forget a birthday or anniversary?

Did I not show her enough attention?

I blinked my tears away as I walked onto *Dirty Black*, cranking her up and sailing across the sea. Chloe sat on the bench in the corner with her arms wrapped around her, her line of sight nowhere near mine. She focused on the ocean. She hadn't said a thing since leaving the condo.

My heart broke for her. I couldn't imagine how she felt. I thought surely I would be able to protect her from ever getting caught—from ever ruining her relationship with my daughter.

I was wrong.

I guess I couldn't do everything.

I was no Superman.

I was the Joker, playing tricks with her mind and body, bringing her deeper into a game that we both knew wouldn't end fairly.

Stopping the boat, I went for the anchor and dropped it in the water then turned around, getting an eyeful of Chloe. Fuck, she was hurt. Her face was pale, her body shivering as if she were freezing. But she wasn't shaking from the wind. She was shaking because she was crying.

I walked her way, silently reaching for her hand. She looked up as I kissed the back of it. Then I brought her to a stand. She looked away, but she stayed close. "I'll talk to Izzy," I murmured. "She can't be angry forever."

"With you," she mumbled. "You're her dad. She can't be angry with you forever. But with me... she can." She sighed, dropping her head. "Theo, the last thing I ever wanted to do was hurt Izzy. There were plenty of times when I wanted to give up on you—us—but I didn't because I was torn. I love you... and I love her. But... I should have known this would happen. Look at us," she whispered. "We don't belong together. It may feel like we do, but we don't."

"What makes you think we don't belong together?"

"Because, if we were really put on this earth to be together, Izzy wouldn't have turned out to be my best friend of ten years, and you wouldn't be her dad. There would be nothing to tie us. No one should have to get hurt because two people love each other."

Her eyes were glossy when she looked up at me again. She didn't blink; she just watched my eyes until a tear slid down her cheek. I swiped it away with my thumb. The question I wanted to ask hurt. It made my heart pound, but not in a good way. I didn't want to ask, but I also didn't want to be selfish. She deserved better. Ten times better than me.

"So what do we do from here, Chloe?"

Her mouth sealed tight as she placed her arms around me. Her lips pressed on the sliver of skin revealed above my chest. Next, my neck. She pushed against me until I stepped back, landing in the captain's seat again.

Straddling my lap, she grabbed the hem of her shirt and tossed it. Then she reached for mine, pulling it over my head. Her eyes drifted down my bare chest and arms. She studied the tattoos carefully, and then she brought those beautiful hazel eyes back up when found the black tribal wave below my left collarbone. She leaned forward and pressed her smooth lips on top of it. Something about that created an ache within me.

I felt empty.

Hollow.

Like I was slowly losing my grasp on her.

Sliding off my lap, she bent over and unbuttoned my jeans. She slid them down to my ankles and did the same with my briefs. Her perfect mouth circled the head of my cock, and she filled her mouth, gagging only slightly, causing a deep groan to fill the air.

"Chloe—wait, let me—"

"No, Theo," she whispered, pressing her hand to my chest and forcing me back. "No. Let's make this one count. Okay?"

She didn't give me time to answer. Her mouth wrapped around me again, her tongue gliding down my shaft in the same amount of time. I watched her, and my eyes pricked with heat when I realized what was happening.

She didn't have to say it.

I already knew.

And the sad part?

I *still* wasn't ready.

And though I wasn't, I was still hard for her, her velvety tongue going round and round. I tensed and pulsed, on the verge of exploding, but she yanked way, slipping out of her skirt and panties with haste. Her body came above me, thighs outside my lap and the entrance of her pussy right above my cock.

Her eyes, they filled with tears that didn't need explaining, and as she rigidly slid down the length of me. Her sadness spilled from her hazel eyes and streamed down her face. Her emotion gutted me. Her tears were the death of me.

I held my knight close, feeling as her body rocked with me, our kisses coated with salty emotion. I hated shedding tears, but as she watched me while making the sweetest, purest love to me, I could no longer control my feelings.

I was powerless as her pussy drenched my cock, and she cried my name, not only through pleasure but also with the pain that cut her deep. Skin slapped together, my hand gripping her ass as she bounced mercilessly.

And then it came.

I came.

We came beneath bright, burning stars that admired us, twinkling with merriment. We came between voracious midnight waves and the silvery light of the moon. Her head fell back, and I sucked greedily on her skin, not ever wanting the taste of her off my lips. I dropped my head, yanking her top down and exposing taut nipples. My mouth stimulated, sucking each one leisurely, and then I brought my mouth back up to hers, forcing her head down and eliciting a thick and heavy whimper.

I crushed her lips, the passion all-consuming, kissing her like my life was ending. I kissed that beautiful girl like I loved her. Because I *did* love her, and I would have done *anything* for her to be happy again.

But most of all, I kissed her like this, because I knew...

I knew this would be it.

This would be our last time.

We stilled, gasping for breath, but it seemed neither of us could supply it. We suffocated as if we were under the water that surrounded us, sinking deep in our dark ocean.

Once upon a time, our black sea was a miraculous place that we could share without worries. It was a place where we could be alone. We didn't have to think. We didn't have to fear. We just... *were*.

I held her tight as she jolted above me, and when those beautiful, watery, hazel eyes landed on mine, I whispered, "I love you so fucking much, Chloe."

And her smile faltered. I witnessed the love she had for me, saw how much it broke her in two. Her bottom lip trembled, the dam wanting to break again. And she quietly whispered the magical words I loved hearing. "I love you, too, Theodore Black," she said through a thick, wavering voice.

We stayed on the boat, floating in the middle of the ocean, for nearly three hours. I held her, and she held me. We didn't say much.

There wasn't really anything more we could say. We'd had our fun. Although it didn't last as long as we'd planned, it happened, and that was all I'd wanted, after all. Another chance. Another shot at becoming someone better. I wanted to love her in all the right ways and with every single ounce of me. I didn't care if she'd squeezed me dry, soaking up all my affections. They were hers to take. I was hers... all hers. I. Belonged. To. *Her*. I would always belong to her.

Later that night, Chloe left me with one last kiss in my condo. No, she didn't cave and come running back to me, confessing her truths and forgetting about all that happened an hour later. She was really gone.

I know because I checked.

There were plenty of unanswered calls and text messages. Fed up, I drove to Primrose Way every day for a solid week and a half about three days after our boat ride and never saw her car parked in the driveway.

I saw no trace of her, and after only a month, I heard from one of my old neighbors that her house had been put up for sale. Her father moved to an apartment in Orange County with the caregiver at his side. Chloe's number had also changed. The number had been disconnected. That drawn out beep and then the *"We're sorry, but the number you have reached..."* absolutely gutted me to hear.

I was ripped apart.

Deteriorating.

Dying little by little. Every. Single. *Fucking*. Day.

I never accepted her leaving. I never accepted it because I wasn't ready to. I wanted us to have our happily ever after. I wanted Isabelle to accept the love I had for Chloe, but my daughter was stubborn, and when she was angry, she was angry. She'd yet to fully accept my apologies. She brought the conversation up almost every time I called or saw her in person, but she was still my daughter, and she still needed me. She forgave me somewhat, but she hadn't forgiven Chloe in the slightest.

She was hard on her for no reason, and I told her that.

I told her over and over again that it wasn't her fault. I told her repeatedly that it was a mutual thing and that she had always been vulnerable to me. If anything, I should have been the one she never forgave, but Izzy saw it as nothing but her friend splitting them apart.

Not that it mattered anymore. It was the past. I stopped going to Primrose because I had all the evidence I needed. Chloe Knight, my beautiful, little knight, was gone, and I knew I would *never* see or hear from her again.

EPILOGUE

CHLOE

FIVE YEARS Later

Time is a tricky thing. It can be a mind game—a passing clock of deception, but it can also carry the gift of acceptance. Over time, I grew and became someone I never thought possible, and though it was hard getting over my past—my failures—I made do. I kept my head held high, even though some nights I would cry until I no longer could.

I missed how it used to be and the people I used to hang with. I missed the smiles, the laughs, the hugs, kisses, and even the momentary confliction I endured. I shouldn't have missed it. After so long, it all just seemed so unreal, so unlikely. I never thought I would end up in a situation like that, losing and walking away from almost everyone I loved. Shit, just being back brought back all the feelings—a deep-rooted feeling that tugged and pulled at my heartstrings, but got me nowhere at all.

It was July 18th. I would never forget that day. It was the day my dreams officially came true.

I had an interview at 12:30 PM the day before, and though my nerves were frazzled, my palms sweaty, I knew I had aced it. I went in prepared, with my head held high and my mind focused on only one thing—becoming a second grade teacher.

I got a call to come back in the next day. I figured they were going to reject me, but boy was I wrong.

"Congratulations, Ms. Knight—the kids will love that name by the way—we believe you have the patience and energy a second grade class will need for Bristle Wave Elementary." Mr. Lint, a man in his mid-fifties with a bald head, square glasses on the bridge of his nose, and a bright white smile that, surprisingly, didn't come off unsettling, held his hand out, and I hopped out of my chair, shaking it swiftly.

"Oh my goodness, thank you!" I tried hard not to bounce in my red wedges as he bobbed his head and then pulled away to pick up a manila envelope.

"Of course. We are glad to have you as a part of our staff." After informing me there would be papers I needed to sign and bring back before August, I was out of Bristle Wave Elementary with the widest grin on my face. I rushed to my Escalade and immediately whipped out my phone to call Sterling.

Yeah... *Sterling Martinez.*

We had become really close, especially after I apologized to him about the whole Mrs. Black thing. He forgave me. No doubt. No questions. No hesitation. At first, he was only a friend. He listened and understood and even gave me space when I told him all about my last night on *Dirty Black* with Theo. Unfortunately, he was still in Arizona, but he was going to transfer to Bristle High the next school year to continue his teaching career. We wanted to be closer now.

It was strange because, all that time I thought Sterling was a weirdo, he just really didn't know how to express himself around me. After months of texting and calling, checking up on me, and randomly asking me out on dates (which I had constantly turned down due to my damaged, no-good heart) he finally got to me. It wasn't during the best of situations. In fact, the situation was ten times worse than losing Izzy and walking away from the first man I ever loved.

Dad died when I was twenty-four. Another stroke. It was very severe and happened when he was walking to his bathroom one morning. Margie and Sterling showed up at the funeral, and after shedding crocodile tears and hiding the pain that truly dwelled in my heart, I told them I would pack up the apartment my dad rented out.

I also didn't want Margie to have to deal with his belongings, the sweet memories of their tough two years together. Sterling volunteered to help me, which totally distracted me from having to think about the funeral. The next day, he asked me to join him for ice cream.

He came down the hallway as I was tying my robe, catching a glimpse of my cleavage, and I covered myself as he cleared his throat, apologizing quickly as he whirled around.

"Shit! I'm sorry." He rushed away from the bedroom, but I called after him.

"No, it's fine," I assured him. "What's up? Need something?"

"Nah... uh, never mind. I don't think I should be bothering you right now."

"No," I laughed as he looked every which way but into my eyes. "Sterling, what is it? Come on, spit it out."

He rubbed his face, and after his nervousness had passed, he said, "I was thinking we could go for some ice cream today. It's nice out— and I swear I'm not asking for a date. I just want to give you a little pick-me-up after yesterday." His smile was charismatic, his grey eyes gentling as he squared his shoulders, most likely preparing for the rejection.

This guy never gave up. Like, ever. "Sure," I said.

"Shit, I knew it." He turned and started to walk out, but when he realized I wasn't turning him down, he turned to face me again. "Wait —that's a yes?" His face lit up.

I grinned. He was so goofy. "Yes, Sterling. I'll go with you for some ice cream. Just let me get dressed. I'll meet you in the living room in fifteen."

His lips quirked up, and a breath of relief passed through them. "Okay. Fifteen." He nodded his head and walked away, glancing back once before disappearing.

Let's just say having ice cream turned exactly into what he wanted it to be. A date. But the crazy thing about it? We actually hit it off. I didn't know too much about him, but I connected with him in a way that was difficult to explain. I was comfortable with him, and I could truly speak my mind without feeling judged or ignored.

We both were full of wonders and had questions that we'd always wanted to ask. Maybe all of those reasons were why I had fallen so hard for him.

"Sterling!" I screamed when he answered the phone.

"Shit, Chlo!" He laughed, and I blew a breath of relief as I focused on the building ahead of me. "Trying to blow my ear drum out?" he chuckled. "I take your excitement as you getting the position?"

"Yes! Oh my god! I seriously didn't think I would! They were asking me all these questions about what I would do if a kid choked on a crayon or got lost during a field trip - ugh, it was insane, but apparently they loved me and they think I'm a good fit for their staff."

"That's great, babe. I knew you'd get it. See, what did I tell you? I don't know why you always doubt yourself."

"I don't know why I do it either." I sighed, and the line went quiet for a few seconds.

As if he had read my mind, he said, "Listen, I know you didn't want to go back to Bristle, but this is a great thing. You can start fresh, and when I get there, we'll make the most we can out of it... together." I could tell he was smiling on his end.

"Yeah." I dropped my head. He knew what being here would do to me. I would remember and then I'd regret. God, I regretted so much, but this position was one I'd been trying to acquire for so long. I loved Bristle Wave. The serene city with little crime and a lot to do. "Hey, listen, I'm gonna go check out the house. The agent said I could view it today, and I also have to meet the previous owner. Apparently the owner wants me to know a few things before moving in."

"Okay. Let me know how it goes. Call me later."

"I will."

"I love you, Haze." That was a nickname he gave me. He swore he would never be able to stop looking into my eyes for as long as we lived.

"I love you too, Creep."

I listened to his deep chuckle, how it hummed straight through me, and then I hung up with flutters in the pit of my belly. We'd been together for two and a half years, and each day seemed to only get better. I placed my phone in the cup holder and grinned once more at the future school I would be teaching at before pulling out of the parking lot and driving to my new home.

The house was right off the coast. A two story home made of tan cement and a burnt orange stucco roof to accent. There was a two-car garage, and the front yard was covered in well-kept, green grass with two, towering palm trees. It was beautiful, but what I loved most about it was the backyard.

It wasn't just any backyard. It was filled with soft white sand that never got too hot. Yes, our new home was right on the beach. I inhaled as I stepped off the deck and onto the sand, slipping out of my sandals and watching the ocean.

My heart thumped a little quicker as bittersweet memories unfolded. That last night on the boat. Our last ride together. The ocean only reminded me of one thing—well, *one* person...

A door shut behind me, shattering my thoughts, and I turned as Rita, the realty agent, trotted through the kitchen in her black baby heels and stopped at the patio door. Her brown hair flew with the breeze as she lowered her thin frames. "The previous owner just arrived," she called. "I have another house to show. Do you think you will need me?"

"Nah! Go ahead! I should be okay," I called back. "I'll call you if I need you. Thank you for everything!" Rita nodded her head, giving me a small glance and a light smile before turning around and pulling out her cell phone. She reminded me of my mom. Always busy. Always on the go.

Speaking of, Mom was living in Brazil... alone. Her young boyfriend broke up with her, which made South America their last destination as a couple. She called me once, crying. I didn't feel much sympathy for her. I was a firm believer in Karma. She told me everything, like how she actually liked it there and wasn't sure she wanted to come back, but how she wished he'd stuck around to make it worthwhile. It was a shame.

She came back when I told her about Dad's funeral but flew right back out the next day without a goodbye. I was used to her not being around. Of course it killed me to know she didn't hug or kiss me or even want to bid me farewell, but I quickly got over it, just as I did everything else when I was a child.

She bawled her eyes out during Dad's funeral. Her emotion was raw. I'm pretty sure she left like the wind because of all the remorse she felt for not being around during his final years. She never should have left to begin with. She was still a very, very selfish woman.

I shut my eyes, allowing the salty air to toy with the loose tendrils of my pinned hair. I could really get used to this. The balcony door slid open and when I recalled Rita saying the previous owner was around, I turned.

"Hi, you must be—" My words flew out before I could see the person, and they quickly came to an end when I met familiar brown eyes.

An audible gasp filled the air. My chest felt heavy, the pressure real, like an elephant stepping on top of me as I lay flat. I thought after all those years the feelings—every feeling—I had for him would surely pass, but that was complete bullshit. Time only made it easier to move on with life, but time had nothing on chance encounters.

Who was I kidding?

My feelings were never going to change.

Not when it came to him.

Not when it came to my first, at both love and womanhood.

They'd never change for Theodore Black.

He walked out to the deck with a crooked smile, his head in that childlike tilt that used to make me so weak in the knees—still made me weak in the knees. His hair had grown out around the edges, and his body was just as it was before, in great shape.

His eyes were tired, though, like all the stressing had finally caught up to him. As always, it was only his eyes that gave away his age. His face was shaved clean, besides the black scruff above his lip. When his hand came up to wipe the sweat from his brow, I caught the silver band on his ring finger, and for some reason, my heart dropped. He was... married?

I tried to cover my hand, the square engagement ring on my finger, but he saw it, his face screwing. I still remained rather speechless, watching as he carried himself from the deck to the stairs that led to the sand. He didn't say anything either. I didn't feel so bad for being flabbergasted.

This was never supposed to happen again. I was never supposed to run into Mr. Black in Bristle Wave because, from what I'd heard, he'd moved out of Bristle to go elsewhere. I had no clue where he'd moved to, but I assumed it was far away from here. That's what I got for going with the rumors.

When Theo was only a few steps away, I swallowed the emotion that'd collected in my throat, tears burning the rims of my eyes. I don't know why I was being so emotional. It could have been the recollections, or maybe even the pain that was still buried deep.

Or, perhaps it was because he looked just as great as ever, with the ink that stained his arms, that perfect, wavy black hair, and the same hard and delicious body. His nipple ring prodded through his light grey T-shirt, and I smiled, remembering the way my tongue had surrounded it a long time ago.

"Little Knight," Theo finally said. His voice was just the same, and it still held some type of power over me. I felt my core clench, but I ignored that guilt, allowing a smile to sweep across my lips. "You are still so beautiful." And he was still so goddamn gorgeous, but I couldn't say that.

"Theo," I breathed. "Wow... um... what are you doing here?—I mean—" My mouth clamped shut, unable to form proper sentences. I couldn't believe it. I felt like the twelve year old girl that had first met him in Primrose. Back then he was a stranger—someone I knew nothing about—and even now it seemed I was meeting a stranger again. Someone that I wasn't sure about, someone that may have changed and I didn't even know it.

"It's been a long time, huh?"

"Yeah." I blinked rapidly. "You are the previous owner?"

He nodded with a press of his lips. "Funny, right? How fate brought us here?"

"Fate and destiny seem to always tamper with our lives one way or another." He moved forward, and I shifted on my feet, the sand squishing between my toes. "How'd you know I would be coming to Bristle today?"

He lifted a hand, running his fingers through his lengthy hair. "That woman that just ran out of here?"

"Yeah?"

"She's my mother."

My jaw dropped, gaping. "What?! No way! No wonder she seemed so familiar! I take it she didn't take your father's last name?"

"Nope." He smiled. "Rita Morris. I told her to keep it secret. You know, it's quite a coincidence that you wanted to move into this house." He looked around. "Seems like a place you will really enjoy, though. Anyway, she remembered seeing you around us before and asked me if the name Chloe Knight sounded familiar." He wiggled his eyebrows. "Shocker, huh?"

"Wow—yeah," I laughed. "That's wild. No wonder she was acting so friendly towards me."

"I told her you were one of Izzy's old friends."

When he said her name, I felt a pinch deep inside me. He caught that small ounce of pain run cross my face and straightened his back. "She feels terrible. Talks about you at least every other week. She misses the hell out of you."

"I miss her too."

"You know she got a job in New York? She got a role for a small film up there?"

"What? Oh my gosh, that's incredible! Tell her I said congrats!"

"I will." he put on a genuine smile.

"So, what is it with you, Knight? Did you go and get married on me?" he asked when I looked down again, guilt-ridden. I could tell he'd been wanting to ask about the ring on my finger for a while now. I drug my gaze back up to his, and he brought his eyes from my finger to my face again.

"Oh... um, engaged actually."

"Let me take a wild guess..." His tongue wiped his lips, and he laughed as he said, "The Sterling kid?"

"Lucky guess, mister," I teased, blushing. I dropped my head, and Theo stepped forward to tilt my chin. His gesture seemed almost natural and brought back so many memories. I would never forget his touch and all it did to me. I would never forget him in general, but I knew better.

Now, I really knew better.

"And what about you?" I asked, backing away without making it too noticeable. I put on a cheery tone as I asked, "What woman has you wrapped around her finger? —Wait, no, let me take a wild guess..." Theo crossed his arms with an amused grin on his face. Laughing, I said, "Trixie!"

And he busted out in a hearty chortle. "That is fucking hilarious."

I snickered. I knew damn well he would never take her back, but I was curious who the new woman was. "Well," I urged, waving my hands for answers. "Come on. Who is the lucky lady?"

He scratched his chin, his eyes bouncing from mine to the sea. "Her name is Sheila, and we got married a little over a year ago. I met her at some bachelor party in San Francisco about ten months after you left. She's a nice girl... great woman."

"Wow. Married?" I gasped. "That's great, Theo." I smiled. "I'm really happy for you."

He changed the subject. "Does he make you happy?" he asked. I caught the protectiveness in the bass of his voice, watched as the joy slid away from the corners of his mouth.

"Sterling is a good guy. Of course he makes me happy."

"Do you love him?"

"Yes, Theo."

"And you're sure about marrying this guy?" He studied me, hoping I would waver. I didn't weaken or waver. I kept my head held high.

Vibrating with laughter, I focused on his brown eyes and kindly said, "Yes. I'm sure." Theo shook his head with his mouth curved upwards, his arms still folded tight across his chest. "What? I asked defensively. I knew he probably still hated Sterling.

"Nothing," he laughed. "I just can't believe he stole both my women away from me. Apparently the kid has something I don't."

That remark, I had to admit, caught me by total surprise. Even though there was a deeper meaning behind it, it was funny. And the fact that he didn't get angry about it made me realize one thing: Theodore Black was content with his life.

He'd changed and had moved on. He found someone else to complete him. I couldn't blame him for that because I'd done the same. I was sure within those ten months, he'd tried to reach me, but I changed my number and email and made sure there was no way he could find me unless he drove to USC. Luckily, he never did. Though I blocked him from all directions, I made way for Izzy.

Unfortunately, she never called.

That day, I could read him like a book. The way he laughed, the way he smiled and still listened to me, I knew he'd always be there. I knew his love for me would always live in his heart, just as my love for him would. It would never change, and it would never fade.

We loved each other as we did during the beginning, wholly and compassionately, and I couldn't complain, bitch, or whine because that was the way it should have remained.

"I'm moving to San Francisco with her tomorrow," Theo told me.

"Then what in the hell are you doing here?"

He shrugged. "I won't be back to Bristle Wave. I needed to see you one more time, make sure we were okay."

I didn't know whether to smile or cry at his response. I rubbed my arm nervously, and he stepped forward. "Don't worry," he murmured. "I will behave." He smirked, and I knew he was teasing me. I knew he'd behave. He had no choice. I had no choice. "You're happy, Knight. That's all I ever wanted for you." His eyes were soft. Something about his gentle smile and the way he looked at me made a stray tear drift down my cheek.

I nodded. "It's all I ever wanted for you, too," I whispered.

His boyish smile tickled my heart. "Can we take a walk?" He bobbed his head, gesturing towards the beach. I glanced back, listening to the seagulls caw, the familiar waves crashing from a short distance.

"Sure," I murmured.

He was excited. I could tell, but he kept himself on a leash. He didn't dare get too close, and though our hands bumped, we didn't bother trying to hold onto that sensation. Believe me, it was hard, and I felt even walking with him was wrong, but as we created this one last memory together, something phenomenal occurred.

I realized that we were exactly what he wanted us to be... *Okay*.

We talked and caught up on almost everything. About my dad passing and how he still thought of Janet from time to time. How he didn't blame her or allow the truths to ruin what he remembered about her. He loved her. And I was glad he could forgive and forget.

But most of all, he understood my struggle in the end. I didn't have to tell him how hard it was to walk away because he could see it right on my face as I explained how tough it was to finish college. He accepted my sacrifice, and he took it for what it was. That was proof enough that he'd become someone better.

I'd always heard that it took men longer to mature than women. Theo wasn't fully mature when we'd first met or even when we'd first slept together. I could tell he used to want so much more out of life during those times after Janet died, but something had obviously shifted deep within him. After losing two loves, I was sure he was making the third one count... his third luck charm as he put it.

He wasn't going to take advantage of his new wife. I knew that for sure.

He vowed to love her, cherish her, and make her feel like the greatest woman in the world, and I knew he'd keep those promises because that was exactly how he made me feel five years ago.

He made me feel like the sweetest and most beautiful girl in the world. He made me feel like his one and only. He told me I was his knight in shining armor. He still thanked me for saving him and swore he would never be able to repay that debt.

See, Theo Black no longer lived by the darkness of his last name.

His life was no longer chaos. It was no longer a dark, tainted catastrophe. His daughter had forgiven him. He saw her once every week, and said she still treated him the same, no longer bringing up the past or his mistakes.

I guess I could say Izzy and I were... fine. If that's what I could call it. I'd received a letter from Izzy in my P.O. box one day. It showed up a few days after my dad died. Only Izzy knew about the P.O. box. She'd used it once before when she bought a naughty toy she was ashamed of people seeing.

The letter read:

Chloe,

Don't write me black. Please, just don't.

I want you to read this, and then I want you to forget about me. I want you to know that I love you and that you will always remain a sister in my heart. All the other girl friends I meet will have to live up to what I saw in you, and that will be hard to do. Why? Because you are the sweetest person I know, and all those cruel things were wrong of me to say. You are nothing like your mom.

I had no right to judge. Instead, I should have taken the time to listen and understand the situation. But I was young and immature, and I shouldn't have taken my anger out on you. I know I should be saying this in person, but forgive me right now because I just can't bear to see you.

Maybe I'm a coward. A chicken. Maybe it's my pride, or perhaps it's the guilt I feel about all those hateful things, but I am so sorry, and I want you to know that you are not a bad person and that I don't blame my dad for falling for you.

I mean, I kinda always knew, but when you really love someone and don't want to lose them, you defend that person in every way. You shield and blind yourself from the truth. You only seem to see the good in them and overlook the bad. I knew it the day after my mom died. I saw you help my dad in the garage. I heard you leave, and I saw the way he looked at you and how you looked at him. I thought you were only helping, but now that I think about it all, I knew it deep down.

I just hope you can understand why I can't face you on this. I love my dad, and in order to keep my relationship with him steady, I have to move forward without you in my life. I'm a stubborn little bitch, and you know this. LOL. I suck at keeping my mouth shut, and I would feel really, really weird about my dad still sleeping with you if you were still my friend. Not that I don't have respect for you, I just can't handle something that intense. You may not think of it this way, but I think of it as my sister sleeping with our dad. Ew

What you two do now is none of my business, but I know you. I know you won't go back. Not because you don't love him—which, I know you really do— but because you care about me and never meant to hurt me to begin with. I know things happen, and I want you to know I am glad that I could grow up with an amazing person like you. It's hard to come across friends like you, Chloe, but remember that I love you and if we happen to cross paths one day, I won't hold anything against you.

I love you, and I hope you can understand my decisions.

So much love,

Izzy

Her letter was understandable. It made me shed way too many tears and was worse when Sterling read it to me again out loud, but I understood and respected Izzy's decision.

I loved Theo, and she knew, but when it came down to the wire, she also had to choose, and she chose her father. It was a good choice. I would have hated to be what came between them. A dad was much easier to forgive than a friend. Every girl needed her dad, especially Izzy. He was all she had left.

This, too, was okay because Theo and I had chosen her. She deserved happiness, even if that meant losing some. Sterling thought her letter was a bit selfish, and that after ten years of friendship, I deserved a face-to-face apology, but I didn't expect that from her. I knew Izzy.

Yes, she had a lot of pride and refused for her ego to be tampered with. There were times when I would have to be the one to apologize when she was the one that was clearly in the wrong. But she was my friend, and in order to get past something, I became the bigger person and stepped up to the plate.

I was glad she chose her father.

And I was glad we chose her.

We were all happy in our own ways.

Theo and I walked until the sun set, and when it was time for him to go, I watched him hop on his bike and ride with the wind. I watched him go until I could no longer see him or hear the growl of Ol' Charlie.

I turned, walking back towards the house, and when I spotted the blue sticky note glued to the door, I took it off, and a large grin took over my face. My heartbeat quickened, and I laughed out loud.

I laughed on the way into the house, walking through the hallway, and onto the deck, spotting the red recliner that once belonged to Mrs. Black in the far corner where I left it. It would forever remind me of them. Of *him*.

I tousled with the paper, and as I stepped onto the sand and faced the ocean, I realized tears were now streaming, a mixture of joy and sadness flooding my eyes.

He was gone, and I was sad, but only because I knew I would never see him again. Mr. Black. Theo Black. My first of many. But I was also overjoyed because he deserved this. We deserved this. We obtained some form of happiness when it seemed utterly impossible.

I studied the paper, his macho handwriting. On the note was a sketch of the tribal wave his tattoo artist had created for him. I remembered his promise—how he'd give me something to remember it by. He swore he'd get the sketch for me, even after the artist told him he didn't give the sketches away or make copies of them.

But Theo was Theo. I was sure he'd had this for a while now because, low and behold, I had an exact replica of the sketch in my hands. And written beneath it were the words, *"Told you I would get it. I guess being a Black has its perks."*

I clung to that note. I kept it in the bottom drawer of my desk in my classroom for years.

I clung to hope.

To fate.

To *love*.

That man's soul was no longer stained, dipped, or tainted in black.

His soul had been bathed in gold, baptized to become someone pure.

No matter how far I went in life, or how being with him was oh, so wrong, I was never going to forget someone so incredible. Someone so wonderful. Someone so amazing—a person I couldn't sum up with words, no matter how many I used.

I was never, in all my life, going to forget that man.

My incredible first lover.

My beautiful Theodore.

My loveable *Mr. Black.*

I'm happy to announce that Dear Mr Black has a follow up book. To read Forever, Mr Black, the conclusion to Theo & Chloe's love story, click here.

AFTERWORD

DON'T FORGET THAT POSTING A REVIEW, WHETHER BIG OR SMALL, IS ALWAYS A BIG HELP AND IS MUCH APPRECIATED.

To get notified about new release alerts, free books, and exclusive updates, visit www.shanorawilliams.com/mailing-list.

FOLLOW ME

I'm an Instagram fanatic so please feel free to follow me! I am always active and always eager to speak with my readers there.

Instagram @reallyshanora

Other Ways to Follow Me:
Twitter @shanorawilliams
Facebook @ShanoraWilliamsAuthor

Want to contact me personally:
Email me at booksbyshanora@gmail.com

ACKNOWLEDGMENTS

There are many people I could thank right now. So many!

First and foremost I'd like to thank my heavenly Father. My Lord and Savior. Without Him I'd truly, honestly be nowhere.

Thank you to my family, my little baby boy for keeping me on my toes. The beautiful man in my life, Juan Carlos. The reason I can create these sexy book boyfriends.

My sister Dajai for always making me feel like I've outdone myself and for reading every single one of my books.

Thank you to Stina Rubio, Tamsyn Bester, Heather Orgeron, Selene Malek, Miri and Yaya, Nancy Flores, Nanette Bradford, Kristie Wittenberg, and Julie Joyness! You ladies have been so supportive and amazing. Not even funny. I love you all!

Thank you to these lovely, super awesome readers on Instagram. You guys are an entirely different (and rather naughty) crowd and I love you all so damn hard! To SmuttyBookLover, KinkyGirlsBookObsessions, xxBookQueenxx, RentasticReads, ButThisBook, TiffanyThe-Bibliophile, CrazyBookLovers, DarkReadings, YABookshelf, BookBabe, BookWhores, BookBellas and so many more! These are in no specific order at all but thank you to each and every one of you for the shares, the teasers, and the freaking amazing graphics/edits! I can't thank any of you enough. I LOVE YOU ALL!!!

Thank you Ena Bena for running your promotional services like a boss! I don't know how you do it, but thank you, girl!

Gotta give thanks to my family for believing and supporting me to the fullest. I love you guys.

To each and every blogger and reader that has taken the time out to read, review, and give me so much love about *Dear Mr. Black*... my word. I am seriously in awe. Sometimes I am absolutely speechless because I have *never* seen so much love all at once. I can't believe how much adoration this novel has gotten but, trust me, I am NOT complaining! I appreciate it so much and I love, love, LOVE you all! Thank you a million times!

Made in the USA
Middletown, DE
14 February 2025